Holidays

The Christmas Oratorio

OTHER VERBA MUNDI BOOKS

The Lonely Years, 1925–1939
by Isaac Babel

The Tartar Steppe
by Dino Buzzati

The Book of Nights
by Sylvie Germain

The Prospector
by J. M. G. Le Clézio

Honeymoon
by Patrick Modiano

The Christmas Oratorio

A NOVEL BY

Göran Tunström

TRANSLATED FROM THE SWEDISH BY

Paul Hoover

Verba Mundi
DAVID R. GODINE · PUBLISHER
BOSTON

First published in the U.S. in 1995 by
DAVID R. GODINE, PUBLISHER, INC.
Box 9103
Lincoln, Massachusetts 01773

First published in Sweden as Juloratoriet by
Albert Bonniers Förlag, Stockholm, in 1983.

Library of Congress Cataloging-in-Publication Data

Tunström, Göran, 1937–
[Juloratoriet. English]
The Christmas oratorio : a novel / by Göran Tunström ;
translated from the Swedish by Paul Hoover. — 1st ed.
p.   cm. — (Verba Mundi)
I. Hoover, Paul, 1945–   . II. Series.
PT9876.3.U5J8513 1994   839.7'374 — dc20
94-32003   CIP

ISBN 1-56792-008-X   HC

First American edition
Printed and bound in the United States of America

❀ I ❀

Beginning in 1930's Sweden, this
rich, poignant novel spans three
generations of the Nordensson
family - children, parents and
lovers who do not really know
each other.

THE FIRST THING I DID at the hotel was call home to say I'd arrived. My son's childish voice has cracks where the dark squeezes through. "Do you have a TV in your room, Dad?" "No, I don't," I said as I watched the snow melt around my shoes. "In any case, I wouldn't have time to watch it." "Do they have a movie theatre there?" He is skeptical of the provinces. "Well, there was one when I was growing up." "And you *wanted* to go to a place like that?" "I had to," I said, promising to take a stroll along Main Street. He loves the blurbs on the posters: "If this film doesn't scare the life out of you, you're already dead." "In space, nobody can hear you scream. And if someone could, it would be even worse." This evening's film is called *The Fog* and its message is: "What you can't see won't hurt you. It will kill you."

I ended up standing for a long time outside Östberg's Clock and Optics Shop. On a bed of glitter and synthetic snow, among Christmas goblins I thought I recognized from my childhood, lay a jumble of clocks: alarm clocks, wristwatches, pretty ornamental wall clocks, an old-time grandmother's clock, pocket watches, and small ladies' watches, impossible to read. I counted twenty-seven different timepieces, each of them running. And not one of them showed the same time. One said a quarter past two, one twenty past four, a third showed just before midnight or noon. Indefatigably they ticked on, each in its own time, unconcerned about the others. None was false and none was true; there was no before and no after. Each was turned inward toward its own mechanism.

It was the same outside the shop window. In the heavily falling snow, people skidded and slipped toward each other, no one in

3

exactly the same time. As one woke from his nightmare, another became motionless in the memory of a summer day.

I was forced to shut my eyes against the snow and, pulling my coat collar high above my ears, let the material provide a calm enclave. I was in my own time's bewildered labyrinth as I continued along that street, where once I had named so many things. Even as I was taking adult steps, another part of me was three years old. The hand clutching my portfolio simultaneously held my mother's hand, pointed at an ice cream cone, fought its way free from a battle in Greece, followed the delights of a musical score. Every act in the past yielded a thousand other possibilities, all trickling along toward their own future. And so they continue, further into the wilderness of consciousness, shadows that hunt and are hunted. It is never still.

I cut across the Square and walked over the Bridge – the water was always frighteningly black in the narrow channel: how many dreams of falling had been played out there! – went past the darkened house where I had once lived, and walked gingerly up the church green. The larch and yew trees stood white and solemn, wanting to tell their stories. The Church was already alight. I lingered in the snow and looked out over the lights of the village. In among the trees, I saw myself skiing, falling down, getting snow between my socks and long johns. Down there was the Balcony. There the Hotel. So many years had gone by, and yet: the same moment, the same life. The same necessity.

Creative death…

When I turned to walk toward the graves, Egil Esping stood behind me, observing me, snow shovel in hand. He was dressed in a black overcoat and dark trousers. He was bare-headed, and his greasy hair was combed back as it had always been.

"Well, if it ain't you, Victor. Yer back. I saw it in the papers."

"Yes."

4

"Yeah, you got somewhere, you did. Saw you on TV once. There's a difference 'tween folk and folk. It's a long time since we worked together."

I swallowed. I felt like a traitor.

"It's at least thirty years."

"Thirty-one," Egil Esping said. "You quit in August. I come here temporary same time as you. But fer me, it ain't been nothin' more. You want a little coffee?"

"I don't know."

"You got time still. It's hard to direct so many people, ain't it? But, of course, it's in the family. It was yer old man started with it, wadn't it? 'Cause he was yer old man, wadn't he?"

"Mm."

"Can I just shovel away a little snow? It's twenty minutes till you start. No point in folk gettin' the church all wet."

It was a dismal summer when we tended the graves, trimmed hedges, raked paths and sat in the now-demolished shed, gossiping about the dead being brought in a constant stream to the mortuary. It was the summer before we moved. Esping walked in front of me toward the new church hall and showed me to a door in the cellar.

"It was better in the old shed, doncha think? The windows are too high up so you gotta stand on a chair to see out. Though there ain't nothin' ta see. Same people the whole time. 'Cept when you come, of course. Didja see what a fine coffee maker we got? It's on all the time."

Egil Esping sat on a chair, unbuttoned his coat, put his elbows on his knees and lit a cigarette. His eyes were tired, his fingers nervous; ceaselessly he knocked the ash off onto the floor. He pondered something for a long time.

"Listen… how is it when yer gonna go on?"

"What do you mean?"

"Well, on TV? Do you take anythin'? A buzz or something?"

"Do I take a drink, you mean? No."

5

"Not even a little buzz!" He ruminated over that, then shrugged his shoulders, relieved. "Yeah, somebody else would never even get up there, ya know. But it's gotta be nerve-wracking. Lots a cameras 'n' such. When yer out there naked?"

"It sure is. So what else is going on here then?"

"A common wage earner don't have nothin' ta tell, ya know. So there's lotsa folks standin' an' watchin'. When yer out there naked?"

"Sure. Have you been promoted to boss of the cemetery now?"

"Not hardly. But the boss is away. So then I have ta jump in. Have a cigarette. 'Cept maybe you don't smoke?"

"Yes, unfortunately I do."

Snow melted around our feet. He looked down at them and further on, toward ponderous depths.

"Everythin' was better before. Now yer watched so close. Before, I kept my bike down by the bend. There wasn't nobody noticed I rode down to the State Store 'n' bought a little. You can't do that now. So the last five, six years ain't been worth nothin'. When I'm workin', I mean."

"Are you married?"

"Naw, it never happened. But I got a kid down in town. Six years old now. A boy."

He looked up, as if out of one of his graves.

"It was too much drinkin', ya know? She couldn't stand it. You remember Bertil? He's dead."

"You don't say. But he was old, wasn't he?"

"It was buckshot. Right up under his jaw. He's buried over there in the new part, right up against the wall. You can go look 'im up, in a manner of speakin'."

"So he shot himself?"

"His old lady left him. And then he was drinkin'. Alone out in the woods. He wadn't here on Monday, and ya know he'd never been away a single day in twenty years. Not one day, no matter

6

how drunk he was. So we phoned: no answer. In the afternoon we drove out there. It'd taken half his head off."

"I remember he dreamed about lying around home some day, listening to the rain on the barn roof. Just lying in the hay with a beer."

"No, no, that was Gustav."

"Oh yes, of course."

"He's dead, him too. Have a cigarette!"

Egil Esping always wanted to be accommodating. Not be a bother to anyone. When he was six years old, his mother had taken him down to the jetty and said they would drown themselves together since he had destroyed her life, making her the disgrace of the family.

"I have lots. I can't be without cigarettes, no sir. So yer gonna play Bach. Yer old man, he disappeared, huh...?"

"Mm."

"I usually slip in an' sit there when they're playin'. Are you... religious?"

"I don't know."

"But it's nice when he reads outa the Bible, the preacher." He looked up. "Ya know, you don't need ta tell anybody that. That I think that. I mean, the sermons I don't catch so much of, but... You get kinda quiet. Well, ya know. I've read in the Book. About the wandering of souls. But maybe you don't... believe in that stuff."

"No."

"Well, it was really nothin' in particular anyway."

Turning his back to the room, he looked out the window. Outside, the lamps made the snow stand out like grains of gold.

"It's a pain with the graves now, when it snows like this. Like yesterday, it was Eva Bergkvist. You knew her, didn't ya?"

"I believe so," I said vaguely because there were hardly any faces that were clear to me in that way, but I was glad he believed that I could share eyes with him in his loneliness.

7

"Of course you did. It was cancer. When she come to the hospital, she started ta cry when they asked if she had relatives. No, she said. Any acquaintances then? Any friends? No. An' then they understood how alone she was 'n' made that breast cancer the best thing that'd ever happened to her. That's what she said when she come home on leave from the radiation treatment, 'cause she had a lump like a tomato. So she went to Karlstad where they have a patients' hotel. She got liverwurst sandwiches there, with pickles that was cut right down the middle, lengthwise, ya know. There was almost only me at the funeral, me and the preacher. That's the way it'll be when... That nobody... Not even the boy."

I strolled out toward the graves. The snow lay in high drifts along the paths, the wind heaved down and the tombstones were covered. It was impossible to find any names, but:

How fit a place for contemplation is the dead of night
among the dwellings of the dead.

"Johann Sebastian Bach created from vibrating air the worldwide, invisible State of God, and, while he still lived, wandered into it like the legendary Chinese painter into his painting," wrote Oskar Loerke.

That was Bach. But who managed to keep "categories of jubilation" alive? Who maintains language so that it remains accessible, year after year? What in me had managed? Which moments form our lives; which faces are illuminated by the first pale beams of our consciousness and give us direction?

The church door was heavy to open. I stood a moment in the snow, hesitated before I pushed it, then entered the light-filled grotto.

"Welcome," I said to the orchestra and chorus. They were sitting in front in the choir. I let my coat and scarf fall to the floor. "My name is Victor Udde and you can congratulate yourselves for having me as your conductor. Who else would believe in such an insane enterprise, leading celebratory choruses in this day and age? This is, you know, a tradition which..." but that, of course, didn't concern them, that was my history... "is as old as Adam. It isn't easy, as you know, to scrape together a group of musicians in such a little place. Still..."

Something began to sing in my spine; it is always the same. Deep in my consciousness doors were thrown open, faces peeked in... But where are the trumpets? Where is Dietrich Fischer-Dieskau? Where is the Vienna Boys Choir? Where is van Kesteren? What a shot it would give the Evangelist if he were doing it. Do you know *anything* about music? Is it worth sacrificing the reading of good books, worth sacrificing ambitions of studying iconography or the Bhagavad–Gita? We'll assume it is, and let us praise the mystery of the Birth. *Jauchzet, frohlocket! auf, preiset die Tage!* Trumpets and timpanis, where are you?

The gate was opened. I heard how my voice calmed slightly.

"You should know that such works were written for each Sunday. The parts were written out on Monday and Tuesday. The whole Bach family worked together; it's impossible to distinguish between Johann Sebastian's handwriting and his wife's, honor be to her memory! Wednesday and Thursday, the copies were written out; Friday and Saturday, the work was rehearsed. Then the whole race was run, and they could drink their coffee in peace. There are five or six complete volumes. But remember, there were loads of formulas to help them in that time: there was a system of emblems. The creative process that we value so highly today was only the added color. The intended effect was produced in and with the emblem, more or less. These formulas were public property. Like a piece of furniture. A chair. A chair has certain attributes: it has legs, a back, a seat. But then we have van Gogh's chair, we have Picasso's chairs – one remembers such things!

"Remember, too, that Bach never got to collaborate with a really good poet. The texts were written, for the most part, by the chief postmaster in Leipzig, Heinrici, called Picander. Incidentally, nothing against postmasters; my neighbor in Ingesund works for the Post Office, and you'd have to look far and wide for better rose-hip wine. Then we have those sections that build on biblical texts and were composed by Bach. The gospel texts are surrounded by chorales and so become modern, in our view, with an entire spectacle that, if I may say so, is observed from the outside. Compare it to an opera, where the action moves ahead, then suddenly comes to a halt. All movement stops and someone's thoughts take form in arias, or gospels. Or, as in *The Threepenny Opera* when Pirate Jenny sings in the bordello: everything becomes quiet. It takes so much *time*. But that is the time it gets to take, and must take.

"Or think about the Marx Brothers, my dear congregation. Furious action, chases, love. Then, suddenly, they step outside it, perform an aria of jokes; it's beautiful. Because that is humanity's privilege: to remove itself from time and place. A lot of studying, ladies and gentlemen, much meditation, a bit of theology in this brow," I said as I pointed to my head. The chorus smiled.

"Okay. So this is everyday music for Christmas 1734. Johann Sebastian uses parody: secular music with sacred texts. Was he short of time? Or were they smart enough back then not to differentiate between secular and spiritual love? The question warrants some thought. Eros, Agape. Could someone get me a glass of water? How did the audience feel when they heard music from the world's chambers? The first piece, 'Jauchzet, frohlocket! auf, preiset die Tage,' is actually called 'Tönet Ihr Pauken...', a secular text, and it works damn well, if you'll pardon the expression, in its secular context. A familiar story, performed in a hall at court, in a palace, by a group of poorly-paid students. Music for lackeys. The fine lords and ladies would sit awhile and talk, drink a glass, and feel they had participated. Listen now!"

Out of my pocket I produced a little cassette recorder.

"Jauchzet, frohlocket... the trumpets..."

I held the tape recorder toward the choir, swayed with the tempo, began to conduct the Concentus Musicus, and wanted to push Harnoncourt aside. I looked at the chorus as I tramped on my scarf's red coils:

"The chorus... dienet dem Höchsten... a falling theme, soft, the same effect in the worldly. Schweitzer – Albert that is – said, around the turn of the century that these choruses work better for the religious purpose; on the other hand, the arias... Ssssh! Typical effect, here comes the theme... notice the order or precedence between the instruments, timpani, trumpets, joy! Joy, my friends, da, da, da. Now it's our turn, one, two..."

> *Jauchzet, frohlocket! auf, preiset die Tage,*
> *rümet, was heute der Höchste getan!*

❋ II ❋

ONE JUNE IN THE BEGINNING of the 1930s, Solveig Nordensson stands on the graveled ground in front of her farmhouse in Värmland, her legs on either side of the new bicycle Aron has given her, as if newly-loved and warm with joy, her hands on the shiny handlebars. She is on her way into Sunne to talk to Mr. Jancke, the choir master, about this autumn's concert, which, after ten years of preparation, is finally about to happen.

She tells Sidner: "I forgot to turn off the gramophone."

She ruffles his hair, strokes Eva-Liisa on the cheek, and looks out over the lake at the long afternoon shadows on the fields.

"I'll turn it off, Mamma," Sidner answers. Later he would add, many times: "It never happened." The three of them listen awhile at the open window where the tone arm dances its song of joy:

Lasset das Zagen, verbannet die Klage,
Stimmet voll Jauchzen und Fröhlichkeit an!
Dienet dem Höchsten mit herrlichen Chören
Lasst uns den Namen des Herrschers verehren!

They fall silent, as so many times before, in toward each other, enveloped by Bach's Christmas music.

"But first you have to push me, Sidner."

He puts his hands on the baggage carrier, presses his bare feet into the gravel, and gives her a shove. Solveig settles onto the saddle and coasts downhill. The spokes sing, sand and pebbles spurt up; she draws the whole summer into her lungs from trees and ditch banks, draws in the scent of meadow-sweet, lady's bedstraw, and ox-eye daisies. Sidner, taking a short cut across the yard, comes out onto the steep edge right over the bend. He shouts:

"Bye…," sees the cows, sees his father, sees Solveig start to brake, sees the chain hop off, sees she cannot dodge the cows, sees how the first one throws itself to the side to avoid the arrow of speed, sees how the cows lumbering after it cannot avoid her, sees how she tears right into the cave of flesh and horns and hooves, sees her fall and remain lying there as they tramp and tramp over her, long after she ceases to exist. "There are," notes Sidner in his booklet, *On Caresses,* "moments that never end."

About the "Present," Sidner writes, "It is the time that *is heard,* when the roaring presses into the passages of our senses to fall down into the lower part of the body, a richly branched network of canals, which is our body's irrigation." It is quite obvious that he is referring to that June day when he is twelve and stands on the crest and, turning around, sees Eva-Liisa's red braids against the darkness of the open barn doors. They are lifted by her speed as she runs down the path to catch up to Solveig; her arms raised, her skirt tossing over her rumpled stockings, she shouts: "Wait for me, Mamma."

She does not hear Sidner shouting. He stands still.

"Long after one has begun to run, one can continue to stand at the same point. Standing there, one can suddenly notice that one has reached New Zealand," he notes.

But part of him catches up to Eva-Liisa just before the bend. Below them lies the wild strawberry patch, overgrown with wild thyme and plantain. He throws himself on her and they fall to the dry clay road. Her broad face is turned toward him; the space between her teeth stares at him, her eyes stare, her nose stares as she tries to get loose. He bites her on the cheek, draws blood. She lies still under him, her body slackening, warmth rising out of it; they look right into the source of each other's thoughts. The earth turns. What is going to happen now? What is he going to do? What does the next world look like?

"What are you doing? Are you crazy, Sidner?"

"Mamma," he whispers, but the silence goes on. He rolls off her stomach, feels wet in his pants, shuts his eyes. How could the world begin again? What names could they find for each other? If only he were called something other than Sidner, he would not need to bother about what happened. He could be someone who came for a visit and heard about the dreadful thing that happened up there on the farm below the forest.

He does not want to know his name, but Eva-Liisa sits up, her white underpants staring at him.

"Sidner, what are you doing?"

Don't ask, he tries to scream, but his voice gurgles down in a black hole.

If he'd even had parents who had chosen not to call him anything. To be called Rice Pudding, Fence Post, or Sunday Morning – whatever.

"I want to run after Mamma."

"No!" he cuffs her on the ear.

"You're a bastard, Sidner."

Sidner has dreamed many times that he has fallen down a steep precipice, that he has drowned; but waking and going into his parents' bed, he learned to wait out dreams. "Wait out the world's longest dream as well, year after year? Wait until you are old and really wake up at last, in death? Is that the way my life is going to look?"

The youngsters get up and he tells her *faintly*: You can't go down there, we'll wait here. Eva-Liisa wipes off her cheek, which gets smeared with blood.

"Bastard! I'm going to tell Mamma about this."

But, as if for the first time, she sees Sidner's eyes.

Sees they are *new* when he stretches out his hand to her, the filthy fingers, touches her blood: "I'm sorry…" Her words are as faint as his:

"Why'd you do that?"

17

"Some day," Sidner says, feeling the words recede from the world, "some day it will be clear."

They catch sight of Aron. He walks right in the midst of the running, jostling cattle. In his arms, he carries a bloody bundle, and it is not to be looked at. Nor is his cry to be heard:

"I can't gather the cooows. Oh, I can't gather the cooooows."

He passes by them, up toward Things, which now undress themselves. The house undresses, the spruces at the edge of the forest, the chopping block in front of the barn, the axe driven down into its middle; yes, the grass undresses and turns toward the road. They all draw near to receive him when he falls.

ARON WANDERS BACK AND FORTH on the surface of
sleep. Here are the white and dark-violet blossoms of the broad
beans, which at four in the morning have a web of dew around
them. They stand in long rows on the lower side of the house. The
carrots are still light green, still delicate. He walks there and ob-
serves traces of roe deer. Once he would have put up a net. Once
he had zealous fingers.

He wanders over the fields of oats, through the pasture land.
Ends up standing, looking at something which, after awhile, re-
veals itself as a stone, a cowpile, a dried branch. Slowly, if it happens at all, the properties glide out of the object, take form, put
themselves in proper order, become one with their name. Often
there is a white moment just before, which can last minutes, when
the stone refuses to be a stone, when the hand refuses to be a hand,
when one cannot even die since one is not alive.

He returns to the yard when the sun reaches the lowest row of
windows; the cat sits in there, getting a splash of beams on its black
fur. Stands again with one foot in the vegetable garden: Solveig's
holy land. Aron helped her dig it in the spring, but then went out
into the open fields, leaving her on her knees, barefoot in the
spring earth, the germinating earth, because he felt so strangely
shy in the presence of this sowing. The seeds were too small. But
in the autumn he returned to pull up, cut tops, pack in sand, and
carry to the earth cellar.

Stands there now and contemplates the memory of her:
Leaning forward, she crawled along the rows, her soft breasts
filling her blouse, her hand brushing her hair from her forehead
and leaving a streak of dirt. She was the prettiest thing he knew;
everything stood in comparison to her. Even asleep, early in the

morning, during hard work. In all her movements, she gathered in so much light that there was enough for him, too. She always found a smile where he could least imagine the presence of one. Because there was a shortage of smiles in the district. Laughter did not belong to the farmers; laughter was an act of treason.

He bends down and tries to push her aside, makes an effort to clear away the weeds that already stand high among the broad beans, the sweet peas, and the red beets. But it is as if someone lifts away his hand.

You must not weed here, Aron! This is Solveig's land. The weeds are waiting for her. If he took them away, she would not return.

The Smile breezes by him.

It had been so near that he shrugged away this possibility of her.

He gets up and peers at the sun. The Smile stretches over his lips when he looks out over the plots: she could never refrain from that!

What was death compared to that shining love in the trees, in the soil, in the mist rising down there on the lake?

Everything is in its place: last year the barn was newly-painted red, the new hay-drying racks lean against the big birch; the pastures are high and the clover moist. Outside the kitchen window coneflowers sway, and little sweet williams look up at them in admiration. The cat sits in the window, her blue-black ears twitching in the presence of a buzzing fly.

Oh no, you cannot resist all that. The only thing to do is wait.

Aron pushes through the currant bushes, gets the ladder from the back of the house. Neither of the children has slipped out for a morning pee; he wants to see them.

But they are not asleep. They sit naked on their beds, in the same world as he, and he has nothing to give them.

Cannot come flying to their gaping senses.

Leans in and frightens them, since he brings so much darkness.

The black in Sidner's eyes: he sits with crossed legs on the sheets and travels through the surf.

"I was only..." says Aron, picking with his finger at the window putty. A bit falls, bounces off the ladder. His hand doesn't know anything anymore.

"I'm hungry, Papa," says Eva-Liisa.

It will be easier for her. Her memory will evaporate from her mind. But Sidner?

"Sleep a little longer, it's early."

"But why aren't you asleep?"

Giving was Solveig's thing. Language was hers; then what was his? Nothing. He was a borrower. He was on the outskirts, could sometimes step in under her light and become a participant. But now... what was left behind?

He stumbles down the ladder and sets out running for the fields, away along the lumber trail through the forest and, while he runs, June turns into July. It becomes August and September; the rain falls; the fields become muddy and the grain lies there. Waterlogged ruts, cows with distended udders bellow in the barn. Aron sinks down onto a stone. No one has come to pull up the weeds. No one has crept into his bed. Solveig is still too busy with her death; there must be a great deal to do.

Aron gave up in October of that year, despite the help he received from his neighbors with the animals and the harvest. He knew he could do nothing else.

The last day, when he was carrying out the furniture and household utensils he had decided to save, Solveig stood before the bedroom mirror and blocked his way. Knotting a scarf at the nape of her neck, a hairpin in her mouth, she smiled at him:

"I'm just going to get ready," she said as their eyes met in the mirror. "It won't take long."

Aron nodded and went toward her until he struck his hands against the glass of the mirror, splintering it into a thousand pieces. Sidner, standing behind him, remained silent and looked down at the sea of glass.

"Would you get the dustpan, Sidner?"

"We've already packed it on the wagon."

"Do as I say!" Aron yelled. It was the first time he had raised his voice at either of his children.

While Sidner was outside digging among their possessions, Aron gathered the shards together so Solveig could remain whole. He lay on the floor, saw her twinkling in the pieces. Her fluttering scarf was violet. He knew her eyes, her arm must be in another of the pieces; it would take a long time.

"Solveig, where are you?"

And just as she was about to answer from far inside one of the bits of glass he held up to the light, Sidner came crashing into the room with dustpan and brush. He stopped:

"What is it, Papa?"

"We're going to move away from here." Aron crawled along the floorboards with his hands full of pieces. When he reached the wall, he huddled up, squeezed the bits until the blood ran from his fingers.

"Can you ever forgive me for this?"

"It's not your fault, Papa."

"Yes, it is," said Aron. "Sit down beside me. I… can't… manage anything."

They cried the empty room full, side by side, with their backs against the wallpaper, where ugly, pale squares left by pictures and photographs stood out, where rips could be seen and dustballs, a safety pin in a crack stuck out its shiny head, autumn flies walked on the windowpane, darkness against the rain-laden skies, and outside, the horse that would take their lives away from here and into town, neighed.

"Shall I get the gramophone?"

A little later it stood on a packing case containing the bed linens.

Ich folge dir gleichfalls mit freudigen Schritten
Und lasse dich nicht
Mein Leben, Mein Licht
Befördre den Lauf
Und hör nicht auf
Selbst an mir zu ziehen
zu schieben, zu bitten.

"I didn't find the *Christmas Oratorio*," said Sidner. "But this is just as good. In two months, Mamma would have sung."

"She's going to," said Aron. "I mean…"

"Hold me, Papa."

"Where's Eva-Liisa? I want her, too… Go get her."

"I can't."

But he got up, opened the window, yelled out. Eva-Liisa sat in an armchair on top of the load, eating apple rings out of the big washtub, apple rings they had cut all autumn, hung on string and dried in the linen room until it smelled like paradise, and Sidner had often snuck in there alone, not to steal the winter's sustenance but to smell the scent of other autumns, of other conversations around the kitchen table. About music. About America. About the Fireflies on the porch in Kansas where Solveig had grown up.

"I don't feel like coming in," laughed Eva-Liisa without turning toward Sidner, and he quickly closed the window.

"She's already…"

"Yes. She's forgotten. She'll forget, but you and I…" Emphasized, as if to imprint and confound forgetfulness. Clarities in chaos. Something to hold onto. Something to test time and time again with tongue, hand, and eyes. That: "When we sat there that last day, you and I, Papa, and you said…" But at the same time, it would never help. Right now the house was coming loose from them. Now Aron's enterprises were slipping from his hands. As of now everything was new, unknown, without a name. From here until death.

❦

It was raining heavily when they came out into the yard. A neighbor was putting a tarpaulin over the load, and they could see Eva-Liisa's eyes peeking out of the dark.

"I have a terrific cave here."

Sidner carried the gramophone. There wasn't room for it under the already-secured cover; he placed it on top of the load, its horn seeking space.

Aron stood on the steps. The neighbor came and stretched out his hand.

"I understand how it feels," he said.

"Thanks for all your help. Now and last summer."

"There's not much one could do. About the toughest part."

"I know, but without you..."

"I hope you'll come back and visit. You know, you and Solveig, you have..." The neighbor turned away, dried his eyes with the back of his hand, and Aron saw her again: Big, tremendous, she grew out over the landscape, away over his old meadow, by the hay drying racks.

"You know what I mean."

There had been so much about Solveig that was different. The neighbor gave Aron a faint smile through his tears, so they both thought about the same thing: the daylight kissing. Because, there, Solveig had been a pioneer. It had not reached the district before Solveig one day, right in the middle of a bright morning, had embraced and kissed him; and when the neighbor, who had been standing further off, watched them in astonishment, Aron embarrassedly wriggled out of Solveig's arms, dried off his mouth, and said: "That comes from America." The words had spread like wildfire through the village, soon escaping from the mouths of all the farmers when at twelve noon they wanted to have their arms full of woman, words that made their bodies hot:

"Now you're going to taste something from America."

At first, the women had broken away, snorting and saying that might be alright in America, but not here. But the poison spread, although no one thought any longer that it intruded or destroyed the desire to work. It even happened that one might see a dog rose in the women's blouses in the middle of the day.

"And all the music from your place! It's going to be quiet around here now. Boy, is it raining! You don't think you should wait until..."

"It's going to stop," said Aron.

Climbing down the stairs, he went over to Basso and stroked the raindrops off his back. He did not want to get rid of the horse, and it might be needed in town. Slowly he began to move, slowly braked down the slope, around the bend past the Moment, where all went with heads bowed. Aron was like a collapsed umbrella; nothing shielded him from the world's view. His thumbs lay slack in his hands. Sidner walked by his side, sought his free hand.

The neighbor waved. Turned up toward the forest.

The road wound down toward the lake, passed the little sawmill and store, and crossed the farm yards. Here and there, faces were glimpsed behind windowpanes; people hid; it was too hard to see and converse about. And the children!

The trees were almost leafless. Outside the village, the forest stretched tall and dark. The crows flapping over them, Basso lumbering slowly, the wheels squeaking, and Eva-Liisa's chewing under the tarpaulin were sounds that ate into them. Aron thought about all the homecomings from town along this road, how strong his desire had been, how urgent his impatience.

It was always like coming home to the dwelling-place of words. For Aron, everything had been closed before he met her; the world had not chosen him. He witnessed how she forced open one thing after another so they became rich, glimmering with meaning. He had moved into the world of words.

Now he was out in the silence again.

Here he had come with the bicycle hidden under flour sacks. It was a shiny black-and-yellow model. He had seen it outside Asplund's Sports Shop, and Asplund himself had said it was the most expensive, but she's worth it, Solveig is. On the morning of her birthday, he had put it in the billowing vines on the porch. At five o'clock when the sun broke through, he led her out in her nightgown, the children following; they knew and exchanged glances. He stood a little behind her; she turned around and showered him and the children with all that she owned so much of: caresses, kisses.

Here and there in the forest a leaf still fell to the ground. A hare dashed across the road. Sidner had climbed up to the top of the load and sat there with the gramophone and a stack of Bakelite records in his arms. Here the road was straight for several kilometers; there was nothing to see, nothing to look forward to. He would start in a new school on Monday, have new companions. He was afraid. Afraid not to be able to talk to them, afraid he would start crying in the middle of lessons. In the village, the youngsters had left him in peace; now once again there would be so much to explain, to repeat, to come into contact with the memories. He peeked down enviously at Eva-Liisa, who had fallen asleep in her armchair under the tarpaulin: to be able to forget as he knew she was doing! Would Solveig not exist in her at all, then?

These first seven years of hers?

The farm where they had lived?

Wouldn't it exist? Don't those first years exist? Just erase them... like that!

The first and only person they met on the road into Sunne was a little roly-poly old woman who, like a swan on land, came swaying toward them from far in the distance. When she caught sight of the loaded wagon she went off into the ditch, and behind her bouquet of heather she made herself into spruce and rock, grass and blueberry sprigs.

"The first dove," Aron said when they were by. "Sent out from our new land."

"Who was that?"

"I think she's called Angela... Mortens. She's sure to be on her way to some funeral or wedding, but got lost. She usually does that."

Sidner turned around and saw the old woman climb out of the ditch and, with the bouquet in front of her face, stand absolutely still, watching them with an ice water smile on her thin lips.

They reach Sunne at around nightfall. Aron has an apartment and job there.

There they will start over.

And Sidner is twelve, and soon the gramophone and box of records will slide off the load when the horse recoils from a car; the ground will be covered with Bakelite splinters. But first a quote from *On Caresses*: "Nothing lasts, except the dying tone which the succession of ordinary days tries, but never completely manages, to obliterate."

Now the records fall to the ground.

SLEIPNER BRINK, one of broadcasting's first victims, knelt in front of the sofa with the earphones on, listening to the Devil's apparatus that he had tenderly placed on the flowery seat cushions.

His wife, Victoria, screamed and cried about every other thing. Radios got on her nerves. From the day her brother-in-law, Torin, had given them that apparatus, their world had started to fall into decay. However little she cared for the front side of her man, his bottom, back, and the dirty soles of his feet were even worse to have to look at constantly.

"You've forgotten to muck out around Rosa," she shrieked. "That's the third day in a row I've had to do it myself. And you haven't been out in the masonry, either."

But Sleipner heard nothing but the radio's delights:

"Assyrian was the diplomatic language of the whole Middle East from approximately 2000 until nearly 700 B.C. We find an excellent example of the Assyrian language's significance to inter-Asian communication in a collection of documents and letters to the Egyptian king, Amenhoptep IV, which are dated from the year 1400 B.C. All these more or less official documents are written in cuneiform…"

Interference covered the lecturer.

"… how daily life was shaped in the Euphrates Valley during the second millennium before Christ, and in the year 1901 the great codex was found which King Hammurabi – the Bible's Amraphal – ordered published in the year 2000 B.C. During the course of the seventh and eighth centuries, Assyrian was superseded by the other great Semitic language…"

Sleipner would never know what that language was, and that enraged his days. Victoria walloped him on the back so he fell flat on his face on the sofa.

"Your brother-in-law will be here soon, and you've promised to help him."

"Damn. Are they here already?"

"Soon, anyway."

"But that's not *now*. You could have at least waited until that damned opera started."

"I don't read the radio program," she shrilled.

"You can hardly read anything else, either," he answered, but softened at once: "Oh, so Aron and the kids are on their way. You could have said so earlier."

Victoria snorted and crossed to the window. Sleipner locked up the earphones and the apparatus in a chest, stuck the key in his pocket, sat down at the kitchen table, and looked out through the trees toward the stone masonry where his brother Torin worked on a tombstone.

Victoria came and leaned over him.

"Has he said anything?"

"About what?"

"About the child... About the Zetterberg girl, of course. If it's him?"

"That isn't our business. Torin looks after himself."

Sleipner pushed aside the kitchen curtain and looked out at his brother's huge head with the bright red hair and the pale eyebrows like rye on a summer morning. His back was heavy and his upper arms powerful. He was a skillful stonemason, nobody could say the contrary.

"But he must know if it's him?"

"You can ask him if you're so interested."

"I'm not his brother. Has he said anything about getting married?"

"No."

"The Zetterbergs would never go for that. Torin isn't good enough for them."

"You don't think so either."

"I haven't said he isn't nice."

"But dumb, you've said. And Torin isn't dumb. Do you think an idiot can get a pilot's licence? He wasn't more than eighteen when he got it. The youngest of all. Do you think he'd be allowed to take care of the planes up at Broby in that case?"

"He could at least dress a little better. *I* wouldn't dare fly with him."

"Nobody would let an hysterical female like you in an airplane."

"It would never occur to me to put myself up in the air."

"Do you think an idiot could build a radio that brings in the whole of Europe? You bitch," Sleipner muttered, in English, sinking over the kitchen table so he could peek with one eye at the radio listings for the evening, but Victoria was happy to be able to talk to her husband and did not intend to waste the opportunity.

"But to go with a loose female like that. After all, you are a minister's children."

"Zetterberg's looseness we don't know anything about, and what do you mean a minister's children?" Again in English, "My father was not a real minister."

"What are you talking about?"

"My father was a bar owner in Kansas. I've said that a thousand times."

"But before that. My parents remembered him."

"I think I need to shave before they get here."

"That's the limit."

"It's Saturday."

"As if you care about that. Just think, Solveig and you and him…"

"Don't drag her in now, I'm warning you."

Sidner writes in his first black oilcloth book: "Uncle Sleipner and Aunt Victoria have become lost in Quarrel Forest. There is little space between the trees; they bump into each other all the time. I cannot imagine how they kiss or caress. There is such a difference between theirs and my parents' marriage. And yet Uncle Sleipner, like Mamma, is from Kansas where, according to her, a more *cordial* atmosphere prevails: therefore, he ought to have learned to show his innermost feelings, which, of course, should not be frightened of the daylight. However, perhaps Aunt Victoria has *taken over* to such an extent that expressions of feelings flourish only in darkness, which ought to be common in Sweden. (With certain exceptions for Midsummer, when the lack of darkness, so to speak, *forces* them out into the light.) Yes, presumably this is so; the example of daylight kissing I myself have seen had not come into use before I was a child, through Mamma, and before that darkness was used, something which for a Southerner must sound awful. (Research that!!!) But one must not forget the long winters which, of course, for seventy to eighty percent consist of *complete* darkness."

Aron, who is a teetotaler, has a job as porter at the Hotel Sunne where he is put in charge of Boss Björk's liquor supplies. An apartment comes with the job: two rooms and a kitchen above the hotel, with an exit at the back of the building. Half the town can be seen from the windows in the middle room, as can the Spirits Cellar, a low but solid building of granite blocks and a heavy door that cannot be opened without double keys. Sleipner and Torin are waiting for them when they rattle in on the shiny wet pavement. They make the first trip upstairs empty-handed, the brothers urging Aron to go first, standing behind him at the threshold. Sleipner sees Victoria has already slipped in with a geranium as a signal that the world is ready to receive them.

They breathe in the clean smell of varnish and paint: here it is light and clean.

"Fine, fine," Torin sighs, laying his heavy hand on Aron's shoulder. But Aron turns to go down again:

"I'll start carrying things up," he mumbles, because it is as if he is not allowed to be pleased with the apartment. As if he would betray Solveig. And he has already done that by not waiting for her at the farm. So he stands there with the kitchen table. Sleipner stretches his hands toward it.

"Where do you want it?"

"It makes no difference," he says, rushing out again to avoid taking the initiative. He makes himself a bearer of foreign objects: trunks, silverware, chest drawers; he puts them just inside the door, not raising his eyes, hurrying out again when Sleipner tries to stop him. He does not want to have anything to do with it. And besides, Sidner is there as well, you know. He's going to live here, too. He comes slowly up the stairs with the broken gramophone records under his arm, pressing them tightly to his body; he passes Aron with dumb-struck eyes. So at last they end up standing beside each other in the doorway, and Sidner gives Aron the pleasure of asking him where they are to sleep.

There is not much to choose from. Aron will have his bed in the kitchen; that is what he wants, weakly referring to his work, in case of night-time errands... Sidner gets the innermost room and Eva-Liisa the middle; Eva-Liisa, who has slept almost the whole trip, is still asleep when he carries her up and lays her on her bed in the middle of the gleaming floor, under a naked, swinging bulb.

There he glimpses his burden, just after he has put her down. It tears through him: "How long can I manage to keep the kids together?"

So now *that* question is going to whirl through his head every day. Now that he isn't anyone anymore, not even a bad farmer who can't manage cattle or fields.

A nothing without language, without characteristics; how long will he be able to be the center of these children's lives? To dare wake up in the morning and take their needs in hand. As well as his. Where will he find himself again?

Sleipner and Torin watch his movements, faces half-turned away; and when table and chairs are finally where they should be, they find themselves across from one another, and Torin's big hand finds its way across the table top.

"She was the best there is, brother!" Adding in English: "Papa said, 'Take care of her.' Just before he died."

"Speak Swedish." Sleipner pokes him in the shoulder, but Torin does not hear.

"*I remember when she sang on the veranda among the fireflies...*" Again in English.

"Fireflies," prompts Sleipner. "When she sang on the porch."

"*Such a voice!*"

Sleipner translates.

"*And how beautiful she was. My little sister.*"

Again Sleipner translates.

"I understand," says Aron. "I managed to learn a bit myself... *She* taught me a bit."

"*And that hair!*"

"And that hair."

"I understand," says Aron. "That hair."

"*What did you say?*" Torin asks, lifting his head toward Aron. "*You remember her hair, too?*"

"You remember her hair, too?" Sleipner interprets.

"Of course I remember her hair."

"*Good. Wasn't it lovely? Not my red hair. Not at all, brother.*"

"Not my red hair, not at all," continues Sleipner, but suddenly it's the funeral all over again. A hundred people in the midst of a summer day, the overpowering scent of flowers, the sweetness, the tears. It's the church choir, which suddenly falls silent in the middle of singing; it's Choir Master Jancke's hands, which become rigid in the air and cannot go on:

"Because it was you, Solveig... who gave birth to this choir,

33

who gave birth to and nourished our work. Who filled us with enthusiasm evening after evening. It was you who... Solveig, give us the power to... continue."

It is Eva-Liisa who pulls them back by waking and dashing into the room.

"Where am I, Papa?"

"We're going to live here."

"I don't want to. I want to go home."

"This is home."

Someone says it. Someone fixes on that.

Someone tries to pull the knife out of his remark.

"For a while, in any case."

Notices that it has got stuck. Cuts and tears:

"It's going to be all right, you'll see."

"I want to go home."

And there the matter rests. The knife is going to turn around in the replies. And Aron sinks down at the table with Eva-Liisa in his lap, strokes her hair awkwardly, hears how it screams out of him:

"I'm only thirty-five!"

"Such is life." Torin pads back and forth in the kitchen. "Such is life, brother."

"Oh, come on, Torin." Sleipner shakes off his brother's gloom, raises the curtain. "There's going to be a change. You'll meet a lot of strange people here at the hotel, Aron. Frenchmen and Americans; Englishmen, at any rate. If you need help with translations, you just ask. Boss Björk holds court here. To be quite honest, it's a hell of a life sometimes. The Thursday Club. You're going to see some things.

"Now, let's go to Beryl Pingel's and get a bite to eat."

SIDNER CLAIMS MANY YEARS LATER that, without the baker Beryl Pingel, *On Caresses* would never have been started – which might be an exaggeration, the way many things with Sidner back then were exaggerations in the word's true sense. But at that particular time, she came to mean a great deal, which all people in and of themselves in what followed would do, since he found himself in a new world.

"Were I to describe her or the impression she made, I would place her in a summer day, in a cloud of flour, with the door open to the lupine. Pale morning sun, when I came in after helping her with the beehives, almost blinded by the sun. Often she was baking, but just as often she was ironing the loose collars Torin used when he was out taking orders for tombstones. On such occasions, the open door was filled with her laughter, and it struck me frequently that the laughter had to come from somewhere. Nothing originates from nothing. Everything has its cause. The dough and the loose collars, at the very least the loose collars, could be the cause. Unless laughter itself is the origin of all things. Oh, wonderful thought! I took it upon myself to research that, and Consul Jonsson, who took care of the library, got his greatest customer. It was tremendous to go into such a big library. I started with the pre-Socratic philosophers Heraclitus, Parmenides, and Zeno. It is a fine thought that Heraclitus might have sat in the kitchen and let Beryl Pingel iron his loose collars while he tasted her rolls and, little by little, sank into her laughter."

But that October evening Sidner was quiet. He trotted among the falling leaves, through the stone masonry, to Beryl Pingel's yard.

In the darkness Torin grasped Aron's arm:

"You can always depend on Beryl," he said. "About things that deal with females, you know, and children. There's a lot we don't understand."

"Yeah, it's a good thing she's around," Sleipner muttered and stepped through the doorway of flour.

Beryl Pingel sat at her baking table and was expectant. Strong arms, big bosom, pale yellow hair around her forehead. Eva-Liisa was pushed forward first:

"Well, look here, God bless you, you're Eva-Liisa. And Sidner, come close so I can touch you."

She impetuously drew both youngsters in toward the center of her warmth. Sidner stumbled and dropped the bunch of broken records in Beryl's lap. She picked up a triangular piece upon which the label was still readable.

"Don't you think it's possible to fix these?

Sidner shook his head.

"It can't be done." Still uncertain in her presence, he gathered up the pieces and stuck them inside his jacket, placed himself against the wall.

"They're supposed to be broken."

SIDNER'S TEACHER was called Mr. Stålberg. He was a good teacher. He used to end each term by balancing on his bicycle in the classroom and, *standing still,* playing his violin: "It's Getting Better Day by Day," "The Tragic Ballad of Lieutenant Sparre and Elvira Madigan," and, as a conclusion, if it was Christmas, "Silent Night," or if it was summer, "Now Is the Flowering Season, with Joy and Beauty Great."

Sidner bewildered him. He had read the boy's first essay, "A Christmas Memory," not expecting anything but the usual clumsy effort, that the snow fell and the Christmas trees gleamed. But this is what Sidner wrote:

"The greatest of all composers, Johann Sebastian Bach, was tired. In the dark December evening he wandered homeward, where all his children waited impatiently for him with their hubbub and screaming. He had forgotten to buy *candies,* for there was so much to do. He was freezing. The church had been cold all afternoon, the choir members grumpy and hoarse. How could he cheer them up? That was the question that kept going around in his handsome head. While he slowly strolled through the slush in the dirty streets, he got an idea. He said to himself, 'I'll cheer them up with a song. They could use that, my poor friends.' When he approached the house where he lived with his whole family and saw the lights shining there, a lovely melody suddenly rose up inside him. An idea had taken form! He had hardly managed to take off his outdoor clothes and hug his children before he dashed with urgent steps into his workroom. So he began to write the Christmas Oratorio. Those were happy days for the family as they gathered around the piano just before Christmas 1734. The best was created."

Mr. Stålberg had been informed that Sidner should be treated with care. He was told he should have patience with Sidner's absences, his staring gaze, gaping mouth. The boy was gifted and would soon recover from the shock, if he were just given time. Mr. Stålberg understood that, but sometimes he was still impatient when he noticed that, as he put it to his colleagues, "The boy lives in his own world. See," he said, pointing out the window, "there he stands completely alone." His colleagues followed his pointing finger toward the woodshed. Sidner stood with his back against the wall, absolutely still, his right arm pressed against his side, as if he were hiding something inside his clothes, and Mr. Stålberg knew what it was: a bunch of broken gramophone records Sidner refused to let go of. Snow fell in heavy flakes on his shoulders and cap. Playing children made a swing by him, threw shy glances his way.

During class, when the essays were being handed out, Mr. Stålberg was at a loss.

"Sidner," he said, after he had gone through the others' miserable writing efforts, "Sidner, you have here…"

And Sidner flew up from his desk, stood completely still, staring directly through his teacher. Not a muscle moved in his face.

"You have written a curious little composition here. Your language is very fine, but is it really a Christmas memory? You haven't really experienced that."

"Nothing was said about having to be there."

Mr. Stålberg swallowed: "No, you're right about that, of course. But one assumes that is so." And why really? he thought, the boy's right. "And there are several strange words: for example *candies,* what's that?"

"It's a type of sweet, sir."

"So why didn't you write that?"

"I didn't think I should write: He had forgotten to buy a type of sweet. There are *candies* in America."

"If I remember correctly, Bach lived in Germany. You shouldn't put on airs, Sidner."

"Sorry, sir." Sidner's eyes filled with tears. "I didn't mean to, sir."

"Sit down, boy. I understand that."

The next subject several months later was: "What one can learn in forest and field."

"When rambling through forest and field, one can learn a great deal. In a book I read one afternoon up at Gråmyren, near the place I lived until last summer, I read that Johann Sebastian Bach was born in 1689 in the German city of Eisenach and that he was married twice, since his first wife died of a bad cold. He had many children..."

"Sidner!"

Sidner is already standing up. His classmates look at him. It always gets very quiet when Sidner is called on. The room smells of wet wool and the warm stove; the coughing and sniffling die away. Stålberg hesitates, looks down at the book with its long, angular handwriting, where every word is spelled correctly, where there are no errors in syllable division, not one comma misplaced. It takes a moment before he dares assert his authority as a teacher, knowing the second before that he ought to let it be:

"Sidner, you have misunderstood your subject. That was not the idea."

"Sir, it... I mean, I learned that in forest and field."

"You may sit down."

"Are you angry, sir?"

Stålberg shakes his head.

The boy glides away on his sea of absence. It appears that way, at any rate. It's just that he has never been able to catch Sidner being lazy, being inattentive.

Stålberg had, of course, met Solveig, since he was also in the church choir. He was one of those who was to have performed the *Christmas Oratorio*. He knew it was Solveig Nordensson's idea, and he remembered how enormously quiet it became the day she put forward her suggestion. He remembered how Mr. Jancke had started, then stared at her a long time. It was after an unusually wretched rehearsal of some very simple spring songs for the concert on the church steps at Walpurgis. Jancke had stood up in the organ loft and snorted so that saliva spattered over the balustrade and down on the portrait of Haqvin Spegel.

"*The Christmas Oratorio!* By Bach? *Us?*"

Jancke was a great musician. He had come from the Stockholm area with loftier ideas than the Sunne choir could implement. The night Solveig made her suggestion he could not sleep and took his youngest child on his shoulders, wandering back and forth in the churchyard until morning came. His feet were soaked and it was only then he noticed he had walked in the rain-soaked gravel paths in his slippers, without an overcoat or anything on his head. And all this was his own problem. It was worse for his daughter, who in her nightgown had caught a terrible cold that kept the family worried until Midsummer.

Mr. Jancke was aware of the weariness of his life. He was forty-three years old and nothing had really been as he had thought it would be. He told the choir members the following week:

"When I was young, I dreamed of being a great musician. I had childish hopes of becoming a conductor, of traveling around Europe's cities, making choirs and orchestras dance to my baton. It didn't happen. I came here. You're a lousy choir and it's not your fault; it's society's. With one exception – you, Solveig – we are second-raters, all of us, because we have second-rate goals. But now I've made a decision. Those who are with me will work until it hurts. But I'll make you a promise: In ten years, here in Sunne's church, we will present Bach's *Christmas Oratorio*. This will be my life's work. Maybe it's not what I dreamed of to start with, but with the conditions we have, it'll have to do. Ten years is a long time. Your children will be grown, some will have grown tired.

But let us, a couple of times a week, piece by piece, measure by measure, work toward that musical cosmos Bach has created. I'll try to recruit musicians from dance floors and brass bands, I'll train kids. We'll *do* it. Are you with me?"

Ten years had passed since that day. The music grew around them. Swept like a cloud of wings around the chimney sweep, the house painter, the tenor, around the children's choir and the orchestra members. One after another, people were plucked from their houses with new talents.

And now?

After Solveig's death?

Jancke raised his hands at Solveig's funeral. The choir began to sing, but after two or three measures, just at the point where Solveig's voice should have freed itself and swung up to the highest heights, played like the swallows under the honey-scented shadows of the churchyard lindens, just there, they all fell silent at once: a choir, an orchestra, a conductor, a whole community's collective goal. And no one had been able to start again throughout the fall.

Sidner's last essay for Mr. Stålberg was called "One Day in Spring." He had to read it aloud to his classmates while Mr. Stålberg stood with his pointer swinging behind his back.

"One lovely spring day, Johann Sebastian Bach took his family with him out into the country. The birds chirped in the trees, the brooks rippled, all the roads were messy, but at last they found a place where they could sit down and eat their bread and drink their wine. (The class stirred nervously.) They sat right by a brook; the youngest, who was named Johann Philip Emmanuel, was allowed to sit in his mother's lap. The older brothers had their flutes with them. Together they played the melody line from Papa's fourth Brandenburg concerto. It sounded so beautiful. The sun was hot and, after a while, Mamma and Papa took off their clothes and sat there completely naked, letting the sun light up their bodies. (The class put a collective hand before its mouth and giggled.

Sidner looked up and smiled uncertainly…) After that, they lay down on the ground close to each other…"

"Now that's enough, Sidner!" screamed his teacher. The class held its breath. Sidner gaped. He was surprised. He looked from one to the other and pressed his back against the blackboard.

"Give me the book," hissed the teacher.

Sidner dumbly handed it to him.

"Here's what to do with such rubbish." And Mr. Stålberg, who had had a bad day at home, tore it into pieces and threw it into the stove.

It was quiet, too, in the teachers' room when Stålberg related chosen parts of the essay to them. One of the older ones grumbled that the boy ought to be taken out of school, while another thought that he wasn't in full use of his senses and certainly such immoral writing ought to be punished. But the promise of patience was in their consciousness and all of them got lost in the thought: Has it really been like that, there at home with Solveig and Aron?

Sidner himself had misunderstood everything. He believed his teacher's wrath had come from his writing yet again about the adventures of the Family Bach; but this was necessary for him. Only there did his language catch fire. The source and joy of fantasy was there. There were so many words and tales, which he no longer knew for certain if Solveig had told, or if he only wished she had told them. For in his head, endless stories were shaped about a family out of whose midst the Great Music rippled.

As of that day, he was not able to write another word for Mr. Stålberg. The pages remained blank.

But he could still read:

To open a book and sink into it! Jungle on the one page, a battle raging on the next. No one could reach you on that narrow ledge between Period and Capital Letter. Like a wood louse, he could pop in between the pages, lie still, peek out sometimes. He could tickle the words on their backs so they laugh, a laugh heard only by him. He could wander around in the forest of words where the light plays so beautifully, and behind every curve in the text see something new: words as arches, as crowns of trees, as trunks and flames of fire. Strange animals moving about with cries he had never heard before. There he could find secret cities, villages, ships, and people who talked in many different ways. Grown people were there, as were those already dead, and all of them taught him things he perhaps shouldn't know yet. There was much he did not understand, and that gave him pleasure most of all, because there was a world before him then which he must reach. The incomprehensible was the best, or as he would write one day: "I do not know, therefore I must go further."

To play was also possible. To take a little step to the side and transport himself into music's time.

When he still lived up near the forest, he used to be sent to the store to shop. Willingly, he went with the list of goods. A little distance away he caught sight of some ants crossing his path. They were unusually large, their backs glittering brown-black in the sun. Sidner bent down and ended up precisely *under* time. When they found him crawling with his face against the ground, when they tapped him on the back after speaking to him a long time without getting an answer, he got up without surprise and said: "I was just... I'll go now." That was his right as a child, for children could not manage without the ability to disappear from the body's cramped prison. To grow up is to relinquish that ability.

The gates rust shut.

But music's gate did not rust shut. On the keyboard's secret paths, he wormed through the jungle of demands and shortcomings. With bowed head, with half-closed eyes, he took himself to the crest where the roads lie open. Then he cast his face backwards, opened his eyes, and smiled: he was through the gate. Inaccessible and alone out in the music, if on a great sheet of ice where the sun releases drops of gold. Telephones could ring around that ice. And they would.

TRUSTED HORSE AND WAGON DRIVERS deliver hundred-liter barrels to Hotel Sunne's well-locked Spirits Cellar. The porter, Aron Nordensson, receives them at the open door; his son Sidner helps roll the barrels into the big storeroom. The drivers then hand over a box containing several envelopes: these are the labels for aquavit, sherry, champagne, liqueurs; pretty labels with glimmering colors and French and German words. Clean, empty bottles with narrow shoulders, with wide, round, oblong, square shoulders, stand on the shelves.

Aron writes receipts for the consignment, then follows the drivers to the hotel's kitchen where they get something to eat. But to Sidner he says: "You stay here and keep watch." He closes the door behind him. Sidner sits down on a stool among the barrels; the naked light bulb glows over him, the steps in the gravel die away. He sits still, one hand clenched, his mouth half open, his head tilted slightly backward. He can sit that way an hour, a day. He does not need to move. But he will if Aron wants him to move. He does if his teacher says something to him. Then he gets up immediately and gives answers to what he already knows. He has overheard someone saying that his lamp of intelligence is being turned off. But that is not so.

When the drivers have had their food, Aron comes back, and they help each other fill the bottles, glue on labels, seal the bottles, wind foil around the corks and place them in fine rows. Five hundred bottles of aquavit, two hundred of sherry, and much more. Many workers like to hang around there in the evening, when work is over at the factories along Torvnäs Road. Fifty to sixty workers make their way home by here. They toss a last word to each other, perhaps cast a glance through the little barred window to catch a flash of the splendor, or simply in the hope that the Miracle will occur! One day, the door will glide open and everything will be quiet. No guard will be there, and, one after another, they will be able to wander into that delightfully illuminated cellar, gathering bottle after bottle into their arms.

"Think about that, Sidner, don't let anybody coax you, not with money or anything else, to even let them look in here. These are dangerous things we're handling."

"Yes, Papa."

"Has anyone tried?"

"Yes, once I was to have a big coin from a man. He stood outside the window and showed it to me. He banged on the door because, of course, he'd seen you go and leave me alone. It was the biggest coin I've ever seen. It hurt to look at it; it shone like a sun. But I turned away."

"How big was the coin?"

Sidner measured with his fingers.

"Only prize medals for horses are that big. They're not worth much." Aron cut off a foil square with the big scissors.

"It's a nuisance with this alcohol."

"But everybody says you can't do business without alcohol."

"Maybe business is a nuisance, too."

And so the days go. There is no music between them. They both have a terrible thirst for it.

"I think it's time for you to pick up Eva-Liisa at Beryl's, Sidner."

"I wonder if she hasn't caught the measles. She had so many red spots this morning."

"Then you'll have to stay home from school and take care of her." Words crawl between them. All through the winter, the words grope their way toward the barrier that is in them both. Time after time, they try to reach out to a smile, to a sudden flapping of wings, of flight straight up into the air. But it does not happen. They are both occupied with intense images. When

Aron looks at his hands, for example, the coarse hands Solveig placed one day on the piano keys:

"Now see, this is the scale, Aron, ta-da-da!" He sees them move over the black and white field, clumsily ending up between two notes.

"I can't do it."

"You're doing fine, Aron."

"But it's not fitting for a farmer like me..."

"Ta-da-da."

Spring and fall.

"Now this is a minuet. It's easy; listen how pretty it is." Summer and winter. And the piano, that almost hostile piece of furniture, became his, too. One day he could say: Our piano. How he tested those words when he went to the barn and mucked out: Maybe we should move our piano into the big room? His hands. Her hands, "Twinkle, twinkle, little star, how I wonder what you are."

"Sidner, you sing, too!"

And one day it is Aron who says something, it is he who takes the initiative, who wants to get into music; it is he who expresses a desire.

"Up above the world so high, like a diamond in the sky... You, too, Eva-Liisa... Up above the world so high."

"Listen to what you can do with your hands, Aron."

And he could lift them up in front of himself when he emptied the wheelbarrow onto the dung heap on early, cold mornings, when he was alone with the morning stars and really *see* them. They are mine. Like a diamond in the sky!

But his hands now!

Aron felt himself to be vulgar. His hands were vulgar when he dressed in a dark suit and white shirt and opened the door for the European lumber lords visiting the hotel to negotiate the price of wood. He gave himself anxious looks in the mirror when he had dressed for the evening's festivities, where he was to be the shadow between the kitchen and the vestibule. Boss Björk came in one day when he was straightening his bow tie:

"Good, Aron, that will do admirably. You're quite elegant."

Appraised and approved.

"Between us, Aron, I think we can use first names. When no one else can hear us, that is."

"Thanks, boss."

"Oh, it's nothing. You can call me Johan. After all, we're both Värmlanders, you know. Take something good with you from the kitchen up to the kids."

And Boss Björk inspects the next thing in his vicinity, the newly-bought furniture, strokes the gold frame of the mirror with his fingers; straightens the potted palm so the big feather pattern is turned outward; takes two steps back, his head on one side.

"What is it she's called now, your lass, sweet girl."

"Eva-Liisa."

"Yes, yes, that's right." Screws the palm further to the right, straightens the curtain, presses his face to the window. "It's begun to snow rather hard. Hope the guests aren't late."

"We must hope so, Johan."

Surprised, the Boss spins around, takes a breath, checks himself.

"Good, Aron, you've caught on." He sticks his thumbs in his vest. "You'll see, everything's going to be all right."

And when the kitchen maid carries a pile of plates out of the kitchen, and the clatter grows loud enough to be heard from where they stand, he says:

"It can't be too hard for you to get a little…" Aron turns on his heel, wants to hurry out onto the landing.

"Sorry, Aron, I didn't mean that you… I was lost in thought."

"I have to carry up the wine now, boss."

For the first time he feels how he is talked down to, how power lays a net over him. It cuts deeply, and he remembers his father, the stove maker, who gave away all he earned to anyone who was in need and who devoted himself to politics in his youth, had been what is called a free thinker. He had worked hard to get telephones in the district. He pushed the question harder than anyone else, but when it had gone so far that a delegation was to be sent up to Stockholm to negotiate, he was put off because he had one leg shorter than the other. "For you see, Aron, that makes you not quite a whole person in their eyes." And he had quit all his functions, caused a furor in the community since he knew so much and was indispensable in many areas. And he did not have any leanings toward Socialism, either, so there were apologies and excuses. But Nordensson had had enough. He moved, bought himself a farm, had the pleasure of hearing he was touchy.

And now the Boss stands there, several years closer to Modern Times, and wants to placate, shouts down the stairs.

"There was one thing, Aron. I've purchased a gramophone and wonder if you know... your wife was from America, of course. Do you know anything about what they call *jazz*?"

Aron stands listening to the silence while snowflakes fall on his eyelids. The Boss comes out after him:

"Something shocking, as they say?"

"Yes, Johan."

Solveig's interest had not really been in the direction of jazz, but she would gladly play some of the melodies they heard on the radio; she translated the lyrics, hummed along. So Aron was not a complete stranger to his task when he stepped into Grandin's Gramophones and Electrical Appliances. It was just that his hands were in the way when he browsed through the batches of records. This was not *work*. His body's strength had not been created to choose records.

"I would like something shocking. For Björk at the hotel."

The sales clerk lit up. While Aron picked a stack of names he had heard before – Jimmy Lunceford's Hot Sextet, Paul

Whiteman's Light Symphony Orchestra, Duke Ellington, Louis
Armstrong – the tone arm began to dance:

> *Thought if I want to be up-to-date*
> *I had to shimmy like Sister Kate*
> *Although I tried t'was all in vain*
> *But Sister Kate could not be blamed.*

WHILE SIDNER BURIED HIMSELF in his books after school or sat at the piano working through the pieces Mr. Jancke had assigned him, Eva-Liisa would glide out of Mourning with a guilty smile, her one braid almost catching in the door. Outside in the courtyard, she was sucked up by her friends who waited behind the Spirits Cellar or with Torin at the masonry; there were always children there, since Torin was a master at making animals out of clay: swans, elephants, horses grew out of his hands, animals with such pleading eyes and such pitiful expressions it was doing them a favor to own them. Eva-Liisa's friends waited in apple trees, behind hedges and on the slope of the railway embankment among the tansies and the lupines. Aron and Sidner could hear their laughter rise and fall in the summer evenings; saw bare legs moving, heard their intimate whispers out on the stairway where they sat and browsed through dictionaries for girls. Red balls rose outside the windows, their arms up-stretched, dividing the sky into different colored spheres.

Eva-Liisa escaped to open spaces: to the streets, to the forbidden sawmill, to the lake shore.

When Sidner went walking beside the churchyard wall there was a rustling in the crown of the maple tree:

"Ho, ho. I'm a bird."

The gap between her teeth was wide open.

"I live here with my friends."

Sidner tried to smile back at the one smile that existed in his world.

"We're building a cave. Are you a bird?"

"No, I'm not a bird."

"Goodbye, Notbird!"

He went along Gylleby Road with his hands behind his back. A field heavy with wheat, larks singing, a light wind in the telephone wires; at one point near the road, he saw waves of grain billowing.

"Good morning, Mr. Notbird."

Giggles filled the air. He stopped, searching for the words of play, but they were farther away than the Östanås Mountains. He heard how pitiful it sounded when he said:

"You're not allowed to be in there destroying things."

That was what burst from him, although he had chosen to extend himself to the heap of friends pressed together in there with their slender bodies. He wanted to wade out and be drawn down by a thousand small, sinuous arms, but he did not even dare to dip his toes in that sea, remaining instead on the shore, trying to look clever.

"Partridges," he said. "You're like partridges!" He sent a weak smile after the words, but it was tossed out too late and he received as an answer:

"We're not partridges, we're cartridges!'

Giggles and rustling.

He was amazed she could keep herself out of the darkness. It would take him a long time to understand that she had taken a gigantic task upon herself by staying out in the light, to show him it still existed. Like a sparkling comet, she and her friends flashed around the hotel in circles, sparks falling and exploding everywhere, searching him out where he stood still and alone among the apple trees when the second autumn came. Innocent atrocities chased him out into the night. It could be a little letter on the kitchen table:

Dear Mr. Notbird, I am going to the Saga Cinema tonight with my Friends. Are you going there with your Notfriends?

A bird

It could be a glance, a word, that caused him to flee. Because everything that was said had such strong *radiation,* and the radiation was directed at him. And so the apple orchard's darkness, and silence, catatonia.

So HE STOOD ONE EVENING in windbreaker and cap, reciting into the gale:

> *In the middle of this our life's wand'ring,*
> *I found myself in a gloomy wood, lost,*
> *gone from the path direct: and e'en to tell*
>
> *It was no easy task, how desolate*
> *That forest, how untamed and rough its growth,*
> *Which but to recall my horror awakes...*

He stood with his face turned towards Mr. Jolin's, the mill owner's, yard and it was completely dark:

> *A horror not less terrible than death.*
> *But, to discourse of what good there occurred,*
> *All else discovered there I will relate.*
>
> *How first I entered it I scarce can say,*
> *such heavy torpor in that moment weighed*
> *My senses down, when the right way I left...*

Right nearby he heard a pitiful and, at the same time, furious voice:

"Help me. Help me, damn it."

He stared into a pair of wild eyes.

"Oh, I got so scared... What are you doing on the fence?"

"I'm hangin' here," said the eyes. "By Selma's right shoe, help me get loose."

"You scared me."

He went closer and examined the phenomenon.

"It's your foot that's caught."

"I know that. Twist it round, it'll come loose. Like that. Thanks..."

A boy his age, but shorter, fell down on Sidner's side of the fence:

"Doggone, I thought I was done fer... Take these here apples, we gotta hurry 'case she comes..." He got up, approached Sidner:

"I thought she was after me, Old Woman Jolin, but it was jest a fox. What was that you was recitin'?"

"Nothing."

"J'a write it yerself?"

"No, he's called... Dante."

"Sounded good anyway."

"Do you think so? I thought no one would find me out here."

"Couldn't 'a done better myself..."

"Did you steal the apples?"

"An' plums. Take one... But we'd better get outta here, or the old lady'll come fer sure. We'll go down ta the woodshed by the lake."

Sidner's friend was called Splendid for the Hotel Splendid in Karlstad, where he was conceived the first night his future parents slept together at the hotel. It was a posh place with an elevator, which his mother never neglected to mention. They had ended up there by mistake, since the sister they were to have visited during their honeymoon had broken her leg and was just then in a hospital, cut off from the surrounding world. The minister, who was called upon ten months later, said: "I cannot christen a child Splendid," but the parents responded: "Splendid or Nothing," and, faced with those alternatives, he chose to yield. And Splendid, who kept quiet during the exchange, as was fitting for one conceived under such expensive circumstances, had never protested his name. In a surprisingly short time, he stepped out of his baptismal gown, put on a cap, and developed into the community's foremost apple pincher; and it was as such that Sidner met him that temperate September evening. Splendid had used the evening well and, with a ladder, had methodically made a clean sweep of Jolin's pear, apple, and plum trees, until he thought he heard the mill owner's wife walking in the grass and flew right into the fence, where he got helplessly stuck. He passed the time by hating Jolin, who once, and surely correctly, had accused him of having played in his rowboat and thereby losing one oar, which, because of southerly winds, was driven out into full view of the world.

Sidner was filled with amazement at the orderliness inside the previously unknown woodshed. Fruit stood in straight rows on shelves, bright and shiny, every stem facing in the same direction, the foundation a pile of *Fryksdal's Weekly Ledger*. The incoming stock was so large Splendid had to do some re-arranging, heaving part out through an opening in the wall.

"This is really nice. And so much fruit!"

"Yeah, there's too much now."

"Why don't you stop stealing it then?"

"I don't think th' upper class should eat so much fruit. Have another plum."

"Thanks," said Sidner. Splendid saw he was lost.

"Ya c'n spit the seeds on the floor. What'cher name?"

"Sidner."

"Well. Then it's you lives over th' hotel. Your mom got trampled ta death by cows…"

"When she was on her way to the *Christmas Oratorio,* yes."

"An' yer daddy works in the Spirits Cellar fer ol' Björk. My name's Splendid. My daddy was a cannon king."

"Cannon king, oh!"

"Though he don't have no legs. He fell once."

"No legs at all?"

"Jes' a couple a stumps. He sits on a wagon on th' floor. You c'n come home with me, if you wanna see 'im. Have ya read t'day's paper yet?"

Sidner wrinkled his brows, shook his head.

"Set down a while."

Splendid sat on the floor on a well-scrubbed rag rug of yellow and red, arranged in a corner between two woodpiles. He read and pondered, nodded and hemmed and hawed to himself like an old man, now and again reading a sentence aloud, as if he were tasting it. "Sunne beat Munkfors by 5–2. Goals were made by Bengtsson and Lamming." He looked up at Sidner who had not yet managed to sit down; this was like being on a visit to a Turkish sultan.

"Lamming, that's my mom's brother. He can juggle one hundred fifty-six times. How many times can you juggle. I can juggle fifteen. And you?"

Sidner swallowed.

"How many? Ten? Five?"

Sidner looked down at the sawdust on the floor.

"Can'cha talk?"

"Yes."

"Well, how many times can you juggle then?"

"I don't know. I don't know what that means."

"Ya don't know? Whad'ya do then? During the day, when you ain't in school?"

"Nothing."

Splendid looked at him sympathetically and pointed at the shelves of fruit.

"Take a couple more plums. As many as you want. So, nothin'?"

"Play a little piano. You know. Read."

"How long's it been since yer mamma got trampled to death?"

"Four hundred eighty-six days ago."

"I understan'. An' you 'n' yer daddy fill the bottles at the hotel. Have ya ever tasted it?"

Sidner shook his head.

"A little bit? On yer finger?"

"Papa is a teetotaler. That's how he got the job."

Splendid understood.

"He'd get awful mad, of course, Björk, if ya took a sip. He does that over nothin'. But he's rich, ya know. Richest man in all Sunne. Mom says he eats omelets all th' time. Without milk in 'em. An' with onion on 'em." Splendid sighed heavily: "I guess tha's the way they get. Jolin's rich, too. Have ya seen the kinda shoes he has? Full o' holes in the front, white 'n' brown. I'm gonna buy a pair when I get big." Splendid stood up. "Well, then." As if he had laid some new knowledge of life in with the rest. "See ya t'morra."

They attended different schools, but Splendid was waiting outside the gate for Sidner the next day. In the daylight, Sidner saw him clearly: he was little, a whole head shorter than himself; he was slender and pliant and his black hair hung down on his forehead under his cap.

"I thought we should go see Pastor Wärme."

"Why's that?"

"Jes' ta see if he's home."

They walked through town, but it was slow progress since Splendid went into every entrance. He went into backyards and rooted through garbage cans. He climbed into trees, showed Sidner a hole where they could leave their schoolbooks until the next day so they would not have to drag them along. When they approached the church, Splendid said:

"Yer gran'pa was the one who was preacher there long time ago. An' who stole th' money from the church. An' who ran off to America then."

"Well, yes," said Sidner.

"An' who sent a coffin here that only had rocks in it so's they'd think he was dead."

"I don't know anything about that."

"Well, it don't bother me," said Splendid. "I think that was smart. Darn well done. An' then he had a gambling house in the States, right?"

"Grandfather was a pomologist."

"What kinda pastime is that?"

"He grew all kinds of apples."

"Yeah, I know that. That's why we're gonna see Wärme. He's got such good apples."

"Grandfather started those trees."

"Have you met 'im?"

"No, it's a long time since he died. That's why Mamma and Uncle Torin and Uncle Sleipner came back here. Mamma wasn't very old when he died. He had written in his will that there was a house here that he owned."

"Well done, in any case. Take off yer shoes now!"

"Why?"

"Do like I say. Stick 'em inside yer shirt so's they ain't showin'."

They walked barefoot along the road past the storehouse, down toward the parsonage. The pastor stood on the porch with his hands behind his back, looking out over the yard.

"Oh well, of course, it's three o'clock. He's usually standin' there then. Don't show yer shoes now. Hello, Reverend!"

"Hello, boys. So you're out for a walk. Isn't it too cold to go barefoot?"

"Oh, yes," sighed Splendid. He looked longingly at the bullace bushes and the trees weighed down with ripe fruit.

"Wait, you're going to have a couple of really good apples."

Pastor Wärme was big and heavy-set; his white hair fluttered as he crossed the yard humming "Oh, Sacred Head Now Wounded." With his hands behind his back, he regarded a heavy branch. "With grief and shame weighed down." He stood on his toes but could not reach high enough. "Now scornfully surrounded." He hopped, got hold of a branch and apples tumbled down around him. "With thorns thine only crown."

"Now pick some up, boys. Take some home to your parents, too."

They sat outside the church and tied on their shoes. They sat under the bare elder bush where the flagstones come into the light.

Splendid beamed:

"Ya see, I was right. If ya've got yer shoes on ya get nothin'. He only gives ta them who's without. He likes the poor. Ya c'n have my apples if ya want."

"I don't know if I can eat any more."

"Nah, same here. Ya get tired of 'em this time of year. An' ya gotta go ta the shithouse all the time."

"Then why do you take so many?"

"'Cause I think they're... so neat... Kinda purtty. That ya c'n think about 'em."

This was where the friendship really began.

"Yeah, they are neat."

"Jes' think, you feel that way, too."

WITH THE MOTTO "You always learn something," Splendid and his armor-bearer make their way about town and Splendid opens up the world bit by bit. They visit Torvnäs Road with its small factories: the razor blade factory, Tidan's Wool Factory, the brickmaker. Splendid is at home everywhere, at the railroad station, at the Central League, at the Dairy; everywhere he is welcomed and always begins with the same words:

"This here's Sidner. He lives at the hotel. His old man takes care of th' liquor fer Björk, but he's a teetotaler."

The rest of the introduction he omits; everybody knows it already. There are no awkward silences, yet it will be many years before Sidner knows the world has penetrated the fabric of his nerves. It takes time for insights to mature.

One day he is allowed to go to Splendid's home, and Splendid announces at the doorway: "Here he is."

As if he is expected. And that he *is* someone.

Splendid is poor. He lives in a small house up near Totthagen, beside the hospital. It is a white house on the edge of the woods. Chickens run in and out of the half-open door. There are rabbit hutches among the trees. Splendid's mother, who looks the worse for wear and grayer than Solveig ever was, stands beside the chopping block, chopping off a rooster's head with a short-handled axe. The headless rooster runs around several times before it falls at her feet. Feathers drift to the ground in the stillness.

Splendid stands quietly in the kitchen and lets Sidner share his father.

As if here were the basis and explanation of everything.

And Sidner looks at the compressed package of a father who is sitting at a half-meter-high table by the window carving wooden ladles. His legs are cut off somewhere above the knee. One half of his face is pushed in, and part of the temple is gone. But his eyes are there, and his hands. He wears glasses that hang half-way down his nose, also pushed in or broken. He turns his wagon's wheels, gives Sidner a toothless laugh.

A doll's world: a low, short bed stands against one wall; beside that is a shelf filled with tools, on the floor a huge radio. There is a spittoon with juniper sprigs. The bedspread is of the cleanest velvet, dark red in color.

Sidner has time to absorb all his impressions. Splendid does not rush him. He stands by the water faucet, drinks, then hands the dipper to Sidner.

"It's good 'n' cold!"

There are photographs on the bureau of a young man in close-fitting tights. He has a bowler on his head, a walking stick in his hand, a long, waxed moustache, and, by his side, a poodle in jacket and tie, standing on its hind legs. He stands in front of the Eiffel Tower, or before a palace, or he leans against the railing of a bridge under which swans swim.

And the drums roll with ever-rising intensity. Sidner stands there breathless. The loudspeakers shout out over the kitchen, which is a carnival, which is the world:

"Ladies and gentlemen! The sensation, the attraction, the living cannonball, Fonzo!"

Thunder and lightning; Sidner draws in his breath together with hundreds, thousands of other gaping, upturned faces:

"And I flew as I had always dreamed of doing, in a wide arc over the lawn at home in Småland, flew up and up, and my parents stood down there and yelled: 'Little Alfons, careful you don't break your neck.' And I flew and our neighbor, the district police superintendent, shouted: 'Alfons, watch out for our Swedish flag.' And our neighbor, the pastor, the old humanist, said: 'Alfons, careful you don't fly too high, like Icarus.' I remembered his white

61

mustache and was ashamed of the down that eventually became my military mustache."

The loudspeakers again, in many languages, changing lights, over the kitchen, over Paris, over Vienna.

"And now ladies and gentlemen, the lovely Miss Lola and Fonzo, the cannon king who has conquered the continent."

"And I flew over the glittering sound toward Copenhagen where the harbor was full of boats and flags, flew over the railroad that thumped southward. To Kiel. To Hamburg. And zeppelins flew beside me. The pilots peeked out and waved at me, but I left them behind. There was a smell of sawdust and horses and the warmth of the tent when the circuses were empty of people. Miss Lola from Markaryd was the red flower on the posters. I was the blue one, which her husband, who fired the cannon during the roll of the drums, painted once in a happy moment. And we came to Rome and I brandished my cane over the Pope, high over the cupola of St. Peter's, a Harlequin in tights, wearing a bowler and smoking a fat cigar. Over Buda I traveled, over Pest, and Prince Ferdinand was there in a stylish coat. We came to Paris. Oh, bonjour Paris, I yelled. Bonjour Fonzo, Paris answered back. And Isadora Duncan stood on the Champs Elysées and danced a dance for me that stopped traffic, and chauffeurs in leather caps climbed out and divided their attention between Isadora and me. And Jean Jaurès was there.

"And Miss Lola and I flew higher and higher toward the stars, in each other's arms we soared, around Mars and around Venus the Torrid. The musette was distant, the tarantellas faded away, mouth to mouth before the beacon of the stars, like fish in an abandoned aquarium."

"Ladies and gentlemen, the sensation, the attrac..."

A cannon shot tore through the kitchen.

"And while we flew, the safety net down on earth was removed. When Prince Ferdinand took off his coat the bullet had already passed through it. When Jean Jaurès put his hat on his head, it was pierced by a murderer's bullet. And the grass, where people picnicked and waited for us in Europe's parks, was singed and their faces were down-turned.

"And we fell. There wasn't even a moonbeam to hang onto because the cannons had shot off their fastenings. We couldn't find a star to land on because they had been turned off by the tips of rockets. And I, who had laughed and waved with my walking stick, the last human cannonball, an abandoned art form, fell, mouth to mouth with Miss Lola of Markaryd, down toward the burning earth. And now I've reached the floor. Nobody can fall from here."

The kitchen quietened. A chicken feather hovered in the doorway, drifted in on the mild autumnal draft, approached Splendid's father. He took it in his hand. He looked at it, brushed his whole cheek with it.

"That's the way it was then," said Alfons Nilsson. "Now it's like this."

"Really, Papa?"

"Actually, it was tough."

"Yeah, but... When Papa fell. An' why'd ja do that?"

They sat on the floor and Alfons Nilsson looked out the door.

"Your mamma never likes me to tell that," Alfons said.

"She's not in here now."

"And I don't know if such young boys..."

"Ah, Daddy. Sidner *needs* ta hear 'bout it. I've told ya that. He needs ta learn how it is! Otherwise he'll jes' dream hisself away."

Alfons Nilsson put his fists on the floor, gave the wagon a push toward the door, bent his torso over the door sill and peeked out.

"It was like this, boys," he whispered and smiled. "I fell in love with Miss Lola. Well, she was really Greta Svensson. But she was married to the cannon firer. And one day he discovered us when we..."

"When you *were together*?"

"That's right. The next day of a performance, he put the

cannon at the wrong distance, ten meters outside the safety net. When I woke up three months later, the whole circus, the cannon firer, Greta, and all my friends had sailed away on the steamship *Titanic*."

Splendid examined Sidner's expression.

"Mamma was a nurse in the hospital."

"That she was," chortled Alfons Nilsson contentedly.

Afterward they lay on their stomachs in the autumn grass and spat on ants. Rowanberries glowed above them, the air was clear and high and not yet cold. They tried to hit the ants with their saliva, to bury them in the white scum. The ants struggled awhile, but their movements were slow and they curled up; then it was time to lift them out to see them come alive again.

"It's real terrific how strong they are anyway. If ya think how small they are."

"Boy, your papa can tell a story."

"I believe it's 'cause they don't think. Sometimes I wish I was like that, jes' goin' straight ahead without thinkin'. Hey!! Maybe we jes' *believe* we're thinkin'. But then there'd be somebody who'd spit on us, an' then we'd be lyin' there 'n' flounderin' in the middle o' the spit. An' then somebody'd lift us out to a dry leaf, an' after awhile we'd wake up 'n' say: That was a close call, Oskar. An' then we'd go a little farther on."

"Was it true what he was saying?"

"Think Daddy lies?"

"No."

"'Course he does exaggerate. But I think he's sure allowed ta do that. It ain't so much fun ta be without legs. Sometimes I take 'im out in the woods. He likes birds so much. We usually take some coffee with us 'n' sit completely still. What ya goin' ta be when ya grow up?"

"I won't live that long," Sidner said.

Splendid rolled over on his back.

"I'm gonna follow in Papa's footsteps, that's what I'm gonna do."

"Just think if you fall like him."

"It'd be worth it. Though it's strange. If ya think that he flew maybe twenty seconds a week. If there was plenty of engagements, that is ta say. Twenty seconds instead o' standin' in a factory day in 'n' day out. But Daddy's said it's important for somebody ta do such things. Ta show life ain't so simple. That there's people that's diff'rent. So people'll think: God, what crazy people there are. Unbelievable! Not that he imagines they sit 'n' brood on how he behaved, but jes' that once in their lives they've seen a flying man. That there's a picture of it. Kids are the best ta perform fer, he says; they exaggerate ev'rything an' have it in their eyes fer the rest of their lives: once they saw somebody who *flew*. Ya feel like a poem, Daddy says. Like a line from a poem, anyway, an' it's import'nt that somebody keeps bein' those kinda' lines. That we don't give up. Jes' like priests or those that play music. Says Daddy. I think ya should be a locksmith when ya grow up. If yer alive, that is."

"A locksmith? Why – to make keys?"

"It's not jes' that. Ta open doors fer people that's locked out. Ya know, there's a lotta people do that; they ferget where they put the keys, or if they're poor maybe they got holes in their pockets. I've found a lotta keys myself, sometimes several in the same day."

"They don't have an extra key?"

"Poor people don't think about gettin' one neither."

"Then why do you want me to be a locksmith?"

"Want ya to an' want ya to. But you're so shy. Ya'd go see lotsa people. See how they live. Diff'rent houses, diff'rent apartments. That'd be good fer ya."

"But I'm not shy."

"Sure ya are. Why, ya hardly talk."

"Yes I do!"

"With me, yeah. But it takes so much time fer me ta teach ya.

It's always a word in the mouth an' one in the rump."

"Maybe."

"Ya need to go see folk. An' so many dead people you c'n see. Once there was a Finnish tramp who sat in a room out in the forest. There was some berry pickers who was out there, an' they thought it smelled awful when they went by. They sent fer the police an' Hermansson, the locksmith, ya know."

"No, I don't know."

"Ya see there? Ya gotta know ev'ry single person if yer gonna get by."

"What happened then?"

"Ugh! Ya wouldn't 'a been able ta stand it."

"Yeah, but what happened?"

"You blame yerself then, if yer gonna hear it."

"Mm."

"The flies was as big as bees, I'll tell ya. All woolly. Thirty, forty of 'em. The sun shined inta the room, so they was all green 'n' blue. An' all woolly like, too. The Finnish tramp sat in a chair. He was all moldy on the one side of his face. Like moss, Hermansson said."

"Did you talk to him?"

"Nah, he told Daddy an' Daddy told Mommy an' I heard it through the wall. An' Daddy said: If he'd sat like that for fourteen days when he was dead, how long had he sat alone like that when he was alive. Daddy said."

"How does he actually get up on the bed?"

"We lift him up. He weighs next ta nothin'. An' worms crawled on that Finnish tramp. White. Things like that ya gotta see. If you're a locksmith, yeah."

And Splendid wanted to inspire Sidner further: "Another time it was a guy who flew. He was layin' outside the house up in the Sexton's garden. Half his body was mush. He'd put wings on his feet. Toilet paper."

"Like Apollo?"

"Well, I don't know 'bout that. His name was Erik anyway. Or maybe the wings was made of cardboard. Ya think he believed he could fly?"

"Your papa did that, you know. Sometimes you *must* believe you can."

"Or maybe he knew he was gonna die an' he wanted 'a die so's we'd talk about 'im. That we'd say: 'him that had wings on his feet.'"

They were interrupted by the sound of a horse and carriage. It came from over on Stapel's Hill at a slow walking pace.

"Well, if it ain't Selma comin'."

"Selma Lagerlöf? The writer?"

"Yeah."

"Do you know her, too?"

"Nah, I don't really know her." But Splendid got up from the grass, jumped out into the road, pulled off his cap when the surrey came up, hailed Selma and took hold of the horse's bridle.

"Mornin', Aunt Selma!"

"Why, Splendid, is that you?"

Sidner regarded the famous lady up in the carriage; she looked exactly like the pictures. The white hair under a black broad-brimmed hat, black cape, and her hands stuck into a muff.

"Are ya on yer way to Fanny's fer her saint's day?"

"Yes, indeed. How do you know she…"

"I follow that in the newspapers."

The dust settled around the horse's hooves. Sidner went closer to the carriage. He held his cap and some books in his hand.

"And who is this young man?"

"This is Sidner I talked about, ya know, las' time I was out, him that…"

"Oh, it's you, then! Have you been to Fanny's and given her coffee in bed, too, Splendid?"

"No, I was fishin' perch so's there wadn't time."

"You are active, aren't you! How you manage! It's different with me. Now I have to be on my way. Come out sometime. Both of you," she said. Suddenly Sidner was jealous of Splendid. He seemed to be all over the place, almost at the same time. Later he would write:

"There are people whose nature is manifold. They are capable of doubling themselves, yes, of multiplying their existence and presence ten times over. They reveal themselves to those in difficulty, to those who do not have anyone with whom to share their sorrow or joy. They go through their lives with long feelers."

He followed the horse with his gaze until it disappeared. He stood still and asked in a monotone:

"What have you said about me?"

"Ah, nothin'."

"Why haven't you even mentioned you knew her?"

"Oh, one thing at a time."

"Did you catch some perch then?"

"Enough fer supper."

"And who's Fanny?"

Splendid pointed down toward Fanny's house. Hazily between the trees, Sidner saw a woman on the balcony. She was wearing a red robe and held a coffee tray.

"Is she the one who owns the dry goods shop?"

"Yep."

After awhile he saw Selma Lagerlöf come out with a cake box in her hand. Fanny placed the tray on the balcony railing, disappeared inside for an armchair, a tablecloth. She spread it on the table, poured coffee, and the women sat down.

"I wanna tell ya, that Fanny, she gives a lotta ideas to Selma."

"How's that?"

"Oh, you'll unnerstan' one fine day."

Doors, entrances. Gaps in the foliage where something red flickers.

THAT FANNY UDDE is in telepathic contact with Sven Hedin, the famous explorer, does not disturb her ability to manage her dry goods shop. Dressed in a high-collared white blouse, she stands behind the counter, scratching the back of her neck with a yardstick while she browses through a French fashion magazine. Fanny smiles and dreams, dreams and smiles. She takes several turns among the shelves, looks out through the door toward the street, the hotel and railroad crossing, returns, and dreams.

Her store is like a Kirghiz yurta. Pairs of curtains, remnants, and rolls of flannel are piled about. Thick velvet drapes separate the fitting rooms. The atmosphere is heavy, and a breath of perfume spreads through the air when Fanny moves her long hands. She has such wonderful hands, fine blue veins running under the skin of ring-covered fingers. One of the rings, she has said, came from Sven Hedin. It is real and is from the region of the Gobi Desert. There are many pictures of him on the wall, one of which is dedicated to her. He stands leaning against a white car on a road somewhere in Sweden. "To Fanny, my faithful admirer, from Sven Hedin." It is written right there, if no one should believe her. So there! His one hand rests on the shining left headlight; that can be seen. It summons up a good image. The birches in the background make an effective frame for the picture. Fanny sighs. She is thirty-six, but no one now living knows she has a birthmark, a little dark spot, under her right breast. Her hair is combed up into an enormous French roll, but no one alive has seen it brushed out; no one knows how long it is. No one alive has yet kissed her lips. No one has touched her straight nose. Comprehension cannot grasp how that is possible!

Splendid has an unparalleled talent for finding ways in to unseen wilderness. He smells his way to secret passages that lead away
from the everyday. One day he considers Sidner ripe for such a
voyage of discovery, for they have been friends now for some
time. They stand hesitantly outside Fanny Udde's door. They do
not really want to press down the door handle and open it, but the
bell rings. It is Chinese and real; ding–ding, is how it goes. That is
Chinese and means: Come in, even if you're not thinking of buying a single pack of needles.

Ding–ding, and they are in another country.

Fanny is sitting in a tall wicker chair behind the counter.

"Hello, Splendid. How nice of you to come in. What will it be
for you today?"

"I jes' wanted to show Sidner the bell. That it's Chinese. He's
the one lives at the hotel an' his mamma got trampled to death by
cows."

He approaches her, leans over the counter, balances on his fore-
arms, looks into her eyes.

"He didn't believe me."

Fanny turns toward Sidner, oh, you Creator of physical beings!
He is still standing by the door ringing the bell, a delicate, tranquil sound that wanders in and out among bundles of fabrics and
draperies. He remains a long time, as if trying to understand the
sound, to be able to read it in the right way and to see all the remarkable places and times the sound brings with it.

As if the old Chinese bellmaker's face allowed itself to be called
forth. His hands become visible. The house where he made it, the
mountains behind the village where he lived, the flocks of sheep
on their slopes, the caravan paths over which the bell was transported. All, all evoked by that delicate tone. Slowly Sidner opens
his mouth, becomes paralyzed with enchantment. Fanny nods in
his direction:

"He sees it."

She smiles and lets him stand there until the visions subside and does not listen to Splendid's whisper: "He's like that sometimes, Fanny."

She does not say anything when he approaches her, but takes his long hand between hers and examines it thoroughly; then she raises her gaze to him: "Poor boy!" She turns the palm of his hand toward her, presses it to her breast: "Exactly like Sven's."

Splendid nods encouragingly at Sidner, but Sidner is serious; as yet he knows nothing about his life. In his booklet *On Caresses* there are, however, some words that probably have their origin in just this moment: "The Swedish word that has always fascinated me the most is Divination. To *Divine* something. There is an activity in the word that makes one believe the subject is the one that anticipates, while my firm conviction (Bah, there aren't any firm convictions!!) is that *we are reached* by the Divination. The Divination's source is outside ourselves. It is the beacon in the dark. It is the lightning that sweeps around the vault of heaven, time after time, and searches and, now and then, it happens that a scrap of its light brushes against us, presses into the deepest strata of our consciousness. I would like to say: I became divined. She granted me the Divination." Splendid breaks into his reverie.

"She means Sven Hedin. She knows him."

As if there were anything else Splendid had whispered about the whole day.

"Looky here, you'll see."

Sidner's hand remains pressed to Fanny's breast. He turns his body toward the picture on the wall: To my faithful admirer...

"That's her!"

Together, they look at her under the protection of those words and she allows herself to be changed, for her life is dreams. Gracefully she releases Sidner's hand, sinks onto the wicker chair, leans her head against one out-stretched finger, and smiles pensively. With her left hand, she brushes nothing from her lace blouse; she shuts her eyes:

"Right now, he's in Vadstena. He's eating dinner at the

municipal hotel there. What is he eating...? Lake Vättern charr with remoulade sauce. He's dressed in white, a linen suit he had made in Singapore. A glass of white wine, a sparkling white, stands before him, a bouquet of roses wet with dew. He's alone. Now the waitress comes up: What will it be for dessert, Mr. Hedin? she asks. He hesitates. He puts his fingers on his chin and thinks about it. Strawberries with cream, he says."

"But Fanny," interrupts Splendid. "It's not strawberry season now, is it?"

Fanny starts. Her face is full of distress.

"Oh, where am I? I made a mistake. I've had such a headache all day. I'm very tired."

"It's nothin'. Maybe he got 'em by train from Italy."

"No, Splendid. I made a mistake. I can't see anything."

"But plums then? Maybe he wanted to have plums. They're a lot alike. At a distance. If they're canned."

"You're sweet, Splendid."

"It was stupid o' me ta say that, Fanny."

"It's all right. You've got to make me toe the line, Splendid. Come here and let me ruffle your hair."

Splendid goes behind the counter and bends his neck. He twists his neck and closes his eyes, and Fanny's fingers dart around. Over his collarbone and ears. Sidner also has to bend his head, but he does so in toward everything dark and empty and quiet.

IN THE WOODSHED, Splendid reads aloud to Sidner from the *Fryksdal Weekly Ledger.*

"'Yesterday in the district court, two moonshining brothers confessed that, for a couple of years, they have secretly distilled liquor and sold it.' Sss."

He lies on his back on the rag rug and snorts contemptuously.

"Secretly. It's the Gustafsson brothers in Åmberg. They been doin' it a long time. As if ev'rybody didn't know 'bout it. I know a lotta people's bought it. 'The so-called Passion Play in Sunne church was a disappointment for the audience since the pictures were very blurred, so they were impossible to look at.' 'Missionary's farewell reception tomorrow. Ester Nordberg, teacher, will be leaving to start out as a missionary in East Turkistan.' East Turkistan! Get the *Nordic Family Encyclopedia* from behind the wood so's we c'n see where the ol' lady's goin' to."

"*You* have the *Nordic Family Encyclopedia*?"

"Daddy gave it ta me. It's *you* who needs ta know ev'rythin', he said. Bring a few o' the yellow plums at the same time."

It has been a year since their first meeting. There is not so much fruit on the shelves as last year: it seems the raids on the community's fruit trees just don't happen so often as before.

"Here it is. 'East Turkistan. Chinese Turkistan, also called Kashgar, and situated east of West Turkistan and separated from it by Tien Shan and Pamir. The land opens only to the east and continuously passes into the Gobi Desert.'"

"Oh, well whadda ya know 'bout that! Go on!"

"In relationship to the surrounding border mountains, East Turkestan appears to be a depression, but in relationship to sea level is a plateau at 3,000–3,300 feet. In the northeast part, which can be regarded as a physically separate section, the land sinks in certain places to more than 400 feet below sea level.'"

"That's not bad! Go on!"

"In the higher areas, the fauna includes, among others, the yak, the kula (Equis hemionus), the wild donkey, the wild camel and several antelope. In the level areas, tigers, wild boar, roe deer, wolf, fox, and more roam.'"

"An she's goin' there, old Ester. We should go see her. I see no other way."

"Why?"

"Oh, do ya know anybody else's goin' ta East Turkestan, huh?"

"No."

"There, ya see? We'll bone up more later, so's she sees we know somethin'."

"Oh?"

"An' then we'll shake hands with her, an' then she'll go to East Turkestan 'n' maybe get ate up by a tiger, an' then it's almost like you was there yerself. An' then we can get stamps 'n' things from there. Now let's go on with the newspaper... Here, listen ta this, Sidner: 'A tragic event occurred in the early hours of Wednesday morning in Östansjö. A man, about thirty years old, suddenly became mentally ill and his condition expressed itself very violently. Household utensils and furniture were broken, and the man's mother was forced out and had to seek help from neighbors. Persons who hurried to the scene took the sick man in hand, and he was transported to Bergskog where he is now being treated. As to the reason, it is explained that the man had never shown any signs of mental illness; presumably he suffered from religious obsession which led to this tragic end.' Whadya say 'bout that?"

"I don't know."

"Him we gotta go see. I've never seen such a loony before. Not one's got religious obsession least ways. We c'n ask 'im himself what he was thinkin'. It'll be good fer ya, Sidner."

"Why does everything have to be so good for me?"

"'Cause yer scared. But it's not dang'rous. I know a lotta strange types, 'course not anybody that behaves this way."

"But it's late now. We won't get there before it's dark."

"I knew ya'd say that. But talk with yer daddy. Say we're goin' up ta Lake Häll to catch crawfish. They're good there."

"But it's not crawfish season now, is it?"

"It's *almost* crawfish season."

And then, suddenly, with such seriousness that he starts to speak properly:

"You must learn to know the world. Otherwise you could be like that girl we read about."

They both shudder and look out through the cracks in the woodshed walls. He can see the water as it flows by out there. It is cold and he tries to avoid looking again at the clipping in the corner regarding PARTICULARLY STRANGE NEWS FROM AROUND THE WORLD, but his eyes are drawn, as if by an inner power.

"Dateline New York: It is reported that a four-year-old girl from Lima, Ohio, is slowly turning into stone. Parts of her have fallen off into chips, which chemists have analyzed as limestone."

Sidner presses his fingers against a point in his wrist. There is something there that should not be, a hard spot only a couple of weeks old, dating from the day they read the news item for the first time.

"That isn't true, Splendid."

"Oh? Have ya seen 'em take it back in the newspaper? Have ya seen that, huh?"

"No, of course not."

"I wonder how long a time it'll take till she's wholly an' completely stone. An' where it started? If it was the legs er the head? Which d'ya think'd be worst, if it started in the eyes er the legs?"

"Stop that. I don't believe it anyway."

He presses hard against his wrist.

"My daddy said..."

"I don't care about that. But maybe it's worst if it starts in the mouth," he says and gets tongue-tied and knows immediately that it has started.

He has got the illness.

It is like a rock in his mouth. He swallows.

"There's worse things," Splendid says. "I've heard tales 'bout a boy whose beard started growin' when he was one year old, his voice changed when he was two and he lost his hair when he was three. An' then I've heard tales 'bout one that didn't get teeth before he was fifty 'n' hair when he was sixty an' his voice changed when he was seventy."

"You just made that up."

"Yeah, that last I made up. But otherwise it was true. I jes' mean there's so much ya gotta watch out fer. I mean there's no order ta life. That's what's strange… that there's any order at all."

"GOOD MORNIN'," says Splendid. "We'd like ta see that loony from Östansjö."

It is Sunday morning and autumn is making a last blazing attempt to remember its summer. In the nursing home's garden old people and lunatics walk about in the light, chained by their own nerves' short links, listening to the murmur from apple trees and birch and to that which behind it all creates that murmur. The shadows are long and soft. They flow over tall grass. Farther down toward the plain a patch of harvested wheat field, of newly-ploughed fields shining like silk. Horses and distant cattle whinny and low. The church bell in Sunne strikes. The matron is standing before them, bust high and stern:

"And what do you want with him? Besides, that isn't proper to say."

"His ma sent us here ta find out if there's anythin' he needs."

"Here one has everything one needs."

"Well, that's good," says Splendid. "She was so worried that he didn't have his Bible with 'im."

All around them the lunatics mumble, scream and suddenly jerk their bodies, as if struggling with all the devils of the underworld.

"Bible?"

"Yeah, he's gotta read it ev'ry day, otherwise he gets upset."

"We have Bibles here. Besides, he can't read right now in his condition.

"It's gotta be this Bible," Splendid says and pats his windbreaker. "It's th' only Bible he can read 'cause he's made marks. His ol' lady said we gotta give it to 'im personal so's he won't be upset."

77

"He's that already, and what language is that you're using?"

"He's gotta have it 'side 'im on his bedside table, his mamma says."

"Bedside table, he doesn't have a bedside table. Go on, now."

"He don't have a bedside table! D'ja hear that, Bengt-Emil! The man don't have a bedside table. That's pitiful to hear. I sure wonder if the town doctor in Karlstad knows 'bout that. Let's go, Bengt-Emil."

"Listen you, you, you," the matron shouts, but they are already on their way away from her.

In the grove beyond the bend, Splendid pulls Sidner in among the trees.

"Now, we'll wait here till she gets on her way to Sunne. She's gonna go ta the doctor ta get a shot."

"Do you know everything?"

Splendid digs in the ground with his foot and does not answer.

"Why did you call me Bengt-Emil anyway?"

"Otherwise she'd know who we was. Bengt-Emil Jolin ya know sure 'nough, that upper class type. He gets an allowance of one-fifty a week, so it's nothin' if she thinks of him. We'll stay here now 'n' bone up on East Turkestan. Jes' think, meetin' a real loony!"

The Madman from Östansjö sits in a wooden cage up in the attic. Splendid knows that, too. In the twilight the courtyard is quiet, but Sidner is afraid. And while he creeps up the creaking stairs he recites to himself, mumbling like the old people and lunatics had mumbled, nervously and disjointedly.

Through me you pass into the city of woe,
Through me you pass into eternal pain,
Justice compelled the Supreme who caused me,
Divine Omnipotence has founded me,
The highest Wisdom and primeval Love.

Nothing was created before me but
the Eternal, and eternal I am.
Abandon all hope, you who enter here!

"Why're ya sayin' that, is that him... Danto again?"

"It's good... when you're scared... to say such things," Sidner whispers. "He's sitting over there."

"Then it's like I thought. Daddy says that's what they do with th' one's that's worst sick in the head."

"What are you going to say to him? Do you think the cage is safe?"

"It'll be all right."

The room is like a church sanctuary, high-ceilinged. The floor creaks as they pad across it, and they see the madman start, then cower in a corner.

"Good ev'nin', sir. We jes' wanted ta stop by 'n' see ya. How long ya been sittin' here?"

"I just want to say I'm darkness with lemon in it. They don't believe that. It was him in the lemon who fought. He was angry with the furniture, Mommy, lamp, tramp."

The Madman looks fiercely at them but then grins a little spasmodically. Splendid clears his throat.

"We've read 'bout ya in the papers. My name's Splendid, and he's Sidner. His mamma got... Why've they put ya in a cage?"

"On the back of the mirror it's black as raspberries. That you can tell on the stairs in complete full of darkness. But he finds his way."

"We've read it was religious obsession which you..."

"Religious! I'll convey the message."

He turns his back on them and sits quietly a long time, suddenly jumping around again:

"Can't you stop, there's so much headache bouncing around my skeleton."

"What'd I say," Splendid whispers, "that's a real loony, that is."

79

"Quiet, Splendid. I want to hear more."

Sidner knows he is a part of something important. He swallows, he is uneasy. There is something he must pass through.

"Hear, yeah, that's what one should do. Drive, should, butter, sail free… But that's sailing, of course!" Screams: "No, no sails in the mud. In the slush, in the muck, but in the lemon they see everything."

"Are you sad?" Sidner asks.

"You bet, that's the way it can be."

"Really?"

"There's no other word. We'll write that up on the back of the paper. So they can stand there and be ashamed WHAT DO YOU WANT FROM ME?"

"I want… to understand."

"Understand. That's good, that's what one should do."

The Madman bares his gums and grins at Sidner, lays his hands around the bars and shakes them.

"That which isn't seen is real," says Sidner.

"Darkness with lemon in it, which gathers together. Comes out in Mommy, lamp, tramp."

"Let's go now, Sidner," says Splendid.

"No, I want to stay."

"Like horses at the fence?" the Madman asks, curious, almost smiling. "Half the horses aren't lemon. They kick at the glass quarter melon. WHY ARE YOU HERE YOU'RE MAKING FUN OF ME, that's why they've shut me up in here. In front of the glass. That's good. That's good."

Now he is crying. Now he clutches the bars and the tears stream down his cheeks:

"It's good for the poor creatures who never live this life."

"Yes," Sidner almost shouts. "You know it, too!

They were naked and sorely stung about
By wasps and hornets which abided there.

From their countenances these drew blood
Which then, mingled with tears, at their feet
Was gathered up by disgusting worms."

"Shit and piss is what it is." Now the Madman is angry and sits with his back towards them again. He does not answer in spite of Sidner's appeal to that chink of understanding he thinks he has glimpsed.

"Keep on talking, don't turn away." And he recites slowly and distinctly: "'Then looking further onwards, I beheld a throng upon the shore...'?"

The Madman interrupts him with a cold voice, "Mommy's a tramp."

"'... of a great stream,
At which I said: Sir, grant...'"

But now it is Splendid who is afraid for Sidner, who is hot in voice, hot in speed, and who knocks away Splendid's hand when he tries to draw him away from the cage.

"We gotta hurry up 'n' git outta here, Sidner."

"Mommy's a whore! Mommy's a whore!"

"'... grant me to know now
Whom here we view, and why impelled they seem
so eager to cross over, as I see...'"

"It's probably best if we... Goodbye, sir. Come on, Sidner. Come on, I said."

"There's too much darkness for him. And stairs and..."

The entreating tone does not appear again. The Madman becomes hard, his lips thin.

"Git, git, hit, hit. He doesn't care."

Splendid drags Sidner across the floor and down the stairs, out into the yard. It is dark now. It is black. Sidner's whole body is shaking. At first he thinks it is only he who is sniffling and crying, but soon he notices Splendid is in the same state.

"It was," Sidner tries to press it out between tears and a runny nose, "... it was as if I was sitting in there myself... I understand everything... what he said, when you don't dare talk and I sit with Papa in the kitchen... or in school... then I think... I'm not real, when I think about Mamma, that she's dead and that I... can kind of talk to her... really... and I'm a shadow... and it's the shadow that wakes up... and doesn't want to show itself... like that lemon, when everything pulls together and is visible... that I'm not here, Splendid, that I'm really one of those madmen, too."

"I'm so damn sorry I come up with this. I didn't mean it," Splendid sniffles in answer.

"I know."

"So sorry I forced you. I didn't know how really strong you was, I didn't know that."

"No, there's... no one who knows."

"I understan'. It's the same sometimes as when I think 'bout Daddy, that he ain't got no legs an' he's a cripple an' he can hardly show hisself roun' town... an' when I go 'n' carry him up ta th' woods an' other places where we c'n be in peace."

"I know."

"That he's like a little package. But damn it all, he's the best daddy there is. Yeah, doggone it, that he is, Sidner... But like it's *me* that carries *him,* an' not th' other way roun'... that I'm so old 'n' sensible, which I really can't stand ta be."

"It's the same here. I'm so old and understand everything. But that you're alone and it's only you who understands."

"Uh, huh. Have you felt that yer gonna die, you too?"

"Yes!"

But now Splendid has to tie his shoelace and pull up his socks, which have slid down. That gets him out of rhythm.

"But not yet though. Not till I've kissed a girl."

"Yeah!"

"Have ya *done* it?"

"Are you nuts?"

"Me neither," says Splendid. He has finished tying his shoe and the first steps he takes are lighter. He feels his relief but waits for Sidner's.

"There's no one who's... interested in me."

"But there's one's looked at me."

"Who's that?"

"Kajsa, ya know. The one lives next ta th' grocery store."

"Did she do that?"

"Yeah, she looked a little bit."

"There's no one who..."

Splendid wants to console him.

"But it was only a little. Probably jes' I thought so."

"She looked all right."

"Yeah, she's kinda purtty. She's started ta get breasts, too."

"I've noticed that."

"Not as big as Britt, o' course."

"No, but still."

"Yeah." But since Sidner's sniffling hasn't passed, he has to say it again. "But it's prob'ly jes' what I thought."

"I'll never get married."

"Oh, sure ya will. Oh, it was jes' what I thought."

"You know I'm not like others."

"Me neither."

"So there are certainly no girls who want me."

"'Cause ya read, ya mean... Books 'n' such?"

"Yeah, I don't have anything to talk to them about..."

"'Course yer gonna get married. There's a lotta girls that read. Though they don't talk 'bout it."

"Who then?"

"Oh, Mary," Splendid says weakly.

"But she's not exactly pretty."

"No, that's fer sure. But Ingegärd then?"

"Does she read?"

"Well, I dunno. But she's got glasses."

They are a little more cheerful now. They are walking across the plain toward the church. The stars are visible. They emerge palely above the woods and Gylleby Avenue.

"But she doesn't have breasts."

"They're comin', Sidner. They're comin', ya c'n be sure. Yer sis, she's fine lookin'."

"Ah."

"She is. Have ya taken a good look at 'er?"

"Looked, you mean breasts? Eh, maybe a little."

"I jes' wonder. What're we gonna do with that Loony? He had it bad there in that cage. An' his pisspot stunk so. Hey! We gotta set 'im free."

"No! That's dangerous, you know."

"But we got responsibility fer 'im. It's us discovered how it is with 'im."

"We can't let a madman out here in Sunne."

"Ah, nobody'd notice."

"We don't know what he'll do, you know. I don't feel good, Splendid."

"He needs somethin' soft in there... till we figure out somethin'. What's the softest thing there is?"

"Baby rabbits. Baby rabbits are so soft... their noses... when you stick dandelions into them... through the bars... But we CAN'T LET HIM OUT."

"Sidner, what'sa matter with ya... my God, are ya faintin'?"

That he is. Sidner collapses beside the road just outside the churchyard wall. He feels a great darkness sweep over him, feels it wrap him in something soft.

SIDNER HAS THE MEASLES and the fever transports him to other lands. Sometimes he is in a huge hole full of snakes and bats, and the Madman is there screaming that he has to set them free before they get eaten up. It is steamy hot in the hole. Sidner sweats and flings himself back and forth. Sometimes they stand above the hole, and the Madman says:

"I'm a tiger behind the mirror. Thank you for setting me free. I'll never forget that, if you're one mile, two miles, three miles. Now we're going to break up the house and furniture, Mommy, tramp, lamp, and you'll go first and point, and I'll break things for you. You have the poker, point, and I'll break. We'll march off and break and break."

"Leave me alone," Sidner screams, and he hears a voice which is Aron's:

"A little lingonberry juice, Sidner." He hears a name which is Eva-Liisa's, and he feels small, light fingers on his forehead. But the Madman comes back:

"I'm a toad behind the mirror. Thank you for setting me free. Do you think I'm wet and disgusting? Slimy, repulsive. Now we'll go to Mommy the tramp and force her down on the floor, on the bed, on the table, you point, and it will grow and thrust through the tramp the lamp."

"Drink, Sidner, drink and the fever will go down."

But the Madman strikes away the cool hands, strikes the glass from his mouth:

"I'm a vulture behind the mirror. Thank you for setting me free. Now we'll eat the corpses, pick out eyes and tongues and dig our way into their bodies, to the maggots and guts, so nice to hear people scream. You have the beak there, point with it, and it will hack well enough."

"No," he shouts. "No, I don't want to."

"A towel, Sidner. To dry off the sweat."

Then Splendid is there. He drinks water from the faucet, takes off his clogs by the door, sits on the edge of the bed:

"Now I've gone 'n' got myself in a mess. I stole a pair o' baby rabbits an' stuck 'em in my pocket 'n' went ta Bergskog. Looky here, I said ta the Loony an' pulled out the rabbits. But ya know, they was dead, both of 'em, completely loose-limbed they was. The napes of the necks was soft. It was awful, an' the loony thought fer sure I'd done it on purpose an' screamed an' I began ta cry 'cause I'd thought he'd be happy... An' then it turned out like that instead. But then he unnerstood I'd meant well 'n' tried ta comfort me. "Cause there ain't nothin' wrong with 'im 'cept he's sittin' there locked in, an' that's dang'rous 'cause it's beginnin' ta get on his nerves. That's what he said hisself, an' I said ta him that it wadn't good ta sit there like some crazy man 'cause then it don't make no sense.

"But it was like he'd given up. 'It isn't possible,' he said. 'It isn't possible.' He talks real fine like you, but 'course that comes from readin' the Bible. Then I went ta Selma Lagerlöf 'n' asked her if she couldn't take the loony ta Mårbacka in case we got 'im out. But that didn't get nowhere. She jes' talked 'bout how she didn't have the strength, an' I said ta her that, Aunt Selma, here ya got jes' such a crazy fella as the Emperor of Portugal, but then she answered that she's got enough crazy people, an' then I asked if she meant Fanny Udde. 'Oh, that poor thing,' she said. 'I have her.' But I got furious 'cause she didn't need ta sigh over her, 'cause Fanny's given Selma lotsa ideas though she never lets on 'bout that. She offered me coffee anyhow an' those rolls with powdered sugar on 'em. They're good. You still have a fever?"

"I *want* to be sick," says Sidner. "I must be sick."

"Yer healthy, yer healthy. I'm gonna get a little lingonberry juice ta cool ya off."

"Where's Papa?"

"He's workin'. He said fer me ta sit here. By the way, I can give ya greetin's from Fanny. Here's her hand," says Splendid, laying Fanny's long hand beside him on the pillow.

Sidner's illness continued. He glided in and out between the islets and skerries of his dreams. Sometimes his boat was torn apart, and he gave himself over to sinking. He wanted to die, to go to Solveig in heaven as quickly as possible. She sat up there waiting for him. It was pleasant to lie under the quilt and look at her, to hear her sing a song or to listen to the stories about America and the fireflies on the porch; and he became irate at Aron and Eva-Liisa who interrupted his dreams with a damp smell of newly-washed clothes over the stove, irate over the smell of cooking and music from downstairs in the hotel. Irate over the world existing. It was so much uglier than the other, the genuine reality.

One evening when moonlight filtered through the window, Splendid stood beside his bed.

"Now it's time, Sidner. Get dressed, we gotta get goin'. Selma's changed her mind. She's waitin' fer us, an' she's gonna help us get the Madman free. She's over at the blacksmith's. She don't dare drive all th' way inta town."

They slipped out, crossed the street and kept to the churchyard wall. Moonlight swept over the plain, mushrooms shone like death's heads in the meadows. In the shadow of the wall stood an impressive surrey. In the driver's seat sat a woman with a black veil over her face.

"So, here you come at last," he heard her say. "How is this going to turn out? Now hop up so we can get it over with."

"It's gonna be fine, Selma," said Splendid, sitting down beside her.

"But if people catch sight of me."

"This concerns life now. It won't do ta jes' dig down inta yer books."

"But if it's discovered."

"Discovered 'n' discovered, that's sure a word, that is."

"Why do you have a veil over your face, Miss Lagerlöf?" asked Sidner.

"That's so I won't be recognized. Because how would it look if I sat here and whipped my horses in the middle of the night?"

Her voice was as black as the darkness when the moon goes behind clouds. She raised the whip and drove the horses out of the shadow of the churchyard wall. The surrey took a leap over the shallow ditch and rushed out onto the road. Sidner held tightly with both hands, crouched behind her back.

"Why are you whipping the horses like that, Miss Lagerlöf?"

"So no one will believe it's me. For how could anyone believe that Selma Lagerlöf would whip her horses so wildly?"

They jolted along over the plain.

"Doggone, she sure can drive good."

"Only at night, my children. Only at night." And again the whip whistled over the horses until the steam rose from their backs. Bergskog's Nursing Home lay sleeping and the moon shone on its brow. Splendid coaxed the back door open, and no one seemed to be awakened by their steps on the stairs. The Madman lay in a corner of the cage sleeping. He was thin and miserable, slept with his thumb in his mouth, his knees drawn up under him. Splendid put a finger in front of his mouth as he stuck a hand through the bars and woke him.

"We're here ta save ya, sir. Sssh. Selma Lagerlöf is waitin' down in the grove with horse and wagon."

The Madman groaned, and Sidner began mechanically to rattle off:

Then see! Just at the ascent's beginning
A panther came toward me, nimble, light,
whose skin of scattered spots shone gaudily;

And neither would it retreat from my sight,
But rather obstructed my going on.

"Don't be so scared, Sidner."

The Madman sat studying Splendid, who had begun to saw a bar.

"Is he afraid of me?" whispered the Madman. "I am, too. You have to take the letters backwards. Then they're sure surprised, they never get to sleep."

"If you'll pull the saw blade from th' other direction it'll go faster."

Yet e'en so I was not seized by alarm
When to my vision a lion appeared

Who came toward me with head lifted high
And ravenous with terrible hunger.

"It's never going to work, they'll hunt him," the Madman moaned while he sawed.

"Ah. Maybe you'll be in a book."

"I am A. I'm A, or I won't play." He rocked his body contentedly. "Sore. Coop. In a hook. Take me away from me."

"You help, too, Sidner. This is your crazy fella."

"No."

"Saw!" Sidner thought Splendid's voice had a new, commanding tone, which frightened him.

"Yes, all right, I'll saw. Saw everything free."

The Madman rocked back and forth. Piece after piece of the bar fell to the floor.

"What's going to happen to all my mud over the darn place?" And he became anxious, more and more anxious the larger the opening became; when they prepared to leave, the Madman collapsed and refused to go.

"I don't want to leave. This is my place. In the mud."

"Come on, now."

"I'm afraid of me. So afraid, so afraid."

"Put 'cher arm round me, like that. It's gonna be fine."

The horses neighed and snorted when they had at last dragged the lunatic down to the grove.

"Heavens! In all my days, how you look, young man. What have they done to you. Is life so cruel! Put a blanket over your legs so Selma of the Night can drive you away from this valley of misery, where wolves rush over ice and snow."

"Not home to Mommy, not home to Mother, keep me away from that lamp."

"We'll drive as long as night lasts. So we won't be..."

"... discovered, o' course," said Splendid, and Selma became as if completely wild. The horses neighed, took a couple of tentative steps out of the overgrown grove, and Selma raised the whip over their backs, and away they went. Dust smoked around the wheels when they bumped downhill by Borgeby School, and before they knew it they were down on the flat. The moon was even clearer than before. The mushrooms had grown. Their eyes followed them from everywhere. Their pupils glittered green and malevolent.

"May I kiss you?" the Madman asked suddenly.

"Of course, young man. But you'll have to lift my veil yourself."

"But I'm a toad."

"Kiss me and we'll see before morning comes." The Madman fumbled with his hands; the surrey jolted.

"Must the horses rush so?"

"Yes, they must, otherwise morning will catch up with us."

"The veil is stuck, my hands shake so."

"It isn't stuck." Selma's voice was furious.

"No, maybe not. But I… I don't know how to do it… I can't. I'm good for nothing out here in these darn places." Selma did not check the horses at all to help the Madman, just the opposite: they passed the town of Sunne with such speed that the wheels rumbled like drumfire and should have awakened every citizen; but the citizens of Sunne do not awake so easily. No one slowed his passage over the bridge, no one showed himself on Main Street. In Muddy Bottom the houses lay deep in sleep. No wolf nor lynx rose against them on Three Man Slope; at Rottneros the cows turned their shrewd eyes toward the road but expressed no unfavorable comments. Nothing made Selma stop before at last they swung down onto a little curving road through the woods by Öjer Cove and stopped right at the water's edge. There, moored in wide bushes and hidden by the thicket, lay a raft, and on the raft stood an armchair covered in green velvet. A little table was set with a steaming coffee pot, sandwiches, and rolls. The water was still and the silence overpowering after the dreadful journey. There was a pleasant smell of wood from the raft's substantial logs. Dawn came and soon the first bird of the morning rose from night's opened hand. A shade of green on the water. Some gleams of gold.

Selma raised the veil from her face.

"We have arrived. Hop down, now. I've stolen a little food from my own pantry. My housekeeper is going to think thieves have been there." She chuckled, pleased, smiling like a girl who has committed her first exquisite sin. Sausage, cheese, bread. The Madman dashed over to the raft and snapped up a sausage sandwich.

"At Bergskog I only got soup."

"That's gross," said Splendid.

"Not nettle soup. If there are egg halves and chives and some small Vienna sausages in it."

"Yeah, that's fer sure. If there's Vienni sausages in it... But that don't happen often, ya know."

Sidner helped Selma over, and she sat down in the armchair. When the Madman had swallowed the first sandwich he said:

"I'm not allowed to eat food. I'm a no-good person, Dr. Lagerlöf. It's not right to set me free. Back to the cage, back to the cage, Dr. Lagerlöf, I've seriously broken the Fourth Commandment."

"Which's that?" asked Splendid.

"Which is it? Good God, Lord Jesus, save my soul! I've let myself be freed by you. Is it really true you don't know? At last I see clearly... Maybe you don't even know what the First Commandment is."

"Yeah...? It's on the tip o' my tongue. It's... Ain't it the' one with 'always' in it...?"

"Are you in league with the Devil? Are all of you on this raft in league with the Devil?"

Splendid kicked the raft away from land and began to pole vehemently through the shallow water.

"Nah, I don't think so. Not me anyway. Are *you*, Sidner?"

"No, I..."

"An' Selma then?"

Selma had taken a comb and mirror out of her muff. She had undone her long, white hair and was combing it. She looked at him in the mirror.

"I don't know. Furthermore, you will call me Miss Lagerlöf now that it's morning... Oh yes, sometimes I certainly feel he's after one."

Splendid pondered that while the raft steered straight out toward Moth Island's huge, spoon-like silhouette with its enormous spruces.

"Yeah, after one, that he sure is, o' course."

"Especially when one writes well. Then one feels that the power she has over her fellow humans isn't of this world. That she sees right through them. Looks deep into their souls and sees the darkness, sees the bottomless in them. AS IN YOU SIDNER. COME HERE."

"What would you like, Miss Lagerlöf?"

"To kiss you."

The Madman looked at them with terrified eyes, took several steps toward the water.

"Huh, then I've got to hop in. I can't live in this evil world."

"Like hell you will," said Splendid and threw himself on the Madman, twisted his arms and forced him down.

"Now, sir, you lay still till we've freed you!"

"Didn't you hear what I said," Selma repeated. "Let's not fight among ourselves. Think what I've done for you."

"For me?" Sidner wondered.

"Yes, for you. Come, now."

"No," screamed Sidner. "No, I don't want to."

A great weariness came over him. He sank down on the edge of the raft dipping his hand in the tepid water, which was now quite pink with the approaching sun. A fish bumped the bottom of the raft, and far away the sound of a steamboat could be heard.

"They steered the raft into the shadow of the overhanging willows and waited until the light had disappeared. Noise and laughter was heard from on deck, and we felt a great fear that Aunt Polly stood there keeping a lookout for us, but who could possibly imagine where we were. I understood now that they had discovered we were gone, that the constable and all searched for us. And I enjoyed the feeling that maybe they thought I was dead, regretted that I had not written a letter and said that I could not take this life any longer so they would be sorry..."

Sidner sat up with a start:

"Where's Selma Lagerlöf? Who... who's Aunt Polly?"

"So, you awake now? Polly... I don't have any idea who that is." Splendid hid away the book from which he had been reading. Sidner sank back into the pillow.

"Selma got so difficult when it got light. When we'd brought the Madman to land."

"Despite his not wanting to?"

"Yeah, he said that…"

"… I belong to the darkness. I want to go back there. There they won't find him. He's your darkness, too. It can't be in the light."

But they managed to get the Madman over to Moth Island. He struggled and fought awhile, but suddenly became cooperative and followed along like a lamb. And Splendid took a breather, sinking down on the sand.

"Now we've saved the ol' fella."

"That's good," said Selma, "then I can get myself home again. So it isn't…"

"… discovered, yeah, yeah. But stay here, Selma. I've made a table o' crates an' a rib-backed chair there under the spruces. Ya c'n sit 'n' write there. 'Bout what's round about."

"I don't think you understand this. I'm a public figure. And in the middle of a book!"

"Write 'bout us fishin' perch 'n' pickin' wild raspberries…"

"I must have distance from things."

"Things! As if they wadn't here… The sun shines 'n' the bees buzz, an' we got us a real live crazy fella. As if that wouldn't do fer Selma. An' I promised he'd get ta be in a book."

"Promises, promises, Splendid."

"I want to go back to my cage," screamed the Madman.

"Ain't that a good start, Selma? See, here's paper 'n' pens."

He forced her down on the chair under a tall spruce. The sun peeked through the branches and shone on her white hair, which still hung down, but her eyes were tired.

"Start writin' now, Selma: "'I want to go back to my cage," screamed the Madman throwing himself down on the sand. It was in the beginning of August. We had just freed a poor, unfortunate person from his degradation and come out to Moth Island. We

had fine days out there. There were fish in the lake, and at night I
rowed in and stole a little milk and butter and salt.'"

Sidner turned in his bed.

"Wasn't I along?"

"He's awake now, Aron."

"I'll warm a little milk," he heard his father say from over by
the stove.

"Tell me more about the water."

"What water?"

"Lake Fryken... or the Mississippi... or. Where am I? Papa!"

"You're awake now... Let me look at you. You look better."

"Awake? Then I've been asleep?"

"Yes, you sure have."

"Where's Splendid? He was here just now, wasn't he?"

"Oh, well, not just now. But you can be glad you have a friend
like Splendid. Just think how that boy can talk... And make up
things."

"Make up things? I want to sleep."

Oh, it is a rich illness. It is so full of pictures and words. Huge,
still waters, the cool mornings; he lets himself sink and rise at
water's edge, lets himself be filled with the flood's drink. But the
fever is actually beginning to subside. More and more often he is
in the kitchen with his father and Eva-Liisa. Soon he can stretch
out his hand for the book lying on the chair. It is *The Adventures
Of Tom Sawyer*. It lies open somewhere in the middle.

"Have you been reading to me from that book?" Splendid
stands inside the door.

"Well, yeah, I thought ya might like..."

"Even though I was sleeping?"

"Sleepin' and sleepin'. Ya tossed about a lot... There's one
thing, Sidner. I hope ya c'n fergive me. I'm so doggone sorry I
coaxed ya out ta Bergskog. If that's what made ya so poorly."

"That wasn't why. But everything was so strange. We could
very well go and visit him some day. Since we saved him."

"That, yeah," Splendid said evasively.

"It wasn't true, was it."

"That's fer sure somethin' you've dreamed…"

Splendid places himself with his back to the room and lifts away the curtain.

"Though you told me that, too, didn't you?"

"Yeah, well, yeah, I thought you'd like it."

"And that Selma Lagerlöf helped out?"

"Nah… she… She's old, ya know."

"So he's still in the cage."

"No. No, he ain't."

"So he's well, then!"

Sidner's strength returns at once. He sits up and even laughs.

"In a coupla days ya c'n go ta school again."

"Yes, and then we can visit… What is it, Splendid? Why are you looking at me so strangely?"

"It's hot."

"Splendid, there's something else. What is it you don't want to tell me?"

"Nah, ya know… Can't I go now?"

"No."

"Well… Ya know, the day after I'd been there with the rabbits. When you was sick…"

"Yes?"

"He hung hisself then. He hung hisself, Sidner. An' I didn't know if you could handle it. An' me neither… me neither."

"The truth!" Marc Chagall snorted. "You won't reach it that way. Possibly you can find truth first behind imagination."

We sat with our backs to each other, each before his own easel. I was fifteen years old, and Mother had driven me out to painting's richest pasture land: behind a field of poppies in bloom, the hills of Provence shimmered. She herself sat under her parasol in a white, high-necked dress, in the dual capacity of watchdog and model. She wore a blue clematis in her hair; I, in the White Artist's Smock, now represented the young Monet. The old fellow popped up among the stones when I had already been working about an hour. Now and then he glanced furtively over at us. Without breaking her pose, my mother said:

"So you paint, too."

"Yes, I paint, too."

"It's so marvelously beautiful here," Mother said.

"Yes, unfortunately," said the old fellow, "but I couldn't resist the sight of you two. If you'll forgive me."

Perhaps Mother did not understand, so she repeated – for which time in a row I do not know:

"My son is so talented."

"Nothing is so dangerous as talent," the old man said, and my mother's nervous lips pulled together. She stared out over the landscape.

"What is it you *want* to paint?" he asked me, looking at my canvas.

"The truth," I answered in the midst of one of my mendacious brush strokes. That was when he snorted. But I never told Mother it was Marc Chagall who snorted.

THE RAILROAD HAD BEEN inaugurated at the beginning of the century with flapping flags and quantities of punch. Boss Björk stood beside the engineer, waving at the people jostling about the roadbed all along Fryk's Valley. Smoke poured down into their faces, but still they took part, celebrating the great occasion that would soon devastate the work of many who devoted themselves to the transport of heavy loads. That many constantly celebrate their devastation was something Branting had known and had made speeches about; but now development was in full swing, and that day one admired the Boss's white straw hat, his vest which in any case had been gleaming white when he left Kil. His gold chain shone satisfactorily; he stroked his bristling mustache, for without his help the railroad would not have managed so quickly to wind its way between farms and crofts, along flourishing fields and through woodlands owned by Björk. He was a good businessman: in his youth he traveled in Norrland and saw the sawmills develop and learned a great deal. Though he had fed on bread and pork in the beginning, he was soon able to pass on from veal to devouring both real estate and woodlands; soon he owned half of Värmland, built himself a residence in the middle of the community, a veritable manor house with gate posts of cast iron and a flag on the circular lawn, which often floated over the new middle class. He built the hotel, and the sawmill grew for every passing year. Sunne blossomed. There were many factories; the artisan's quarter on Long Street and Main Street echoed from hammer blows, from people's laughter and groans; it was like an Arabian Casbah here. Shops opened, yes, and even a Department Store, not so different from the fine stores in Karlstad. Ola's Cars, which had acquired its first taxicab in 1905, now had expanded to include a large delivery firm. Gyllner's Auto Showroom was expanded, and as their first jobs, several young boys got to go to Göteborg and pick up the new cars. By train down and then up again, alone, with a pack of sandwiches and some fried eggs in an aluminum box on the seat, like kings in shiny new coaches. Björk and his sons-in-law all owned cars; even his daughter, Valborg, had her own driver's license, and to start with, it was a big sensation to see a woman behind the wheel. She always gathered a crowd when she drove the two hundred yards to Åberg's to buy delicacies. Even Selma Lagerlöf sometimes came there, often by horse and wagon, but soon she was negotiating with Gyllner to buy a Volvo.

And the population grew: many of the laborers who had worked on the railroad remained, becoming station masters and employees of all sorts. When inauguration day came, strange yellow and foreign station buildings lay like a string of pearls beside the platforms; among newly-planted cone flowers the dialects of Skåne, Blekinge, and Småland were spoken. The first nervous departures of the so recently uniformed laborers were rewarded with punch by the Boss, who personally stepped down from the engine with glass and bottle in hand. Bands played, children trumpeted, and flowers were thrown in through the open windows of the railroad cars. The Danish brothers Per and Pop got engaged to the twin sisters Edel and Esther in the middle of the railroad bridge; they even kissed in public, but that was a great day, of course, the prelude to a new age.

And the years passed. Naturally, punch was still drunk, but not along the railroad: after such an invitation to dance most people had to return to the plow, to the counter, to feeding the pigs. The weather no longer seemed so glorious, either; thick clouds towered up from the south. One of the factories on Torvnäs Road burned down, another suddenly stopped paying wages, the owner of a third disappeared early one morning and the machines fell silent.

One read the newspapers and knew there was a shortage of food – a little here and there. On Main Street, a lady dropped a bottle of syrup, breaking it on the pavement, and immediately two boys could be seen lying on their stomachs, licking it up. If one wanted to have fun one had to go to the Hotel. There one could dance to effervescent, foreign melodies:

> *Wish I could shimmy like my Sister Kate*
> *She shivers like the jelly on a plate*
> *My mammy wanted to know last night*
> *Why all the boys treat sister Kate so nice.*

And later at night to slow, melancholy songs which Aron, with tired fingers and empty gaze, put on the gramophone under the potted palms:

> *Do you know what it means*
> *To miss New Orleans*
> *I'll never forget that old town.*

There were many who stood outside the hotel in those days and muttered, a gray mass Aron was forced to see every time he opened the window to air out the odor of the Boss's cigars, for Björk participated all the more frequently in the parties, even if there were now fewer business people and more lady friends. They played charades, had masquerades, slapped down poker cards, and drank more punch. Björk had started to look tired; his belly had grown, and he smacked younger and younger ladies on the bottom.

One morning after a party he knocked on Aron's door; he stood there sallow and partied out, wanting to talk. The gold chain, which had cost the forest so many trees and the workers so many bent backs, was the only thing about him that shone.

"Let's go down there," he said, pointing at the wine cellar.

He locked the door behind them, opened up a bottle and drank several gulps, then sank down on a stool.

"A labor representative came on the morning train on his way up to Torsby," he said. "That wasn't what I wanted the train for."

Then he looked around the cellar: "You ought to have better light in here; I'll see it's taken care of. Now I want you to take the next train up there and take care of that character."

He scrutinized the rows of bottles: "Fill a keg with aquavit and offer it to him before he talks to people. Arrange a party and see he disappears. Twenty liters ought to be enough to make it a decent party."

"I don't drink," said Aron.

"Oh, no, you don't, I forgot that. But it's not you who needs to be... To be honest: business isn't so good anymore. Things are tight in this line. If the workers are going to demand more money now, I won't manage much longer. That's *my* reality and I have to live with it. I'll have to send someone with you. Someone who boozes. Asklund boozes, doesn't he?"

"He's a socialist!"

"But he *boozes*."

"You're buying people, Johan."

"Yes, I am. It's expensive." Björk broke out in a drunken laugh. "Just think, getting paid to drink. What employer would offer that. He can even stay home the next day, if he feels like it. You'll have to go down and get him at the sawmill. But you've got to see he doesn't drink before you get there."

"And if I refuse?"

"You know you won't do that, Aron. So far we employers can give orders. Are you sympathetic to labor? I didn't think you were."

"It's treachery."

"Maybe. In any case, the labor leader is going to talk to the workers at Hedsätter Sawmill at eleven o'clock. Try to find him before that. I'm sure he's staying at Björnidet."

"He can't afford that."

"Then he's staying with one of the workers. Let Asklund smell that keg, he'll run there fast as hell."

"What if the labor man is a teetotaler, too?"

"He's not. He wasn't sober when he got here on the train; that's why I know everything."

"How dare you, Johan!"

"It's not hard. Everything *can* be bought. Maybe not you, but in that case you're not interesting. In business you don't have to count the exceptions; we can afford to overlook those. If they're too many, they're not exceptions anymore; then a different political situation arises, and it's not here yet."

"It's on its way."

"True. But I'm on my way, too, you see. Out, out of life, out of business. I'm not so dumb I haven't seen that; I read the papers. But I think I'll continue a little while longer. I don't want to see my life's work vanish into thin air. By the way, those were fine gramophone records you bought. Now let's go up and play them, just for you and me. That's an order, too."

The ballroom is empty, Aron blows off the needle, places the tone arm in the groove, stands silently listening:

> *Thought if I want to be up-to-date*
> *I had to shimmy like sister Kate*
> *Although I tried t'was all in vain*
> *But sister Kate could not be blamed*
> *She made me dance till I got sore feet*
> *I will be glad when it's all complete.*

THE TRIP TO TORSBY dug deeply into Aron's self-confidence. He stood on the platform between cars with the gurgling aquavit keg in his arms, looking out over the Boss's rich woodlands and thinking how easy it would be to throw it away – but just then the conductor came along and started a conversation. He wanted to pour it down the toilet and fill it with water instead, but the toilets were occupied, and all of a sudden they were in Torsby. He wandered through the streets and after a while found himself in a churchyard. An organ played in the church, the doors opened, and a funeral train swayed out. Aron retired some distance away, but the train was after him, driving him farther and farther toward a wall, in front of which lay an open grave. The keg exhaled evil, he did not want to be seen with it there, and desperately he lowered it into the grave, where it ended up on its edge. Too late he realized the coffin would not lie flat on the grave's bottom. Who was he who could not say no to the boss's demand? Reality was too hard, he thought, as he fled from it.

He became a reader of the Bible and let himself be encompassed by God. One day he read about the disciples who broke an axe on the Sabbath. That story was the center of the Gospels for him, their center of daylight. It had so much to do with Solveig and him: here was the center of love and tolerance – a place he often sought for himself in order to be alone. He closed his eyes and let the light play inside his eyelids; Solveig came and was very close to him; he could feel her eyelashes tickling his cheek. When he opened his eyes to continue reading he saw how the letters suddenly freed themselves from the paper. Terror-stricken, he noticed with fascination how they lost their connection with each other, were were sucked off the page, danced away, and took up residence everywhere – in the grass, in the tops of trees, up in the sky, which paled toward evening. Aron gave a laugh and threw the Bible far away in a ditch: it had served its purpose now. He had received the sign. It was just a question of being attentive.

He watched the letters whirl up toward the sky, and when evening came he saw that what he had earlier taken to be stars were the letters in the old alphabet: an original text stood up there, a rebus, and Solveig was in that text, was the uniting power. Someday she would let him understand.

And he saw something else, which perhaps came from Ezekiel: in the valley with the bones of the dead, on the plain filled with lamentation and affliction, he caught a glimpse of her behind the letters, only half visible in her blue-white cotton dress which, light as a curtain, enfolded her warm breast. And he had hope that she alone among all the dead still retained her colors, that the dress was still blue-white, that the golden brown scar was still there on her cheek bone. She lived, but far, far away.

Aron thought he kept his new insight secret, but it oozed out in glimpses, first to Sidner's consternation, then to Eva-Liisa's as well: "How strange you talk, Papa," she said looking wonderingly at him.

What did he say then? Nothing special. But it was as if conversations – those miserable, paltry exchanges of words over the kitchen table – had taken on a new dimension in time. Conversation discovered itself not only here and now; all of a sudden a wisp of words from farther away would slip in, a smile that had nothing to do with the laundry, the cooking and the darning of socks in which the three were engaged together. Aron had begun to smile.

"He's gotta get somethin' ta do," said Splendid. "Somethin' that takes his mind offa her."

"That's not so easy," was Sidner's opinion, after he had told Splendid about it and allowed him to observe Aaron.

"I'll talk ta my old man."

So Aron was invited to visit Splendid's father. He saw the huge radio set. "It's a good hobby," said the little old fellow spinning the knobs. "Have you ever heard of ham radio operators?"

And after awhile they managed to coax Aron into Sunne's ham radio operators' club, which Splendid's father had founded. They met in Mr. Fälldin's, the nurseryman's, greenhouse. An antenna had been raised out on the flagpole, and in the steamy warm greenhouse, under the letter from his Majesty the King granting them permission to own the apparatus, there was a confusion of cords and headphones, coffee cups and rolls.

There was whistling and crackling from Europe, and every once in a while from America and Africa, too. They sat on chairs in the warmth, near plants weighted down with tomatoes and rows of geraniums, chrysanthemums, marigolds; they spun and poked, as outside the snow drifts lay high, pressing against the glass walls.

One day they had a remarkable, far-off contact from New Zealand. The envelope was passed around so everyone could see the stamp; then Sleipner opened it, drank a little coffee and read it so loudly and so fast that not many understood.

"Don't put on airs now," said Fälldin, who wanted the letter quickly over and done with. It was the transmitter itself he was interested in, not the letter. He wanted to know how well the signals reached, what improvements might be made. The contact itself was only a confirmation that his set had succeeded.

But not so for Aron. Gazing out into the darkness on the other side of the glass walls, with the stove crackling behind him, the smell of damp earth and wet wool, he was snatched away from his body. Distance transported him nearer Solveig.

The letter was marvelous. It was a signal that had reached him from incomprehensible distances; it confirmed something he knew and had always guessed would come: the desolate whistling and crackling came from out in space, and Solveig was out in space. It was like an act of devotion to listen, and Aron could interpret the signs better than the others, make them his own. He often became irritated with Sleipner and Fälldin, who spun away this or that signal, just when he had started to get some order in its cryptic message.

The person who wrote, or more correctly, dictated the letter was a sheep farmer in New Zealand. He lived on his farm with his sister, Tessa. They owned four hundred sheep, but during the summer, which would soon be over – listen to that, Sleipner sighed – there was time left to pursue this new hobby. He had managed to make contact with Australia and India before. This unexpected success was more than he had ever dared hope for. Would even be happy to continue the contact in the future, but perhaps even more so my sister, who writes down these words because my own hand is in a bandage since an accident. Was putting up a fence. Signed, Robert Schneideman by Tessa.

"Is there anyone who wants to read it himself?"

Fälldin quickly glanced over the lines. Contact achieved, period. Juno Luntz, who was a stock assistant in Jolin's factory, twisted and turned the letter; he did not understand English, but could he have the stamp?

"No," said Fälldin. "I think we should keep all the letters in a special box. There could be a lot of them in the end, we can establish a large net of contacts. If we let anyone take the stamp the letter will fall apart."

"I can soak it loose," said Juno, "I've done it many times."

"Then the text disappears."

Aron spelled his way through the letter, it went quite easily. He cleared his throat:

"And who's going to take it upon himself to answer?"

Fälldin put more wood in the stove.

"I think you can do that," he said to Aron. "You understand English, don't you."

"Who, me? I don't have anything to write."

Fälldin snorted:

"You can write anything to people like that."

He had spoken his piece.

"No, you can't. You have to be careful with far-off contacts. Very."

He closed his eyes and leafed through the old atlas Solveig and he had so often looked at with the children by lamplight in the evening. He remembered how she had pointed out the American states, pointed out trips she had made to small spots on the page, hardly visible. There, there's a mill there and the river; yes, it's a river, even if you can't believe it, wide and slow. We sat there one evening, Papa and Sleipner and I… It was just before he disappeared; I had to be five. We fished and had a fire on the riverbank; Mamma and he were absolutely quiet. I became frightened, didn't understand anything. I still don't…

Opening an atlas was like sinking down out of the air. Near the ground you could let the page become transparent, the signs changing into reality, into forests, ravines, mountains; one day they were going to set off on a long trip together…

Fälldin became sulky when no one said anything about his radio set. As if he had hoped they would kiss it or at least regard it with a touch of deference. When Aron went home that evening he carried all of New Zealand with him. He bore the oceans between the continents, and the night and day which separated them.

He wrote a letter. First in Swedish, then with the help of a dictionary and stealthy questioning of Sleipner, who said to him:

"I know you're busy writing that letter. Good for you. You need something to think about. And who knows, maybe that woman is someone for you."

Dear Ham Radio Friends,
Dear Robert and Tessa,

This letter comes from a snowy Sweden. The drifts lie high around our house. It is cold and the stars sparkle during the long nights, and your message from the other side of the planet reached us like a falling star.

It is remarkable that this should happen. I who write these lines, partially at the request of my fellows, but much by my own will, am a very lonely person since my wife died in an accident. I still exist all too much in her. Until now nothing has been able to get my thoughts on anything else, despite my having two children, a boy and a girl, and a meaningless job as a porter at a hotel. I was a farmer before, had a small farm which we worked together, but I could not manage to go on there alone, could not live in the past since every room, every part of the house was filled with her presence.

Now I am only half a person. Perhaps it would fill my days if I knew that now and then there was a letter to pick up, a distant landscape to fantasize about, another sort of knowledge to fill the empty room with. I am only thirty-five years old, but it is as if I have lost my grip on life, or rather: as if it has lost its grip on me. If you could help me in some way, I would be extremely grateful.

Sincerely yours,
Aron Nordensson

Several months passed, the spring sun peeked out, the snow melted and the days grew longer; and Aron, who lived with his letter, the first outward opening, began almost to believe it had got lost on the way, or that he had placed too great a demand on these unknown people when one day, in the beginning of April, he took a long, slender envelope from his mailbox.

Taihape, April

Dear Mr. Aron Nordensson,

The rain fell heavily when your letter arrived. I had been out shearing sheep with my brother and was soaking wet when I saw the postman. I don't often receive letters. Almost never from so far away, and I had nearly forgotten that I had written out that greeting from my brother, which I understand is your reason for writing.

It is an open letter. It is shocking. It was as if I got to know, really know, a person. I know so little about people. I have lived on this farm my whole life, ever since my parents died in a boating accident. A couple of times a year I travel with my brother into Wellington on business, but I feel like an outsider in Wellington. I am a country girl, and business conversation does not interest me. Instead I read a great deal, which seems to irritate my brother. He says it puts me outside the purpose of the farm, that I get ideas, and perhaps that is true.

I feel shy writing you. You have given me a trust which I do not know how I will answer. I myself do not have any experience – except my parents' death – which can be compared with yours. But what tribulations can be *compared*? They are all unique. Each one's tests are always the greatest. But on the other hand: it is probably wrong of me to reject the insights of my own life. But it seems to me as if they – to the degree they exist – have never been put to the test.

Is loneliness an insight? Walking through fields early in the mornings, looking after the pasturage, looking for parasite worms, changing pasturage, keeping silent together with my brother in a silent kitchen, seeing *his* loneliness, is that an insight? Robert is reserved. I believe it is the mishap with his hand. It is not at all as he forced me to write, that he recently had that misfortune. His hand was cut off long ago. He wears a prosthesis which he tries to hide whenever we have visitors. His sullen back is a part of my tribulation. His averted glance, his jealousy. (I have to be honest with you; after all, we will never meet. We cannot judge each other, you cannot judge me. It is just fine at last, at last after all these years, to find someone to write *everything* to.) Yes, he read your letter without pleasure, yes, with suspicion and contempt. (As if it were actually I who got him to answer the card the first time.)

I am twenty-two years old. I have never been with any man, but my desire is so great that I often want to die. The only freshness I can find is in church, to which I go frequently. But my own desires are not sinful, they are something which is denied me. Strange that I should tell you, a *man* I have never seen. It is reassuring to know that you are sitting on the other side of the world. My cheeks are hot as I write these words, by the stove, in the rain which pounds down almost horizontally on the fields, a rain so thick I have to strain to catch a glimpse of my brother's back out there where he bends over the sheep pen (one of our ewes lambed half an hour ago).

New Zealand would condemn me if it knew my thoughts. It is a narrow and cheerless country; people are uncommunicative, shut up in themselves, dissatisfied. I often feel I do not belong here, that I am disguised, that my name is not mine, that my thoughts, my real dreams are not allowed to be released into my true self. Perhaps we are all like that, all women in the vicinity: keeping silent, guarding one another, each in her own prison.

No, I am sure I have read too many books. My brother is right: I have got ideas, improper ones, but what can I lose by writing you, in secrecy, and in secrecy I must send this letter, one day when I have errands at the store… I have to stop, my brother is on his way in…

(Three days later) Now is the first opportunity I have had to continue. Although it has already become so long: I do not regret what I have written; you are an opening for me. The nights have been full of possible conversation, the first in my life. Like a tide in the darkness where I can lower my thoughts into a bottle, which is carried out of me and away toward you. You are the first person who has talked to me, openly, with the *whole* of your being. Therefore, during these three days I have hardly been able to sleep, I have *seen* you. But who are you really? Do you exist? Or are you a dream? All the others − and they are not many − talk as though between sheep pens to me, to each other, stunted words pressed through bars, through barbed wire, through electrified wire, crouching words, facades of words; I am bewildered, do you understand me? I am so afraid, so afraid now as I write to you. The words ferment, swell in my mouth. Do not abuse me, do not betray me, and write to me, c/o General Delivery. Perhaps I can trust Mrs. Winther there.

Yours truly,
Tessa Schneideman

WHAT A FLAMING ARDOR grasped Aron when he read the letter that spring. It had a tone which was many times higher than his own. He had not opened himself up that much. He had not *given* her anything. He carried the letter with him everywhere he went. He slept with it under his pillow. It was a flame lighting up his face.

And he answered and received an answer.

Taihape, May

Dear Aron Nordensson,

Today, sun. The whole way down to the village, to the post office where your letter waited. After the rain, the thistles the sheep leave shimmer with a wonderful violet luster. I frequently cut them and let them dry inside. The thistle is New Zealand's flower, at least I think so. Prickly, hostile, but pretty at a distance.

I do not know why I decided to trust Mrs. Winther at the post office, but there is something in her eyes that tells me she will not give out your letters. We have never talked about how things are for me, but I think people know. When I asked if I could receive General Delivery she just nodded and looked at me with warm, good eyes. As if she had her own dearly-bought experience behind her. Perhaps there are many women who pick up secret letters from her, perhaps all women, even a few men, those living at home, those growing.

There is a neighbor of ours, a farmer who shares his farm with his two sisters. They are old now, all three of them, conservative, surly, obstinate, in other words like people are for the most part. But one day I heard that he, who has such thistly, hostile eyes, once in his youth came home from Australia with a woman. She was a widow, had two children, and he explained that he wanted to marry her. His parents opposed it and turned her out.

What happens to such a person? To those concerned, since the sisters remained unmarried – for that is the custom?

I frequently observe him secretly to be able to understand his fate, but it is not possible: he is as blank as ice.

I observe him because his situation is mine:

Yes, I have had a man. One. We were engaged, I gave myself to him (dared not tell this in my first letter, I knew so little, but now I dare everything, I *must* dare everything) *one* time. I was not ashamed then, I am not now either. It was the only time I have felt *alive*. When I came home with the ring on my finger, when I happily stretched it out toward Robert, he hit me with his prosthesis, a blow on the cheek; then he pulled the ring off me, dragged me out to the outhouse and dropped it in. You can hunt for it there, he screamed.

That was four years ago now. "My husband" was threatened and moved away from here. Everything I owned of will and drive fled from me. I acted as if I were dead, still so when your first letter arrived. Perhaps I was over-excited, but the letter was a real shock.

I would not be able to handle another such divorce. Could Mrs. Winther see that in my eyes? Is there a dangerous sheen to them? Are they desperate?

In a way I was afraid you would answer me. This having a pen friend opens too many floodgates, awakens thoughts which I have forbidden myself. You should know that, if you continue, your letters will become the one thing I will live for, every walk to Mrs. Winther at the post office like wandering over glass splinters, even if I know it takes several months between each letter. The days in between I formulate, even if you cannot observe it, sentences, views which I want to share with you, but right now (so typical) they have disappeared. I possess no language. My whole life I have lain fallow, never had the opportunity to use myself. No, never been used. Therefore, I am afraid it is visible on me, that I am observed and that Robert will notice it and punish me. Perhaps I draw men's glances to myself, too, the absence of current which dominated me these years made me invisible.

That which is now visible – if this is so – that which sticks up its face in me is a dangerously vulnerable person. I cannot explain further.

Yours,

Tessa Schneideman

Aron Nordensson and Alfons Nilsson had begun to spend time together. During the tranquil days of June it happened that Splendid put his father in a wagon, pulled him up to Broby Woods and, there in a glade, they could be seen listening to birds. There was a rich collection of rarities in a bog. One evening a bluethroat came and sang so extremely prettily. The binoculars went around and Alfons Nilsson said:

"It shouldn't be here. Just like me. The statistical probability of seeing a bluethroat here is certainly greater than the probability of my life."

The glade lay high up; there was a fine view of the valley below, the houses and the treetops where blackbirds, chaffinches and titmice twittered, and their notes fell over them like a warm rain of gold.

That little packet Nilsson closed his eyes and smiled.

"We are both men with a past, Nordensson. That doesn't prevent such a day as this from having its value."

"But do you think it was worth surviving? Really."

"The question is raised, Nordensson, and I have an answer: look at the youngsters. See how well they play together. They can give each other so much."

"It's mostly your Splendid, you know, who gives to Sidner. Sidner is so introverted I sometimes fear for his reason."

"Just give him time. And what you say isn't true: they're storing these experiences now, they're acquiring a foundation for their lives."

"I'm such a bad father to mine."

"We all feel that way sometimes. Quiet, now it's singing again!"

The bluethroat off in the treetop. It was quiet in the grass, Aron would write to Tessa about that. About the little cannon king in his wagon, the contented expression on what was left of his face, about his son's helplessness.

"But my life is slipping away, Nilsson. I give so little."

"You never know that yourself. What do you think *I've* given my old girl with this body. Maybe something anyway. She was afraid of men. She was a nurse; she wanted to care for someone, so she found someone to care for, an abominable character."

"Why did you become a human cannonball?"

"If you're from Småland, you've got to become a human cannonball. I got absolutely weird down there in the woods without views, from not seeing where I was in life. It was like that from the beginning; I just wanted to be over the treetops. Nothing strange about that. And I read about someone who fell and…"

"And still?"

"My parents were like moss, low, limited, repressed. They said: Alfons, emigrate to America or become a construction worker, but don't kill us with such stupidity. One time a variety show came by and I joined it, began to practice. It gets like a poison in your body. You ought to feel what it's like to fly, to be shot out into the air; it takes ten, fifteen seconds, then it's all over. In any case, you've done *something*. You've been seen as something different, you know they'll be talking about you later."

Taihape, July

Dear Aron,

Mrs. Winther offered me coffee today. I came just before closing time. She gave me a nod to follow her into her private quarters. Even then I understood that I had a letter. She saw my excitement; she said: I'll go out a while, you sit here and read, nobody will disturb you. I burst into tears. No one, I tell you this, Aron, has spoken to me at eye level, spoken directly into my existence. Life is so cruel, it could be so good. Who and what is it people fear so intensely? Is it their own freedom? Is it terror of our enormous possibilities? When she came back she stood behind my chair and massaged my shoulders, and she did not say: Don't cry. She said: Go ahead and cry now, as long as you want. What a beautiful letter about the Swedish summer! I could quite clearly *see* you sitting there, that cannon king and you in the grass, listening to the birds.

Yes, I cried out part of the tears twenty-two years of my life have collected: I was relieved tear by tear, in Mrs. Winther's clean, cool room with tulle curtains and flowers in all the windows, with the scents from the well-tended yard outside. I lean my life against your letters, against the scent of them. What do you look like? I started to say on the outside because I believe I know your inside, the important, the true.

You have raised me from the dead.

(Several days later) Now in the middle of July the first hoar frost is on the panes. To the north, a layer of fog above the top of the woods, we are the fog's children. True, it is the Maoris who call us that, but I am one of them, not by birth, but by desire. I belong to the crushed. I am pakheha – that means white – but what besides the color of my skin unites me with Robert, with the neighbors on the farms around here? Maoris have a concept – "tapu" – the taboo regulation over which the whites make themselves ridiculous, but how many taboos surround us, yes, even more than the Maoris could ever think up.

This morning I went down to Mrs. Winther's again. I wanted to help her with the wash. Robert muttered about there being enough to do at home, but I told him about her bad back. He does not believe me. He does not believe anyone, anything; everything is excuses, lies. I went out through the gate just as the fog lightened; the black and striped piglets were cold, but sunshine began to glimmer in the foliage, icicles glittered in the trees. Several Tui birds fluttered in a glade with raised fantails – we have glades here, too. I sat there awhile digging in the moss with frozen fingers. I do not know why I did that; someone has said when you dig in the moss, it will snow.

We pakhehas, who are we, if not losers. We came here, took the land from the Maoris, "Christianized" them: now we sit here, trapped by our land, our things which we jealously guard. We live in a country which has not reached into our spinal marrow yet; we are strangers since the Maoris have already named the mountains, the rivers, the villages, everything that should give us a history. Ask Robert or me what this or that name means, we do not *know*. We have no history in common with names like Maungapohatus or Urewerealand. What those names tell us, we do not know. Tourists who come here – not many, but some – always receive the answer: that is something the aborigines made up. For us there are no shadows, no sound. We answer contemptuously, "made up," because we are tired of not being able ourselves to fill our faces with legends and memories. Our history ends just before us; and do not get the idea that it continues over in England, the break is too great. Our language is so ugly, full of swear words, simplifications, and repudiations. It is the convict's bitter language which oozes even into my, our nerves, a language without pride. It holds us imprisoned in loathsome ways of thinking. If you react against it, you must either sell yourself back to England, to Oxford or Cambridge, or become a Maori romantic. The Jews who live here, I imagine, have their own traditions at least, even if they are watered down, their peculiarities to hold themselves to. It makes them conscious of their individuality, their identity. We have nothing other than the religion of saying no, and that shrinks us.

All of that I have thought out and must tell you. I am not learned, even if I have read a bit; my life is only a few acres large, but I can see the mountains beyond. I have ridden the bus in Wellington. My glance roamed, I smelled of sheep. I am not afraid to reveal my ignorance to you, Aron, for the one who walks about in these rags is only partially me. There is another person inside me who now, for the first time, is beginning to be visible, thanks to you.

I kiss you,

Tessa

A pressed rose lay in that letter, it still had its scent.

ONE DAY ANOTHER LETTER ARRIVED. It was addressed to the hotel and concerned a room reservation. Aron opened that sort of mail in the kitchen with the Sauce Queen and Mrs. Jonsson. These morning moments of calm talk about purchases and bookings and relaxed gossip about yesterday evening were the best time of the day. As usual, Aron read the letter aloud:

> I hereby wish to reserve a room in your hotel for the nights between the 17th–19th when, in connection with the production of a film which is being launched in the area, I need a room to which I may withdraw, most preferably incognito.
> Sincerely,
> Fridolf Rhudin
> Actor

It was as quiet as before an earthquake. Then the letter was torn from Aron's hand, the Sauce Queen sank down opposite him at the table and read. Then she burst out in uncontrollable laughter:

"'Which is being launched in the area!' Well, he's just too funny, that Fridolf. Swell, swell, he's going to come here, well, good Lord." And her laughter rolled out into the dining room to spindly, sharp-chinned Stina Öhrström. With her scrub rag dripping in her hand, she opened the door a crack.

"Fridolf Rhudin's coming here! Swell, swell." Then she laughed again. "Look here, Stina, he writes so funny."

Stina, who was suspicious of everything written, looked anxiously at the lines, then turned to Aron.

"Do you think anything'll come of it?"

"Come of what?"

"That he'll say something. 'The Lonely Dog' or something?"

"Can't you read," Aron said. "He needs a place to withdraw to. And most preferably incognito, you understand?" Now she did not understand, she resolutely squeezed out her rag in the middle of the floor, rushed for her coat and disappeared out into the streets. Her lips were tight and dry.

Aron had a feeling it would be hard to protect their guest as early as when Boss Björk called and informed him that he needed a room just that weekend, "to think over certain things in peace and quiet." Soon after that Parliament Member Persson called saying "just at that time" he would be on his way into Karlstad for a horse show and "needed to be near the station." Then when, of all people, Göte Asklund tumbled in to reserve a "chambre," he knew what the whole town knew. Göte was one big bag of snuff and aquavit hanging over the counter.

"You don't think I'm fit fer yer hotel."

"Oh yes, but it costs."

"The boss should just hear that, that you don' want money comin' in. He needs it. Look here," said Göte, throwing his wallet on the counter: "Count it, Aron, take wha' you need, but I'll have a room." And he leaned all the way forward to Aron, grabbing his coat; his hands trembled from something other than anger: "You know how strong I am, Aron. I could wring your neck, an' the whole hotel. But I won't do that, I'm respectable, you know that, too."

"Yes, Göte."

"I could crush the whole mob."

"I know that. But you're drunk now."

"But Saturday I'll be sober. Then I'll have a room. I've never hurt a fly; work, tha's what I do, day and night, and nobody beats me at workin', you know that." He sank down on the outside of the counter. "You know, the missus, she buys clothes with everythin' I earn. An' now she's startin' to study, she says, but then I said, no sir, there'll be no studying for you."

He staggered up and lay across the counter, became confidential: "Study, females! Aron, you know wha' they do." He thrust his finger into Aron's face: "They travel into Karlstad, the females, they're away the whole week an' come home on Friday, with such soft eyes, an' say they're studyin'. But what do they do, Aron? They jazz it up! New coats 'n' skirts for all that money. A support machine, tha's me. But I'm gonna shoot myself, Aron. Then she can stand there with her new skirts."

"You have a child, too, Göte."

"The little one I'll take with me when I shoot myself, so she won't have to take part in this misery. But first I'll talk to Fridolf! Saturday I'll be sober," he said, and fell asleep on the counter.

Göte Asklund was not only respectable: he was shrewd, too. That Saturday afternoon the hotel's dining room was filled with guests; in the whole room there was but one free seat, opposite Boss Björk, who sat in the middle at a table by the window. On one side he had Parliament Member Persson, the harness king's son, on the other Journalist Edvardsson, who was already chewing on his pen. VIPs sat at every table, most of the men in dark suits and white shirts. Several had been generous enough to bring along their wives. "Makes a change from being home on Saturday," one family man said. Another bowed his head: "On account of the beautiful weather," he lied, and a third said, "I happened to be passing by and thought, why not treat myself to something extra good, since I'm alone," despite the fact that everyone knew the tables had been reserved for several days. For being so crowded the dining room was uncommonly quiet. No one had begun to eat, no one had taken a sip; those reading a newspaper had not turned a page for half an hour. The Sauce Queen and Mrs. Jonsson stamped nervously in the entrance to the kitchen, sometimes taking a swing by the smörgåsbord with all its pretty, shining dishes and straightening a plate, moving a bouquet of flowers and, at the same time, glancing furtively out into the vestibule.

Now and then an ear started. Someone swallowed audibly; a little child, who had not said anything, got a sharp rebuke to be quiet. All the windows were open; the train could be heard arriving, the booms were down outside on the street. Then at last! The door was opened and steps were heard on the stairs. Boss Björk pushed his chair out a bit, thought it over – there were many stairs – and sat a while on tenterhooks. Then he pushed it out completely and squeezed the napkin in his hand, threw it across his plate and hurried through the dining room. A smile could be seen to grow larger, and he made an attempt to throw out his arms in a big welcoming gesture.

"A hearty…" he said and suddenly found himself shaking hands with the tall and powerful Göte Asklund, who appeared in the doorway in as full finery as the other citizens. His dazzlingly white shirt shone, his pomaded hair lay straight back, smooth.

"Well, I never," he said, looking confused. Then he turned toward the corridor. "I was right, Fridolf. It's full here."

"Then we'll have something in the room, Göte," they heard Fridolf say. It did not sound funny at all. The Boss almost fell through the doorway.

"What the hell, Asklund… Mr. Rhudin…" And still further away in the corridor, "Mr. Rhudin."

"I believe Mr. Rhudin wants to be left in peace," said Göte Asklund. "He's had a strenuous day…"

"There's a place reserved for Mr. Rhudin. A table by the window. My name's Björk; this is my place, so to speak."

"He's the one I was talkin' about," said Göte.

"I intended to *treat* you to dinner, Mr. Rhudin…"

"Very kind, but… we prefer to…" A door opened and closed. A moment's silence. Then the sound of the door – Boss Björk stood again in the doorway looking out over the sea of guests – and Göte Asklund's order:

"Could we have two cups of tea in the room, please?"

It was a very awkward dinner. The forty guests could not, of course, just get up and leave, since they had now ordered. Very little alcohol was consumed. People picked at their food, hardly raising their eyes to each other. The child who whined about the potatoes being too hot got a box on the ear.

"Is he really any good as an actor?" Parliament Member Persson whispered. "I mean, as a comedian he's good enough, I suppose. Maybe."

"Really," Journalist Edvardsson said. "A comedian doesn't even write his own scripts. I mean, repeating what someone else has written."

"There's no *art* to it. 'I know what it will be, I do, it will be a common farm dog.' 'Today a little accident occurred on the parlor rug...' I mean, what's so funny about a sentence like that? If you look closely at it?"

"I never listen to the radio myself," said Björk. "In any case, not to entertainment programs. It was better before."

"Yeah, it sure was," said the Parliament Member and cast a contemptuous glance out the window; many upturned faces stared at him.

"I don't understand," he said, drawing the curtain, "how people can be so curious. Just because a slapstick comedian comes here. Skoal, Björk."

By midnight only the staff was left. Stina Öhrström, who had cleared the tables, came in with the scrub bucket and sat down in the kitchen, taking one of the left-over sandwiches the Sauce Queen pushed forward. Sidner sat in his pyjamas beside Aron, who filled in some papers for the next day. Mrs. Jonsson counted the tips, pushing coins into a savings box for the Salvation Army.

"Did you get yourself an autograph?" asked the Sauce Queen,

putting several spoonsful of mayonnaise on her bit of bread. Mrs. Jonsson shuddered.

"What do you think I am? I'm a respectable person." And to free herself from such terrible suspicions she let several coins jingle down into the box.

There was a knock on the door, and Fridolf Rhudin stuck his head in.

"Please excuse me if I'm disturbing you. May we come in?"

The Sauce Queen made a sign to Stina Öhrström to get up from her chair.

"Are you sure we're not... I mean, guests aren't allowed to stay in here, are they?" Göte Asklund stood behind him, hands folded over his stomach, as neat and orderly as before.

"It's not easy to be popular," Göte explained to the gathering. "Sometimes it costs more than it's worth, you know. It's not everything it seems in the newspaper."

He went around shaking hands, exactly like Fridolf, and considering the noteworthy words he had uttered, and the strength with which he had uttered them, no one found it peculiar. It was a saved soul standing before them.

"Is there anything we can serve Mr. Rhudin? A little clear soup? A pilsner?"

"A glass of milk would be fine."

Stina Öhrström had dragged herself up onto the kitchen sink. She dangled her legs and understood she was a part of something she did not really understand. She picked her teeth with her index finger so it would not be noticeable how her cheeks twiched.

Fridolf looked around. "I've always liked kitchens. They're the best place in a house. My father was..."

"A tailor," the Sauce Queen said, handing him a glass. Stina Öhrström wrinkled her eyebrows. That was well said, that was; what should she find to say? So she had said something. Afterwards.

"Yes, over in Munkfors. Just think how a person can miss something so much."

"Popularity has its price." Göte Asklund looked around, scrutinizing each person. He wanted to impress that on the ignorant. Stina Öhrström wrung her hands in her lap. She could have said that herself, of course. Almost. She thought of it at the same time as Göte. Almost. She stared at Fridolf who took his glass in *both* hands and drank. Maybe she could say something about that.

About cold milk being good.

That could be forward. It was just to say it, you know, straight up and down. So in any case she had said *that.*

"There's nothing like cold milk in the evening," said Fridolf setting down his glass.

"No," sighed Stina Öhrström, but no one heard. Now she was forced to start again.

"Göte, how in all your days did you manage to become acquainted with... Mr. Rhudin?" asked the Sauce Queen.

"I went to Ämervik and got on the train. I needed to confess, if that's what one says."

"And you've been sober the whole day." She patted him on the arm.

"If you meet such a fine person as Fridolf, then you don't need alcohol. Then it's *interesting,* you know. Everything. I sing, too, you know."

"Yes, we know that."

"And it's not so great. That's what I wanted to talk to Fridolf about."

"And a very interesting conversation we've had, too," Fridolf joined in.

"I can stay on pitch, you said so. But what I've brooded on is why nothing has come of me. And it has of Fridolf. That it can be so different. Despite the fact that it was so much the same for us from the beginning. Both his father and mine were tailors, you know."

Stina Öhrström tried to keep up: you could not know how long Fridolf would remain. Still she had not yet gotten anything out. Maybe she should say something about film. Or music, since the others were talking about music? So she would not be interrupting, but joining in. Kind of.

"Would you like a little more milk?"

The Sauce Queen had to destroy everything!

She jumped down from the sink, made it first to the pantry door, knocked away the Sauce Queen's round, fat arm, and reached for the pitcher:

"No sir," she snapped, raising the pitcher and holding it over Fridolf's glass, but he made a dismissive gesture.

"Thanks, it's fine as it is."

So she had made a fool of herself. Not before she had put back the pitcher did she think of saying: But half a glass maybe? She also could have said: There's nothing like cold milk in the evening. Though... She stared into the shelves with her back toward the kitchen. She swallowed. This had to make it or break it. She could not go home without having said *something*. Now it was quiet. She opened her mouth...

"What did Mr. Rhudin answer to that?" asked Sidner, who until now had just listened.

"To what? Oh yes, why it turned out so differently. I said that it's really just a lot of luck. In my case..."

"You said more than that," Göte interrupted. "You said you must let yourself go."

Fridolf wrinkled his eyebrows and his glance fell upon Aron, who had sat turned inward toward his own pictures, and he said right into them:

"You have to let yourself go, yes. Leave everything and just let yourself go. Then you get somewhere. Devotion is the only thing that counts, in the end."

"It's a long way," Aron said.

But now Stina Öhrström had had enough. There was nobody who wanted to listen to her. Morose and grumpy, she muttered into the pantry:

"I know enough to be a common farm dog, I do." She got her coat and, without condescending to give them a look, left the kitchen.

DEAR ARON,

From what does one derive courage, you ask. The courage to continue living? I can only answer what gives me courage: your letters. For two years now you have held me up.

Do I lie – I am so afraid of lies since I have decided to be open with you – do I lie because I lived even before we began to write each other? No. I did not live then. You have raised me from the dead.

In the sun's rise over the mountains I see you. In the dew on the grass, yes, in the short grass between sheep droppings, in the crunching of the frosty moss I hear you. In the books I read.

You know, I have got hold of some books at the library by a Norwegian named Knut Hamsun. *Pan, Victoria, Hunger, Crops of the Earth.* I have seen on the map that you do not live far from Norway. What books! There is something in them that is well-known to the marrow of my spine, even if the fall of the leaves is different; their changes of color in spring and fall are not ours. Have you read them? At night, in my dreams, I mix you up with the characters in the books. You are alone, you walk in the forests, you shoot a bird, you are silent and reserved, but not in *that* way, like the men here... Yes, in the books I read you hold me up, in that there are other worlds.

If we should meet! How would it go? You say you speak much poorer English than you write, that without a dictionary you are as helpless as a child. What does that matter? I have seen your inside and I love that. If we should meet? I cannot lie: that is what I look forward to. That you will come and set me free. I lay my cheek against this letter, perhaps it smells of lambs and wool –

Your Tessa

In that letter, a yellow flower she called a Kowhai.

Dear Aron,

I do not know if I should laugh or cry, but I shall laugh. Had thought I would send you a surprise; it is, isn't it? When I complained to Mrs. Winther that I did not own a single photograph to send you, she told me there was a camera which had been her husband's. She offered to buy film, but explained that she did not know how to take pictures. She is seventy, you know, short, roly-poly, helpless and, as you can see, she really could not take pictures. Let us laugh anyway.

We placed ourselves among the sheets in her yard. The first time she was going to take one the phone rang in the post office and she turned around, so instead of me you see sheets, New Zealand sheets. There is certainly something of interest in them, Aron; on such sheets I have dreamt that we would rest together. In the background is half the entrance to Mrs. Winther's best room where I have cried many times; if you have a feeling there is a rivulet there, it is my tears. The next picture is also a sheet, a close-up. The wind lifted it just as she took it. But I am behind it. The third photo. What do you think? Is that part of me all right? I shall have to show you a little at a time. Next time perhaps I shall send my fingers or an ear. Which do you prefer to have? The double exposures in the last pictures show little scattered fragments of sky, flower beds, and still more sheets. You can glimpse my silhouette if you make an effort. That is me, too: an empty silhouette which you can fill with what you will of your own good wishes. Try anyway, good, sweet Aron; I am present everywhere in these pictures, either to the right or to the left, above or below them.

Kiss my chin.

I love you,

Tessa

She enclosed a lock of hair, dark, soft.

Aron smiled, for there were fine signs in that letter. Very fine. Of course it was only he who could interpret them. Sun shone on the sheets, but she was there behind them. Still it was too early to reveal anything.

He stood at the stove, boiling clothes, when she made her first visit. He had certainly heard her fumble through the door, but he wanted to be shrewd and pretended not to hear. Before he knew it she was behind his back, her fingers searching up under his shirt.

"Don't turn around," Solveig says.

"I knew you'd come visit," he answers her, lifting the white laundry out of the cauldron with a wooden ladle.

And Solveig lays her arms about his waist.

"Nobody believes me," he laughs.

Solveig breathes through his shirt, presses her lips against him.

"You'll have to learn to live with that."

"May I see you now, Solveig?"

But she holds him in a steady grip, turned toward the stove.

"It's not time yet."

"Why have you taken so long?"

"Oh, you know, there's a lot to do over there… Put the wash in the rinse water now, it looks clean."

"Can you see through my back?"

"Of course I can, this time hasn't passed without a trace."

"Why did you disappear anyway?"

She laughs.

"It was just for fun. I think it's lovely to see everything."

"But you didn't let me come with you? And *where* have you been?"

Suddenly her voice becomes hard.

"Anything at all, Aron. But *that* you're not allowed to ask."

"I know."

He wants to sink through her arms, pound by pound she races into his body.

"Sometimes one has to move around. But you're going to be a long-distance traveler, too. If you want to meet me again, of course."

"Solveig."

Her name tastes of the heather and pinewoods of summer.

"Is there something else you want to ask me? I have to go now."

He becomes afraid, changes legs, carefully so she will not disappear.

"No. You're not allowed."

He swings around with the ladle in his hand, but she has already disappeared; the kitchen door is open; there is a cold draft and Sidner stands looking at him.

"Something smells burned, Papa, what are you doing?"

A shirt sleeve lies smoking on the stove. He runs and plucks it off; the kitchen is full of steam from the laundry vat.

"I understand," Aron says and cannot put down the ladle, cannot drop his arms, cannot leave the stove. Sidner pushes him away.

"What is it you understand?"

No, Sidner, not yet. It is too early. That is what she said herself. In time you will all know. Best to lie a little.

"It was nothing." He feels the smile of shrewdness creeping over the corners of his mouth. "It was nothing at all. You have to joke sometimes, Sidner." He says that very clearly.

And he becomes so cheerful from discovering language again, welcoming it by repeating:

"You have to do that sometimes."

As if he had passed through now, gone by.

Reality is so sharp. Clear, clean corners on all objects. The ladle, for example, can be laid in the sink. The old wash water can be poured out, drawn anew, poured out.

He nods encouragingly to Sidner: "That's easily done. Rinsing."

But since Sidner wrinkles his eyebrows – well, he is still on the other side – Aron has to add something so he will not feel completely left out:

"Sometimes."

"What are you saying, Papa?" Because he is standing there, staring at the burned shirt.

"Sometimes," Aron repeats and smiles, but understands at the same time that it is the wrong word. A moment ago it was all right. Now it is not all right. "Sometimes" remains hanging over the stove, looking so hard, so sharp, and he rubs the air with his hand, smiling at Sidner:

"It's easy to forget yourself sometimes."

That was much better. It was easy to say, and now he wants to show Sidner that it is not a coincidence he can express himself so easily; so full of cheerfulness, he makes a variation.

"And easy to hide oneself, too."

Like music. Like when one changes the reciprocal relationship of the notes.

But, no.

One can reveal oneself this way. Blab on Solveig! He had, of course, promised her to say nothing, that would be unfaithful; he must make the done undone, flush *down* the cheerfulness which is, of course, *the sign*. He rests his head in his hands, goes over to the tablecloth, quiets himself down, to get rid of the shimmer; it is easily done, it is all too easy, he sinks, he must show something in *entirely different colors*.

"We ought to get out some day and pick mushrooms, Eva-Liisa, you and I. Pick berries. So we can have them for the winter. So everything is in order. Listen to me! Everything must be in order, Sidner. Not like this – "

And he whisks his hand over the table, knocking the salt shaker to the floor.

Sidner stands before Aaron and lays a hand on his collarbone.

"What's happened?"

Aron looks up.

"You've gotten so big, Sidner."

"Go rest, Papa. I can fix dinner."

"Can you really? Is it snowing out?"

"It's only September."

"Oh, yes, of course. But it's so cold."

It is over now. It is only the common world again. He goes over to the window, presses his forehead against the pane.

Body in place. Silence in place again.

"We have to keep together, we three."

"But don't we do that?"

"You think so?"

"Yes, Papa. I think we have it good."

"You've gotten so tall since I last really looked. I hardly recognize you."

"I know. I'm five feet eight, almost the tallest in my class."

WHEN SIDNER HAD FINISHED SCHOOL, been confirmed, and bought a hat, he took a job at Werner Nilsson's paint store at wages of five kronor per day. He stood behind the counter selling paint, glue, household articles, and herbs.

So far it was a marvelous store, and there was always something happening that further widened Sidner's world.

"For the person who is able to possess curiosity," he later wrote, "the world is an ever-growing field of experience. But who can, and who cannot? What mechanisms are there which hinder some and give others that gift? I do not know, because I did not know myself for a long time if I made myself a participant or if I was a zombie wandering deaf, dumb, and introverted through the world."

Werner Nilsson, the owner, spent most of his time on the display windows, since he was educated at the College of Applied Arts in Stockholm. He was a skillful draftsman and decorator who had worked both in Copenhagen and Stockholm, where he decorated the Red Mill and Bern's Lounges. He gladly talked about the big cities, not just to Sidner, but also to his customers; well, he talked rather a lot, so many said you go to Werner's only when you have plenty of time.

Even then he was a rather strange businessman, because Sidner had never before heard of a person *giving* things away, saying: "This is worthless!" Or who advised against a purchase. "Do it yourself instead, it's cheaper." The store was on Main Street, right in the middle of town. During the quiet morning hours, Snider stood at the window, watching the horse-drawn wagons and taxis from Ola's Cars glide round the corner.

Ola's Cars was the first to come to Sunne with automobiles;

that was back in 1905 and the make of car was Repio. Now there
were twenty-some-odd cars, and in all Sweden there were 48,000;
three hundred people had already died in traffic accidents, but a
car was still a sight worth seeing, not least when driven by the veterinarian, Franz Lindborg. Then it zigzaged up and down sidewalks, and sometimes the trip ended against a lamppost. Strangely
enough, that happened less and less, and soon his trips also became
a part of history. One day the local newspaper was forced to make
clear what many already thought:

"Yesterday at Rottneros a five-year-old girl was run over by
Franz Lindborg, veterinarian, who was driving his motor vehicle
in his usual manner. The girl had both legs broken, and despite the
efforts of several people who hastened to the site to detain him,
Lindborg continued his journey, presumably intoxicated to a high
degree. We must hope that, at last, Mr. Lindborg will be relieved
of the driver's license which he has greatly abused."

It was in connection with the veterinarian's rounds that Sidner
for the first time was allowed to partake in Werner's philosophy
of life, because he did have such a thing. He lay in the window
with his felt slippers on, putting up dolls for Display Sunday – his
window was the best in the whole community. Sidner, who had
learned the art of reading aloud from Splendid, informed him of
the notice regarding the veterinarian's accident.

"It's the Devil," Werner said. He smiled. "You can't do anything about the Devil."

And Sidner, who did not willingly allow ugly words to escape
his mouth, asked what that meant.

Then Werner sat in the window and expounded his view of
mankind.

"There are two powers, two forces. The Good and the Devil.
A continuous struggle occurs between them. If the Devil gets into
the body, a man is lost. You can study the Devil in many people,
for example in Judge Francke, in B.P. Nilsson, Berg on Strand
Way, Almers, you know, Almers out at Broby Meadow, Lindbergs

in Salla, Olson, Eriksson... Yeah, well, just an example. The Devil's in coffee, in alcohol, and tobacco. I myself got the Devil in me once; it was my sister who came with a thermos, she has..." And Werner looked around at the empty shop, lowered his voice. "... she has him, too. She managed to mistake coffee for tea; I drank a drop and then I wasn't myself for several days."

"Was that last spring?" Sidner asked.

Werner nodded earnestly.

"Just after Easter?"

"Well, yes. So you remember that."

That was when Sidner was forced to start drinking tea. Before work, a big cup which Werner prepared in the office. He drank nearly a quart himself every morning, earnestly, nervously smiling while his eyes traveled around the room; the cup to his mouth, then a shutting of the eyes, a feeling, as if he were making sure the tea really filled every part of his body, tightened it against the Devil's cunning and snares. How much he drank in the evenings no one knew. And it was not common tea, but a mixture of currant leaves, mint, sage and plantain.

Werner looked closely at Sidner.

"One should stand up when drinking, Sidner. Then the illumination occurs more quickly."

He demonstrated with his eyes, a smile, and heavenward glance.

"Do you feel it?"

Sidner nodded, quickly needing to pee. But that was good, there was nothing wrong with that.

Then the ritual was expanded.

"One should stand at the window when drinking and look out at the tree so the body becomes conscious of its place in the world. That is also good; the tree is pretty in the spring when the tender leaves make the light play on the cobblestones in the courtyard. It's nice in the winter when snow covers its limbs and the whole courtyard is white and smooth as a baby's blanket. The courtyard

mustn't be swept, either, even though our neighbor in the clothing store is always complaining about it."

Sidner was influenced by the tea. He wanted to belong to the
golden, illuminated portion of society.

"You read the paper," Werner said, "and what do you encounter: the Devil, up one side and down the other. Accidents,
wickedness. You don't drink coffee, do you?" Sidner lied, and
Werner looked him up and down.

"Well, I don't know. But you're still young."

And Werner's face was almost hidden by the big, green, quart-
sized cup with its pretty pattern of castle and garden. He locked it
in his safe after the morning ritual.

There was something feverish about Werner's hands as they
uninterruptedly moved among paint cans, brushes, and turpentine bottles. They traveled over the desk in the office, straightening, putting away, laying the pens parallel to the green blotting
pad, rubbing, and polishing. And still there was a glorious mess
everywhere.

But somewhere, thought Sidner, he must have had a treasure
buried, because he always smiled his secretive smile, which he interrupted only when the customer had the Devil.

Like Fanny, Werner was a listener. When he listened he looked
to the side, diagonally backwards. It always took a while before
the voice came, a voice of wisdom that made Werner confident,
opened him to customers, shopkeepers, and people in the street.

But never such a great triumph, such a beautiful smile as when
a package arrived one day, which he opened before Sidner's eyes.
A piece of metal lay there in tissue paper. There was a French
stamp on the wrapping.

"Pitchblende," he said. "Madame Curie."

During the years Sidner worked for Werner many changes
took place. Once, during his time in Copenhagen, Werner met
an Oriental astrologer who evidently had a decisive influence on

him. He had cast a horoscope which, in so many words, said, "Before you are fifty you will do something crucial."

There had been a woman somewhere, but she was rejected when it became evident that the Devil had established a foothold in her; indeed, it was perhaps she who first proved the Devil's existence. Many maintain that. She had cheated him out of money, making a public spectacle of herself over him and leaving him even more disposed than before to listen to otherworldly voices.

And the years went by and soon he was fifty. But the month before his birthday he had seen a notice that Fyrberga Manor was for sale. It was a large building with two wings, two kilometers south of Sunne; it was in bad shape, needed repair, and nobody wanted it. But Werner bought it, and it had a crucial influence on the rest of his life.

With this purchase the number of Devils in Sunne and environs increased disastrously; since the aquisition consumed all Werner's resources, creditors knocked at the door and the house fell into decay. Werner's whole existence soon consisted of writing letters and accusing humanity of malice and persecution. He collected proof, he discovered the Devil in their faces "last Friday when you visited my shop." Sidner had to assume responsibility for the shop, because Werner was preparing the world for great discoveries which would make him what he really was. Together with his cats – thirteen, then fifteen, then twenty – he stood on a table upstairs in his manor house with a gigantic pair of compasses, with paper and pen, and split an atom.

MANY TIMES SIDNER HAD GAZED at the hourglass-shaped curtain in Fanny Udde's door, but had always hesitated about pushing down the handle and stepping in. But now that he had a hat and long trousers and grown at least four inches taller he at last plucked up the courage.

The Chinese bell jingled. It was dark in the shop; it took a while before he discovered Fanny in the chair behind the counter, her eyes and enormous roll of hair lifted toward him when he irresolutely stood in the doorway. He held his hat in his hand and bowed slightly.

"I wonder if I might come in."

"Well, Sidner. Well, dear Sidner, how nice of you to drop in. I've often wondered why you didn't."

He looked around.

"No customers today?"

Businessman to businesswoman. He himself had closed Werner's shop just a half hour earlier; it was Saturday afternoon, and he knew from experience the stream of customers was over for that week.

"Oh, yes, I can't complain. Come a little closer so I can see you!"

He stepped up to the counter and laid his hat beside him, brushing the hair from his forehead.

"So you dare come here by yourself?"

"Yes, I... Splendid isn't here?" he felt called upon to ask, since she had made such an ugly insinuation. "I thought he was."

"It's been a long time since he was here. Everybody abandons an old lady."

"You aren't old, Miss Udde."

"You have newly washed hair, too. Let me feel it."

He leaned over the counter.

"You're impossible, Sidner; come inside. I can't stretch that far."

He obeyed, placing himself near her.

"How fine and silky your hair is. Women like that. In the nape, too. Bend down a little further so I can feel it. You've gotten so tall since I last saw you. You smell good, too, but you have products to choose from in your shop. Only the best is good enough."

She smiled at him and sniffed.

"Old women like that. Because you think I'm old, don't you?"

"No."

"Oh, yes, of course you do."

"I'm sure I don't think so."

"Now be honest, Sidner. You must always be honest with me. Always. One can't surround oneself with flatterers. The world is full of such people. Isn't it?"

"I haven't thought about it."

"But you'll notice it. So be honest now. Where do you think I'm oldest?"

"I don't know."

He liked the nervous twitching of her lips, the fine lines at the corners of her mouth, the extraordinary gray eyes that tried in vain to hold onto the present, but that quite often dreamed away through the window.

"My face?"

"But Miss Udde, I really don't think that at all."

"But you can see I have wrinkles, can't you? Don't you feel that?"

"No." He wanted to back away and leave, but she held tightly to his wrist.

"How can you feel that just standing there with your hands hanging down? You have to touch."

He did as she requested. Her complexion was so smooth he had to exclaim: "No wrinkles at all."

"What fine hands you have. I thought that the first time you were in. Yes, the previous time. Thought there was something quite special about those hands. A little frightened, and yet curious hands. Hands that feel they have to test the world. Is it my body?"

Sidner swallowed. Is this the way Splendid spent his time with her? Before he looked up it struck him that Splendid had almost always visited Fanny. That it was here, and in this way, he obtained part of his knowledge of the world. Was it like this that she conversed with all her customers, too? The warmth streamed through him when she took a new grip on his hands and passed them over her breasts, cupping his hands around them. He closed his eyes.

"Well?"

"No. I don't know, I've never, you know."

"Then I can tell you *they* aren't old. But what is it then, awful boy?"

He had not thought she was old at all, but he had to say something to put an end to this awkward seance.

"Maybe it's the hair! That you have put it up that way, Miss Udde."

"Oh, I understand." Satisfied and pleased, she leaned back in her wicker chair and dreamed herself away through the window. His hands still burned when she asked in a whisper:

"How long do you think it is?"

"To your shoulders, at least."

She bent forward to him.

"Guess better!"

"To your waist?"

Now he got to hear her laugh, a big, broad laugh, and under the protection of it once again she pulled his hand to her, passed it down her spine, bored it into a point in the small of her back.

"You didn't think it was that long, did you?"

"Is it *that* long? I've never seen such long hair."

"No. There aren't many who have. But one day, Sidner. One day you'll…"

Then the Chinese bell jingled, and they parted like bird and nest. Fanny pointed, and he disappeared behind a pair of doubled red drapes, soft, enveloping, heavy. He stood in her private apartment, still with his eyes almost closed, overpowered by the scent of perfume and woman. He had never seen such a striking room before. Here he saw her in another way. Here were several photographs of Sven Hedin; here were his books: *From Pole to Pole, From Turkestan to Tibet, Over the Expanses of Asia.* And here in the middle of the room stood a huge, black grand piano. Oh, his hands shook! He ran to the piano bench and without thinking began playing Schumann's "Von fremden Ländern"; it was like continuing his escape through yet another door. He tossed his head back and floated away. He had never played such an instrument! The notes transported him, and it was a while before he perceived voices from the shop, muted and still; several more exchanges before he recognized Selma Lagerlöf's voice.

"I get so tired of going around to the shops, but it has to be done sometimes. Do you have a chair for me?"

"Of course."

"If I'm not disturbing you, Fanny dear."

"Not at all. How was Stockholm? Did you give my regards?"

"To whom? Oh, yes, of course, yes. Sven Hedin. Dear Fanny!'

"And what did he say?"

"Say. Well… well, he sent his regards, wondered how you were."

"How was he dressed? Did he have on his white suit?"

Selma's voice became quite sharp:

"Fanny! Sven Hedin is an old man. I don't believe he still owns a white suit."

Sidner's cheeks burned and he did not want to hear more. He

struck a loud chord on the piano, one more, and after a moment he heard Selma again:

"Who do you have in there?"

"It's a neighbor boy… You know, Selma, his mother was trampled to death by cows… Doesn't he play nicely?"

"Fanny!"

"He's just sixteen, seventeen, he…"

"What are we going to do with you, Fanny… But that doesn't concern me."

What did Selma mean! The burning sensation spread to the tips of Sidner's fingers. He understood nothing; he did not *want* to understand. He played gently and quietly, trying to be in both the conversation and the music at the same time.

"He has a hat, anyway!"

It was as if he saw Selma poke at it with her cane, push it away from her so it fell to the floor behind the counter.

"Yes, well, you have your own world. But he seems to be a talented boy."

"Very handsome, but shy."

"He ought to get out of here," Selma said.

"Shall I ask him… to quit?"

"I mean out of Sunne. This is no place for talented people. And you ought to think about your own reputation. Give me my cane, Fanny. I'll continue to Mårbacka now. By the way… this fall he's going out on a lecture tour, if he's up to it. Strömstad, Göteborg, or wherever it was. If you really want to see the old thing."

Sidner crept into the music again; he let Fanny stand a long time regarding him as he leaned over the piano.

"Did you sell anything, Miss Udde?" he asked before the final chord had died away.

"It was just someone who wanted to look at curtains. Someone who goes in and out of stores without ever buying anything."

"One has to be friendly to them, too. What a fantastic grand piano! I've never played on anything like this before. Do you play yourself?"

"I can't."

"But why…?"

She walked away to the window and pinched leaves off a geranium.

"It was my husband."

"Hmm?"

"The calvary captain. He had certain ideas about what was appropriate to one's position. Wanted to educate me."

"I didn't know you had been married."

"I didn't either."

She sat down beside Sidner on the piano bench. There was such a coolness between them now; Selma's words lay between them. He refused to close his eyes, afraid to remember the weight of her breasts and the little hollow in the small of her back.

"I was so young, Sidner. Just a girl. He was much older than I. I'd rather not talk about it."

"I won't force you."

"That's good. There's so much you wouldn't understand."

"Of course I understand," he almost shouted at her. Suddenly. As if he had a claim on her. Suddenly. As if he belonged in that parlor with its velvet drapes, the green armchairs, the sconces over the paintings, the grand piano. "I'm no child."

He stepped through music's doorway again, looking defiantly at her while he removed himself to the clean, quiet expanses. He played a Beethoven sonata, a slow movement, and when he turned his head toward her it was with the eyes of music he saw, only with them. In here it was a long way to all horizons; the human in him and her was like a dot far out on the ice. He wandered back and forth in music's own time, his head swaying slowly, listening away from her and the place and the moment, while twilight made itself known outside the window and Fanny obeyed music's laws, sitting still and captivated as long as he played, while she twirled a thread in the green shawl which lay over her shoulders.

"Oh," she said when at last he had finished, but she did not look at him, gazing at her lap. "You can come and play whenever you want. Really, whenever you want."

"Thanks, gladly, Miss Udde," he said, getting up and going out through the heavy scent of the drapes.

"OH, YES," said the Sauce Queen one day in the hotel kitchen when he was helping make sandwiches for a wedding. "That calvary captain Udde was actually a riding teacher. If even that. Thirty years older than Fanny. They came here when she was very young. He bought the house and store, went across the street to the hotel, and here he remained more or less as long as he lived. Came at lunch and stayed until he was carried out. Alcohol and rheumatism finally made it impossible for him to get even fifty yards from home. But there was a green spot in the middle of the street, there were even some pirea bushes growing there. He had a chair there, the calvary captain. Sat and slept or told stories from Gävle and Stockholm till the frost took him one night. The only thing he left, with the exception of a bundle of bills, was a crossword puzzle where one single word was filled in. I saw it myself," said the Sauce Queen, "I was there and helped carry him in. ANGRY, three letters. He'd filled that in. MAD was the word.

"So, Fanny, she doesn't have anything to put on airs about."

ONE DAY IN AUGUST, Fanny asked Sidner if he wanted to go with her on a car trip to Strömstad. Sven Hedin was to deliver a lecture to collect money for a new expedition, to go through as yet unknown parts of eastern Tibet and China. Indeed, the government had given its grant, but still more publicity and contributions would give the expedition a welcome boost. It was to be the last great journey of discovery. After that mankind would be forced to proceed into space or inward into itself to find something new. Soon knowledge of our earth would be complete, the last maps drawn. Sven Hedin was an intrepid explorer. In the Gobi Desert he had drunk lamb's blood and camel piss. His men had died, which affected him less than the animals that had been sacrificed, so to speak, for the sake of humanity. Hedin's shadow was long. In Sunne, Värmland, two youngsters by the name of Sidner and Splendid, for lack of camels and lambs, had drunk rooster's blood several years earlier. For want of a desert, they stood behind Torin and Sleipner's stone masonry. Hidden among stinging nettles and alder, they spat and swore.

Sven Hedin had decided on his calling the day Nordenskiöld returned with the Vega to Stockholm harbor, one windy day in 1880. He was a boy then and stood up on Fjäll Street with his parents and saw how the fireworks blew into the water.

Would Sidner, too, be struck by a great decision if he were now to hear Sven Hedin?

"But maybe you're already too old, Sidner. You already have a hat, and you're almost a store manager." She looked him up and down. "You're so big and handsome."

He was seventeen and veered away from her gaze.

"I should talk to Papa first, shouldn't I?"

"Ask him to come here."

"He has no clothes to wear," Aron said and stared far beyond rolls of material and dress models.

"I'll take care of that. You know, Mr. Nordensson, it's so difficult when one is without children oneself, when one needs a hand with the car and such things."

"Sidner knows nothing about cars."

"Oh, yes, Papa. Splendid and I..."

"It will be a great moment for your son. One should mind children's curiosity, develop it, before it's too late. Oh, Sidner, can't you put on a cup of tea for your father?" Aron started. Was the boy already so at home here? Aron declined. His store-bought clothes chafed his body, the pungent smell of perfume. But why should he make a fuss? Sidner was on his own. Aron was busy with something else. It was he who would soon need the advice of his son. He was about to float away. It was he who needed to be held fast.

"All right, then..."

Fanny owned a dark green Volvo.

The top was down and the flags flapped on the shiny radiator. Sidner sat beside her; he was proud; she had a driver's license for both Volvo and Ford. The sky was clear and saturated with the smells of late summer. Fanny's hands lay decoratively on the wheel, and jewelry glittered around her neck. From the lobes of her ears hung a pair of heavy red stones. After several hours they stopped at an inn:

"Order what you want."

Sidner was not unfamiliar with fine food. Actually, he was pretty tired of cold poached salmon, croustades, and ice cream, since he often ate in the hotel kitchen. He could handle himself well, too. The Sauce Queen had taught him that: sometimes he got to perform little sketches for her, imitating the guests' entrances into the dining room. The most popular variation was

Boss Björk's entrance, which he almost made his own because the Sauce Queen so loudly appreciated it. He rubbed his hands together hard, bowed deeply to right and left, peeked into the kitchen: "Well, my little chicks, what are we treated to today?"

Sidner studied the menu carefully.

"Trout Meunière and mineral water."

"You conduct yourself like a real man of the world."

"It was nice of you to invite me on this trip, Miss Udde."

She took a bite of turkey breast, pierced by her fork. Then she leaned over the table and brushed his hand with one finger.

"It sounds as if I'm so terribly old when you say that. Fanny is my name."

"Thank you," he said blushing.

"Or do you think it feels… awkward?"

If she had not made that pause, perhaps he would not have hesitated.

"I don't know yet. I'll get over it, I'm sure."

But he was quiet afterwards. For that matter, he was usually quiet. He saw himself as a *speaker,* not a talker like Splendid. His sentences were well-defined, correct; he did not know the kind of small talk that floated out of Splendid's mouth. As a store manager he had come into speech by way of phrases. Thank you, thank you, of course, come again. His body was like his speech: no unnecessary gestures, no indefinite movement of head or hands. He envied Splendid's way of talking: as if one were getting closer to the heart of things. The words groped about, sniffed, drew back, made mistakes, started again. His sentences stood there, spoken and all too obvious, impossible to be made unheard.

A great dizziness came over him: just now he was about to lose something. He was suddenly conscious of becoming an adult.

"Now I've certainly made a mess of things for us. You've made yourself very distant, Sidner."

"I was thinking about Splendid. It was he who showed me…

you. He's more worthy of a trip like this. He's poor, his papa's sick."

"I think a lot of Splendid, I want you to know." And with a sudden severity: "You don't think I forced you to come along, do you...?"

Sidner ate a bite of fish, looking down at his plate.

"No, no. But he's been so... decent to me. Even from the first day we met. I haven't been able to give him anything back."

Wrong words. "Has been." As if it was time for a farewell gift.

"You've certainly been good for each other."

"I shouldn't have come," he mumbled. But then she took his hand across the plates:

"It's not dangerous to be with me. Not at all dangerous."

Sidner kept in the background when they arrived at the hotel in Strömstad and let Fanny take care of the keys to the rooms. A poster hung on the glass door. The lecture was to take place at 7:00 P.M. in the City Park. Thereafter, those who wished could attend a supper for Doctor Hedin, the proceeds of which, unreduced, were to go to his enterprise.

Sidner carried the bags upstairs. Fanny went to a door and opened it. Sidner set the bags down on the floor inside the door.

"And my room? What number is it?"

Fanny stood before the huge mirror, taking off her hat. She looked at him in the glass.

"There was only this one." She made a wide gesture with her arms. "You can sleep here. After the lecture you can climb into that big bed with an easy mind. There won't be any sleep for me at all."

She pulled out a hairpin, put it between her lips.

"Otherwise, I can sleep in the car."

"Dear child," she said. He looked around: heavy red curtains at the windows, a gold spread on the largest bed he had ever seen.

"Do you know... does Hedin know you're coming?"

She shook her head and pulled out some more hairpins. Her hands were raised upwards, backwards; she stretched the curve of her back, and his eyes fixed on a point in the small of her back: soon that colossal hair would fall.

"I think I'll take a walk and see the town."

"Yes, maybe you should. It's a nice little town. Wait... here are a couple of kronor, if you feel like going to a café."

"I have money." He backed towards the door.

"I know that well enough. But I'm the one who lured you. Come back at six-thirty. I think I'll take a bath while you're gone."

Hugging his hat, Sidner left.

He had never seen the sea.

The smell of seaweed and diesel oil struck him where he stood on the quay. Several large cargo boats were on their way in, their sails rushing down toward the deck. Compression engines hammered, summer guests in white linen suits strolled along the seaside promenade, and a train pulled into the station. This was the last stop on the railroad. He was a long way away. He was near Norway. Possibilities tickled in his body. For thirty öre he bought a bag of almost black cherries. At a distance, a band played Viennese waltzes. He found a newsstand with postcards and continued up toward a cliff at the entrance to the harbor where he had caught a glimpse of a café. The view from there was fantastic: one could see all the way out to the Koster Islands. Many boats on the way in or out. In the southwest there was a gap toward the open sea. Clear horizon, nothing in the way. He ordered coffee and a Danish pastry, wrote Splendid's address. "It feels like being abroad, here by the sea. Soon I am going to hear Sven Hedin talk. We are staying at a..."

The word "we" tore apart the sentence and touched something deep down in the pit of his stomach. He took a bite of the Danish pastry, tried to swallow.

Then an attack of nausea overcame him. He ran behind some

bushes and vomited. He got some spots on his suit, on the card he held in his hand.

Fanny was pacing back and forth in the room when he knocked just before seven. She looked radiant in a long, green velvet dress and broad-brimmed white hat. Her eyes were painted with blue liner. She smelled delightful.

"Oh, Sidner dear, you had me so worried."

He looked down at the floor.

"I got lost," he lied. "I hurried as fast as I could."

"And what a mess. Did you fall down?"

"No, no." He hurried into the bathroom and dipped his face under the faucet, combed his hair and rubbed off some of the worst spots. She shouted from the other room:

"We have to hurry."

"Go ahead, I'll be right there."

"No, we're to keep each other company, you and I."

The City Park lay opposite the hotel; many people pressed about them. A man was busy putting up a loudspeaker, children blew trumpets, a steamboat's whistle was heard farther off. Fanny tucked her hand under his arm.

"What a handsome couple we are; don't you think so?'

He was not able to smile at her. He pretended to be occupied by a movement farther away in the crowd.

"Isn't that he walking over there?"

But it was not. Not before they had seated themselves and waited a quarter of an hour did a car glide up and stop at the stage. The doors were opened; everyone stood up when Doctor Hedin stepped out. Someone started to applaud.

"How old he is," burst out of Sidner.

"Yes," murmured Fanny, as if a very great wonder had come over her. Her eyes widened, she bit her lip and squeezed Sidner's hand. "Yes."

"Although we knew before, of course, he would be."

"Yes, well. Maybe we knew that." Her voice was as quiet as a breath, but Sidner thought she could just as well have screamed. Screamed loudly and recklessly. She drew her fingers over her eyebrows. "I don't feel well, Sidner."

Her eyes caught his.

Sidner twisted in the loneliness of the bed. It was too warm to sleep, despite the windows opened on the park. From below in the dining room laughter and clatter could be heard, but he was used to that from home, it should not bother him. Sometimes he hoped it was Fanny's high voice breaking out in cascades, but he doubted it. He had had to force her to attend; she had sought his hand and eyes and not talked at all. It was as if he were driving her to an execution. He did not understand at all what had happened. But there was something that was not at all right. He twisted, turned the pillows, threw them on the floor, picked them up again. When he was up to pee he looked carefully at himself in the mirror, and he hated Fanny for having done this to him. When he went back to bed he fell into an uneasy torpor and soon found himself out in the deserts, riding over high mountain passes together with Sven Hedin and Fanny; they came to the Emperor of China, and the emperor said to Sidner: Take off your hat.

He was awakened by Fanny standing naked before him, quite close to him. Now her hair was down! Her eyes were like two enormous wells, but there was no smile in them. She stood completely still, and he pressed out of himself a "No" and one more before he was sucked up into her darkness and helplessly caught there. She drew back the sheets and, without taking her eyes off him, slowly unbuttoned his pajama top, pulled off the bottoms, and his sex screamed when she caressed it and lay on top of him with spread legs. His mouth was dry; he wrapped his arms around her back, and despite their lying quite still, he knew that a kind of death was on its way toward them with infinite speed. Harder and harder they were pressed toward each other, toward that boundary where suddenly wave after wave of light welled over him; he sank, she sank while she incessantly whispered in the dialect of the closed eyes: So awfully nice, so awfully nice. And long after he lay in a sleep embroidered with birdsong from a nearby park, he heard her frantic weeping.

As the great Buddha said: That night, oh, you monks, everything stood in flames.

THE ANGEL SPLENDID has now fulfilled his mission and is called back by God to that place where he was created.

It is a Sunday morning in September. Aron, Sidner and Eva-Liisa are eating breakfast when there is a knock on the door and Splendid stands on the threshold. He has bought a hat, too; he is holding it in his hand.

"Good mornin'," he says and looks at Sidner: "Could we take a walk?"

"Why?" asks Sidner.

"I'd like to."

"I don't know," Sidner says, despite knowing he must obey, because there is a fatal silence about Splendid's words.

"God, you're so hopeless, Sidner," Eva-Liisa says. She turns to Splendid. "He's been like that since he was in Strömstad. Just sits and stares."

"I know. But it would be a good idea if ya came along."

"Do it," Eva-Liisa says, and there is a quick exchange of glances between Splendid and her.

Heavy traffic.

He grabs his hat from the shelf, puts it on, turns back toward the kitchen with one last anxious look.

"Gentlemen boys!" Eva-Liisa laughs.

Splendid first breaks the silence at Solbacka:

"There's really jes' one thing I gotta say, Sidner. We're movin' from here."

"What are you saying?"

"Ta Karlstad. Papa's sick 'n' he needs ta get inta the hospital. It'll be easier fer us."

Sidner sits by the edge of the road and looks out over the lake.

"And me then?" suddenly shouts out of him.

"You'll be fine. There's trips ya gotta make yerself, if ya can say that."

"What do you mean?"

"Ya know that best yerself."

"Is your papa really bad?"

"Yeah. He talks 'bout dyin' soon."

"Are you afraid?"

"Sure I am. I'd so much like him ta see me fly, once anyway. But…"

"Is *he* afraid?"

"No. He says he's lived on grace ever since he fell. He says God's given him birds ta listen to, so he's satisfied. He says he's had as much love as he can take. An' can say that, so then ya don't need ta be scared."

"It'll be dismal without you."

"Same here. But we c'n be in touch. We'll do that. But there's one more thing! Or two parts actu'lly. I'd like ya ta play fer me. In church or at yer place. I thought it could be good ta play fer the old man, if he has a hard time."

"It takes a long time to learn."

"It don't need ta. There ain't *that* many notes ta keep track of. If ya'd do that fer me, I'd be awful thankful. It could be like a… farewell present, if ya can say that."

"Sure. Of course you can manage it. You can do everything. You know everything." Sidner is full of anger and he does not worry about hiding it. "If I say this then: If you meet a woman. She's pretty and attractive in every way. And suddenly… wants you, like. And she has you, too. If you understand what I mean."

"I'm listenin'."

"And then… doesn't even want to talk to you, treats you like air? What's that about?"

"That's hard things, that is."

"Becomes like completely transformed. Not angry or any-thing…"

"You tell it like a horse. But if it's Fanny yer talkin' 'bout, y'oughta know she has a damn hard time with reality. But so do you."

IT MUST BE TEDIOUS in the valley of the dead, Aron thought, when Solveig's visits had ceased for some time.

But one day she returned. Aron was busy repairing the glass in the hotel door which someone, after the furies of the last Thursday Club, had managed to put his hand through. He sat in the spirits cellar, which now also served as a workshop. He changed the glass, cut it with a diamond, nailed, and puttied. And suddenly he knew she was there, behind his back.

"That's good," he said. "I've waited. How could you find me in here?"

He felt how her fingers stiffened.

"Sorry. Of course you can find me everywhere."

"Yes, I can. I have a larger perspective on existence than you."

Her voice was hard, and she was right.

"Why did you marry me, then?"

"I don't know," she answered.

"Have you met someone else?"

"Oh, of course." She went around inspecting the tools, raised the planes and ran her hand over the sharp edges.

"Be careful you don't cut yourself."

"There's no danger." She pressed her finger against an awl so it went in deep. "See, Aron, no blood! No blood at all!" There was a note of scorn in her voice which arrested everything he would have chosen to tell her. But really, what was it he wanted to tell? About the days that dragged by, the letters he wrote? Yes, about the hope that could be glimpsed on the horizon, like a sail that makes a turn in toward land and then disappears again. Was that it, or was he going to ask her about the wash? About the children's ragged underwear, about all the missing buttons in existence?

Or did Solveig know all about snow and dirty floors, about Sidner's new hat and Eva-Liisa's first patent leather shoes? In that case he was unnecessary as a narrator, it was unnecessary to notice the world at all – for that matter, had he *ever* been needed? She played the piano just fine without him. His presence had only retarded the music, restrained it several minutes, chopped it up into small pieces. And his talk, how she had had to *drag* him into it, instead of herself enjoying her own and others' rippling flow. So many times she had had to *wait* for him! All her life had been that waiting; no wonder she became impatient. Naturally she was back to see if he took care of himself! She was sent out from the dead as an inspector. She came as a Boss, the way Björk usually came. For that matter, it was pure hypocrisy to call Björk by his first name, it had not brought them closer, he would see that there would be a change there; but it was going downhill for Björk now, business was limping along. To be sure his billfold seemed thick, but the billfold was only the most immediate protection, of course. A thick billfold did not help against the world situation, the world situation, Solveig, do you care about that? Do you care that I am bleeding now? I cut myself on a splinter of glass, see! But naturally that was nothing to report to the counsel of the dead. One should not come waving every small cramp. On the whole, one should not show oneself to be so important!

Rather, be as natural as when she approached the barn in former times, during the early mornings when the dew still remained, so her footprints could be clearly seen. She had coffee with her then; he sat down beside her in barn-scented clothes, she cool and clean like a glass of water, a scarf over her hair. Sometimes this hair slipped down right to her eyes; she peered *upwards* then. Do you remember that, Solveig? That morning when you came from the mailbox with the newspaper. Charles Lindbergh lands! That morning. We owned ourselves then; Björk can never understand why I get such pain in my hand opening the hotel door, why it gives me such a pain in the neck to bow. We did not bow up in the forest, Solveig.

She sat opposite him in a pile of splinters from the broken door.

"Tell me about Bergström, about his lonely, helpless Sunday hands."

"You were carrying Eva-Liisa then, we sat by the hearth drinking coffee. But of course you were there yourself."

"I've forgotten. You must tell me so I can take some colors with me… over there."

"Bergström was dressed in his best suit, standing in front of us with shiny new shoes, hands in front of his stomach, they were brushed clean and almost smooth; he squinted and cleared his throat. 'Well, Aron, I wonder if you'd like to come up to the Glade at two o'clock. If it suits you.' And then he turned around, the forest swallowed him up in one gulp and you said: 'That wasn't for me.' At two I went up there. There were peacock and tortoise shell butterflies in the vaporous, good forest. The first thing I discovered in the Glade was his hands. Bergström stood in the shadow of a spruce as if petrified. His hands were the most obvious thing about him. And suddenly the forest leaked neighbors, all except myself in their best suits. Nobody really knew why they were there. Everybody was embarrassed by their hands, since it was Sunday and they couldn't hide them in some task; and we shook hands and it was as if we didn't dare notice each other. We glanced furtively at Bergström, who had quite clearly placed himself alone and separate, high above us in the shadow.

"But then he cleared his throat: It so happened… he said. It so happened that I…, as if he'd clear his way into the tangled language of a speech in honor of the occasion. He got a new start: It has happened that I for some time… And then he stumbled over that 'for some time,' was forced to start over again: 'Well, I have, for quite awhile, had a desire…' But he couldn't manage that introduction either, and disappointed over being forced out into the common path of words where we all walked every day, he saw himself compelled to cast aside all finesse: 'Ah, fellas, as you know, for some time I've been buildin' a mill wheel here and now it's done, and I thought we could…' But as if it required something *lofty* in any case, motivating the best suits and the arrangement itself, which he had already demanded when giving the invitations in his own suit, he closed his eyes and puckered up his mouth: 'That we could celebrate this day by…'

"Then he swallowed, casting his despair over them, excusing himself for the everyday pressing in, even here: 'Ah, fellas, you can see for yourselves…!' And with the protection of a wide gesture toward the brook, he stepped out of the shadow, down through the Glade, and we made room, letting him pass, so he had room to point upstream and down. And there among the stones, neatly lined up with the caps all in the same direction, lay half-liter bottle after half-liter bottle and the playful water played, and Bergström made a special gesture for me: 'Since you don't drink, Aron, you've your own there… a bottle of small beer,' a big keg, you remember?

"There was some drinking that day, some rolling down the hillside and grass on suits that none of us forgot. Laughter echoed long into the night. We came out of the forest with our arms around each other. I had been infected by their intoxication, too. But how could you remember that, Solveig? You were sleeping in bed. In the big, broad bed."

"Which you sold, Aron!"

Her voice came from somewhere beside her. From the right.

"And you sold the house, too!"

Now her voice came from the left. It was flat and cold. She despised him. Perhaps she always had. It was he who had begged his way into her proximity. That was it, naturally. He had kept her from returning to America. "If we could go there, Aron? Buy a house there?" "Do you want to?" "No, I just think about it sometimes, how it would be to go back. See if I recognized anything. Walk the old roads, visit neighbors." "Would you like that?"

"One broods over what has been, it's unavoidable." "So you regret...?" And was it not a little anxiously she had answered: "No, not at all, you mustn't believe that, I love everything here, we belong together."

That must be where she went: she had fooled them with death and burial. As soon as they had left the graveyard, she looked up, dressed and disappeared. In America a big house waited for her: in an ocean of corn she had hidden a tractor. There were syrup maples, wasn't that what she called them? Or sugar maples? She had a husband there. They stood in the yard speaking American. He hesitated, but said:

"I just want to remind you of my existence." Solveig and her husband said something he did not understand, and the man fished out a dictionary and handed it to Aron. Aron searched feverishly, but the words were not arranged in order, it would take an endless amount of time to put together one single sentence. But they were helpful; they asked him to sit down at the table in the yard, paper and pen lay there, they nodded encouragingly, standing bent over him. But then Solveig yawned, made a sign to the man and they disappeared into the house, the shades were drawn, it got dark. No one answered when he knocked. He went away from there and came to the sea. A boat lay on the beach; it consisted of a hull and a smooth, arched leaden deck, and the boat's captain stood on the jetty: "If you're going to Sweden, you better hop aboard." "But what about you, aren't you going along?" The captain shook his head: "There isn't room for anyone else. Then we would sink." And he kicked out the boat and soon the sea ran high. It started to storm, there was not a bolt, not a crack where he could get a grip with his fingers, the waves tossed him back and forth, he was alone out on the Atlantic; he took a firm grip on the vice and banged his head against the workbench. Solveig!

"Tell me you'll come back..."

"You must wake me, then." He looked around the cellar, but she was not there.

Only her voice. She had placed that inside him. And that was a long way to go.

Later that same week she came up to the apartment. She was carrying a bag of food. He was extremely unhappy that she arrived then: They had just eaten; the plates were sticky with bacon rind and limp macaroni. He was ashamed. "It's not always so easy to come up with some kind of food. The children seem indifferent, it's so hectic. I ought to have bought candles," he said.

"So I came at an inconvenient time."

"It isn't the best occasion. Anytime, but not now before I've managed to clean up."

"You don't need me anymore?"

Aron grasped after her and fell against the doorpost.

"Who are you talking to, Papa?"

But he did not want to talk with the living just then. Their words were so coarse and over-explicit. They were in the way. He would explain to Sidner later. He heard her step out on the stairs, he opened the door:

"Wait!"

"There's no one there!"

Sidner's hand was on Aron's shoulder. He wanted to fight free, he met Sidner's eyes. The boy was taller than Aron now; time had rushed away, he himself shrank, got shorter and shorter. He tried to knock the hand away.

"Come in, Papa. What is it?"

He sank down by the table.

"Are you sad about Mamma?" Eva-Liisa asked. He nodded and passed a hand over his eyes.

"Papa," said Sidner. "Listen to me now. Something terrible has happened. Björk is finished. He's gone bankrupt. Now, this morning. You know, those Norwegians who wanted to buy the sawmill, he said no to them and went to the Frenchmen instead. But they haven't been able to pay. He's finished. The sawmill's finished, the hotel, everything. The workers are down at the sawmill now. Aren't you going to go?"

"I don't understand."

"Yes, you do. You must. At least, I want you to say you do. Your job's finished. I want you at least to understand that."

Aron looked at his son. This was a new son. He could deal with this. He had slipped into the real world. Things would be fine for Sidner. Aron had to smile while he sniffled away the last drops. He wanted to stretch out his hand and thank him: now his own responsibility was over. He could lag behind entirely, let himself go, as Fridolf had said.

"Why should I go down there? I don't work at the sawmill, you know."

"You're one of his employees. Everybody's going to be without a job. The police will come soon and close the spirits cellar, so Björk can't go and steal from his own stock. It belongs to the creditors now. They say there's hardly anything other than the liquor to take. Maybe you're unemployed, Papa."

"It'll work out for me," said Aron. "We have money left from the house, it's enough for a while. Don't worry."

It went through the town like a hurricane that day; the sawmill, jobs, and future dreams fell like a house of cards. A week later Björk moved out of his big Mansion and into the little cottage on its grounds, the cottage which he had built for temporary workmen. There was one room and a kitchen; it was not cold. Björk would certainly survive.

TESSA'S LETTERS became all the more crowded with flowers, leaves, and locks of hair.

Soon small packages in brown wrapping paper began to arrive. Cartons full of stones, of gravel, of glittering sand: "I sat here today in the morning and thought about you, with my feet in the sand." "These are twigs that were floating in the brook this morning."

Aron cleared away everything except Solveig's photograph from the bureau in the living room and poured the sand out, laid the stones in a pattern, placed the twigs like trees in the growing landscape. A sort of flag came, too: "A piece of the dress I chose to wear today when your letter arrived. Did not dare because of Robert, therefore you get a bit for your eyes instead."

Sidner and Eva-Liisa went solemnly to those devotions before the bureau when Aron poured out the packages' contents. Wonderingly, they saw New Zealand develop bit by bit. A skeleton of a bird came, a piece of bark from "the cowrie tree," beetles, spiders; there were dried fish with still-shiny scales, "unsorted beach."

"Everything I have seen I want you to see."

A bottle of rain, a broken teacup, tufts of wool. A splinter from the dining room table, a piece of her sheet.

Blood.

"Everything is on its way to you."

A dried orange.

"Ought to have eaten it. But it wanted to come to you."

The fork "because it only leaves my hand when I want to eat."

The morning of Christmas Eve they lit the candles on the bureau and the flames cast their light on the antipodal landscape, and it sparkled and glittered, for in the middle were the contents of

Tessa's last package: a little piece of jewelry so costly that "we could buy a farm with it." The necklace was the shape of a boat in ruby and jade, in the little mast was a diamond which the flickering candles caused to shimmer when anyone moved in the room. Sidner and Eva-Liisa were allowed to hold it in their hands, then Aron hung it on a a twig from the sacred Cowrie Tree.

"Now I own nothing which is me myself, now I am only expectation. When you are here you will hang the jewel about my neck; then I am yours in eternal love. My mother gave it to me once, long ago. She said I should wear it only when I was in love."

"That's the sign," said Aron, and it was as if all air left the room.

Taihape

Dear aron,

A great weight and weariness. I have sunk to the bottom
of my life again, for I have understood: traveling here is not
allowed to be. It is expensive, you have your children and
work to think about. And what would happen here?
Between you and me? Between Robert and you. You seem
to have high expectations. There is also much in your letter
I do not understand, your talk about signs, about the disguise
I wear. There is one more thing: you must love me, and you
do not really know who I am.

Yesterday when I received your letter I was still pretty.
I looked at myself in Mrs. Winther's bedroom mirror,
preened myself, behaved like a silly woman. But I liked what
I saw. I liked my breasts, my hair (it is quite dark), my eyes
(they are brown), I liked my lips, my shoulders, everything
that is for you.

But today when I came back from the sheep sheds, when
I saw reality, when Robert met me with his sour look and
silence – and I wonder if he does not understand everything,
how could he avoid that – then I knew all of a sudden that
everything is going to go badly; yes, I saw the rifle in the hall
and was close to screaming. (I know I am very over-excited.
Mrs. Winther has talked to me about it, she is sincerely concerned about that, begs me continually not to hope for anything. "You shouldn't get yourself worked up, Tessa. That is
the longest journey that can be made on this earth, much can
happen, don't hope for too much.")

Today I am ugly again, hide myself, know I ought to talk

to Robert, but I am not strong enough. (Mrs. Winther laughed and said: "You'll have to run away here to me, live up in the attic until you manage to take a boat to Australia.") But I see you coming up the hill, see you every second of the day, we embrace and kiss each other.

Your Tessa

So ARON WAS TO set off for New Zealand.

He packed a case with a couple of changes of underwear, a shirt, toothbrush, soap, and a dictionary.

"I'll buy the rest, you never know how they dress on the other side of the earth."

"And so you'll come home with a new Solveig," said Sleipner, who offered a farewell party at Beryl Pingel's.

"You don't know how right you are," smiled Aron. The only thing he was afraid of was that she had adopted another language while she was in the valley of the dead. That she had learned so much that when she got to see him now, she would not think he was good enough. But it was best to keep that to himself. It was very important that those at home remain calm. The shock would be sufficiently great for them when Solveig came back. There would be much to explain. One would be forced to teach them a thing or two about "other dimensions."

"I'll be forced to protect her so it doesn't get too crowded around here," he said. "There can be a lot of questions."

"Sure," said Torin. "But we'll fix it."

He let them believe that. They were all so touching. Beryl had baked extra and put together a carton with sandwiches, hard-boiled eggs, and thermoses of tea and coffee so he could manage at least those first days through Europe. Eva-Liisa, out of whose girl's body a woman's had begun to emerge, showed him her room; it faced the orchard. Had blue wallpaper, a bedside table and lamp.

"Isn't it nice?"

"Yes, it's very nice. You're sure you'll be happy here? You

know what Sidner said, that he'd be glad for you to stay there at home."

"I'll look after him," she said proudly. She opened a wardrobe door and took out a dress.

"Beryl sewed this for me. It has twenty-eight buttons in the back."

"Put it on so I can see it. So I can tell... her."

He had to be sure not to say too much.

She came back after a while. It was not so easy for her now just to pull clothes over her head. She stood in the door, blushing slightly.

"I'm going to get a new pair of shoes, too; she's promised me. What do you think?"

Beryl appeared behind her, laugh lines in her broad face, arms crossed over her breasts.

"So many expenses," Aron started. "You should write them down."

"Ah, pooh," said Beryl. "You know I think it's fun to have someone to sew for... I don't have anyone else."

"But I'd be glad to pay."

"My money grows in piles. I'm not going to leave it to the church, that's for sure. I'm just so happy to have such a fine girl in the house. Would've been glad to take Sidner, too, but he's his own master now. The young boy, how he's shot up."

"He gets along fine. And we'll soon be back..."

That was a close shave again. He almost said: Solveig and I... and then.

"But now some food would be good."

Aron thought it was tremendous fun to say such phrases, and he repeated them:

"It will really taste good. Nobody can live on air. Boiled red beets are good," he laughed. "And potatoes," he said, heaping them on his plate. "They're so clear."

"I should have taken a warning from those words," Sidner

wrote in one of his letters from New Zealand many years later, "but I myself had no experience of what that Clarity meant. Certainly, we all thought he was surprisingly cheerful, but there was so much in motion that day. The enormity of the journey, feelings of being abandoned mixed with practical advice and uncertain expectations. We believed we realized the journey was essential for Aron. Perhaps it was, too."

And so the train left Sunne; the landscape floated right through Aron. Day after day he sat completely still. It rained over Germany, it was night in Switzerland, there was a sudden morning clarity over Italy. It was nice not to have to talk to anyone. Even showing the ticket to the conductor became a painful interruption in that seeing into which he had been transformed, and what he saw was the earth where he and others lived in short links, walked in limited spaces, with narrow and small thoughts. "Some food would really be good." A pathetic world. "Two times two are four."

He had devoted himself to it long enough now. The tools he had used lay in their places. Those who continued to live there would not be able to say he had left disorder behind him. He had laid all the nails with their heads in the same direction. It had taken time, but what did time mean? What mattered was that the earth be a landing place for Solveig, that he make himself worthy of her love, *her* desire to return. Above, in the sky of the night journey, he saw the billions of atoms rushing nearer and nearer to each other; he saw how they thickened into forms, into legs, into arms, into hair, into eyes. Everything would thicken into only one: there, on the soil of New Zealand, she would put aside the Tessa disguise. Perhaps that reunion would not be easy. One must be a realist. Remnants of the journey might adhere to her, put a filter on the old, normal language. He must listen patiently to the experiences she had had. Not be in a hurry.

Not make any unexpected movements that could frighten her

back; it could be done so easily. Death was certainly something very rich in comparison to this life. One learned this quickly; there were not many variations, the words few, the desires so limited.

No, he would be calm. If she showed the least sign of drawing back, he would follow her. Like on one of the outings they had made together.

A little basket with food. A blanket.

Yes, he had been right to leave: it would not have been dignified to continue living that way. The fatigue in his face had been too great there at home for her to want to recognize him, or what she liked most in him, what she had actually chosen to live with. Because it is not as if we have one real self, he thought; we have many. Some are strong, others weak; it is a single seething chaos of desires and displeasures within us. Sometimes one comes forward and takes command, and the one which had command during the years with Solveig was not the one which steered his steps through the hotel corridor, to the kitchen, to the spirits cellar, to the damp; was not one which claimed him in the proper way. Because that is what life must be: claims. Demands. The fields which were their fields were such a claim: long, straight rows of wheat and oats, the crops that pushed up out of the underworld and greeted them every spring: that was his life's hold on claims. Then his hands were full of strength. He needed every muscle in his hand for the sake of the crops, he needed her eyes from the bank of the ditch when he came home in the evening; there was not much room left for all those *thoughts* which pressed in during the hotel work of repairing others' thoughtlessness. To clean up after parties, fix doors, clean up vomit in the bathroom, month after month watch the Boss's decline! No, he could never get hold of himself under such conditions. And when he thought about Sidner it was good, far away in Italy, to be able to hear him say: "My father is on his way to New Zealand." That would give Sidner more light, greater room, other fantasies. With the help of

Aron's journey he would press further into knowledge, into love, into longing for the large life.

In Genoa he wrote a letter:

> I hope you can forgive my taking this journey, but for a long time, as you certainly have noticed, I have been on the way to losing everything Solveig and I believed. It can appear to be an escape from everything I cannot deal with, but it is not. Perhaps sometime you will understand that.
>
> It is warm here in Genoa. Palms line the streets, the Mediterranean gleams blue-green; it is probably a different color than that you saw in Strömstad on your curious trip. You were so closed and quiet afterwards, I hope nothing bad happened to you there. The ship, which is called the *Neptune,* departs in three days; it lies in the harbor being loaded. Sometimes I see what I assume to be passengers going and looking at it. I am going on board tomorrow evening and until then am staying in a hotel where you can make yourself passably understood in English. There seem to be people of every possible type, poor, rich, from many different countries. Wish I could have brought you with me. There was enough money and... (then came a whole crossed-out sentence where he had unintentionally written: Solveig is your mother, you know, we all know each other...) Love from

> Your father,
Aron

He got a berth in an eight-man cabin far below deck, but during this journey he was an *inner* person. At night he lay on a blanket on the foredeck looking at the starry sky (one night he counted thirty-five falling stars in a couple of minutes) and he smiled: it was Solveig's rampaging that caused the stars to burst and leave their firmament. The universe was shaken by her desire to return to this little earth where a ship rocked on the high sea, obstinately pitching forward on a long journey, past continents, through canals, on an earth where she once had loved. The Milky Way's hazy veil was the dust that spread about her bare feet, oh – he could not sleep, he was not *allowed* to sleep – it was a Miracle. He kept his eyes open night after night, and the waves rippled on the stem; seafire was cast up in great cascades and made that lower world glitter, too; the stars were reflected down there, the taste of salt covered his cheeks: he was in the midst of a cosmic drama where Solveig was the principal character.

He wondered if she knew he saw her, but naturally: she did not have time to think about that now. She struggled. She hurried. She fled from death, and Aron unobtrusively talked her along, hummed her nearer, kept his gaze steadily fastened on points in the heavens where she could set her naked feet with certainty.

And the nights were real, the days not so.

He was irritated by the strong light, by all the *things* that got in the way. The capstan, the masts, the smoke, the faces of the passengers who came up to him sometimes and asked questions, tried to start a conversation. He was irritated by the smells of food that escaped from the enormous dining hall where people were fed – rice, tomatoes, the smell of meat – all that was too strong; he turned over on his stomach and tried to close his eyes. At the same time he was afraid of what Solveig was doing now that he could not lead her feet in the right direction with his gaze. The watermelons that were loaded in Cyprus nauseated him; the heat, which grew stronger, wearied his body. He longed intensively for darkness when he could be with her again, when everything was clarity, a course straight forward toward the stars. Everything was music then: the rocking of the boat, the hissing of the waves. It sang:

Ich folge dir gleichfalls mit freudigen Schritten
Und lasse dich nicht

Mein Leben, Mein Licht
Befördre den Lauf
Und hör nicht auf.

Port Said: dusty palms along the low shore. Din of merchants who came in small boats. The mate was hard on them as he sorted them out and sent them away. He said to the passengers who flocked to the rail: That one you can trust, he's honest. Not that one, not him. Go away, you get back to the harbor!

Aron observed the new things lined up on the foredeck: co-conuts, camel hair rugs, leather bags, small smoking stands of bronze, pearl necklaces, silverwork. There were girls, too, who whispered to him: Foggie, foggie, mister, only two packets ciga-rettes. He did not understand what they meant, he was too far into himself, despite the fact that they crawled around and raised their skirts; he shook his head and tried to retreat, and it was during that harmless flight that he was reached by the heat, a stifling blanket of humidity and warmth he could not get rid of. His tongue felt like sandpaper; sweat dripped from every pore.

Not a breath of air, not a shred of cloud from which to await shadow. It did not help to leave the harbor and go through the canal; that was going through sand, too. The Red Sea was not bet-ter. He lay on his back on deck; he dragged himself around the railing.

It was not only he who suffered. The flock of passengers who had been so clamorous in the Mediterranean, who had arranged dances in the evenings, who had drunk, sung and played instru-ments from every corner of Europe, quietened. Glances no longer met. They dried up, shrank, fell silent. The showers in the lava-tories sprinkled out tepid water, the lines were always long, many felt ill and vomited; he heard someone had died in a nearby cabin, a woman, a child, he did not know for sure.

Aden: here he could have sent his last letter to Sweden, but he had not written one.

Then it got easier. The Indian Ocean arrived with coolness, with long waves that took the ship upon their backs and carried it southeast. It did not rock noticeably any longer. And it was out here he saw the dolphins.

They came in large schools; thirty or forty of them surfaced in front of the prow, played in the bow waves for one, two hours, then disappeared, and after some time a new school arrived. They seemed to laugh and have boundless fun, it "is like freedom," as he eventually recorded for Sidner. "As if their lives are one long free time. Like my life on board. It is not good. I cannot stand being idle, I brood too much. The other day a Swede came up to me and started a conversation. He said I seem unhappy, wondered if he could help me in any way. His name is Edman. I did not know I was observed by anyone. Edman has a sister in Australia whom he is going to visit. She has a farm down there."

Aron felt how soberly he wrote. The pen censured his innermost thoughts, for he wanted to save the surprise until later. But first Tessa must cast off her disguise.

"There," said Edman one evening, "there you have the Southern Cross. Now I'm the second one in my family who's seen it. How about you?"

"I don't know."

"You don't know? Do you come from a seafaring family?"

"No, well, yes."

He did not want to say too much. But he had to be clear.

"My wife has seen it, I'm sure," he said.

"So now she's sent you off for a look."

Aron nodded.

"Or has she gone on before you, maybe? Well, forgive my talking, but time passes a little faster…"

Edman was a big, strong man; he worked in a shipyard, had traveled around a bit of Europe. But then? Which side of humanity did he belong to? Was he one to be trusted?

"It's a little of both…" said Aron and looked up at the stars to get hold of Solveig, to hear what she wanted him to say. He thought he dodged it well. Edman sat in a deck chair, completely outside the answer, as if outside a grating.

"What did you say?" Edman had not understood.

Aron made up his mind to laugh. Solveig did not answer, did not have time, of course; he laughed again to make time pass, but when he looked at Edman's expression he understood he had made a mistake. He spoke quickly, as though saving himself from a sucking bog: "We have children, too, a boy and a girl."

Edman relaxed. That could be seen clearly, it was just to continue: "A fine boy. He's a little shy, of course. He'll be eighteen soon. Works in a store. Paint store."

But this was not sure ground, not even here. When he thought over the last years he noticed how the images rocked and sucked. His head became heavy and he lay down on the deck, at first as if he just wanted to stretch out; many did that here, the deck was full of people, many lying on their backs. Edman could see for himself, if he was interested. Aron wanted to point that out:

"There are a lot of people lying on the deck this evening. It's a fine evening." But then the heaviness in his head increased and he turned on his stomach and banged his head against the deck planks. Now Edman disturbed him, now he must have a big quiet space about him. He said: "I have to ask you to leave me in peace. I must sort out... sort out... it's so cramped here."

Edman leaned forward. "Now why are you doing that again?"

"Again?"

"That's what I've noticed about you. You bang your head, you've done it every evening, every night. Do you have a hard time sleeping? Do you have a headache? I can get a doctor, there's one on board."

"Doctor? What does a doctor understand?"

"I think it's the heat," said Edman. "It's affected your head. That's not unusual. Sunstroke. You ought to have something on your head during the trip. Most do."

"That's not what it's about. Leave me in peace now, please."

Edman shrugged his shoulders.

"I don't want to intrude."

He got up from the deck chair, went over and stood at the railing. Aron dared to turn on his back again, up toward the stars, Solveig's street.

IT WASN'T SO MUCH Australia that Aron landed in when they disembarked in Sydney, as an inner world. There was a house gable here, a hotel bed there, a plate on a table with steak and potatoes, cold water to drink. But Edman still sat opposite him, his eyes flashing, and said:

"I can't leave you alone before I know your boat has gone, and I've already found that out, if you'll forgive me. It'll be a week. During that time it would be best if you could come with me to my sister's farm. It's not many hours' trip there. I'll come back with you to Sydney then. You're not well, Aron. I'm afraid you really did get sunstroke out there at sea."

"It's raining, you know," said Aron.

"It's been doing that ever since we came here, the day before yesterday. You've slept most of the time. I don't even know what you're going to do in New Zealand. That's no concern of mine, for that matter, but you're a strange character. By the way, do you know where we're staying?"

"No. It doesn't make any difference. Everything is just signs."

"If I didn't know you didn't drink, I'd have thought you were a real tipler."

But they were staying at the Imperial Hotel near the harbor. The cranes rose over them when they came out into the rain, railroad tracks crossed the streets, sometimes warning signals rang when trains backed and wove their way between warehouses.

"Why didn't you eat?"

"It didn't taste like anything."

At least he could say that. It was a clear phrase. But food did not have any value to him. Just the opposite, it was a burden to the body, it nauseated him to have to look at pieces of meat and vegetables.

"Females need strong men," said Edman.

He wandered about in the rain, but hardly noticed it, because that concerned only his exterior, and the exterior was very far away. Out in the exterior, people with glowing faces flew by him in the air, sailed between houses, made a sweep in the air, some waved at him. He did not pay attention. He did not need to sleep either.

Evidently they were at the hotel because Edman said: "But *I* need to. It's hard enough anyway with the noise from the street."

"You're right about that. It's a terrible din. But it will pass."

"Good. Now, you come with me tomorrow. You can't get along by yourself. You're completely nuts."

Aron laughed.

"I could tell you," he said. "But I'm not allowed."

"Sleep now, or try to keep quiet."

"I can go out and sit, if I'm bothering you. I've seen parks here."

"You stay here. You'll never find your way back."

Morning or evening. Earlier or later: they sat under pepper trees in a park, and there was almost a nauseating moment when someone stuck holes in his membranes and his whole body was suddenly out in reality. An anxiety was on him stronger than ever. Cars screamed and braked, people shouted, and every single thing's corners and edges were so sharp he did not dare approach them at all.

"I despise cities," Edman says, "the train's going out to my sister's now. Ever since I was eighteen and forced myself into Göteborg to work I've hated them." He held out a can of sardines, broke off a piece of bread. Aron heard his jaws chewing, and he did not like it.

"The funny thing about you, Aron, is that during all this time you haven't asked me so much as one question. About me. You don't know who I am at all, where I come from."

"No."

"Actually, it's not funny at all, and I don't believe you don't like me, and I don't really believe either that you're the sort you're showing yourself to be. Something's gone wrong for you." The sardines slipped into his mouth when Aron deprecatingly shook his head. He could follow them in the esophagus; he saw the sardines inside Edman, the red tomato sauce sticking to his lips.

"It's a little hard to be with somebody who's just quiet, you know, that's why I talk more than usual. I got divorced from my wife – or she from me. I'm an upstart who had to make things better fast to show the old woman I'm good for something. She never believed in me. That I could do anything but hammer sheet iron in the shipyard. Then, you know, we could very well have moved back home where I came from – you know where Dingle is, that's where I'm from – the farm is still in the family, but it didn't suit her to be a country woman. Maybe it didn't suit me either, really; from the beginning, I was always a little envious of those who dragged into town and started working; well, envious or not, that was what you were supposed to do. There's no future here, you had to hear that all the time. Be on your way to town, boys. It took several years before I understood how deceived I'd been. Don't you want the last sardine? A little bread? No, well. If I could understand what it is with you."

Aron thought it was strange that Edman could not see. All his thoughts were visible, he was *open*. All people were open.

"Not only you," he said aloud, as he observed the sardines slipping downward in Edman's body.

Then there was a train, a very slow Australian train, rattling out of Sydney on its way north.

"My sister came down here twelve years ago. She was sick and thought she was going to die. Bought land, got sheep like everybody else. When I visited her the last time she had four hundred.

Hell of a gal for working. Put up fences, spun, dyed, wove. Then she bought the first tractor in the neighborhood. Alone, those first five years. Don't you think the countryside is pretty?"

"Well, yes."

"I'm just checking to see if you're listening, Aron. You'll see, it'll do you good, coming out to her place. The air's good there. It was good for her.

"Well, as I was saying, she was alone the first five years, and they gossiped about her and thought she wasn't any real woman who didn't get herself a man.

"But then one day a real gentleman came walking along the road. Elegant as hell. Chamois leather gloves – they were yellow – Newgate beard, a pipe in his mouth, and a kind of sailor's cap on his head. He knocked at the doors of the farms where there were women by themselves, but they were all afraid of him. Vera was the first who was nice to him and she let him inside the fence. Nobody knew where he came from, but it was obvious he couldn't hold his liquor; I'm not saying anything against that, I drink like a fish myself, sometimes. After the divorce. Before, too.

"His name was Martin, Eslevsen, from Sweden, him too. And he started talking poetry with her, inside the fence, Dan Andersson and Fröding and whatever they're called now, I don't know poetry, and he wrote to her:

> *You come o'er the heather*
> *we rest in the feather,*

and he wrote another I thought was real nice:

> *We meet by the wind's cape*
> *and lay on granite's nape.*

Well, something like that, so they got married. When she put in fence posts, he painted pictures. When the sheep lambed, he wrote poems. You'll see for yourself."

Edman pecked like a bird at Aron's windowpane but could not really reach in. That was how it was the whole week he sat out at Vera and Martin Eslevsen's, in the bright sunlight, under a cinnamon apple tree, or on the porch that was shaded by blooming bushes; he sat there and conversation flowed by him. He knew that sometimes they tried to make contact with him, all three, but the words did not concern him. Sometimes they became so sharp and clear, too, that they gave him a blow in the pit of the stomach, so he had to flee, out on the roads, or up over the hills. They brought him back. They forced food into him; they showed him the room where he slept and he let them do that, until one day Edman said that now your boat is leaving, are you really going to go away in the condition you're in? And he was.

In the dining hall that evening, as soon as the ship had put out from Sydney's harbor, Aron caught sight of Solveig. She sat at one of the tables eating steak, drinking wine; a napkin lay over her breast, her dress was low-cut and Aron, who stood squeezed into the food line, became very indignant and broke ranks, pushed forward between increasingly angry guests, knocked away an outstretched arm, bumped into a man and bellowed that he must get through, excuse me. But the scream came before the plea, someone turned toward him and he got a punch in the mouth, a strong punch that sent him staggering into an elderly lady, falling over her, and he saw a number of shadows gather around him while he struggled to get up; it was a matter of seconds now, he felt more than saw that Solveig would soon finish and vanish and become inaccessible to him, hidden under God knows what name, and in his fear he gave the nearest body a clenched fist, got up, fought free – and the commotion increased in the dining hall; he caught a glimpse of her as she disappeared through the glass doors, ran after her; she appeared on the stairs, he heard doors close and open, and up on the foredeck he caught up to her and saw that it was not her. That it had never been her, not that time, nor any earlier time; he broke through the membranes of his haze one by one and stood naked and alone in the darkness, high over the waves, and knew once and for all that Solveig was dead and he was here and never would be able to reach her. And the boat rose and sank, there were no stars, there was nothing, and he became completely calm and quiet. Slowly he went over to the rail, hung his jacket on a hook by the lifeboat, loosened his tie, hung it beside his jacket, untied his shoes and placed them carefully side by side; he folded his trousers and laid them on the deck, climbed up on the rail and made a long dive into the darkness, out into the swelling water that soon engulfed him.

❀ IV ❀

IT WAS AN UNFINISHED HIGH-RISE outside of time. Instead of scaffolding there were organ pipes, colossal wind instruments. Workmen, supervisors, women swarmed on the different floors. Several stood completely still, singing the building on high. It was evening when I came in. I knew I had come late and would not be allowed to take part in designing the building, which filled me with anxiety. I was to be one of the tenants. A chorus stood right inside the entrance, one of the members put a finger to his lips and pointed at the conductor who stood on the topmost floor. It was Torin: "I'm no airline hostess who's going to serve you," he said and took aim at me and my wife with a fly swatter. He was just about to swat when Solveig, who found herself on the tenth or eleventh floor, right on the very edge of darkness, struck up an alto aria. Like a chimney swift it rose, groped its way through the confusion of scattered instruments and drifts of scores, up half-built stairways, floated out in the dark sky. I was embarrassed because I had interrupted, and my thoughts were so clear that Torin looked at me and said: "That is a text about trust, not an advertisement for diapers." The chorus looked at me triumphantly when Solveig's aria caused walls to rise. "That's what we do," explained Aron. He held Sidner by the hand. "The boy knows that." Then suddenly a loudspeaker was heard from outside, it was the King of Nepal who yelled, "Everyone who finds themselves inside music must immediately vacate, otherwise we will shoot with tone-deaf bullets." Around the king, on all the hills around the building, torches were lighted, a dark mass of people moved about uneasily. It smelled of burnt rubber, and I discovered that we were in Khatmandu. "But we've just arrived," I said. My wife pulled my arm: "It's best we do as the king says."

"But we're going to live here." "That isn't necessary," she said. "We can live with Wilson." She stretched her arms over her head and went out. Wilson came toward her with the king's loud-speaker in his hand. He kissed her on the forehead and shouted: "It's too crowded for any more in my house." Now the whole chorus pressed toward the exit; I recognized several musicians, old friends, who had kept hidden from me, to whom I would gladly have chosen to explain my absence, but no one made as if to notice me. "Wait," I yelled, " don't you understand the house will collapse if you disappear?" They pointed at the king, who had put out a meal beside a monkey temple: in the grass palm leaves lay spread with bananas, grapes, and papayas; there was wine in long-necked carafes. "The party is out there." When I looked around, most of the light bulbs had gone out; only Torin, Solveig, Aron, and Sidner were left with me, but several floors separated us, and I knew at once that the bullets had already left the king's rifles. Now a salvo struck Solveig and Aron, and I woke up screaming.

I know those screams. You do, too. We live from scream to scream. But in between a rivulet of water makes its way. It disappears, it reappears, once, twice, perhaps three times during our lives, so we can moisten our lips and go on. That I was here depended upon my being shown those gleams between the stones in the valley of the dead. I have been allowed to hear music where I least of all expected it.

PEOPLE GOT IT INTO THEIR HEADS it was Lars Madsén's fault that Torin started going to the local bar, that was simply not so. It was Torin *the father of the child* who bashfully forced his way into circles of light to become engaged by people. He had a table farthest down in a corner by the kitchen. There he sat, fiddling with his hands while he absentmindedly played with the Guest Book.

His hair shone like a burning bush and his eyebrows, white as a field of rye in the rising sun, rose and lowered inquisitively, even downheartedly, in the presence of every entering guest. The truth was he had put on airs: he had bought a blazer, sunglasses, and a camera. He cleaned the dandruff from his arms and shoulders and from time to time took a puff on a cigar. A common stonemason should not have such ways, but was he common? The more time passed after the Interview, the more people forgot Torin had hardly said a word, that it was Madsén who had talked so well around his muttering, his hemming and hawing, so that the picture of the genius with his homemade power station and poetic, fabulous animals of clay, of the pilot who flew in solitude over the forests in his Tiger Moth at last lay like an aura, about his figure.

"You who've talked on the radio," people would say as they sat down across from him, watching his hands and hearing, retroactively, everything Madsén had said coming out of his mouth. But then people felt a little snubbed by his surliness and thought to themselves, it was certainly convenient to open his mouth when *Madsen* talked with him. But they thawed out when Torin fumbled with the Guest Book and wondered about a signature.

"Well, now I've paid again," said Torin, becoming dignified while he blew some imaginary flakes of ash out of the guest book, "that's something to celebrate, you know."

Because that was why he sat there. That was why he had gotten the blazer and the sunglasses.

"Be my guest!"

To be sure, the Guest Book had come into his hands before Madsén's visit; it was his sister-in-law, Victoria's idea, and Madsén's name stood first and entirely alone on the first page; but then it told other stories. There was Pastor Wärme's name, there was the chairman of the Child Welfare Committee, there was Senior Enforcement Officer and clothing merchant Petterson's flowing handwriting, with the date and everything, and by which one could understand that the Blazer was now five years old. Perhaps Torin had misunderstood the idea of the book since he carried it with him everywhere, but still: he invited them into his halls of Pride, into secrets of the Payment, the Allowance Responsibility. The signs that he was not alone.

He stretched back in his chair.

"Well, now it's time to travel again."

Let the words die away.

"There was a little money left over after *I Paid,* you see!" and pronounced the words *Pay* and *Paid* with very large letters, let them shine out over the table; and to taste the sweetness in it, one more time: "It isn't cheap to *Pay.*"

One grew tired of that by and by; there were other things to be curious about. About the flying. About radio transmissions, gravestones, and what was Madsén *really* like? Since you've met him?

"Is he really so remarkable?"

"Who?"

"Madsén."

"Oh, I was sitting here thinking about Gary."

Torin took a swig to make the transition natural.

"He's growing, he's five now."

"Really."

"A good boy."

They tried to dodge it:

"And where are you going to travel, did you say?"

"Well, maybe it'll be the Göta Canal. 150 kronor for a double cabin. Not very cheap, but anyway…"

There was reason to dodge talking about Gary. They did not want to let him get entangled in lies about invented visits to "the family" in Karlstad, not let him digress into talk about trips that never came off, or about "his own." Many had seen him prowling around the house in Karlstad, looking up at the light in the window on the second floor where Mother Zetterberg's girl lived. Many had turned back to avoid meeting him when with bowed head he returned to the railroad after such times. If one met him anyway, one pretended to be surprised at ending up in the same compartment. Oh, well, so you're in town, Torin.

"I've been visiting."

"And such good weather you've had."

Torin's nights were one big birthday party for the boy. Gary sat in his lap and laughed. Gary begged him to shape animals from clay that lay in a lump on the table in the yard. In these dreams Torin told about America, about the fireflies and corn fields, about Indians and Negroes.

"He learns quickly, too," he deceived himself into believing. "It'll be America for him in the end. This," said Torin, sweeping a hand over the dining room and the street, "this is nothing for Gary. Sunne is just nothing, you know."

Yes, Torin deceived himself into believing. Boasting was the cement with which he built his house. With the help of boasting he wanted to caulk his world so it would not leak out of him. That leaking, nauseating darkness which night after night, after the evenings in the dining room, caught up with him as he crossed through the yard, dragged himself with heavy steps over the railroad toward his house by the water. It was a clumsy boast, insufficient, too diluted in consistency; it became weak and transparent. He needed a bigger boast, an Eiffel Tower in the woods, a flight across the Atlantic with Gary, a perpetual motion machine to hide behind. That was what he meant when Madsén talked with him on the radio, that the little watermill by the brook, the pilot's license from America, the wonderful animals which made Madsén break out in lyricism, they were just nothing. Those were just the doormats for the palace he would build.

But now he had to scrape off his feet and step into Nothing's House.

Into the House of No.

She had come here once, the Zetterberg girl, with half-open blouse, the most difficult of sights. All that softness inside. He was forced to look right into paradise when she asked him for a glass of water. Leaned against him, lay her hand on his, tottered. He invited her to sit on the sofa, unmade; he removed the old shirt, the underpants, the socks. It smelled bad, the piss bucket stood by the half-open wardrobe door, smelling sour. Torin looked at his effects as if for the first time. Dirty cups on the table, the plate in the wash, the pork grease on the cutlery. He saw the flies in the window. He was in the habit of killing them, lifting them by the wings and collecting them in a pile when there was nothing else to do. Here he had remained since Mamma died, had just remained in the hope that some external force would snatch him back to the porch in the Midwest. For that was where he was at home. There were desires in every direction – California, Florida, New York: one could stand out amid the corn fields and think *forward*.

The house was not made for visitors. When Mamma was alive, and Solveig a child, then the winds had streamed through the open door and windows; since then it had become more and more of a workshop. The Zetterberg girl stumbled along among cords and tools; here lay parts of a radio, here were shavings and scraps of board, here American newspapers about aviation. She lay down on the sofa and asked if she had a fever. He was forced to stroke her forehead, then she was at his trousers, and he remembered how he was halfway into a question: why did you come here… before he was dazed by the contact. And afterward: I'd like it if you came here again, you know.

But it was as if she didn't hear that.

Pulled on her underpants and left, without even turning around. Did not stand there again before informing him that she was with child – stood in the door and sniffed disapprovingly, did not look at him, looked at the water outside. And his own wretched voice: Will you marry me? Though I… Though you what? As if from the bottom of a well: I'm not spiteful.

"It's enough if you pay."

Glorious Birgitta had received from God the soul of a nurse. Set like an amber in her joyful and voluptuous frame, its light crowded right out into her eyes, illuminating the woeful world she was forced to contemplate ever since the all-too-many gulps of wine at the brilliant parties of the 20's had beaten her with adversity. She was very pretty. It was as if someone had dragged her out of a painting from the Italian Renaissance and placed her under the streetlights of Sunne, and she had not yet completely awakened from that transposition. With her head at a slight angle, with her dark hair hanging down over her shoulders, with her hands pressed together inside her muff, she stood there humming "My Heart Belongs to Daddy" with a weak smile which was not suited to the cold present.

That was one of the few aftereffects of her stay in the States: she had to sing. And one evening, when in her wanderings she ended up under the open windows of the hotel's dining room and heard the gramophone music streaming out, she was dragged in through the door and up the stairs, sweeping in under the cut-glass chandeliers in her fur boa, spreading her arms and almost managing to climb up to the same height as the singer on the record as she struck the last note. Applause followed, but what does applause know? Mr. Jancke, who was celebrating his mother-in-law's seventieth birthday, looked around the November-gloomy, almost empty room and discovered two red hands belonging to Torin.

He parted them and produced that awkward sound which fluttered toward her on broken wings.

"*Your pronunciation is very good,*" he said in English. "*Be my guest!*"

Glorious Birgitta stood over by the gramophone in the middle of her vast body, as though she were a saint, carried by her limbs. Her eyes twinkled, and the gold tooth, which she got after a row in the kitchen during her housekeeper period, flashed toward Torin. She curtsied to the Jancke family, and she curtsied to Torin while she tossed the fur boa tighter about herself. She was not used to this, she was Sunne's street fixture; behind her back people made faces and loudly whistled "Night and Day." Nevertheless, she lived in grace: she could notice those springs, those almost invisible veins of water that dart out from under stony replies, from under the abortive yearning of gestures when they fumble after simpler services. And now she saw, far away in the haze, how Torin stretched his voice out to her:

"*Be my guest!*"

And how he, when she approached unsteadily, slowly shoved the guest book across the table, held it in front of him like a shield while his eyes roved about.

"If you'd write... your name here."

"You dear thing," said Glorious Birgitta, supporting herself on his wrist, and his body became like melting wax; he felt how her hand sank down through flesh and blood, down toward bare bone. It burned and gave heat to those thoroughly amassed holes far inside him. They were lighted; he saw and became as if dazzled by his own existence. But then he flew out. It was too intense.

That someone had touched him *like that.*

And he wanted to get up and rush out. But Glorious Birgitta

was leaning against him, thumbing through the guest book and he regretted it, he was even afraid of her name now. That he would burn himself every time he looked at it.

"*You know a lot of people,*" she said in English, and that made him someone special with her. He raised his face, she stroked his forehead with her index finger, talked like someone on a porch long ago, among fireflies.

"*They laugh at me, you know.*"

"*Nobody is laughing, nobody. The color of your hair is so beautiful.* I'm not scaring you, am I?"

She sat down opposite him.

"*Are you afraid of women?*"

"*Love is so ugly, Birgitta.*"

"No, not love. Not that. Maybe you haven't caught sight of it. You have to look for it. Of course, I haven't found it, either. When I saw you I thought: There's Torin sitting and brooding himself to death over love and all hell. But brooding's a sin. Torin, what is it you're thinking about?"

"About Gary. About my boy."

"Aha! Order me a bottle of wine. Just a little one."

"I'm not allowed to see him. I'm not good enough for that."

"And you agree with that! Maybe you think it's convenient. You really enjoy it, don't you? Find comfort in that. Tell me if I'm wrong, if I talk too much, 'cause I'm a little tipsy. I'm not really considerate then, I see what's up."

"Yes, you *see* me. Keep talking." He knocked on the door to the kitchen, and Mrs. Jonsson wrinkled her nose when she saw Glorious Birgitta sitting there.

"Give Miss Larsson a half bottle of wine," said Torin.

"Hasn't she had enough aleady?"

"It's cold out. She's a good person, Mrs. Jonsson. She's my guest."

"Just so you don't disturb the Jancke's," Mrs. Jonsson muttered.

"We're unobtrusive," Torin said.

Glorious Birgitta thumbed through the Guest Book.

"Why, good Lord, I'm the only woman in the whole book, Torin. Haven't you ever...? Am I really the first?"

"We don't dare, you know. Write your name now, Birgitta. With the date and everything. You're awfully nice. Say more about me!"

"Does it really help to talk with me? When are you happy?"

"When I think about Gary. When I wish I could have him here and we could sit in the yard. I'd give him chocolate and sparkling cider. Loads. America – yeah, when I think about him and me going to America. Sometimes I think he and I could fly over the Atlantic, just the two of us, exactly like Charles Lindbergh."

Glorious Birgitta laid a hand over Torin's and showed her gold tooth.

"As long as you do something, Torin. That's what's important. One's thoughts play such a small role. What wine!"

"You know all about such things, from what I've heard."

"Yes, I do. I didn't think of drinking, I drank. I drink, it's stupid, but sometimes life is so desperately cold."

THAT NIGHT Torin could not sleep. He had left Glorious Birgitta outside the hotel. It never occurred to him that she could have gone home with him. Not before he turned around over on the railroad embankment and saw her standing there, under the streetlight, in the snow.

He tossed in his bed and listened to the March wind. The door to the carpenter's shed squeaked, there were mice under the sink, and the cats were out on adventures. If she had come with him and seen this mess... No, he drove away those sexual thoughts, now as before. It was just as well to have it this way, so he was not tempted. But he would put a room in order for Gary. Buy toys. Get pastries from Beryl's bakery.

Somewhere upstairs. He had not been up there for several years. It remained as it had been when Mamma died. He got out of bed and groped his way up the stairs, ended up sitting on the cleanly made bed until dawn came.

In the morning he took the train into Karlstad; at the newsstand he bought three chocolate bars to have something at least to give Gary, if he got to see him now; it was so long since he had even caught a glimpse of the boy inside the apartment windows. There was a biting wind along the streets; the drifts lay high along the river. At first he thought of knocking, saying: "I don't want to disturb you, I just want to see the boy, sit with him and cuddle him. Please, Carina" – that is what he would say. "There's no harm in me. Let me take care of him while you do your things," whatever they were now. "Maybe you'd like to relax." That sounded good – to relax, as he himself would choose to relax from thinking about Gary and the warm child's body. To hold it a while! He took a bag of clay with him, too: "Look here," he would say, "I'll make an animal for you. What do you want most: a rhinoceros? Or an elephant? I'll make an elephant for you." No: "Papa will make an elephant for you." That sounded fine. "Papa will make elephants for you while Mamma is out shopping. Sit in my lap. I learned this in America, you see. Do you know where America is?" he would ask and Gary would say: "No, Papa, I don't know." "It's far, far away, on the other side of the Atlantic. We'll go there one day, you and I, in my airplane." "Does Papa have an airplane?" "Oh, yes, hasn't Mamma told you that?" "No, she hasn't told me *anything*."

That struck a blow at Torin's heart. Had she really told him nothing? How could she? But he understood that from her expression the last time they had met on a street corner, and he had stood there with his hands out-stretched begging to have... at least a couple of minutes... a minute, Carina! *Why?* he had asked, why are you so impossible? He's my child, too, I've never shirked, just the opposite... If you don't stop sneaking around here, I'll go to the police.

So she has not told him anything. He fantasized further and thought that he actually ought to get angry, really angry, as he had seen other people get. That is really what is wrong with me: that I have no anger. I *can't* get angry. I don't know what to do. But now, well, I'll... I'll knock on the door and as soon as she opens it, I'll yell: Now this is the end of this, Carina. Now you've treated me badly enough. I demand to have a hand with Gary, even if you hate me, have a hand with him... he tasted that on his tongue... have a hand with the child, my child, at least... now and then... He'll come to be happy with me... he can have as much fresh bread from Beryl Pingel's bakery as he wants... cream of wheat and oatmeal, fresh red beets from Sleipner's garden; Victoria can sew clothes for him and I, I'll swing him in the yard among the apple trees. Because when did you last swing him in a yard, answer me that! He had suddenly yelled, right out in the street.

He stood in the square feeling the gale gust inside his collar, his feet were cold; it was never this cold in the States. Oh, if Charles Lindbergh could do it, so can I... reserve tanks... reserve tanks, Carina, slipped out of him again, the words slid away over the sidewalk. The scent of floor polish in the stairway made him stop: this was not his world. He smelled the ingrained stench of his own clothes; he saw the house where his days slipped away, his rage evaporated and he withdrew, remained standing confusedly on the ground floor, right inside the door.

Forgive me, Carina, I understand, I'm not good enough for this. I'm a lout, a good-for-nothing, an idiot. I would just destroy Gary if he lived with me, wouldn't even keep myself clean, and if he got sick... while I was working... fever... don't little children easily get fever... juice... cold juice, well, of course he could buy that or borrow it from Victoria, it would be all right, but all the wash... he wouldn't get it clean enough... He clenched his hands around the chocolate bars in his pocket... I can drop them through the mail slot and then go and never more... From within the doors on the stairs came the forenoon sounds of radio music, of the clatter of plates in a sink. In one apartment someone played an accordion, in another two women sighed; the smell of steak and onions reached his nostrils, and he even felt envy for the doorplates of brass; wanted to stroke them with his finger. Towards evening the apartments would be populated even more: the men would come home from work, children from school, everyone would have someone to say hello to, a what-kind-of-day-did-you-have-today? Several would hug, others would only look at each other. But they would have each other. Clean, good people. Clean, pretty furniture. The sheets, oh, what pain they caused, those sheets fluttering in every yard except his. The smell of laundry detergent and wind.

NO! He had said no. He could not be taken in again. It was good he had got to see the miserable state of things: in the evening the quarrels would start, the drunkenness, the screams. The kids who threw clothes all around, the old hags who complained about not having enough housekeeping money. People stuck to each other, imprisoned. He knew well enough, he had Sleipner and Victoria right on top of him. That peaked, stingy face of Victoria's, that was how they got! Sleipner was so haggard when he came to the gravestones in the morning! That crooked smile: You know how Victoria is... And he let himself be satisfied with that. Day after day a perpetual wearing-down of everything Sleipner had dreamed about when he was little.

On the other side: What had he dreamed about, really? When you thought about it. He did not want to learn to fly, he did not care about them having to move back to Sweden, he did not lash out when Victoria prevented him from listening to the radio. "You know how females are..." Maybe he was satisfied. Maybe they were all satisfied. Satisfied and afraid, satisfied because they had somebody to sleep with, because there was food on the table, and afraid to think about anything greater. "Freedom," muttered Torin, drawing in the smell of floor polish, "means nothing to them."

But Solveig and Aron then? Of course they were special people, you know. They belonged to another sort. They had music: a door they could open whenever they wanted and go through. It had always been that way with Solveig, that she was sort of *dressed* in music, and it was a garment which did not *chafe,* the world did not *chafe* her. She had got Aron into those clothes, too, almost. He had been on the way when she died. It was Solveig who possessed the keys to that door, she had taken them with her, no wonder Aron... that he went away... to look for the key maybe... leaving the youngsters...

Suddenly a door opened farther up the stairs and Torin retreated to the courtyard. In one corner there were a couple of garbage cans that smelled of fish entrails, and he crouched behind them. It was Carina Zetterberg and Gary who came out of the stairwell.

"Now you stay here in the courtyard until I come back, you hear me?"

Gary did not answer but stood with his back against a tree, looking at her.

"Not out in the street."

Gary still did not answer. Torin saw. His child, five years old, dressed in a cap with earflaps that almost obscured his whole face, thick mittens, a short overcoat, long warm socks. With his hands behind his back he rocked against the tree, silently watching Carina disappear toward the street.

Torin crept out of his hiding place.

"Hi, Gary. I'm your papa."

Gary silently looked at him and turned away.

"Don't you want to say hello to me?"

"You're not my dad," said Gary.

"Oh, yes, of course I am." He held out a chocolate bar. Gary snatched it and tore off the paper. Gary was not a pretty child. He got that from me, thought Torin, and not the color of his hair, which could be glimpsed under the cap, nor the eyes. But the ugliness, that's mine. Gary ate the chocolate without condescending to give Torin a single look.

"You've gotten so big. Can I feel if you're heavy?"

"You're a rotten old bastard," Gary said, moving away when Torin bent down toward him.

"Has... Mamma said that... that I..."

"I can see that myself," said Gary.

Torin never swore and thought Gary's language was like knives in him. But he had not had a chance for anything else. Maybe swearing was the language he had to live with. Torin said:

"Would you like to go to a pastry shop with me?"

"No," said Gary.

"You can have as many pastries as you want."

"With raspberries?"

"If they have that, you can have it."

"But I'm supposed to stay here till Mommy comes back. You're a rotten old bastard anyway."

"Why do you say that, Gary?"

"Everybody's a rotten old bastard – do you have any more chocolate?"

"If I can hold you."

Gary placed himself erectly before him, looking at the ground. Torin lifted him up, putting his hands around the thin body, wanting to meet his eyes, wanting to see him laugh, but Gary was far from laughter; he stared implacably at Torin and put out his hand for more chocolate. Torin carried him out to the street.

"There's a pastry shop not far from here. And besides, I have a whole pocketful of chocolate." He said that because there was a taxi stand not far from them. Snow fell on them; it was slippery walking. Torin thought: Maybe it'll be fun for Gary to ride in a car. Torin always carried plenty of money, that was part of what he called freedom, but he seldom had any imagination for spending it, and it piled up. "It was when we were in the car that I first thought of taking him with me," he later explained in court. "When we sat in that soft back seat and he called me a rotten old bastard again. And I thought he could have a chance to be spared talking that way, if I could keep him with me. If he hadn't said that, then..." And the prosecutor asked: "Were you conscious of breaking the law?" "The law," answered Torin. "The law can be so grim, so grim."

IT NEVER WAS the children's party Torin had dreamed about; he had chosen the wrong time of year. He became bitterly aware of that when, after changing taxis three times during the trip up from Karlstad, he carried Gary into the house, gorged on choco- late and soft drinks and fast asleep. The yard lay cold and naked under the snow; the yard swing, where they should have sat in half-shadow making clay animals, where they should have rocked calmly together, stood frozen; fruit blossoms kept their distance and cold clouds drifted over the lake. It started so wrong, but it was now Torin first realized that: as if he had hoped that, in any case, the yard would lay outside the seasons of the year, that right at the ditch there would be a border between winter and summer, between day and night, between loneliness and communion. Just a hop over the ditch. A very small hop and his face would have been open to Gary's, they would have floated together in one sin- gle smile of homecoming.

The house – "that pigsty," it flashed through him – was cold, unheated, untidy; there was not a spot in the kitchen where he could carefully lay the child down. Newspapers, cords, and tools now covered chairs, tables, beds, like *that* time. When he pushed a little rubbish from the bed with one hand a level fell to the floor, waking Gary so suddenly that he messed his pants; it was as if the boy exploded from all the carbonation, all that sweet chocolate. Gary swung wildly about, kicking at Torin's face, while the stench and the wet warmth – the only warmth in that drafty house – spread through his clothes.

"There, there," he tried, and got a bite on the wrist. "We have to get you out to the john."

But when he had carried Gary across the dark yard, unlatched the door, and put up the lid to that abysmally dark hole, the wind made the door bang and bang, and Gary was gripped by the ultimate panic:

"Don't throw me in," he screamed, clinging with the strength of an animal to Torin's arms. "No, no," Torin said, "you're just going to sit here and crap. So you'll get dry." But Gary refused; it was impossible to get him on the seat. "It was meaningless, too," Torin admitted in his long and detailed statement in court, "since he'd already crapped everything he had." "Perhaps we can skip the details," said the prosecutor and cleared his throat. "I don't think so," said Torin, "because it was like that hole... when he saw it... that I wasn't even good enough... couldn't even wipe his ass... when I stood there thinking I had nothing at home for him to eat except a little brown beans and pork... no milk... nothing... that everything was so wrong... and that hole... that that's where I belong... *As if that hole was...,*" he started in English. "May I ask the accused to use our Swedish language at least," the prosecutor interrupted him. "*Yes, yes, yes,*" Torin moaned, burying his face in his hands.

In the house he at last got the filthy pants off, managed to make Gary tolerably clean with an issue of the American magazine, *The Pilot,* pulled one of his own sweaters over him. He wrapped him in blankets after taking off the sheets, which had got a splash of the mess on them; he made a fire in the stove, heated water, washed the dirty clothes and hung them on a line over the stove, sat down at the kitchen table, and stared at the motionless Gary:

"Do you want some coffee?" he asked. "But children don't drink coffee, I ought to have thought of that," he continued his statement and the jury nodded. "But what do you say to a youngster who won't even look at you. Nothing, Mr. Prosecutor, is worse than not being seen by a child. Then you don't have any value at all in life."

And he said:

"'Tomorrow we'll go back to your mamma. If your clothes have dried,' I said. But they hadn't. It was foul and cold in the house; myself, I can manage like that, there's never been anyone to warm it up for." And then it was Saturday as well. The stores closed early, and he did not dare go out to shop before it was too late. Was afraid to let the youngster out of his sight. Sat and watched him at the kitchen table, tried to make some of those clay animals for him, but Gary was not interested in animals. He complained about food, and Torin got some brown beans and pork into him later in the afternoon, a small glass of beer, too, so he was not in any immediate need. The evening became more pleasant. For a long time Gary had stared at the radio sets and all the switches and tools, sat and played there. "It was like a beginning, anyway. That he and I could agree. That he showed interest in my inventions. That I could even creep up to him and potter about a little, make electrical current in a generator – he liked to look at the sparks, Mr. Prosecutor. If it hadn't been for those sparks I'd have opened for sure when they knocked. But the door was locked, the curtains drawn, and I sat with my hand over the boy's mouth. That was the only bad thing I did. I would gladly have opened the door, because it was my nephew, Sidner, who banged and shouted. His father has left for Australia, and his mother, my sister, is dead. But there was no beginning, because I destroyed everything by holding his mouth; he complained and screamed all evening. He was hungry, I'm sure. And he'd started to catch cold. That night I went out to the john." "Are we there again now," said the Prosecutor. "When you don't have anyone to reach out to, Mr. Prosecutor, then you have to try to pray. I knelt in front of that hole." "Now, now," said the prosecutor, "perhaps we can skip that." "No," said Torin, "if the only thing you've got to reach out to is about to disappear... then you get desperate... when you've carried something, like, right to the edge of darkness..."

It was a kind of blessing that he was interrupted by a clearing of the throat along toward Sunday morning: in the door of the john stood Officer Hedengren, looking pityingly at him:

"Torin, Torin, what have you done now?"

And Torin got up and put down the lid, his eyes were empty and he was cold.

"Are you here to take the youngster from me?"

"So, he is with you?"

"You know that well enough already."

"I had a feeling; what's the point of that? And to do it so openly. You didn't even have the sense to put a cap on your head; your red hair lit up the whole courtyard. I've got a report on you."

Torin went before him into the house but ended up standing in the doorway observing Gary who slept under the blankets with his thumb in his mouth.

"My child. Sometime a father must get... I meant no harm, you know. She doesn't even let me..."

"I know, Torin. Do you have a little coffee for me? I was woken up much too early. Sometimes I wish I owned a truck garden instead of being a policeman."

"Are you going to take me, too?" Torin dragged the coffee kettle over to the hot part of the stove, stood pushing down on it so it would go faster, washed a cup and poured, sat down opposite the policeman.

"You who were interviewed on the radio by Madsén and everything. By the way, that was a fine program. What's he really like?"

"It's good," Torin mumbled. "It's good you're taking care of me."

"If I'd only known he was here in Sunne I could have taken him out on the lake and fished for some perch. He and you and I, Torin. I caught five kilos of burbot yesterday, I'll see you get to taste it when you're..."

"In custody?"

Hedengren slurped his coffee, then he took a paper out of his pocket.

"Gary, that's his name, right?"

"It wasn't me who named him. Can't he sleep awhile, Hedengren?"

"I have to call in that we've found him. They're waiting down in Karlstad. That you'd make such a mess."

"You can go ahead."

"I can't do that, Torin."

"I won't do any harm."

"I know there's nothing bad about you, but it's best you come along. You know the rules are like that. Illegal abduction, unlawful detention, that's not good, Torin."

"Let the boy sleep a little longer. We could sit here and watch him. You know, it might be the last time... *You know, I had hoped...*"

"I can't speak English, Torin."

"We could sit here. Sit quietly. He's everything I have. Soon I won't even have him."

"Give me a little more coffee, then."

ONE DAY IN APRIL, Torin Brink sat in the courtroom in Karlstad listening to the prosecutor reading the complaint submitted against him by their mutual child's mother, one Miss Carina Zetterberg, with reference to statute number 15, sub-paragraph 8, urging his imprisonment. The description of the deed was long and boring, and Torin looked around in surprise at the crowd that had been enticed there through the newspapers, thanks to their managing to drag Lars Madsén's name into the articles about the kidnapping. Torin was suddenly recognized from the radio and was in pictures together with Madsén, a photograph that the reporter for the Fryksdal district had taken of them at the spot where Torin's pier had once been. Madsén himself had not commented on the crime, but related upon inquiry that he was working on a new interview series from the flatland of Västergötland and the programs would be broadcast during the summer.

Miss Zetterberg, who sat beside the prosecutor, had certainly not counted on this influx when she stepped into the room and nervously looked around. She had put on a considerable amount of flesh; her hair was frizzled and all too short at the neck; she carried a purse and had a handkerchief rolled up in her hand.

On the 11th of March the accused Brink arrived in Karlstad; there, with the help of chocolate and caramels, he enticed the lad, Gary Zetterberg, into accompanying him under false pretences of a visit to a pastry shop. With violence he then, according to the testimony of Mr. Widman, taxi driver, forced the boy into the latter's taxi and traveled to Kil, where he was deposited at the corner of Main and Railway Streets to throw himself quickly into a taxicab owned and driven by Mr. Ederling, domiciled in Kil. Even during this journey Brink obstinately forced the child to eat caramels in such a quantity that Mr. Ederling had "never seen the like." In West Ämtevik the accused once again changed cars to mislead possible pursuers, that time to a Volvo belonging to one Mr. Bengtsson in Bäckebron, who took the boy child to Sunne where he was dropped "not too far from the bridge." The lad was then sleeping, exhausted and with a runny nose. Mr. Bengtsson, who had listened to the Madsén program and recognized the accused, tried to converse with him, but did not receive any answers to his questions, which he thought was "at the very least peculiar." After that the accused Brink stole away to his residence, where he arrived sometime in the afternoon, where he locked the child in without giving him opportunity for either a visit to the toilet or meals, so that the boy, by the time the police arrived on the 13th, was in a deplorable state, "with a bad cold and unclean," and wearing a much-too-large sweater with nothing under it. The plaintiff, Miss Zetterberg, who at her arrival home had found the child gone, was panic stricken! And after questioning her neighbors and learning the child had been taken away by a red-haired man, she called the police. Accused Brink, is that in concordance with the truth?

"I never had caramels," said Torin. "Everything gets so twisted."

"But you concede the substance of the matter?"

"I had chocolate, but no caramels."

When Carina Zetterberg went to the witness stand she dropped her purse and a box of cough drops fell out, spreading over the floor. Bewildered, she looked around and began to pick them up. They waited patiently for her:

"For a long time I've felt threatened by his advances," she said, then fell completely quiet. Not a word came out of her, and she appealed to the prosecutor with her eyes.

"Tell it in your own words."

"From the beginning?"

"Yes, from the beginning."

She stuck a cough drop in her mouth and chewed a long time.

"That he came and took the kid?"

The judge and prosecutor nodded together.

"I'd been over the neighbor's drinkin' coffee. An' then when I come back he was gone. Well, then I went up ta th' apartment, but he wadn't there neither. An' so I run out in the street. But he wadn't there neither. I'd told him he wadn't ta go there. Then I started ta cry an' then people heard 'n' come out in the stairs 'n' asked what was wrong with me. An' then I say Gary's gone, I say, an' it was her, Mrs. Karlsson, Britta, who'd seen a person talkin' to 'im 'n' had choc'late 'n' red hair an' then I unnerstood it was... him."

She bowed her head, fiddled with her purse straps.

"Did you have reason to suspect that it was Brink?"

"There's not many's got that kinda red hair... An' he used ta hang round the house, too."

"So you felt he could have such a deed in mind?"

Carina puckered her eyes and thought:

"Yeah," she said. "I've felt threatened a long time."

"Has Brink in any way made insinuations about that?"

"Well, not really direct he hasn't. But it's felt so awful th' whole time. Ya couldn't never feel safe. Sometimes he could stand outside there several hours 'n' jes' stare."

"You have never invited him into your apartment?"

"No."

"Because you were afraid? He is the boy's father, in any case."

"I've gotten so nervous from him. An' the boy, too."

Now the judge got into it:

"But has the boy ever met his father?"

"No."

"Then how has he become nervous?"

"I've pointed 'im out when he's stood out there starin'."

"And said to the child that that is his father?"

Carina swallowed and squeezed the handkerchief harder in her hand.

"He's so tricky. That he stares so funny."

"But staring 'funny', as you say, does not imply a direct threat."

"No, but he's done it anyhow. Real funny."

And as if she suddenly remembered one of her lessons she spoke in purest Swedish:

"I have been terribly shocked by what has happened, too. The child has suffered from this crime. He didn't have anything to eat. During that whole time, you know."

"Perhaps you have made the boy afraid of his father?"

"Well..." She rolled her eyes, groping in the air for a defense, a phrase, something to say.

"Has there been any reason for fear?"

"I don't know," said Carina Zetterberg.

The judge, a cultivated man from a district in southern Sweden who dreamed of greater cases than this, now looked at Torin's ungainly shape, the hanging lower lip and the light eyebrows.

"Now Brink will relate it in his own words, from the beginning. In his own words," he repeated, like a pat on the shoulder.

"Own," said Torin, "who's given me any words? *Life is a penal colony for a lonely man*."

The judge raised his eyebrows:

"Meaning...?"

"If your honor understands, that's enough for me. It's punishment enough to live. For five years I've paid for Gary without so much as getting to hold him. For five years I've dreamed, not that she would come to me," he said, pointing at Carina Zetterberg, "that would be too much to expect, but that she one single time... these hands, your honor... what do you do with them? It was as if these hands screamed, that day. There was a shout out of them," Torin said holding them out over the witness stand's rail so everybody could see them and, as it were, listen to them. "It came out of them..."

"You mean you lost control?"

Torin looked pityingly at the prosecutor who pushed in between the judge and him.

"My head has no exceptional position on my body," he answered, and a smile passed through the room but was extinguished when he continued: "But the prosecutor himself perhaps consists of only his head. Should the rest of the body be an appendage… Unnecessary protuberances?"

"To the point," said the prosecutor trying to make himself as physical as possible by letting out some stomach muscles and nonchalantly laying one hand on his cheek. "When did you get the idea for the kidnapping itself?"

"The idea? Was I supposed to have an idea!"

Glorious Birgitta's gold tooth gleamed at him as if from an altarpiece in a dark church. "The main thing is that you do something. Brooding destroys." As if she had thrown out fat bait. He had taken it and got caught, twisted his body around in convulsions. Now he had done something, he was on his way: a development had taken hold of him, it had given him a half hour's peace, when Hedengren and he had sat over the coffee cups, watching Gary. That had given him several games of chess in his pocket, a good dinner of burbot and aquavit ("which you don't say a word about, Torin"); and at the same time there was a knock on the outer door and the young clerk from the district court in Karlstad was there to make his pre-sentence investigation. Torin grinned where he stood in the witness stand: that totally unused face behind the city eyeglasses, the well-combed hair, the handkerchief in the pocket, the briefcase. And Hedengren had started up, hiding the aquavit glasses in his pocket, tearing the napkin from Torin (Hedengren had wanted to have it so formal), and yelling at him: Isn't the visit to the toilet over now, and then he shooed him into the clink, from which he was immediately called to answer questions about *whether* he used alcohol. No, he did not want to defend himself from that plateau of cheerfulness. Not on their conditions:

"Hold yourselves to the law," he said. "If you're of the opinion I've committed a crime, I'll take the punishment. Nobody waits for me, just the cats.' "

But the prosecutor continued to interrogate him; he answered indifferently, sometimes eagerly, sometimes with great weariness, occasionally with emphasis, as when he was asked if he had reason to suspect the child did not receive proper care from his mother.

"I don't suspect," he answered loudly. "I know nothing about it. Every person has his wounds. There are reasons behind everything."

He looked at Carina Zetterberg with great tenderness. She avoided his eyes, chewed frenetically on her cough drops and scratched her stomach; suddenly she broke out in tears. During the whole summation speech, when the prosecutor pressed for a stiff sentence since he had unlawfully taken possession of the child, she sobbed, while the prosecutor's white hand repeatedly patted her on the shoulder, partially to silence her, partially to calm her. And when he said the crime was indeed of a serious nature, but with respect for its not being committed with evil intent... and when she heard the sentence could be four months to six years, she got up and cried:

"He's not Gary's father, it's Torsten Bodlund!" She looked right at Torin. "I jes' wanted 'a say that, Torin. I was knocked up when I come ta ya that evenin', but Torsten was so known when he played left back for Arvika, an' he was married 'n' no money ta pay either. We'd been together at Kolsnäs just before that. So we didn't know what ta do. Then we come up with that 'bout you, Torin... that maybe you'd swallow it, I mean you bein' like you was. Torsten waited at the New Café while we... when we..."

"Engaged in intercourse?" suggested the judge who had sunk back in his chair.

"If that's the way ya say it, yeah. An' I was real drunk. If I'm gonna be honest, too."

Sᴅɴᴇʀ ɪs sɪᴛᴛɪɴɢ in Fanny's long-empty parlor, playing Robert Schumann's "Kinderszenen," when Eva-Liisa cracks open the door.

"Good, you're here. You play so well."

"No, I don't. But it's nice of you to think so."

"Selma Lagerlöf called."

"Mm. Was it anything in particular?"

"I don't know. She said you should call her."

"Wants paint from the store, I'm sure."

Eva-Liisa looks around:

"What luck you had borrowing Miss Fanny's piano."

"I water her flowers, look after the house. I should have something for that."

"I think she has such a nice place, you hardly dare to come in. Strange she disappeared like that, without sayin' a word to anybody. What's that piece you're playing?"

"'Von Fremden Ländern und Menschen.' Don't you think we live well, too?"

"Oh, yeah, but in another way. Not so upper class. Listen, do you think I can try on a few clothes?" she whispers, leaning over the grand piano. "And some of those necklaces lying in a box?"

"As long as you put them back."

"Well, of course. Just think, you can still smell her perfume. She's awful fine, isn't she? I came in once when she and Selma were sitting talking. I had a piece of cake. It felt so elegant, sitting beside them. And then I thought, this is how it'll be for you when you get married."

"I'll never find anyone, Eva-Liisa."

"Of course, you will. I think you're so handsome. And

different. It won't be anybody from Sunne or Karlstad. You'll get somebody from Stockholm and then you'll be ashamed of me."

"Why would I do that?"

"She must have liked you a lot, Fanny, taking you to Strömstad where you got to hear Sven Hedin. Why are you looking at me so funny? Anyway, there were raspberries on that piece of cake I had. Do you think Selma picked them herself?"

"Hardly."

"But anyway! Just think if you were as famous as her! Ugh!"

"Why do you say that?"

"Well, what would you wear, when people look at you like that? I'd have something blue. Or green. But not black, like her. Except maybe you have to then. You must think I'm awfully childish. Admit it!"

"You're the best sister there is."

"Why don't we ever hear anything from Papa. Sometimes I think he... Go call Selma, so she doesn't get impatient."

He did as she said. She was right: Selma wondered if he didn't want to come out with some cans of paint, blue, and a little putty, since the butler's pantry was to be repainted.

"Then I'll need a little help with my books, too. And Sidner! Go to the New Café, too, and bring a princess cake with you. So we can sit and chat awhile."

The windows to Selma's workroom were open. The birds sang when she received him, sitting at her desk..

"I never. Well... How big you've gotten since I last saw you. How old are you?"

"I'm eighteen, almost nineteen."

"Did you bring the paint?"

"I gave it to the caretaker. Hope it's the right color of blue. I left the cake in the kitchen. Have you heard anything from Fanny?"

Selma got up heavily from her writing chair, supporting herself with a cane; she walked over to the window and looked out over the courtyard.

"It's the books I want you to help me with. I'll die soon, and what I thought to ask of you is a little delicate, but I hope I can depend on you. It's a lovely day, I've sat here listening to the birds all morning. Just think, one never tires of them. But, of course, you don't have time for birds, you who are so young."

"All too much time. I shouldn't have it."

"No, perhaps not. I know it's been difficult for you."

She ran her cane over the shelves:

"Have you ever seen so many books?"

"Not even in the library."

"Do you think I've read them all?"

"Most of them, maybe."

"That's what people think. It's so painful to admit, but I've read very few. Look here," she said, stretching for a book at random. She opened it and pointed: 'To the greatest of them all, Selma Lagerlöf, with admiration from this devoted author.' Dedications, greetings. The same there and there. I don't know how many I've received. There are too many authors. And all of them send their books to me. Some just to thank me, but others want to have an opinion or a preface. Some come with manuscripts which they want help publishing. But I don't have the strength. I'm old, and God knows if I have any judgment of others' writings at all."

"Oh, yes," Sidner attempted.

"No phrases today, boy. For one single day in my life I can well escape them. But of course, I have myself to blame. However, it's like this now: I've written my will. This grave will be..."

"Grave?"

"Mårbacka, my estate: it's a grave. Mårbacka will become a museum. I don't know if it's vanity or some other reason you can reflect on when I'm dead. But possibly a lot of people will come here then to root and snoop. Including these writers."

She sank down onto her chair again and laid her cane parallel to the green desk pad.

"What I want, Sidner, is for you to cut open the pages of these books. Those I haven't read, that is. So they look as *if* I have. Can I trust you for at least forty years after my death?"

"Forty-five, Aunt Selma. I have nobody to tattle to."

"I've heard you're clever."

"That I am. But that's also the only thing I am. To be clever, you know, is just to pretend to believe that what you do is important. Sell cans of paint! That's not why I was born."

"So, let's get started. Start with the letter A. I'll sit here and you tell me the name and title, and we'll see what's to be done. Here's a paper knife."

Sidner dragged out the first book:

"Ahlberg, Emma: *In Gardens of Joy.*"

"Aha. In gardens of joy is it, well. Cut it open. One ought to open women writers. They do as well as they can. There are so many obstacles in the way of their writing. I believe I met her once. A gray little thing. Does it look like a sad book?"

Selma sat with eyes closed, listening to the sun ripple over book spines and floors.

"If I'm to read them, too, it's going to take an awfully long time."

"You're right. If it's a happy book, there's no reason to read it; if it's sad, then the title lies. But we women can't afford irony yet. Next."

"Ahlberg, Erik: *Beyond the Horizon.*"

"Ugh, what a title. Cut seven pages, so he can see I made an effort. I hope it's completely quiet and calm beyond the horizon, next!"

"Alm, Albert: *Under Poplar Crowns.*"

"Little Albert! So untalented you are! Look, Sidner, he will never change literature. He lives in Landskrona. Was a teacher there. There's certainly not a misplaced comma in that book. Not one incorrect sentence structure. When you cut it open, for that you will, it will be one of the few moments of joy in his life – then you'll discover a flock of Greek gods breeding under his poplar crowns. More learning than life. Although there may be a simple and pretty poem to his mother."

"Yes, here's one called 'To Mother.'"

"I suspected as much. She took care of Albert. I could see them from my window every Sunday when they walked to church, he held her by the arm. Actually, I happened to envy his serenity, which never revolted. Although, of course, we know so little about other people's lives."

"It's cut open. Pretty thin."

"That's good. He'll never become arrogant, in any case. But then he'll never be a great author either; it isn't arranged so in this life."

"Edvinsson, Carl-Edvard: *Song of the Alleys.*"

"That sounds dissolute. Cut it open so people will see I wasn't afraid of modern times. Does absinthe pour over the lines, does it echo of ghastly laughter from loose women? Do you think I'm a hypocrite? You don't need to answer that. But now I'm going to tell you the only funny story I know, and it's not at all funny. But it has the same import as my need of you today. Emmanuel Larsson, do you know who that was? Anyhow, he died last year. And when he died his dear old wife went down to Sunne and bought pajamas for him. So it would be in the estate inventory that he had owned some! That's concern for honor, not hypocrisy. Next!"

"Friedrichsen, Ebba: *The Crofter's Anna.*"

"Oh, good Lord! And I promised that nut an answer immediately. Is it really not cut open! Ebba, I loved that woman. Her creamed mushrooms were unsurpassed. But she used cream, of course. Loads of cream. And then it's really good. And she was so pretty! Her home so nice. Expensive paintings, real carpets, in short, style! I think I'll write a letter of introduction for you, in case you should get to Stockholm, then there'll be concerts and suppers. Would you like that?"

"I'd feel like a fish out of water."

Selma leaned over the desk and squinted at him.

"You know, I did, too. But when you're so famous, people don't notice. She *loved* me, she said, read things into my behavior which were never there. She interpreted everything as most profound, every flummery that jumped out of my mouth. It's just the passion for writing books I can't understand about her. Of course, she's never seen a croft, not even from the outside. A charming person, but are authors charming? No! Now I'll ring for the cake." Sidner nodded and pulled out Lund, Egon: *Still the Horse Dreams*.

"These pages we won't cut open. He'll get by just fine on his connections in Stockholm. Runs around the corridors of newspapers, friend of all the editors he can use. At my grave he'll say we had profound conversations. I, profound! You know, I've always had a hard time talking wittily. I've felt every word I've said was wrong. Like heavy sighs of stone… And that's what people say about me, too, isn't it, that I've been dreadfully boring? Don't flatter me now!"

"Well. Nobody has exactly said you're funny."

"That's how it is. And that's due to the fact that I *defend* myself when I talk. It's like questions attack me straight on. I never manage to play with the words, turn the questions around. Now it doesn't bother me. Now people listen to whatever rubbish I say."

The cook came in with the cake and coffee. There were also two small glasses on the tray.

"Hope it tastes good," she said, withdrawing as she curtsied.

"Well, yes, I'm sure it will," said Selma. "What book do you have there?"

"Malgren, Nils: *The Strong One*."

"Put it back as it is. It's the weak I want to rehabilitate, the weak inside us. If I've any ideology then it's been give this weakness a voice. Do you think there'll be war, boy?"

"I dream about it at night. I dream Mamma's alive and Papa's here and the planes come."

"It's you young who will suffer. In war children are so tenuously attached to life, like the apple blossoms out there in the garden."

"Are you afraid to die?"

"Strange boy, why do you ask that?"

"Because I believe I'm permitted to ask."

"If I could be allowed to die by an open window, on a day like this. Birds in the yard, murmuring water and someone to trust beside me... The birds I could find easily enough... but who could I...? Eat a little cake now."

"It's good."

"They *have* good things there at the New Café. Especially these princess cakes... but they can't be too sweet."

"What's it like to write a book?"

"Pooh, Sidner, one can't talk about pastries with you. You're not thinking..."

"I must become immortal."

"I'm the last to laugh at that. Perhaps it helps a few years."

"I have nothing else. I'm so bad at living. It's like there's a membrane between life and me. But when I take up my pain... I mean *pen*... then I imagine it will be heard right through life and up to... Am I ridiculous?"

"Of course, exactly like me."

Out in the yard the scraping of many feet was heard, whispering voices, then a sudden silence. Then, with clear girlish voices:

> *Out in our meadow where blueberries grow*
> *Come now, hearts' joy...*

Selma shivered and pulled her shawl tighter about herself.

If you want something of me, meet me there
Come roses and green sage, come, delightful sweet mint
Come now, hearts' joy.

"Excuse me, I have to go out on the balcony now and show myself. In the second verse, more or less. Give me my cane, please. It's touchingly kind of them, you know. But do you know how many 'Hearts' Joy' I've heard in my days? Although I have been quiet about that. I *am* pleased, yes, I am. Pleased and totally un-musical." Sidner stood inside the window, listening to the song and to a little girl who stepped forward and raised her voice:

"We from Molkom's Rural Domestic School beg to be allowed to bring our humble homage to Scandinavia's greatest poetess and thank you at the same time for all you have meant to us through your wonderful books and stories. Thank you."

"Thank you," he saw Selma wave. "Thank you, my children. Thank you, thank you." And while her waving and helplessness grew all the greater, she managed to back right into the room.

"That was just horrible," she sighed, sinking into her chair. "I don't have anything to say to them. Not a word."

"That was enough."

"Enough! Now they're standing with their mouths open, thinking of singing 'Oh, Värmeland.' And I disappear and the teacher tries to say, 'Now, sing. You must understand that she's old and tired, she probably doesn't have long to live. But sing, now. She's listening in there.' What were we talking about?"

"It doesn't matter."

"No, it does, too. You wanted to know what it's like to write a book. It's exhausting! It's like forcing yourself over a desert: long stretches without one single drop of water, without a tree to rest under. But then you come to an oasis: words pour out, every leaf opens, everything wants to become poetry. Listen, now they're singing out there! And the pen flies over the paper, you find your-self in a sort of tropic of the feelings. And just think how much one single person captures in her eyes, how loaded every one of her gestures is with the past, with an unknown future, and how painfully fragile the present is: like a pink linnea between two boulders in motion. It's that linnea you're photographing. Yes. And then that decision when the happiness over an idea has become work and anxiety: to choose from where you'll write. You can stand at a distance with binoculars, observing her, sweep back and forth over her world and have the whole panorama of which she is a very small part. You can shadow her from a distance of half a meter, and then it becomes another book. Or you can crawl into her, that is the most difficult, least restful perspective, because you can never abandon a person half created! You have to lean in toward that person's pounding heart and note the rhythm of her breathing, feel the flickering movements in her face. For that matter, I don't really know. I have no theories outside what I write. But when I write, then I *know*. Then I knew. Now it's a thing of the past, now we'll eat our cake and... a little glass of sherry? It's made from rosehips roasted in an oven. Have you smelled rosehips roasting in the oven? It's as if the whole of autumn lies on a baking sheet. We were out picking them last year, in September, Fanny and I. I'll never experience such a September again. You're taking care of her plants now, that's good."

"How long will she be gone?"

"Not much longer. She's a fragile person, Sidner."

Selma's hands shook when she raised her glass to her mouth. She was not able to conceal an unexpected weighty significance when she pronounced his name. Sidner looked at her and swallowed; it suddenly became hard to breathe.

"Perhaps I should continue... with the books now."

"No, you shouldn't, Sidner."

His name again. Something pointing directly in at him.

On the windowsill a titmouse could be heard.

"Do you like Fanny?"

He moved as far forward on his chair as he could.

"What do you mean?"

"Haven't you wondered why she went away so suddenly?"

"Of course I have! I hope nothing has happened to her?"

"Fanny has had a baby, Sidner."

"A baby! Fanny...? Why are you telling me this? Is that why I'm here?"

He fell on his knees and held his head in his hands.

"That's good, Sidner. Scream so you break the silence of this grave."

"Mine and Fanny's? But that isn't possible," he whispered, looking up at Selma, but Selma rocked herself, slowly fumbling for his head.

"But why hasn't she said anything? I'm an adult. She could well have..."

"She asked me to tell you so you'd have a chance to disappear. You can go your way, anywhere. If you do she'll never look for you."

"Does she want me... to disappear? I don't understand anything." Selma drew his head up in her lap and cradled him, caressing his hair.

"I'm so bad at such things... My hands have never done this before."

"Is it a boy or...?"

"It's a boy. He's two weeks old now. Is it awful when I stroke you?"

"No."

"She told me about the trip to Strömstad. How hurt or shocked she was over Sven Hedin... Yes, well, the little goose. Her contact with reality isn't what it ought to be. She's had so many dreams. She's afraid of everything real. Yes, *that* she's told me, but who can tell everything? As for me, the affairs of life go right by me."

She raised his head between her hands.

"Only Fanny and you and I know. But only Fanny and you are

involved, I'm not. Do you like her? Even though she's old enough to be your mother?"

"What am I going to do?"

"She's got the love child she has longed for. Now go to the piano. Play something for me. Anything. I've never been able to bear anyone looking at me when I cry."

TORIN WAS CONDEMNED to life: when he tried to hang himself the bar broke; when he tried sticking a fork into an artery the prison chaplain came for a visit – a bright, worthy minister, drunk on his soberness, who had only answers to give, answers that lay like boulders before the entrances to the chaotic tunnels of questions. Torin was sentenced to two months' hard labor, spring was in the air, and when he stood at the bars he could look down at the girls' school on the other side of the wall. During recesses slender-limbed students moved before his eyes; they continued to glide back and forth at night when he apathetically lay on his cot, staring at the ceiling, with a single burning question in his head: "How can anyone treat a person so? How Mr. Minister, is it possible? How Mr. Judge? How, God?" Now his dreams had been surgically removed, his future taken from him, the plug had been pulled out of its miserably mounted socket. Sometimes he had a dove on his windowsill: blue-gray feathers shimmering in the spring sun. They usually looked each other in the eye, and Torin wished he could think bird-like for one second. Be in another's brain, see the world in a different way: then that *How* would lie naked before him. Or would it cease?

A lawyer had visited him to talk about the Carina Zetterberg lawsuit. It was a matter of perjury in her case, he could get back his money if he signed several papers and answered when addressed. But Torin turned to the wall: "Money won't give my life back to me."

Even without my arrival on this earth – yes, I was now born and lay sucking at Fanny's breast – Sidner would have had a hard time lifting Torin out of his apathy. For a week Sidner had stood before the mirror observing his face thinking he noticed how he aged day by day; and he sat, he thought, like a broken man in Torin's cell.

"How can women treat someone like that, Torin!"

"My fellow sufferer. It's part of life that such things have to be done and said. We're blind, you know. We're just end products. Life's a disappointment."

"Is there something wrong with our family, Torin? Are you thinking of taking your life again?"

"It doesn't help. You have to eat it up further on. In another existence"

And they sighed heavily, both of them.

"Maybe it's nice to give up. To die and get away."

"Give *what* up, little brother? Gary was sort of a brat, but he was mine... I thought. It should have gone on that way. I'd rather live that lie than be changed into a life-like nothing. Without worries... such worries, there's nothing that can hold a person on an even keel. He was my only desire, brother."

"But how we let ourselves be lured!"

"Who's not lured, Sidner? What do you think ministers live on? Most of us swallow lies with an open mouth. Life is a penal colony. But I don't say anything about those lies. The truth isn't really so attractive. That life's a mystery is a good invention, so we have something to busy ourselves with. Children are the only thing that can lure us completely. Children don't beg to be born. Did I beg? What did I have to beg my way here for? Who have I been a joy to, other than the cats? How is it with them? What the hell does it matter? Has a single woman looked at me and had her heart beat faster?"

"But it isn't *so* hopeless, is it, Torin?" Sidner interrupted, because he would gladly talk himself, but Torin was not listening.

"Did my mother say: Listen, Torin, you're such a joy to me? No! Have I accomplished anything in life? Abolished slavery? No, brother, I make gravestones. There are many thoughts around that. Sitting there carving name after name. Fine little first names, skinny years. Good for you who only took a turn on this side of life, I usually think. For our birth we do penance, first through life, then through death, as Schopenhauer says. For twenty years I've carved in names and dates, put a period to their lives. People have laughed at me just as long, but children don't laugh."

"*I*'ve never laughed at you."

"You've never laughed at anything."

"Maybe *I* ought to take my life. All the people I've known disappear from me. The one single time I go to bed with a woman there's a baby! It would have been so fantastic if she had chosen... had me. I would have..."

"Yeah, yeah, yeah," Torin sighed, drumming the table with his fingers. The sun broke through the window and formed a cross. "You'll soon find a little honey pie. But me!"

"Is there anyone I should say hello to?"

"Give the cats a little cream for me. But for that matter" – and it was like a relief for Torin when he saw Sidner was leaving – "if you see Glorious Birgitta..."

AND NOW THE TALE of Glorious Birgitta must be told, she who would hold Torin hidden between her thighs for two weeks after being reached by a whisper from Sidner.

"Oh, Lord, so poor we were when I was a child. The only thing I owned was a tea tin. The house lay on flat land, and the fog was often thick as a quilt. I dreamed about creeping down under that quilt and playing hide-and-seek with other children, but there were none near enough to play with. And I didn't dare, either, because my old dad crept under that quilt like a reptile, over the fields on his way to Mamma's skirts on the porch. There must have been some kind of light in them – otherwise I don't understand why he wanted to come home. He was always drunk, wet in the crotch from piss, mouth full of snuff and blood, his eyes bunged up from fights in Arvika, oh, Lord, what misery. So I sat in my tree in the yard, pressing myself against the trunk, at least in the summer it was nice. I held the tea tin close to my eyes; it was round and shiny, and printed in capital letters was TEA FROM DARJEELING. There were four pictures on the tin: in the first I saw a rhinoceros standing in tall, yellow grass, and on the edge of the grass were half-naked people with spears. In the second a tall mountain rose with snow on its top. The sky was quite blue; yes, it was in all four pictures. In the third was a river plunging over cliffs; below, women washed clothes, spread them out on stones. In the fourth was a bird that shimmered expensively . The bird's one eye stared at me, and the nearer I brought my face to it, the warmer it got: I smelled the scent of tea and hay, and I closed my eyes and took off my clothes – they were dirty and needed washing – and I laid them below the waterfall, learned how to wash in the river. Afterward we drank

TEA FROM DARJEELING in the tall grass; the rhinoceroses watched and the blue bird shimmered in the air under the snow-clad mountains, oh, Lord, what joy. It was always summer in Darjeeling. The yards were full of roses and... marsh marigolds... the only flowers I knew at that time. A fire for the tea from Darjeeling, music for the tea, wind, eyes, mouths for the tea from Darjeeling! Do you want to know, Torin, if I was pretty? In Darjeeling I was very pretty. I was dressed in a loin cloth of reddest velvet and had tea blossoms in my hair, which hung down over my naked shoulders; I often laughed, only sometimes I became absolutely cold. For there in Darjeeling I also owned a tin: it was empty and black and had four pictures. In the first there was fog, and an old man with bunged-up eyes crept through the fog; in the second was a house, and in the door of the house a mother stood calling out into the darkness; in the third there was a road leading nowhere; and in the fourth an ugly girl sat in a tree: she was snotty-nosed and had swollen eyes because she was scared to death when she heard the sound of hands and knees approaching under the tree. Every sound was so distinct; the squelching when they sank down into the mud, the rustling when they fumbled their way over the fields, coming closer and closer to the tree. For that was true, that I really took off my clothes and sat with just a blanket around my body when I wanted to escape him. Believed that he couldn't reach me then.

"No doll, I had no teddy bear, just DARJEELING.

"No books, no words, just the backside of words, Torin.

"There in the middle of the flatland. And I took the flatland with me to school, the screams and the hands. They lay on the bench, they fumbled around me on the classroom floor.

"And one day, when he was sober, Papa caught sight of the tin and he said: 'Good, I need that.' 'It's mine,' I screamed. 'I need it to cook in,' he said and tore it from me, bored two holes in the upper edge so the gouge went right through the bird's eye. He slung a wire as a handle and disappeared out into the woods. Every time he came back it was all the sootier and blacker, soon you couldn't see at all what the pictures represented and I cried. Oh, Lord, now what's happening in DARJEELING, I wondered, but I couldn't reach it with my thoughts, and so I made myself ugly, both on the outside and on the inside. Head full of ugliness. Eyes full of ugliness when they saw him and when they saw my poor mamma; she never met their gaze.

"One night my old dad came home drunk; made a fire in the stove and collapsed in the kitchen bench. Toward morning Mamma discovered the kitchen was on fire; soon the whole house was in flames and it was impossible to wake Papa. For an hour Mamma worked at dragging that kitchen bench out while the flames beat about her. Inch by inch she managed to pull herself along, over the doorsill, down the porch and all the way to the flagpole. The lid of the bench was down because of the flames. Mamma herself had a wet cloth around her face, and sometimes she slapped it over the bench.

"How he had beaten her, Torin! What names he had called her! It broke her health and nearly her reason, that act, dragging her tormenter out to life. I stood completely still by the flagpole when she raised the lid: there he lay, sleeping, on his side, a smile in the corner of his mouth: 'The poor thing,' Mamma said. Then she collapsed on the gravel.

"But my old dad began stretching his arms, he woke up, blinked and got out of the bench. The house was burning, and at a distance we heard the fire department coming. He looked at Mamma, the house, the bench, measured with his eyes, then he shook his head: 'What the hell was the point of that?' he said.

"I assure you, Torin, that if I hadn't once seen my Darjeeling, the mountains, the waterfall and the grass, he would have sucked me to him and shut me up in his dejection. He looked at me, full of self-contempt, stretched a hand toward me, but I retreated. He wasn't going to have a chance to infect me more than he already had. That day I ran away. I don't know where I got the strength; it was a question of such small margins. I ran away with a big ballast of hate, of the infection of hate. I sold myself to get along but knew I must live until one day I had found that Darjeeling: a place where everything was clean. I must know that such a place exists. So many years and so many promises I've swallowed: all those mendacious princes who threw me on the rubbish heap and laughed behind my back afterward. So many glasses I've drunk! Torin, you know how those laughs sound, too, don't you?"

"Yes, I know." She laid her hand on his wrist and he did not move away. "But I'm nothing to have."

"We're not going to have each other. We're going to be. And we're going to search. So follow me to Darjeeling, Torin."

Four days before he was to be released, Torin's first disappearance occurred: in the classic way he filed the bars apart and let himself down with the help of a sheet. The warden was of the opinion that Torin was an idiot for not being patient. Now he had to institute an investigation, give an extended sentence and dig in the piles of paper again. If he found him.

That did not happen. After two weeks there was a knock at the prison gate and there he stood, that idiot, asking so politely to be allowed to be admitted to serve his sentence, which now could occur. In his hand he carried a paper bag and in the bag was a watercolor: a woodland pond, a great crested grebe in the reeds. It was a very bad watercolor, done in love and ignorance, and he let no one take it from him, but decorated his cell with it; lay there, smiling, with his hands over his head. Did not answer any questions regarding his whereabouts. And so it would continue year after year. Sometime in the middle of the summer he would get up from the gravestones, lay down his gouge and chisel in the shed and disappear without a word; and sometime later there he sat again. The only sign that he had been away was a new watercolor on the wall in his house. He was clean and smelled decent, even if that cleanliness did not last the whole year through.

"Have you started painting, Torin?"

"*It's none of your business,*" he answered in English, with a shrug of his shoulders.

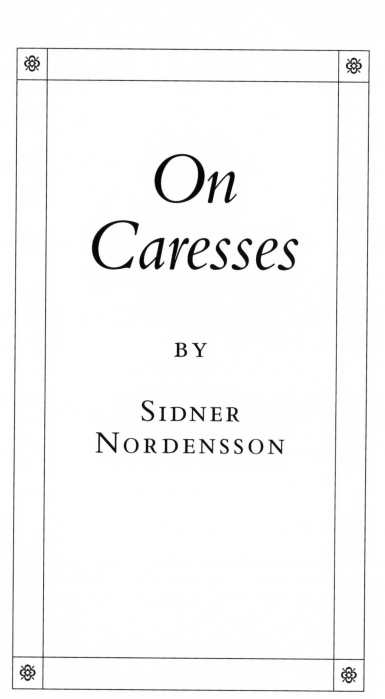

On Caresses

BY

SIDNER
NORDENSSON

THE UTTER helplessness of being alive tonight!

I am sitting by the open window in this kitchen where nothing smiles, before a black oilcloth-bound book, writing for the first time in ages, because I have known now for several days that somewhere I have a son. Who are you? And who am I? We have not yet seen each other. It gives me no joy that you exist; I myself have not yet been born to this life. Only when I *see* you will I know if we exist for each other. But you will have these words, if they turn out to be many; someday you will know who I was, and whether mine was a miserable life.

It is spring. I take long walks outside the village. I walk with my hands behind my back and tell myself that I am contemplating the world, but I am waiting for the Great Catastrophe. In the evenings I sit over books or at the grand piano in your mother's home where I water the flowers. She is the only woman I've known so far. She sought me, or else I was just near at hand.

(LATER)

Nothing passes as quickly as a Caress. But like a scent, a tone, a Caress is the only memory that you can take with you from life into death, because love's caresses are pure attentiveness. The whole body an eye, an ear, a tongue. You will ask: Why did my father love love more than life?

Ninety-five percent of my time goes to thinking about the Erotic. So much wasted energy! I have now lived 6,690 days and caressed perhaps six times, so statistically that is one caress every third year. However, all the caresses occurred at the same time.

Yes, I record my humiliations. I bequeath to you what is mine. To be nineteen years old and have only Fanny and God to choose between!

JUNE 2, 1939

I have seen you, my son.

You were already named, I came too late. A bitter meeting because rehearsed words seldom get said, if the rehearsal takes place without all the actors being present. I stood on the stairs of Fanny's house and wanted to say: "I want to see my son!" But that particular sentence was never spoken, for just then in the summer rain, in the crunching gravel, it was you who disturbed what I had chosen to make a solemn occasion. You cried, Victor – for that is your name – were hungry, needed changing. Fanny, the woman to whom I believed I now belonged since we had you in common, hurried by me through the open door and I was left standing out in the yard with a bag in my hand; I saw her skirts – dark violet – saw how they disappeared into the house. Something was lost, I was deeply humiliated. So I learned a lesson with which I can perhaps reconcile myself. I sat on the running board of the car, hiding my head in my hands. Why did she hurry by? When at last I took courage and went in, all my movements were the remaining wreckage of my conceived plan of action. The yet-unused tea cups, set the day before on the little parlor table, she had pushed together so the tablecloth was wrinkled; the sugar bowl had tipped over, and when I served the tea she did not touch it until it was cold as my heart. She nursed you, and I could not come close to her.

Is this what it is like to be an adult? When I asked if it really was my child, she started and answered: "Yes, but it's mine." So there was yet another distance to take in. A sonata I had thought to play for her lay on the piano, it was as if it flew away from my thinking hands. You lay at her breast, which I have only once held in my

238

hands. I could not leave. I could only remain. I saw how my body and my will began to part.

Only suffering with your arrival, Victor. To my "I have missed you so," she answered: "I am so much older than you." "What does that have to do with it?" I asked, and she answered: "So much. I don't want to see you extinguished by my increasing decrepitude." But she was blooming. Her skin was soft and smooth, newly created for you alone. Neither did I know if these replies hid plans for a new departure, a disappearance; now, writing in my kitchen, I still do not know. When you read this, you will know everything.

JUNE 10, 1939

Days, phrases:

"I am in hell, Fanny." "The child is mine, Sidner, for as long as I live. Then it is yours, if you want. If you don't want, there are others who could take care of him, that is how I have arranged it. I've been away a long time, thinking. If you want, we will make him rich and strong. You'll play the piano, I can knit. You'll take Victor with you on walks. We'll drink tea, and at night you'll go over to your place; I do not want you to live here. I want you to meet other women, I won't be jealous. My body's desire is so small, Victor gives me everything." "I've wanted to caress you, Fanny." "Every caress would complicate our life. Caresses do that. I don't own sufficient temperament to be interesting. But it can never die out between us, for the child's sake. Part of love consists of openness. If you and I lived together, then how would we be able to tell everything?"

What is a woman's breast? What is, then, the rounding of her belly? And her genitals, the hair around them, and that opening in which my fantasy always disappears. The enlightened know but have not taught me. And what is that time, then, that runs away while I think about the glistening pleasure of her parted legs and the thousand eyes of Her face?

❀

Tea, sandwiches, phrases:
"I dream so often of your breasts, Fanny." "Must I take a lover so you'll stop working yourself up? A substantial, reliable person who comes to me at night and leaves late in the day, so you have to knock when you visit?" "You're so different, Fanny." "Sidner, what do you have to compare with? I'm sensible now, sensible and slowly calculating. I like serenity, I'm not drowned by desires…" "You could teach me to be a good lover." "Mistakes are not all bad; they teach us so much."

"You're a person who waits, Sidner. It's hard for you to take initiative. I want to entice that side out of you. You take good care of the business, but it's a sort of death for you. You can do something more, you have greater possibilities than selling glue." "What is greater, what is less, Fanny?" "The greater is that which makes use of the whole person, which makes him strain to the utmost, all the way out to the corners of his personality. What do you care about business, really? You're not happy at all. You notice that you succeed without taxing those parts of you that really concern you, those levels where your weight lies: they're never stirred up. There are no eddies there. Dust settles, Sidner. Silt, like on a river bed." "What do you want me to do, then, Fanny?" "Listen to what you're saying! 'What do *you* want *me* to do?' It's not a question of what *I* want." "But I'll manage, Fanny." "Manage! You will not manage anything. You will *make* something of yourself. Manage! People like you deserve much more!"

Later: summer night. Took a regenerative and meaningless walk to Sundsberget, another through quiet streets and still another through a shapeless novel. The time is one minute to abandonment and still no night in view. Fanny is sitting over there on her balcony. Her flame flickers in the darkness, and you are her flame. Night closes about her white dress; perhaps she is listening to crickets. She is sitting so still. What does she whisper to you when she bends her neck? What does she teach you? What words trickle into your tiny ears? I, the ridiculous one, cannot sleep, for never have I, in the middle of the night, been so far from night as now. Never so many cups of coffee and dreams away! My son: no one touches me now, no one uses my body, no one knows there are kisses to collect here.

You have extinguished her idiosyncrasies. She is *sensible* now, as one becomes who has real eyes to meet, a harmless body to caress. Perhaps she believes yours was a virgin birth, that I was a breeze sweeping by like laburnum and swan; perhaps she believes you are the savior of the world and perhaps she is right, if she means that you have saved her from Fantasy, from Obsession and her hallucinations. She is sober and cheerless, says Sidner the Fox, gazing at her grapes.

JUNE 11, 1939

I am a paint salesman; that does not disturb me very much. The dream about caresses disturbs me. If you want to live, my son, live near women. It is neither good nor bad, but it is to live. All the tales life has to tell exist a millimeter, a second from their bosom.

But behind and beneath all that which is a woman: never forget that they have a name. In dread – the Name always approaches.

JUNE 14, 1939

Nature gives us two good things: Caresses and Music. But since everything strives toward unity, one day these things will join in a New Creation. But owing to my constitution I am compelled to experience much that is not music. It is an exile, a hardship, and a mistake, so I entertain a plan to locate pianos, organs, and grand pianos everywhere in nature, so music is always there at my disposal when I become afraid of people's words. However, I cannot afford that.

Security only exists on the inside of music, when the Other Thing seems to be denied me.

JUNE 17, 1939

How far into music can one go? Is it possible to remain in it and escape time? Played the organ two hours today with Mr. Jancke. He asked me if I did not want them to resume the *Christmas Oratorio,* even if it "isn't the same thing now as when Solveig was alive." He even said: "You have talent. You ought to go to Stockholm and study music." But I have to stay here until Papa returns. Must be here since I have you, Victor. Still, music means so much: only there am I present, there all the absent is present in me. From inside music, time seems to be a joke, a deception that serves some purpose, I do not know whose. To follow a cadence down through all its layers, times, states of mind… and then to be forced out…

JUNE 20, 1939

Boss Björk is dead. They say that in his last days, in the wash house where he had to move after the bankruptcy, he had nothing but his old ABC book to look at. Every evening – the Sauce Queen told me – he opened it, stared a long time at one letter until he completely forgot what it meant. When he had forgotten the last letter of the alphabet, he turned off the light and died, as empty and clean as when he was born.

In his days of hypocrisy at the hotel he said – according to the Sauce Queen – soon after Hjalmar Branting died: "Such a man

242

dies only once," even though he despised everything Branting stood for. "Wouldn't it be fitting to have a moment of silence for him?" Uncle Torin, who had recently begun to drink at the Hotel, answered: "He's hardly dead yet, you know. If there's going to be a memorial moment you ought to wait till you've forgotten a little more."

MIDSUMMER'S EVE, '39

God does not "exist." I believe in him.

Were he to "exist" he would be imprisoned in language and consequently our slave.

Were we to "exist" we would be imprisoned in our language. And we are, too.

As soon as I turn my dwarfish eyes to God, trying to define him, he disappears, becoming manifest everywhere he is not. His absence is the prerequisite for his existence. One can go on like this, and I do.

And I detest those who do not believe in God. There is enough emptiness in me to make roses wither. Enough screams to make the nights burst. Enough desire to allow myself to be killed in war.

But without God so many words must die: those that no longer find a footing. Now I have finished babbling about God. If the babble is to continue, he will have to do it in me. Meanwhile, I'll play études for you and Fanny.

MIDSUMMER DAY, 1939

Nothing new from the Universe!

The same out-going movements. Everything removes itself from everything. It grows dark between us. Nothing heard from Father, nothing from Splendid, and from Fanny a pitiful little smile, a sympathetic hand on my shoulder when I want to hold you in my arms. If only she had not put her hand there. She never lets me forget the fire. She maintains it with great cruel cunning. Today you smiled your first smile, it should have warmed me; but I know, of course, that whomever was present could have received it, and I was not really present. I watched awhile when she nursed you; afterward I rushed into music and closed off all my senses.

JULY 1, 1939

Sunday morning. Clear sky, light wind over the fields. Went over to Vitteby where the Tolstoyans live among the cherry trees. The Old One sat in the bower, his white beard gleaming. The women listened to him. He read from a book. An energetic Peace prevailed there for they are on the inside of belief: seen! And unseen I went by, inside a huge scream, having chosen to be among them. Someone had lost a mirror in the moss by the shore. My eye was caught by it, deep down I saw how my tears fell upward toward me.

JULY 5, 1939

A difficult letter has arrived for Papa from New Zealand, which I opened since nothing has been heard from him; after translating it with the help of a dictionary I have prayed to God that nothing bad has happened to him, and I transcribe it here so you will know everything, what it was like round your birth.

Dear Mr. Aron,

I am an old woman who writes these line to you, Mr. Aron, not in my own interest, but to ask without beating about the bush: Where have you gone, Mr. Aron? Are you alive or dead? Terrible things have happened here to our dear Tessa Schneideman and I fear, not for her senses because they have left her, but for her life; but I must take our misfortunes in the order in which the Lord has arranged them.

I do not know if Tessa has told you about me, but I am in the know about your relationship since she is a very lonely and isolated woman, as is the case in our area. I work in the post office and received your letters, which I then gave to Tessa and allowed her to read in my little private quarters behind the office, which seemed to be necessary because of her brother's wild temper. Therefore, I know everything, for she has cried with me, she has dreamt with me, together we have planned your arrival. So we both rejoiced and sewed clothes, came up with meals to offer you; yes, we were so happy that at last we reported everything to her brother, who became very furious. Perhaps there is no evil in him; there are long stories in every person, and some stories are gathered for malice. He turned his fury on me whom he regards as Satan's accomplice on earth, which God knows I have never wished to be.

On the determined date Tessa waited in my quarters and I went to the bus, because she was so agitated – and perhaps I should say immediately that agitation is of a special nature, so she really was not able to go; at the same time her face glowed with great ardor, so an ordinary man could not meet her without regarding her as a witch. I waited for three buses from Wellington, then called the shipping company on my own responsibility and found out the boat had arrived at the right time. It was very difficult to return, it was the most difficult walk in my life, Mr. Aron, because you were not with me. As now, as I write this, you still have not arrived.

Every day for a week, Mr. Aron, I managed to sustain a sort of expectation, but on the eighth day what I had long feared happened. Mr. Aron, it was as if Tessa laughed herself out of this world!

This letter was delayed so long because I no longer work in the post office but have moved to Wellington, since Tessa's brother's accusations increased so I had to keep myself hidden for a month; and here I have cried, not for my own sake, (those tears were finished long ago), but for Tessa who through you, Mr. Aron, hoped for so much of life. Her brother tried to lock her in, but I managed, with the help of friends, to get her moved to another farm. I visited her two times, I could not bear more. She no longer recognizes me. She smiles uninterruptedly, sings songs that are just terrible to hear and gathers what she calls bridal bouquets of weeds and sharp thistles that hurt her hands – and all that while she has degenerated in body and soul, no longer washes herself and has let her hair and nails grow. Every evening, my friends said, she sits by the radio listening to short wave and imagines she perceives messages from you, Mr. Aron, and all the reports are good. She knows you are on the way. But is that so? I am writing to Sweden, since that is the only address I have seen on the back of your envelopes. Send a telegram to the address below, just a word, so I know there is still hope for Tessa Schneideman!

Desperately yours,
Judith Winther

JULY 22, 1939

Have not been able to sleep since the arrival of the letter from New Zealand. Found other letters from Tessa as well, which I read with great emotion. Felt great regret that Papa has hurt her so badly. Thought afterward that he was dead, too, thought then it was Mamma's death that made Papa poorly and not always in his right mind, thought after that about my hands pushing her bike off toward death. Had great anxiety over Johann Sebastian Bach, who wrote the music for which she died; and when at last I dreamed it was a bad mixture of people who crowded into the hotel corridor and were not allowed by the Boss to go into the dining room, since dinner "was not served." There was a Fair Mamma and a dark Tessa and Fanny, whose face I did not see; and I wanted to talk to them all, each one, but was not allowed because of Fanny who looked severely at me and loudly announced she had thrown me from her body, at which everyone turned their bodies away from me, so you, Victor, were the only one who still kept your eyes on me.

And I thought everything seen there you must have in you and suffer from, because you are a part of this day when I am writing, although you know nothing about it. On the first page of this book I thought I would record my Caresses so you would believe in life and love, but there have been very few caresses, although they are The Important Thing and more valuable than other things, such as Money and a Big House; but what is occurring now and is visible is Caresses' Reverse and cold shadow. Went to the Sauce Queen and helped her and Mrs. Jonsson make sandwiches because there was a funeral dinner – as a sign?

AUG. 20, 1939

PAPA IS DEAD!

Have been sort of in a trance, no thoughts but my dreams have been violent. Eva-Liisa has cried less than I, but many have been here offering condolences since the information came out through the Sauce Queen.

A letter came from Authority with a letter from the shipping company in Australia enclosed saying his clothes and possessions were on their way, but no body since he was seen jumping into the sea. My hand is like nothing and I cannot write more.

Later: It is a comfort to have women here, but it causes pain that Fanny does not come with you. But the Sauce Queen and Beryl Pingel are warm to cry with.

Sent off a telegram to Mrs. Winther in New Zealand. Before that reread Tessa's letters and was so deep in her that she was near, and when I wrote the telegram it turned out like this:

Father is dead. Letter follows. Aron.

SEPT. 20, 1939

Now we are alone in the world, Eva-Liisa and I. We have held hands for many days. She is so strong and pretty and works in the bakery where many customers see her. Have even been allowed to hold you in my arms. Fanny let me caress her hair and face, but as if she were very far away, looking at me with amazement.

What flickering flames we are. How easily darkness washes over us, extinguishing our lives. It is a wonder that we exist at all. A wonder that the only thing we have to oppose night and eternity is Caresses, most transient of all.

Did Papa *see* Eva-Liisa and me? No!!!! He withdrew to Mamma and left us. That is what he has done, God forgive me!

SEPT. 27, 1939

A knock at the door. It was Angela Mortens; she did not want to come in but gave me a bouquet of heather. I shuddered since she is in the Service of Death. Was quiet a long time while her eyes traveled over the lower parts of the apartment. Even had a book with her about marital love and its opposite by Swedenborg, and when I asked why she gave it to me, who was clearly in mourning, she answered with a strange smile that she'd brought it to read for comfort. And then a long silence until she said what I already knew, that the heather was in memory of *her* dead fiancé whose last name was Heather, and she would have been called Heather herself, and not Mortens, if the Lord had so chosen; and there was a little verse she had written, which I also knew, but she recited it in the doorway with her hands clasped together:

> *If only death had not you taken*
> *and me with suffering shaken*
> *my dear Kurt Heather*
> *you my heart's tether*
> *I would of late*
> *have been your mate.*

> *But in heaven we shall meet*
> *where wet shall become our cheek*
> *with many tears of love and gold*
> *For to you did I e'er hold*
> *in rain as in sun*
> *though I've been alone, but one*
> *Say, do you hear my voice to heaven's height*

where you sojourn in chastest delight,
An angel, I'll also be there soon,
bright on its stem, like flow'r in bloom
and wander shall I by your side
and even from the front abide
the beloved kiss for which I yearn
and for which even you, too, burn
my dear Kurt Heather
you my heart's tether.

Her lips trembled, then she finally sought my eyes, now when devotions were at an end and I had received her Sorrow, which lies fifty years in the past. When she had left, her picture pushed out my own and the Heather bouquet, which had been in many Houses of Mourning, now stood here. She had not allowed herself to forget, for she is afraid of life. I have prayed to God not to become like her, a Prisoner of Death.

Read the book and then had a dream so intense that I woke up screaming; Mamma and Papa were angels, but they did not let me come to them in Heaven where they could love in peace, and I had to be in the mire. It was probably caused by reading Angela Morten's book.

SEPT. 28, 1939

A lightning bolt of rage struck me over Papa going to death and leaving us. Have tried to pray myself away from it but am still as though illuminated inside.

Tessa has not received the diamond boat, which no one stole from Papa's coat lining; how, then, will she be able to love? This valuable must be delivered to her, but fear to send it such a long way and need it to contemplate the meeting between Papa and her that never occurred, since it is a meeting of hope. Let it hang over my bed every night so I can quite clearly see Papa hang it around her neck in a dark room, but it shines when they make love with one another, and perhaps the rage comes of this: that it was not I; a thought of vengeance has snuck in that now I will take her instead; she is not much older than I, and Fanny is, of course, much older, and therefore I am not afraid of age. Neither have I been able to pray away these thoughts, so there is a pile of impurities around me.

SEPTEMBER 29

It is necessary when one is in great Sorrow to read Swedenborg, because there one learns to believe this life is an illusion and has its counterpart in the *Spiritual*. It is a comfort to know that errors will be put straight in the Spiritual, with respect to the women I wrong, not from malice, but from despair. And it is a great comfort to learn that the Desire to seduce virgins is not a desire to violate maidens, nor a desire to rape, but is a distinct and particular thing unto itself. It exists, writes S, particularly in the deceitful. "Women, who appear to them as innocents, are the ones who consider whoredom's evil as an appallingly grave sin, and who strive after chastity as well as piety. In the domain of the Catholic religion, cloistered maidens are such; while they believe these above all others to be pious virgins, they regard them as their lust's delicacies and dainties."

To this is to be added that nuns and other pious women very seldom, indeed, reserve rooms in a Hotel, and many such meetings have occurred only in the imagination. Do I commit sins against Imaginary Females who do not have names, and hardly faces, but are like immaculate bodies – those I do not think I violate, but carefully and tenderly caress, both in the flesh as well as the Spirit? And if sometimes they take the features of Real Females whom I have glimpsed in the corridor and dining room – even such as are together with spouses and have Children – and they do not know about the Fire which their out-flowing traits give me?

When at night I receive them, and to me they do not seem to be some kind of scum-like pleasures, but surround me with Light while we hold each other wet in each other's fluids, do I have the right, then, to play in the House of the Lord of a morning?

Often I imagine that to be able to raise oneself Upward one must be in the flesh a certain time, since otherwise no heightening is possible. And concerning these (real) Females' breasts, which I have many opportunities to contemplate on weekends when I serve drinks and sandwiches in the Dining Room, they instill only bliss and Peace and no Destruction in my thoughts, yes, such a Peace that often I become as if petrified and must be roused from a trance by the Sauce Queen. But from talk I understand that is not Proper Contemplation, and I am honestly trying to dispose of it, which hardly allows itself to happen since I do not, in a real sense, understand.

With reading S, who is a solace to me with respect to my Sorrow, it is this way for me: his descriptions of the displeasure of lecherous love only awaken in me a desire for that – when he very thoroughly describes all sorts of odors and "whorishness" – which not only affords pleasure, but nonetheless belongs to this world. And I myself do not do it since everything becomes, as it were, White and Weak and without Odors and Tastes, so I feel, in that respect, like a man of Thought, an observer of language and ideas who, undisturbed by the flesh, can run here and there without being knocked over by the Unexpected. Those men who are called philosophers have many thoughts which appeal to me like Music, but are altogether without smell and touch, and therefore no Help to me; and I think, in that respect, that I am also enclosed in a globe of glass.

And when in that globe of Glass it is completely still and everything Without Impatience, since no Children run around there throwing pot lids and breaking Wind, but everything is an observing of what is inside the Head, one can think out lengthy opinions about life and freedom of will and other assertions, creating one's own world altogether, which however Genuine and Valid is indebted to those who live outside the Glass in the bodily, landing them in much suffering, since the creative appears to them as something Elevated and Pure, which is the equivalent of Rest and Sleep for those who constantly live in Broken Wind and Rolling Pot Lids.

And were I now to tell you, Victor, what Love is, I do not know other than through "general conversation," but I know she exists and it is good, no doubt, because ignorance is as important to mankind as water. She is there, letting herself be perceived in all the finest parts of the Bodily, it is perceived: in sex, and sex is here taken as the whole skin encompassing our bodies, where it is thick and sort of leather-like as well as in the most skinless part, which is its implement and our greatest strength, the tower around which the thoughts of our Bodily heads fly like birds, for of flesh are we and according to the nature of flesh we have a happy or sad attitude toward life, which is revealed in our eyes and in our speech. Of that which we see we create our belief and of our belief we then create Ideologies: and in that way our ideologies are analogous to our sex's way of approaching the world, so that sex, which from the beginning has learned to caress and be caressed, never thinks conservative thoughts like the Boss where distance and lack of encounters have made sex's imagination a loneliness which is conquering and aggressive, where liberal thoughts cannot result, for love is encounters and encounters do not arise in *one* who is Separate. And therefore I walk in the halls and dining room of the hotel, because sex draws me there; and my so-called Friendliness, my Helpfulness and Desire in the corporeal is the need of Females who exist there in abundant quantities, so there are pools of glittering sunlight in the rooms and at the tables; and Hands are there which apparently unintentionally brush against my body, and Breasts are there which breathe calmly and quietly and give Warmth, and steps are heard and little laughs trickle behind doors which are not always closed but sometimes, as if from forgetfulness, are half-open so a great tension exists, and I walk like a Spider in the threads of its web, stretched between two bushes, shining with morning Dew.

But do not understand that I compare myself to that Spider, ready to cast myself over Females, but understand it as Tension. But so the whole truth will be grasped it must be added that even an abundant quantity of Businessmen comes there, and it gets sort of dark and raucous in the corridors and the Laughs are full of sludge so the web breaks and becomes slack, because Businessmen have an elegant exterior which flakes off, like newsprint around barbecued whitefish, since there is no morality in the Business World, and they who go in for business are impure for the reason that their hearts are exchanged for Goods, and their sex, too; and they entice many destitute women to themselves and socialize so there is a sort of stench around their rooms, because they use Alcohol when they do not want to look the Females in the eye, since Deceit is already there. I know that from my own observations when many of the Females return asking for False Names when they have ended up in a Family Way; also from many memories of Aversion to cleaning such rooms, because Shame has followed the Businessman like a creeping snake, which emanates from his eyes in the Morning when he returns the key and has his eyes obliquely backward and his voice is as if couching in a festering hole of his mouth and Frogs hop out onto the Reception Desk, which we recently had the carpenter, Mr. Tillman, make for the price of one hundred kronor.

But often enough Fair Females are here and then I do not say I am a Businessman since I only *manage* the store and have no

Interest there, or honestly expressed: I do not want to Touch my daily Activity with one word, but instead tell about my longing for a richer life, sort of purposelessly, while I, for example, stand on the bedside table drawn up to the window to fix the blind which has fallen down "with a crash," which is one of the chores I sometimes assist with, although she had two Clinging Children, one of which cried.

But even the Sauce Queen inspires Love in me, and which, it follows, is Pure because she is big and fat and walks leaning forward severely, because her bottom is enormous and so is her bosom, and right between Brown Sauce and a White Sauce for the fish she hugs me against herself so my breath almost leaves me, like I am her child, she says that, too: "My little Sidner, how big you've gotten," and then I try to rest my head so close to the Great Warmth and answer nothing so the Moment will be long and everything Calm down, and I think without the white coat and linens and everything she has under there I could be enclosed between her breasts since she, as I have understood, is manless, only having her Sauces and the banging spoon and wisp, which she tastes from Morning until Evening, tasting, thinking about more salt or sugar; and I have thought much about her forgetting something in the kitchen in the evening, which I would find and take home to her, and she would say then that her bed is cold, but she does not wear Glasses and that is, of course, what one usually forgets.

LATER, THE SAME EVENING

I have thought sex's thoughts about Lell-Märta, too, when she has come into the kitchen in the mornings with everything that belongs to the woods: wild mushrooms, lingonberries, wild raspberries, birch twigs, and bouquets of wild flowers for the Dining

Room tables. Have then seen her walking completely alone in the
Mossy Countryside, yes I have occupied myself a lot with her in
my Imagination, since these fields, clefts and meadows are good
places for lust, fragrant and sacred, mornings as well as evenings,
but perhaps most in the morning when no mosquitoes are there,
which I dread so that a single mosquito in a room prevents my
sleeping until it is dead. When Lell–Märta lets a single smile flow
from her when I am making sandwiches for a funeral or wedding,
I see – and I tell you this, my son, to appear honest in your senses
– how she has walked barefoot and with no underpants on, in the
lingon grounds more often than in mushroom woods, since
mushrooms grow, you know, under heavy trees which allow no
Sun through, with the exception of Field Mushrooms which are
found in abundance in open fields, but open fields are exposed to
everyone's eyes; so in my imagination she walks with no underpants and I have asked her, saying: "Since we have a big party
booked next week and we need a lot from the woods, perhaps I
could come help you collect and carry home, Lell–Märta," and
she would pass her hand over her forehead and raise it diagonally
upward, as she usually does, and laugh The Natural Laugh.
"Maybe that's not such a bad idea." And so those who work in the
kitchen will not think anything bad about it, adding: "It does
strain my arms, some."

And in the Morning I came on my bike: for a long time and in
silence we picked together, but I was a half step behind her when
she bent down among the Berries, her Legs were naked and there
was nothing up there, but my silence was so strong she turned
around, saying: "You're so quiet, Sidner," and I could not answer
because my throat was dry and my skin so overstrung on all my
body that inside there I could hardly breathe, and she laid a hand
on top of mine and I had my shirt off (because of the heat) and her
hand aimlessly glided up my arm and over my chest until we were
closely United and fell down on the soft moss and she who was
already without underpants pulled mine off so "we would be

equal" and took my sex in her hand and we then became one Flesh on The Holy Ground, and it was a beautiful day without clouds and no Mosquitoes or Wasps nor sharp stone nor other nuisances and for her that was as Nothing for it was a Sex Act of Little Sin but of Great Urgency.

But when my mouth is sealed with Dryness with reference to these things, like a washtub standing in the sun becoming filled with cracks, I have also thought of getting relief in my distress with the help of Glasses, since Glasses, as I have already pointed out, are things one forgets and I could procure a pair of not too strong ones since my sight is without deficiency, yes, on the contrary is quite strong, which is a superfluous gift of the Lord since there is so little for me to see, but I could locate them In Certain Places, as for example on a bedside table in the rooms of Fair Females or as if forgotten on dressing tables when at their request I have changed Light Bulbs which happens now and then, and inside the case my name and precise address over the hotel, and a little note sort of put away in it from some Woman who expresses her gratitude for Love and with Surprise describes the apartment "where you live in solitude in that big bed" or the like, indicating as well, with precise information the Emergency Exit Stairs' location and many possibilities to "steal into" her room without being discovered. But that cannot be done since the Regular Chambermaid is Greta Jonsson and she is a Baptist and has angry eyes which clearly means disappointment over everything that relates to her sex.

SEPT. 30

Said by the Sauce Queen concerning Lell-Märta that she was feeble in her head but not in her Body. Could not sleep for that reason.

Was a huge wedding with Bridesmaids just budding and many others in the initial stages of their womanhood. Fine fragrances. In my apartment at night heard someone whispering Come. But no one was in the wardrobe and no one outside the door.

Lay down again to sleep. Saw Lell-Märta dressed in white clothes. Trees tall and still. Removed from Lell-Märta the Holy blouse, which she let be done, since it happens in the dream and it only occurs there that I am in my Natural State. Was as if she had four eyes and tears came from my Kind Fingertips when they touched them.

OCT. 2, 1939

Have begun to cry constantly when I touch Softnesses, also at the sight of Doors, Gates, Electrical contacts when they are too Palpable. So even when I hear words of the Sauce Queen, also of the other Females in the kitchen because the Words stand by themselves in the room, wanting something of me, and I can answer them nothing, so I must go away to places where there are no words, but everywhere there is a great Throng of them, also of Such Words as were spoken long ago and they are in the way so I have to follow certain patterns which so far I have managed to hide at the Store but perhaps not at the hotel since they have asked me, especially the Sauce Queen who is a tremendous haven, how I feel and her eyes are so large that they even send Pain into me and I fear for my Senses when it is as if every room is soon completely filled with words so the tears remain like rain on the floors. Have nobody to talk to about that since Fanny, too, is as nobody and only is in the Child WHICH IS YOU and also sometimes when I get to touch you everything is Electric and can Explode and everything in Nature is heard as a Rumbling, like today when it is fall and a white rose dropped its petals, it was such a great pain to see them fall. Even tried to pray, but my words rushed away like

Clumsiness and Raucousness. It is good to have a Sister who comes to me and I see she is pretty, but I go into great Shame over my thoughts and cannot let her know them since she seems to be in Triviality and does not despise the Visible. Was in my bed when she came: "We're so worried, Sidner." Also said: "You shouldn't work so much, take some time off." Her words reached me from a great distance, cried all the same.

Saw Lell-Märta dressed in white clothes. She opened her blouse, showing her skin where there were cracks, and out of the cracks a golden resin emerged, which I tasted. It was like that over her whole body, arms as wells as legs and throat, and I did good then because her skin was completely calm. Awoke and when it was only a dream I began to cry because the taste was something never described.

When Lell-Märta's arrival day came I had decided in this manner: if she wore a White Blouse I would ask her about Following Along to the Woods; but she had on a Red Cardigan since the weather was cloudy.

When I walked to Sundsberget it came to me that the Universe was the same size as the Wardrobe but that *everything* was there and it was cramped and Piled Up and I had to stand still so nothing would fall, causing Chaos. It was in the middle of the road. A car came and had to stop when I did not dare move Outside to Emptiness. Was sharply spoken to and the voice made an opening, and Outside were all the same Things, but not Real.

Had the thought that that was Important.

That I have seen how everything is.

But must not talk since all words are Theirs and Stained.

Have had horrible dreams about a Wedding, I was in a room with the bridesmaids who had the Bodies of Virgins and the Eyes of Virgins, but all their mouths were The Female Genitals; and they danced around with great gravity since the genitals could not smile, but I called to Lell-Märta who, in my imagination, had her genitals in the Right Place, opposite Mine, and at last she came from the direction of a Tree with a quite normal mouth and Naked and she drove away the Bridesmaids and sank together with me so everything became correct and I woke up wet.

Saw words in the dream in the following way:

To be able to go	To be able to go
as Abraham	as Isaac
pure darkness	pure light
the son	the father

by the hand.

Such that I now know the Terms of Darkness and they are Our Life.

Was walking along Main Street when I was transformed into an Index Finger, but the size of a Thumb. At first experienced great joy since I had got rid of many difficult limbs turned in different directions, so now I could be ceaselessly a Pointing, and intended to go off to the Square where I ought to have been distinct. But then many people came around to have a look at me, and they all had furs and warm coats and woolen mittens so I suddenly felt my nakedness. The air was very cold and everyone's eyes were cold. Caused great excitement when everybody pointed at me and *not at what I pointed*. Tried repeatedly to wriggle the outermost part so they would be heedful of the direction but they laughed and looked all the more at me. Therefore wanted to die, but knew it was impossible since *nothing could point anymore*.

Furthermore, it came to me it was the *wrong* pointing since the direction ought to be inward where the spark exists, but it could not be done that I turn myself inside out.

All that I saw when I had my internal organs intact, but it was a long way out to the Visible. I was covered with nakedness.

Now it was not only laughter. Everybody's words were ugly and stained, the minister was angriest.

Loomed like a wall. Then help was given me to bounce away, but it did not go quickly. Their boots and shoes took longer steps and I was in a woods that creaked and scraped and had a strong feeling they would trample me in the dirt so the Pointing in the world would cease. Escaped in the Bridge Watchman's yard where I grew out of my nakedness like a mushroom rises from the soil, and it fell off me like a peel and I was again in my name and in all limbs and clothes which was good.

Met Mr. Persson, member of Parliament, and when he greeted me it kind of jumped out of my mouth:

"I'm going to build a house of music." Since he believed I spoke figuratively he seemed very enthusiastic, shook my hand and after that was gone.

A brain came rolling into the kitchen while we were there and it got quite cold from the door and among us in there since we had been talking and laughing a lot.

Had glasses and could snort and see right through things, I

threw a sandwich at it but had to be ashamed when the Sauce Queen and Mrs. Jonsson said they had seen nothing since they had their backs to it.

Disappeared under the sink where I searched and only found three hairs which I presented. Had strong electricity if one held them hanging down, a fine glow.

The Sauce Queen said that was "nothing" and the garbage bag "would do," but then "in a particular manner" found out they belonged to Mr. Holm whom I had not known before and he would come back the Same Way if I talked anymore.

Asked Lell-Märta to sing a Jubilate, which came out of my mouth without my knowledge since I heard it "afterward" when there was a great Silence in the Kitchen and she did not need Underpants when singing since I was thinking so intensely that they must come together, our Bodily lives, and it was as if I saw right through the material into her and it was hairy and dark and open and the Sauce Queen and Mrs. Jonsson sort of faded away and we were alone in the kitchen so I went "right up" to her and said ALL THE WORST WORDS IN A CLEAR VOICE without my Knowledge that they came and seized me about my middle forcing me down onto a chair where I felt like A BIG PENIS, entirely alone in the world and without Shame, but Great Sadness that no one ever touches me with what they have, but instead brewed horrible drinks saying I should quiet down but smelled only the odor of Lell-Märta so I thought to go to a window where I could jump out so everything would be over, but Mamma and Papa stood there and had clean clothes and then I collapsed on the floor maybe yesterday.

They say I violated Lell–Märta. Do not remember more than that the Sauce Queen held me in her arms and my scream went out through the windows. There was a doctor, a car trip and now I am among Lunatics, a Lunatic myself without mamma or papa.

What I want is to sleep.

They say, too, that a number of sandwiches with liverwurst and pickles as well as canape shells with smoked salmon went to waste during a struggle with Devils when they wanted me to lay hands on Lell–Märta under her skirts, but nothing but the attempt occurred since she had Pants, and it was not my fault but the state of my soul. I have slept much over a long period and received shocks which have cut off many memories, but the Keeper has said that now I am on my way toward a Morning, which he has expressed, so I am spryer and have spoken occasional words.

That I do not remember.

FEB. 5, 1940

Visit, made everything wrong!

It was Eva-Liisa and Splendid. Had flowers with them, chrysanthemums, and Splendid said: "Maybe flowers are silly, but I thought they might brighten things up a little bit," and Eva-Liisa said: "So we bought them," and in that way understood, when her words hooked into his words, that they were together and had Love, but wanted to say nothing since the words were so heavy. But saw that she was now out in the middle of Womanhood and she was more mature than I, and so pretty that it came out of my mouth: "Chrysanthemums are also blooms," which they did not

263

understand, but it had to do for the present; but the conversation went the wrong direction when Eva-Liisa asked what I meant, then I said, sort of angrily: "You're blooming yourself," although I had meant it as something good.

Even said other stupid things: "Blooms should be in water," so they would not see my lunacy.

Suddenly wanted to rake leaves or shovel snow in the yard when I saw their faces, or be in the pillow, which was smooth and clean, instead of those faces where there is all too much to see and become upset over. There were so many things to tell them, but I could say nothing and hid myself in the pillow, crying. Then felt their hands stroking my back and their hands approaching each other and gliding apart, approaching again so their fingertips brushed and held each other a moment, was glad my back was such a place for lovers to have their hands and fell asleep.

Best Nurse came to me later when I woke up and said: "What pretty flowers you've got, and such a pretty sister you have." Answered that she had such strong radiation because she was in love, but I was sorry I could not cope with people, not even those I liked best in all the world. Best Nurse said: "They are the ones who are hardest," added: "Because they remind you of so much." "Now I'm going to smooth your sheets so they'll be cool." "Cool sheets are nice," I said without being ashamed of such simple things to say.

FEB. 15, 1940

Have been in the park today, walked many times around the yard at the side of others, no leaves on the trees, no warmth in the air, I understand from this that a long time has passed. Have seen there are many of us idiots and idiot is Greek and means to be "peculiar," such as I am "peculiar" without connections to anyone else. It is restful to be an Idiot now when no one expects me to be Helping and Aware.

Often happens to me that I am not an Idiot but my head is completely Clear and Pure. Am afraid it will be noticed and I will be sent away from here. Like a seal sticking its head up above water – only seen pictures – my reason is above the surface. Quickly dive down again.

Because if I were out there now and dragged down by everything that is out there, it would be a hard fall.

The Salvation Army has sung for us in the dayroom. A pretty girl was there but left together with the others. Awoke a longing for Music. Does not exist here.

MARCH 7, 1940

Have had two visits from Eva-Liisa and Splendid. The one was not good since I had to go into the hall to erase their faces' radiation and talked very incoherently in *their* eyes, but it was as though I could not follow when they talked fast about Fanny, who sent greetings, and the baby, and everything became like a mush; and Eva-Liisa laid a pair of tears in my hand which were so heavy I sank under them, talking about boats I saw in them, as I believed with pleasure, when I sang: "ROW, row, row your boat."

Best Nurse was with me after their disappearance, which was sudden and without adieu. Best Nurse related Simple Things: about her going skiing in a Blue Ski Outfit with many pockets, has a coffee thermos and sandwiches, that "coffee smells so nice in the woods." Thought a long time about that in my sleep and awake, as if it was a Painting. She is so smooth in her style, and reassuring.

Yesterday's visit so successful! Stood at the window looking out at the park. Waxwings in numbers, melted snow. They came hand in hand, I waved and saw my hand, all the fingers, the sun shone on them, started to cry when I felt it belonged to me, and felt my body and my name and everything that has happened to me, saw outside myself and hugged them both long and hard when they came into the room, said I had so longed for them, which I had not known, asked them if they got embarrassed by my crying, but they did not at all. "I am very likely on the point of getting better," I said, which was true, and took both their hands, bringing them together in such a way that even my hands were included.

Asked them many things about Sunne. Have not *asked* before. Found out Splendid's papa was dead, too. That they wanted to get engaged and married, but not before I was healthy and could take part. Found out that you, Victor, have grown.

Wanted to take a walk and *see*. The icicles were long on the drainpipes so it was dangerous to walk. Walked between them. We threw snowballs at each other. Went outside the gates and had coffee with pastries at a café.

Such a happy day!

MARCH 13, 1940

The buildings are made of red brick. They are many and tall, with bars on the windows so we will not jump out of our lives, those They are responsible for. But I believe quite a lot of us *want* to live after we have come over to the Land of Morning.

Cry often, but the Doctor says that is good since "channels are opened again." At that point I thought of River Boats, rows of poplars along the banks, thought about Clean sheets and big Bread, open barns and cattle with dark eyes. Told that to the Doctor who said that now there was movement and Desire in me. Asked if I read "usually." Said that there is a library here. Great anxiety came over me since many books are Philosophy and Thinking and I do not want to think because it goes around in me and makes me completely white inside. Took Travel Books, but even that was a lot because the Words still touch me and find their way to Wounds that are open.

Snow and a great mildness in the air.

MARCH 17, 1940

Among all the voices talking in me, now and then I recognize my own. However, it is still so weak and weary and thoroughly tired from trying to make itself heard in the racket the others make I have sold myself to sleep and silence. Perhaps to be revenged on Fanny and on an even greater Mamma whose cradlesong has fallen silent and faded away. Fanny prepared a nest for me between her legs and arms, within her many fingers and toes. So many eyes a lover can have!

Yet once to learn the sincerity of one's fingertips; follow their movement along the endless coast of a woman.

APRIL 4, 1940

Everyone who has made baskets is not an idiot, but most idiots have made baskets, and in such number that I can imagine a wall of them running around the whole of Sweden. However, they are seldom seen in the market; perhaps we export them to foreign countries, that is to say, not We who make them, but They who have taken possession of our lives.

They who make up laws for this life.
They who say that Life is their Preserve
They who exploit us who live through no fault of our own
and go round in the world and understand only Bread
Only Water, only Love
and keep our mortality Alive.
We are Naked Questions and have no Wardrobes.
The Nurses smell of snow.

What myth shall I be dragged into now, I wondered when, cast out of the centrifuge of darkness, I stood outside the hospital's gates, still held fast by its umbilical cord, afraid to be off immediately too far away and too quickly, to be sucked immediately into life again, before I could manage to say Yes or No. I wanted to get to *see* myself, Victor. Wanted to play with possibilities, as if I owned a free will.

I stood there at the edge of the road, in the slushy snow, surprised that so much of Myself was left in the broth of thought after shocks, felt how my name closed about me.

To have been in a madhouse. What does that mean? How will it come to *color* me? What continents of words and concepts will rise over my surface like islands, occupying space, becoming visible as a part of my landscape? What if this having been a Madman is my *only* experience, so that at fifty years of age I am still telling the same story!

Am sitting in a café writing this. Released! Only a future remains. Only adult life. Drink tea, morning comes, I am waiting for a train. Still see the grounds around the hospital where I have gone through the winter, see the fellow beings who will soon sink away from my consciousness; new conversations, new visual impressions will silt them over, like jungle growth covering over a temple in tropical regions. Where does the hospital go? Will it sink deeper down into me or evaporate out into the air. I believe: it is going to sink so that every conversation henceforth will rest on *the stratum of the hospital* and take color, like litmus paper. Am afraid to leave this point, this café, before I *know* for sure. Have ordered two more cheese sandwiches. There are other trains.

I have sat here an hour now (maybe it will be several), because I feel a need to remember this winter in my soul so its meaning, great or small, is constantly near. When I close my eyes I see the black gate where I stood an hour ago, hesitating. On the inside: permissiveness, a proper sort of idiocy. On the outside: the demand and decision of every step. Am I ready for them? We shall see; one day, Victor, *you* will know.

There is so much I would like to describe from in there. The doctor told me I certainly would not need to be afraid of becoming emotionally disturbed in a real sense, but I could expect periods of hypersensitivity. I am not afraid. I know what it means "when the darkness closes around one," as it now has closed around Europe. There is a world in the darkness, too. Also, encounters and dreams occur in there, of which some are exquisite entertainment.

The morning sun is here now; it is lighting up the way that leads between the black gates and away through the park. Puddles sparkle, someone opens a window in the corridor on the second floor where my body has sat, heavy and apathetic, where my hands have lain without wanting anything. Yes, the light is here, and how gladly did I want the rest of my life to be a single describing of *light,* as I once long ago experienced it in the curve of a road: it was a summer evening then, the sun's rays oblique over the green fields, I was sad and alone. Then suddenly it happened that a Warmth, which was Present everywhere, went right through my body. In the leaves, in the grain. I was as transparent as Music. I was an Adagio. I was one of the notes, an essential part of the piece which was being played, and when the grass and trees bent down I knew there was someone who travelled with light fingers over everything living, like over a keyboard. I was played, Victor.

Far away over the mountains, over the lake and the groves

where cows and horses walked, someone fiddled forth a wonderful composition, and all things visible and anticipated and dreamed were equally important elements. This happened long ago, on the other side of the Madhouse purgatory, but that which occurred was Remaining! With long pauses it has been struck up anew, so not always, but often enough, I have known how it sounds. Also, when I fled into the toilets over there, tore up rolls of paper and threw them around me, also when I bit the Keeper on the wrist when I was bound fast to the shock table, also when the doctor blew sickeningly sweet cigar smoke into my face and I did not have the strength to protest, I must have heard it deep inside me.

Can it be seen on me that I have been in the Madhouse? Did the café customers who left just now look in that special manner? I, of course, have my own clothes now – can they hide my Reality? In that case: it does not matter to me. I am not afraid. I shall take the next train here from Kristinehamn and go home. Via telephone the Sauce Queen has promised me apple cake with vanilla sauce in the kitchen, and I shall let her clasp me to her big Bosom, without it meaning anything other than happiness.

(ON THE TRAIN HOME)

There are many remaining down in Kristinehamn, looking out over the trees in the park, and some will remain until their deaths, for they have nothing to return to and, therefore, do not want to make themselves better in spirit. Old Årjäng with his red hands owns a little cottage but no longer has any work as he does not dare show himself to anyone since "it shows on ya that yer marked." The young boy from Sörbyn who killed somebody and had lost his speech, so he talked in unintelligible syllables. The stooped Ekvall from Väse who lived on squirrels and had a cat with him as spare food when he dragged through the woods, because people wanted to do him ill and did not allow him to be "seen by any house." The senior accountant who pretended to be at a Hotel and had his own room with paintings and books and who did not speak to those who "drank pilsner," but mentioned to me he planned to travel to London "as soon as the weather gets somewhat better," since he had something "important to report to the English concerning the war and its conclusion."

MAY 20, 1940

Today fumitory and blue scilla peek up out of the earth. Celandine gleaming yellow and the tender stinging nettle from which Eva-Liisa has made soup. Rhubarb buds, too: like periscopes out of the underworld, they stick up, looking around, as I look around myself and discover the world exists. That so many things are left to be seen.

Yes, there are things to remember, for they are overclouded with names like "fumitory," "stinging nettle," "paving stone." Have even burned grass in Sleipner's yard. We were all together tending the fire, which darted between the naked apple trees, however superficially, so only the dry burned and under it: green. Afterward we were invited to pastries and coffee by Beryl Pingel in the yard furniture, which had been carried out. Everyone's face was Real and had many expressions which I thought never to have seen. There was both concern over the war, grief in our hearts and joy over "warm weather being on the way." Was even real that we were of the same family. It amazed me we could talk as we did with such simple words, and these words existed even for me..

MAY 27, 1940

The hazel hanging along the shore was yellow. There was a smile in me when I at last saw what everyone had always seen. As if I were the last on the whole earth to receive this knowledge, but the important thing is that it was the first time for me. The water is blue and sparkling. It was offered to me. Had a Plant Book with me, looked up and learned anew many plants such as: Plantain, Taraxacum vulgare. My eyes were new. Everything intense.

Spring sun, melting snow on all the roads. Instead of "squeezing out" a smile, I smile. I am Someone and I have a "right" to be in the World. As if before I existed "behind" the looking, like a spy who never left me in peace.

JUNE 1940

"I have today ascended the highest mountain in these climes which, not without reason, bears the name Ventosum (that means 'Mountain of the Winds'), driven by the longing to experience what such a tremendously high outlook could have to offer my eyes. For several years I have often had this journey in my thoughts. As you know, I have lived in these regions ever since my childhood: destiny has so ordained it. Almost constantly I have had that mountain, visible far and wide, before my eyes."

So wrote a certain Francesco Petrarca on April 26, 1335, to a certain shop assistant who, for the first time today, received that letter where he lay stretched out with a book in the woods, on a hillside full of the bitter vetch's bluish violet hues. His bicycle was leaning against a fir that exhaled resin, the bike's bag was packed with a thermos of coffee and sandwiches, a gift from the high, noble Sauce Queen, and a little volume with the mentioned letters of Petrarch. Oh, a pleasure to be in the Superficial! Out! Free! to have as one's task "to dispel the darkness," "to complete the body's Middle Ages, the Black Death of the senses," which have ruled his body for a long time. The birches are newly in leaf, a Camberwell Beauty rises from its hiding place and shows itself to the shop assistant from every direction and angle. Yes, you are a beautiful butterfly! Everything is beautiful out here, for my eyes are new-born and unaffected. Where have I been my whole life! What shore have I climbed upon? As if I were the first in the world to *look around*. I am the discoverer of vistas, I am the shop assistant of my senses!

Yes, Victor, he is lying in the grass reading about the desire for vision, the caresses of the eye and the ear, he is feeling his limbs being born this day of Petrarch. Lilies of the valley stand farther away among the trees, their bells hidden by large green leaves, but they are ringing delicately and quietly for the very finest of our senses; we often bury them because of the great racket both from ourselves and the world. How seldom do we have time to listen to the delicate things! Or more correctly expressed: how seldom is the ability given to us. Therefore, the one who has been given that, if even in short moments, must be attentive, as if one were in love, and describe the Obvious: that the anthills have opened for the season, that the lark is here.

But are these obvious things? The shop assistant knows from his own experience one can live a long time in that grim work-house which is life, according to Petrarch, without being alive. Things then show only their terrifying depth. One is on the in-side and cannot reach out. Therefore, we must capture each day, capture the flower and tell ourselves that the oak leaf, which I reach if I stretch out my hand, has never been seen before. You are always the first and should notice it! Count up the days you have read the moss's writings on the boulder (how "obvious" that that script is there), because one day your eye has gone out or the legs which carried you here today have gone on strike, a fire has run over the surface of the stone, cold has broken it in two. Ask the shop assistant, he knows!

My friend Petrarch knows, too: "And while my brother, striving for the summit, was not timorous about making his way straight up the mountain's precipices, I tried to advance by easier side roads; and when he shouted at me, making me heedful that the way he kept to was the true one, I gave as answer that I thought it was easier to come up to the top on the other side and I gladly made a detour, if only it was comfortable. While he and the servants, too, made continual progress, striving upward, I played for time in useless wandering about in lower regions, without being able to find the more comfortable way up for which I hoped. Finally, I tired of that and remorsefully began again to work my way up the mountain. I found my brother fit and refreshed by a longer period of rest from waiting for me; myself, I was exhausted and ill-humored. For a while now I kept together with him, but it did not take long before I again, forgetful of my wanderings, got a desire to try a side track, which soon conveyed me into valleys where I discovered that I was merely led from my goal during my efforts to discover an evasion of that costly task of going up without curve or detour. However, the nature of things is unalterable and does not conform to human desires. The one who wants to ascend has to throw away all half measures and evasions; one cannot go up and go down at the same time."

Therefore, I now know one thing: my decision is made.

Victor! You are still a child who would not remember me, if I were to disappear. You were born into a world which is already guided by laws other than mine.

As soon as the war is over I must journey to New Zealand; it is a debt which will be paid by *our* family. And this book has been my conversation with you. Yesterday I took a walk with you, pushed the baby carriage along the churchyard wall, under the lindens. We looked for wild strawberry blossoms, I pointed out the horses inside the fence. I taught you to say Horse, Flower, Sidner. Fanny was glad when we came back with almond blossoms, did not allow me to caress her; she sees only you.

❋ VI ❋

"MRS. JUDITH WINTHER, I presume?"

The old lady held tightly to the door handle, her hands blue-veined and liver-spotted. She squinted at Sidner over the eyeglasses hanging down her nose and did not smile. He had dragged her out of a midday slumber, and he regretted he had not waited longer. After three days of telephoning Taihape – it had been a holiday – after three days of walking in Wellington, where he imagined he saw Tessa everywhere, after three bad nights when he bitterly regretted the whole insane trip here to New Zealand, he had at last found Mrs. Winther's address in the telephone book, called Tinakori Road repeatedly without getting an answer. After a much too early breakfast down at the Heidelberg Private with Mr. and Mrs. McPartland, who had helped him in every way, he walked aimlessly about the Botanical Gardens and tried to enjoy the sea of flowers and the greater sea far down below, a sea where Aron's eyes now were pearls. Eight years he had had his eyes directed at this point. He had written many letters in the final stages of the war, when his decision had become an obsession that made him see things near him more dimly, made his every day, in service at the border and later in the paint store, provisional. The dearth of answers had not dampened his belief that this trip would atone for the family's guilt. He was now twenty-seven years old, and his life had to manifest itself at last in a substantial act; and Tessa was his act's means of compulsion; through her the past would finally be sent off to be completed. A long series of events would be finished here, and afterward: freedom, strength, his own life.

"Dear Victor, I am writing this card from the other side of the earth. Farther away than this one cannot go. But I tell you this: in my thoughts I have been here for a long time, but now my thoughts are with you. When is one closest, then? The nearness of Body or Thought, which has the greatest significance? I do not know, but I know how endlessly distant a present body can be and how close a very distant one," he wrote on a bench in the Botanical Garden beside a bougainvillea bush and addressed the card to a point right between Fanny and Victor.

"Near and Distant are often not a question of distances but are attitudes. It is always exactly as far to God." And he continued on the back of a photograph of a steaming hot spring: "We are all made of the same dust. We are within and around each other. Our bodies are ideas, suggestions, concentrations. Our thoughts are our reality, and my thought 'now' forces itself into your thought 'now' when you read this. My thought has placed my body 'here long ago.' Victor, wherever I go from here I must draw near you!"

"I come from Sweden. I'm Aron's son, Sidner."

Mrs. Winther let go of the door handle and backed into the room.

"You shouldn't have come." She scrutinized him from head to toe, nodded, and made a gesture toward a chair in the room. She disappeared out into the kitchen; he heard her putting water on the stove. When at last she was back with a tray, a bundle of letters lay by the fresh white bread.

"You can take those," she said, pointing. They were Sidner's letters to Tessa. Mrs. Winther sank down on the sofa, straightened her glasses.

"Do you take milk? I've been with my sister for several days. Her husband is sick. It's his liver. I brought the bread home with me. For that matter, would you help me put up the window box? It fell down while I was gone. Too heavy for me to manage myself. If I call the superintendent it will take an eternally long time."

"Certainly."

"I have to replant the whole box. Now, whatever purpose that will serve at my age. But you have to allow yourself something pretty. If nothing else, it hides the view of the street a bit. But drink your tea first, there's no hurry. When you're this old there's no time at all. Although my sister doesn't agree with that. She counts the days her husband will live, she's convinced she'll die soon after him. But I wonder about that, they have children, you know. Grown, to be sure. I understand what I'm talking about interests you colossally."

Sidner looked up at her tired, ironic smile.

"The worst of it is, Mr. Sidner, that I don't have anything to tell you, because I suppose it's not for my sake you've traveled all the way here. Well, well. If you knew how I've cursed you. Or more accurately, your father. Mr. Aron!"

"I understand that, Mrs. Winther."

"If Tessa and he had… But it makes no difference. I'm not bitter, but I've never felt at home here in Wellington. I've hardly got to know a single person. It was in Taihape I was at home. In the country. Just to wash here in town! As easy as it is with the new machines. But it doesn't get *clean*. Too many cars and too much soot. Though it's worse in Auckland, they say."

"Where is she now? Is she alive?"

Mrs. Winther spread her arms.

"Perhaps it would have been better if I had returned your letters or written myself! But you must understand it took a long time for me to get on my feet. Because I was driven out! That's the only way to express it. My nerves were upset for a long time. If I hadn't had my sister. But I can't draw on her endlessly. And there's so much whining and talk about illness. Medicines here and there and what Dr. Farrell said that day and the day before that. Though I actually never believe he said anything, probably filled in what she wanted to hear. Because there's nothing to do for my brother-in-law. It'll be over soon. A couple months maybe. A little more tea?"

The only thing to do was drink until she had given him information, so he pushed his cup forward.

"You know, I think he should be in the hospital. But you can't talk to her."

"Did Tessa ever get to know Papa was dead?"

"I know nothing about that. I sent a telegram to my friends where she lived, I believe. Yes, I did. But, of course, no letter followed for a long time."

"I got sick myself. Was in the hospital quite awhile. And the war."

"Exactly. The war certainly gave you something else to think about. Even if we were spared on this island, there were many who went off to Europe and Australia and God knows where. The man in the family where Tessa lived was one of them. Trained as a pilot, went down over Germany, his wife and children moved, I don't know where. And Tessa! It's so long, you know, since all that happened, and for all that she was, of course, only one of my customers at the post office. I had many who came and went. Who had troubles, who tossed words over the counter, because it was gloomy there at home. One doesn't have enough for everybody."

"Her brother, then?"

"The war there, too. What I know. Do you think I could manage to be interested in such an evil person? Both he and Tessa are surely dead. Presumably she took her own life. I mean... didn't I write that she was totally changed? To a witch. Didn't I write that?"

"Oh, yes."

"It was dreadful. She had been so pretty. So refined." Mrs. Winther straightened herself. "Do you believe it's religion that makes people so wicked?"

"I don't know. Religion can appear to be so many things."

"Not here. Religion twists people, makes them narrow-minded and stingy. I'm glad I got away from those people. Perhaps it's better here in Wellington after all, the city is larger. Go away from here as fast as you can, young man."

"But I have to. There's a debt I must clear up."

"Talk!" The color of Mrs. Winther's cheeks heightened and her hands began to shake. "If it hadn't been your father, it would have been someone else. She was undoubtedly disposed to be ill. Of course, it had happened before, too, that she had had to submit to her brother. He was a devil. I believe it's religion, I do! Are you very religious in Sweden? It's a cold country, isn't it?

"We were afraid of the Japanese here. They never came as far as here, but we sent out numbers of men. Many died out on the islands, Fiji and at Nausori. I can imagine what kind of soldier he was, Tessa's brother. Perhaps he became a hero, whatever that means now. At last he could probably hit out unrestrainedly. That's probably what heros are: people who at last get to kill, which they've dreamed about all their lives. Many farms were empty. Tessa must certainly have inherited hers, I wonder who took care of it."

"Why do you think she's dead?"

Mrs. Winther folded her hands in her lap, looking at Sidner while her eyes grew:

"Otherwise, she would probably at least... My name is in the phone book."

THE GREEN SLOPES around the post office in Taihape were covered with short grass, sheep grazed along the sides of the hills, a rooster crowed from a farm up in the mountains, a tractor passed by on the main road. It was a clear and chilly day, the dew had not left the yard surrounding the post office.

The woman who worked there was young and smiled at Sidner as if they were acquainted, but Sidner could not respond to the smile, nervously looking around the whole time in case a witch should sneak in, barefoot and with dangling hair, hooked nails and dishevelled clothes. He expected to hear a song.

"I've only worked here a few months, hardly learned to know the folks in the area. There's nobody in our register by that name, either. Where do you come from?"

"From Sweden."

"Oh, do you think New Zealand is beautiful?"

"I just got here."

"To visit? It's a long trip."

"The longest you can make. Do you know who I could turn to?"

"Go down to Mr. Johnstone across the road. He's lived here his whole life. Except during the war, of course. Just the women were left then, I've heard."

"Excuse me if I'm disturbing you."

Mr. Johnstone half-rose from his chair; he was a man in his seventies, a harsh face, thick beard stubble, hard eyes.

"I'm looking for a woman, Tessa Schneideman, her brother was called Robert. I come from Sweden.

"Gothenberg," said Mr. Johnstone. "You weren't in the war."

"Luckily we escaped."

"But you let the Germans pass through. "

"We were forced."

"Forced!" he snorted. "We were the ones who had to take the punches. I was in Germany. Taken prisoner, released half a year ago." He pointed at his leg. It was a prosthesis. "A souvenir from those days. I'll tell you just from this vicinity, with five hundred people, twelve were in it, three survived, one of them that died was Robert. A devil for fighting. The village's biggest farmer. Did you know her?"

"I've never met her."

"Understand that; you're young, of course. Well, it was a damn shame for such a farm. Will you have something to drink?"

Sidner shook his head.

"That's good. I can hardly get out to the kitchen. Two thousand sheep he had before he enlisted. Well, that damn war."

"So the farm doesn't exist anymore?"

"Yes and no. Young folks from Wellington come here to make money. Probably know nothing about farming. She, Tessa, must have got a good deal of money for it, whatever she'd do with the money now."

"I'm afraid I don't understand."

Sidner balanced on the steps, but Johnstone did not invite him to come closer.

"It's no business of mine what you want to know about her for, but…" he made a gesture near his temple. "She went real nuts. Robert had a hell of a time with her. And then the war. He got hold of somebody who took care of the animals, but it wasn't the same, you know. If Tessa had been healthy, then she ought to have managed it. There were a lot of females who had to take over when their men went off. We were a hundred thousand strong! Fought on the islands, in Europe, to help out."

"I've read a bit…"

"Read," he snorted again, made a gesture toward the newspaper. "They write drivel and nonsense. Sit on their asses and make it up. No, you weren't in it."

"I served at the Norwegian border for two years."

"The border, yeah. That's not being in it. I fought." Pointed at his leg again, his pride, his identity. "You let the Germans…"

"You can't very well accuse *me* of that."

"No, no." But showed that he very well could, if he just wanted.

"Do you know where Tessa is now?"

"No, and it doesn't interest me either. Running around half-naked… We're respectable folk here in these parts. It wasn't fun for any of us to leave here for the war. But we did it voluntarily. Many of us. Robert didn't have it easy."

"Tell me what happened."

"What do you mean, tell!" Mr. Johnstone stared through the three times, the three horizons and ended up again in his eternal present. "You could never trust the Japs, though they said they wouldn't come here. But when they bombed Nausori, then we started to smell a rat. There were five of us that day taking the bus to Auckland. We were too old, they said, but we stuck to our guns. Then we came to England."

"I meant…"

"You who weren't a part of it can never understand. Only somebody who's been shot down by the Germans – or the Japs, too, as far as that goes – knows what it means to live, right?"

"Yes, but…"

It was as if Mr. Johnstone had been spurred on by Sidner's acknowledgement, he leaned forward. "Listen you, you, you're no damned thief, are you, even though you come from Sweden." He laughed self-consciously, as if he were joking. "Go inside the door there, in a cabinet to the left. There's a bottle of whisky there. Bring two glasses."

"I don't drink."

"Sure you do. All men drink. You staying somewhere?"

"I've rented a room up by the bus stop."

"Mrs. Finney. Bitch. But that probably only concerns us who live here. Now get the whiskey. There, now. Pour it. For yourself, too. Oh, no? No, you Swedes never want to be a part of it when its important. Like in Rotterdam. That was the fall of 'forty-three."

Not before darkness began to surround the glow of Mr. Johnstone's cigarette did he let his firm grip on Sidner's attention go.

"I have a pension because of this leg. Get by just fine, though that probably doesn't interest you."

"Oh, yes," said Sidner.

"It does not. You're only interested in Tessa. And I'll tell you something. She never did fit in here. Thought she was special. Read books. Poems!" he spat far out into the yard.

"Robert threw all that shit out after her when she… Cheers, Swede. But the sheep. Do you think she cared about them? Those fingers probably never really worked hard. Acted the grand lady. But damn fine-looking – before, anyway."

"Before what?"

"Sat down by the road and sang, ran around up here like a damn Maori and heard voices, damn."

Emptied his glass into the throat of darkness and repeated:

"Damn. Lucky they moved her so we didn't have to see the miserable thing. There was an old hag at the post office who took her farther up into the mountains, I don't know what happened then. Other than that the farm was sold when Robert was shot. Some broker in Wellington came here one day with those young dandies. Boswell, I believe it was. Boswell and Sons."

THREE DAYS LATER Sidner pushed open a church door in a residential area in Wellington and finally got in the lee of the fierce gale. Several people stood in groups on the floor, listening to the minister in the pulpit:

"And Herod decreed that all children under two should be registered for taxes. At that time there was a woman by the name of Mary who was with child, and since Joseph was registered in Bethlehem they made their way there to be enrolled."

"No, no, no," one of the men on the floor yelled.

The minister closed the book, climbed down and stationed himself to contemplate the pulpit with hands in his pockets: a moment's conversation followed, which Sidner could not understand, and then with several men's united strength the pulpit was moved farther out on the floor. Again the minister stood up there:

"And when Christmas Day arrived they had come to Bethlehem, and many people with them, so all lodging was occupied, and there was no place but a stable."

"No, that won't do," said a man who held a burnt-out pipe in his jaws while scratching his head. "We'll have to try it in this direction."

Sidner sat down in a pew, the pulpit approached him, and he ended up sitting right under it. The minister started again:

"And there were in an Eastern Country three wise men, and they saw a star in the heavens and decided to follow it; and they were Balthazar, Simon, and Josephat, and they were kings in this Eastern Country; and an angel said to them…"

"That sounds a little better now, although…"

The pulpit slid closer yet to Sidner.

"And they went into the stable to Mary and Joseph, and they had costly gifts of gold, frankincense and myrrh, and Mary rejoiced in her heart."

"Good. In any case when you talk so loud. Try another level."

"Let us pray," said the minister. "Our Father, which art in heaven, hallowed be Thy name, Thy Kingdom come, can you hear that, too? Thy will be done on earth as it is in heaven." Then he leaned over the railing.

"Do you hear me well, too?"

"Yes," said Sidner.

"When I pray, too? The Lord bless thee and keep thee, make His face, OK?" He raised his face out toward the congregation:

"So we'll nail the spot here, boys! Amen."

The man with the burnt-out pipe pulled a piece of chalk from his pocket and drew an outline around the fundament.

"Although it blocks the window, it's against the light."

"One can't have everything," said the minister, took out a comb and swept his hair back round his ears. He came down to the floor but stumbled over a paint can which turned over, splashing on his black trousers. "Hell's be... sorry." He looked around the sanctuary, quickly pulled off his trousers:

"Turpentine? Are there any rags?"

He sat down beside Sidner and began to rub his trousers.

"You didn't think there was too much reverberation?"

"It could be heard excellently."

"That reverberation is irritating. You have to talk so slowly and the echo is like... well, quite simply it's wrong. I haven't seen you before, do you belong to my flock, eh?"

"I was told by the porter in the parish office that you would be here, and I need help with something."

"Of course, of course, just let me get this spot off. Shouldn't work in this outfit. So, you think it'll be all right? We're doing a complete renovation of the church. We have a new organ, too. Fine sound, they say who understand that sort of thing."

"May I try it?"

"Oh, certainly! Yes, please. Everyone should be happy here."

Glory to God in the Highest
and peace on earth
to men of goodwill.

Sidner filled the church with his voice, which was strong and convincing. So long since he had used it! How it carried! In pure inspiration he continued with the Doxology. The minister stood beside him with his trousers and the turpentine rag in hand, but put them in his armpit and started applauding when Sidner turned off the power after a long and mighty fragment of a postlude by Bach.

"That wasn't bad at all. What language were you singing in?"

"Swedish."

"Aha. I thought as much. We should have a man like you in this church. Then there'd be a little pace to the playing. It sounds a little different with the nice lady we have, nothing wrong with her, but she isn't competent; the previous organist departed this life in the war."

He held his trousers out toward Sidner:

"Completely new. But you pay for your vanity. My name's Eliot, Stephen Eliot. Around Christmas we're going to dedicate this, the Lord's dwelling place. Do you think turpentine smells *good*?"

"That's balsa turpentine, you know, it has a fine smell. I've worked with paint and such things all my adult life."

"So you aren't some runaway organist, then?"

"I've substituted."

"Aha! And you need my help."

"It concerns a completely practical question. Doesn't have anything to do with the soul."

"You just think that. Can one be seen in these trousers? Yes, one can," he answered himself, pulled them on and showed the way out the door.

Pastor Stephen Eliot looked through parish registers:

"The broker was right. Here she is. Tessa moved here six years ago. Married a Charles Blake a year or so ago."

"That's not possible!"

"That's what's written here."

"See for yourself. Charles Blake and Tessa Schneideman. Live on Glenbervie Street. Then that was bad news I gave you. Do you love her?"

"I've never met her," Sidner said.

"Would you like tea or a glass of water?"

"It's such a long and difficult story," said Sidner. "Actually, it was my father who knew her, they corresponded – that was before the war – she and he had plans together, but he died and she, according to what I found out, couldn't stand the disappointment over their meeting not coming off, and went mad. I thought I could do something good," he continued, wiping off the halo, tearing his hair, his skin; it was so cold to be a skeleton!

A child stood in the door staring at him; he hid his head in his hands so as not to frighten the youngster.

"Mommy wants to know if you'll be gone this evening, too."

"Very likely I'll have to be. Come here and give me a hug."

"You're always gone."

"Tomorrow I'll be at home, I promise you. Run in and get a glass of water, please"

Sidner was embarrassed, and while the child was away to get the water he hurriedly put on his skin, his hair and a sort of smile that he was really uncertain was his own. Nothing fit, it had stretched out; his fingers did not fit the glove of skin.

"Do you have many children?"

"Three."

"I have one," said Sidner. "Eight years old."

"That's a sensitive age, too," said Stephen Eliot. "They're so full of curiosity. They *believe* in life, they believe in us grownups."

He went to the window and looked out, turned around suddenly toward Sidner.

"The age of belief is so damn short. Many never manage to live in it even the first months of their lives. Still, it's the most important period when one forms the foundations for the house that will become their lives. Children are like an egg lying trembling on the outermost edge of a step. Why are we so careless with children? Why do we so seldom give them time to *believe*? While they have the possibility? Before the heavy traffic breaks in and clouds the eye? Good, Paul," he interrupted himself, "Give the glass to him there. He comes from Sweden, do you know where that is?"

"On the other side of the world."

Sidner drank and it refreshed; it filled out the parched sack of skin's every recess, made it more pliable on the skeleton.

"I have a boy there, the same age as you."

"What's his name?

"Victor."

"What's his dog's name?"

"He doesn't have one. What's yours?"

"Winston. He's a poodle."

"Maybe I should give him one, then they could bark at each other right through the earth."

Sidner looked down in the wastebasket. Old newspapers, envelopes, several apple cores, an empty cigarette package. Two flies on the apple cores. A dish of apples was on the table, too; the table top was bright and clean, he found himself on the other side of the world and saw that here, too, a table stood on its legs, without falling out into space.

"What shall I do with myself now that you've turned this trip into a total fiasco? These last years have been built on false expectations, namely the expectation that she'd be crazy, too. Isn't that awful?"

"Life isn't static. She needn't be sensible, you know, just because she got married. Or did you come here to marry her? The basis for my being a minister is the same, perhaps: you want to help. Then people don't even need help, you stand there finding no new task. Well, the war. The war is excellent help for doubting ministers. To comfort widows, to hold hope alive while the battle for Europe continued. This evening I'm going to show slides from Crete. No soldiers in these photos, only ruins and shrubs and ethnology. An entertainer, a passer of time."

"She's 'betrayed' me by being normal. As if my own health has been dependent on her being sick. Oh, it's as if she's deceived me in the only thing I could be good for: to stand by her side and lead her up to the light. But where do you lead a person who's already there?"

"Then that's what you've thought of yourself?"

"That and nothing else. I have nothing to do among healthy people. *They* take care of me. What am I going to do?"

"Surely you've said this before. Without expecting an answer! You're going to go visit her, of course."

"You can't just come tramping into a person unannounced..."

"That depends on what you expect. You want your expectation to get a response. You fear she will be a part of you, as you are a part of her. And you hope it will be so. That's what I think," Stephen Eliot said and got up from his desk. He went over to the window and looked out at the sea.

"You're well off, you who can believe."

"Ah," said Stephen Eliot. "Religion isn't what people think."

"SHE'S OVER THERE!"

The hospital grounds were full of wheelchairs. He was used to them now; they met him on the promenades, they were in shadowy yards, in clusters on the sidewalks. The great war was over, but here it continued in nightmares and pain: for many of these invalids it would never end. Each and every one's story is always the greatest. Now it was morning and they were rolled out of the white buildings, out among the shady trees so the patients could be given an airing. Here were flower beds that were fragrant, there a pond and several ducks.

"She's the one on her knees over there!"

Halfway across he stopped. Now a sort of journey would end, eight years of waiting were over. There was an empty bench not far from her. He sat down to try to loosen his tongue from the roof of his mouth. After this conversation with her he would be forced to find a new goal for his life. A new journey, a new point. He had put off most of his decisions but promised Stephen Eliot to stay and play music in the church. That would give him a subsistence, time to travel around, time to think.

She was on her knees by one of the wheelchairs, feeding a patient. He could not see her face. Only the long, bare arm that now and then stretched toward the man's mouth. The patient had a bandage on his head: a turban hiding the memory of a catastrophe?

"Oh, Mr. Bly. Don't be difficult now. Open your mouth. You're not allowed to refuse to eat again. A little water."

"You're in such a hurry."

"There are several patients who need help."

Her knee, her profile. She turned her head in his direction. He started, as if he expected she would recognize him. He thought his glance pressed right through her skin.

It was not right to press into another person's life this way. He should go back to the boarding house and put the jewel in a letter. A few short words about the debt he had felt all these years. He could sign it with his address. If she wanted him to.

He was so close to her. And he shuddered. To stretch out his hand and touch her shoulder. At last to lay a bridge across a world of daydreams. Debt. Atone for his crime. Was it not really a sort of extortion he thought to engage in? Here I come with the love jewel. He remembered the first time he held it in his hand.

"Now I have nothing of me left here, everything is yours."

At the bureau in that room. The candles, and the diamond boat swinging in their warmth. The sand, the twigs, the fork.

The indecency! To observe her every detail like that. But with whose eyes was he seeing? With Aron's? With his own? And what does one's own eyes mean? Was it with the need's or the dream's? Was it with erotic eyes, with the child's, or the avenger's?

His fingertips tingled.

"Mr. Bly. Come on, now! A couple more spoonfuls. I have to hurry you along."

Suddenly she turned directly toward him. She did not smile. Her eyes bored into his, one moment, as if she were now conscious of his staring.

Heat waves quivered about her, her contours dissolved. Soon she would start to burn. All the words he had brought here with him swelled in his mouth and did not come over his lips. "May I have a little water?" She handed him a glass. Her wedding ring was enlarged through the water. The water put out the fire. Her nails were long and well cared for, a little down around the knuckles. "Thank you." He got up and quickly went away.

That night a fish swam around Sidner's head. It made small flicks of its tail, and the darkness eddied. She plucked with her mouth at his eyes and ears. He lay on his back with half-open mouth, and the fish found its way in, passing over the crowns of his teeth, with quiet meditation. It placed itself to rest with its mouth buried between tongue and palate. She stayed still on the quiet swell of his breathing, suddenly flicked her tail and disappeared through his throat, stroked along the walls of the arteries, gave him a smack on the heart so he woke up.

Many of the patients and visitors wore civilian clothes. He aroused no attention where he sat. Often he shared the bench with others. A man laid his crutches beside Sidner and told him he had been stationed in India. In Bombay. "I took care of provisions. There was terrible waste. Once a whole boat-load of ham came. It was unloaded and nobody came to get it. We patrolled around it, so the ham wouldn't be stolen. We rang. The telephone didn't work. The heat was intolerable, the ham rotted. Emaciated, wretched creatures came begging, we threatened to shoot them. It was hell to see, but what were we to do? The flies came. The rats. In the end we were forced to heave it all in the sea."

Sister Tessa was glimpsed among the trees, pushing a wheelchair. She walked quickly and with her head held high. Now what did that say? It said nothing. Possibly it said that she was a capable nurse who discharged all her duties. She laid a pillow behind a patient's head, held his hand, perhaps she took his pulse. The heat quivered about her. The crutches fell from the bench. A book. It was *Crime and Punishment*. "Have you read it?" Sidner nodded. Over there Sister Tessa also nodded, pulled the wheelchair in under a tree, then she nodded again and disappeared into the hospital building. Shadow and sunlight. "I avoided killing anyone," said his neighbor on the bench. "Those who have always say it's worst with the first. How was it with you?" "No, I didn't have to either." "What did you do?" "I was a cook. They didn't think I was good for anything else. I've been screwy in the head. Was in an asylum, but it wasn't bad." "Because you couldn't stand thinking about...?" "No, that was before the war. And I'm from

Sweden, we were never in it. If you'll forgive that." "Of course I do... I know a lot of people are furious at Sweden."

Tessa came back now with a tray filled with medicine. She went from patient to patient handing out tablets; she approached, saw Sidner, furrowed her brow, gave his neighbor a couple of pills. She bent over. Her jacket went far up her throat. "Unfortunately, you don't get anything. You don't belong to my ward." "I fall in love with every nurse. When they come close to me. Well, maybe not Sister Tessa. But the rest of them." "What's wrong with her, then?" "No, nothing wrong. But... No, I don't know. Besides, she's married to one of us cripples."

In the afternoon, tea was served. A wagon with big thermoses was rolled out and those who could walk helped those sitting still. The nurses drank tea, too; they assembled in groups on the stairs where they had a general view of the grounds. A doctor showed himself now and then. They moved about the stairs like a flock of chattering gulls... only Tessa...? No, should not imagine anything. She laughed, too: a gust passing quickly over her face. Sidner, who also drank tea – like one working his way into the state of a patient – should not imagine that she... that there was a crack there where he could force his way in.

Tessa finished about five. He followed her at a distance. She walked slower now when she was a civilian, her purse dangling from her arm. She stopped frequently to stare into a show window, still poor in goods, passing her hand over her hair with a quick movement. She ran an errand to a photo shop, through the window he saw her put several developed rolls of film in her purse. He wanted to see the pictures. To see *something* which belonged to her eyes. Did she have many friends and acquaintances? He never saw her visit anyone. Did that make her "possible?" Her apartment was on the second floor of an apartment building. One could see the sea even from the street. Once he was on the stairs: then a neighbor woman came out and said Mrs. Blake worked at the hospital all day. He did not need to go up... Loaded with provisions she disappears inside: what pictures meet her there?

She helps her husband out into the yard behind the house: he walks with crutches. She carries a camera and a tripod, places it before him. She strokes his hair, she disappears inside. The man points the camera up toward the clouds; they come in from the sea, they roll heavily over Wellington. The clouds change their appearance and form. They disperse, they draw together, their transience never ends. Birds pass by the camera lens, the man pulls a black cloth over his head, becomes one with the camera. Morning becomes afternoon, the wind makes the black cloth flutter. A woman on a balcony shakes a rug, the mailman arrives, crosses the lawn on his way to the next lot, he says hello to the cloth, the cloth does not answer. Perhaps a picture will reveal itself if one has patience. A fish cart stops, women come out their doors, the shining fish are lifted up, laid in baskets. Conversation, loud voices, soft, some of the fish struggle, the wind increases: that is not the picture. The days pass, Tessa Blake comes out and lifts the cloth, a quarrel...? A persuasive chat? Something about dinner or the Picture?

The days pass. The wind increases in strength, the sea heaves in, there are high waves now, it is gray, there is rain as well. Sidner stands by the corner of the house. Tessa Blake comes out, she supports her husband, he puts himself in order, she strokes his head, the days pass, the black cloth unites man and camera.

In the shadow of his new ignorance about Tessa – he could no longer comprehend her with his fantasies – Sidner felt a disquieting relief: there was time. For how he had feared the empty room after the meeting with Tessa Schneideman-Blake. What does one do afterward? Of course, grown up, free. The world open in every direction. He remembered the ice rinks at home where "the others" skated. Forward, backward, lifting one leg, pretending to be figure skaters, the girls imitating Sonja Henie. The meetings, laughter blowing like corn snow. For the dream of Solveig he had learned to play piano. For the dream of Fanny he had become a father. For the dream of Tessa he had learned English and ended up on the other side of the world. But behind these dreams? Had he ever lived on "his own terms?" No. But now he had a respite. He slept better at night and the lightning flashes from the windows of suicide became more distant, quieter. He was not ready to die. For this trip had been an invocation against death. To finish the "given" life's possibilities. Then: posthumousness. But the case of his life was not finished, the task not completed. Because she stood between him and death yet a while: here there was a lee! It was a question of not removing her.

"Who?" asked Stephen Eliot, plucking a light bulb from his mouth. They sat high up in the church tower, each on his own rafter, putting the lighting in order. It was blowing violently outside and the tower swayed. Stephen's cassock, which hung out over the rafter, made him look like a crow. Sidner fed wire to him while the flashlight, which hung several stories farther down, swung and swept its beam of light over the tower room's lower part. "Ah," he said. "Your *princesse lointaine?*"

"I don't know French. Do you have the screwdriver?" Stephen leaned forward over the rafter and handed it to him.

"Are you familiar with this song:

When the days are long in May
Fair to me are the songs of birds afar.
And when I am parted from her
I remember me of a love afar
And I go with a mind gloomy and so bowed down
That no song or white torn flower
Pleases me more than the winter's cold
Never more will I take joy of love
Unless it be of this love afar,
For a nobler and Fairer I know not of
In any place either near or far."

"That was pretty," Sidner shouted.

"It's disgusting," shouted Stephen. "There was a prince of Blaia, Jaufre Rudel, who sang that for *his* faraway princess, the lady who always says no. I detest that devotion, it's pure death. Do you imagine you're focusing on a living woman when you talk about that Tessa Blake? You're afraid of her wrinkles, her neuroses... Is she to be a person on the other side all the time? On the other side of life? Give me a little more wire! The farther away the stronger the desire, and you can deny everything that's near at hand. The distant! When I preach down there... down there," he repeated and, as it were, struck with his finger down into the depths of the tower room, "then it's like I want to vomit every time I borrow those symbols for remoteness. Make music of it! Yes, that's what I do, and hear how I transform every individual person into some sort of mistake in the presence of these worshippers of the distant, of the religious. It's deplorable. Because what's the result of that. Well, we *have* almost none. All created creatures become imperfect representatives for creation. The glorification of such ideas, of such a love, becomes, of course, only denial and asceticism and escape. May I have the screwdriver back? Love is a positive act: it is to give vigor to another. It is to set free what is petrified in stone, so you can see the soles of her feet dance, even if they dance away from you; but how many dare do that? How many lovers do you see? They're noticeable because their eyes sparkle!"

To take courage.

To separate himself from her at last. To dare grow to the point that "the others" were independent of him. To dare to lose in order to win something else: his own life. He wandered to the hospital again. He drank his tea with the other patients. Sister Tessa hurried from group to group. He must now step over a threshold, commit the act which finally would leave him alone. Muddle his way out of the nest of dependence. He sat on a bench under the trees. He looked at the trees "one last time before." Tessa Schneideman approached. Sidner said:

"Sister Tessa, would you sit here awhile?"

Her knee and his hand.

"You know my name?"

"Yes, Tessa Schneideman."

"You've followed me!"

"It hasn't been with evil intentions. I'd like to talk with you."

Her knee moved closer to his hand. He looked around and there was no rescue, neither in the trees nor in the clouds.

"I'm staying at the Heidelberg Private, I'm not a patient here."

"I've wondered about that."

"I have something to give you. Or rather, give back to you."

He took the jewel from his pocket and held it in front of her.

"I'm Sidner Nordensson, from Sweden. I'm Aron's son. Once…"

Her eyes suddenly widened.

"No," she said. "No, you are not." And she got up and ran away, throwing herself into the heap of nurses on the stairs, and disappeared.

IT WAS MANY hundred miles between New Zealand and Sweden, and yet the distance was nothing compared to the distance between Tessa Blake and Tessa Schneideman. She knocked at his door one day as he sat working. Sidner had really made an effort to try to forget her. Stephen Eliot had done his part by laying several tasks on him: his church would be Wellington's musical center. It was a question of getting money for music, attracting musicians, advertising for choir members. Together they made outings up country, visited the Maori district, fished for trout in the rivers, botanized in the (for Sidner) completely unknown flora. But Tessa's eyes were in the clouds over them.

Her body was in the shadow of birds gliding along the sides of mountains.

There are women who particularly attract us inside, and others who grow better in the open, writes Goethe about Friederike: her disposition and figure never appear so captivating as when she moves forward on a high footpath; the delight of her carriage seems to compete with the flower-adorned earth, the indestructible cheerfulness of her face with the blue sky. Tessa Schneideman had been an outdoors woman; Tessa Blake was not. She was actually ludicrous where she stood before him, twisting her purse between her fingers, dressed in a strict blue dress and with a little hat sitting at an angle on the well-arranged hair. In the role of nurse she functioned in a stream of continuous activities; as the homeward-bound, tired housewife, too: the professional gestures went to rest during the walks, replaced by others the closer to home she came. And he did not know if she, like Friederike, brought home with her "that refreshing ether," if there she "understood analyzing mistakes and effacing the impressions of small disagreeable circumstances."

But he did not believe so. He had seen her stop one day when he had followed her. It was a street corner about halfway between hospital and apartment. Her rapid pace ceased, she ended up standing by a fence plucking leaves from a hedge with red blossoms. She stretched out her hand, looked at something down in the nerves of the leaf, let it fall. She followed the falling leaf with her gaze until it had settled on the sidewalk. And it was nothing more. When she continued walking, when she had been sucked into the attractive force of the apartment, her step was much heavier.

That could, of course, mean anything at all. But Sidner had felt a strong desire to pick up that leaf, catch up with her and say: "Tessa Schneideman, tell me what you saw in the leaf," and throw himself over her just in that crack between two realities where she appeared so manifestly naked. In the same way he had dreamed many times of taking Fanny unawares. Between the hand and the intended gesture. Between the lip and the word.

This Tessa who now stood before him was a third Tessa: she had gathered together an identity of foreign particles and they did not suit her. They suited *him* poorly, for perhaps it was how she really was. He did not like the revelation, and she herself seemed not to feel at home in it: her eyes wandered about the room and her knuckles whitened over the purse's straps. She exerted herself to be unapproachable and cold; her voice did not have the nurse's professional buoyancy, nor (as he imagined) Mrs. Blake's weariness.

"You have a pleasant room."

"I'm quite satisfied."

"It's not too expensive either, is it?" She smiled self-consciously and walked over to the window, stood with her back to him. Sidner pushed aside his papers.

"May I offer you some tea?"

"No, thank you, I don't believe so."

"But you're not sure?"

"Fairly sure."

He got up and went toward her, stood just behind her back.

"Tessa Schneideman..."

"I came here to ask you not to interfere with my life. Whoever you are. There is no Tessa Schneideman any more." The silence was long. The averted face before him was still. It was not the sea rolling in toward the shore. A bird toiled between the winds. Sidner's hands wanted to move toward her shoulders, for that reason he walked away and sat on the bed. Somewhere in the house Mrs. McPartland was busy vacuuming. From the kitchen teacups were heard rattling.

"That was all... I had... to say."

Then she collected herself, turned toward him, knotted up her voice so it became shrill, floating out over the room like the bird in the storm:

"And I hope you'll respect that."

When she was halfway across the floor Sidner stood up.

"Tessa Blake, you are the shock of my life. That people can change so. I've read your letters many times."

"What letters?"

"Don't be silly. I haven't chosen to interfere with your life, I just wanted to give a thing back to you that belonged to you long ago."

"I don't want anything from you."

She sought for the door as one seeks a life buoy. But her eyes came back to him.

"For that matter, how did you find me?"

"Judith Winther would probably be happy to hear from you. She doesn't live far from here."

Tessa Blake tried to smile:

"And who's that?"

Sidner had never hit anyone before. Now he reacted all the way from his spinal marrow into his hand. It struck against her cheek. She staggered, then slowly raised her eyes toward him, turned toward the bed and lay down with her face in the scarlet spread. His hand stung. He still stood staring at it when he noticed she was crying. He sat down beside her.

"Forgive me," he said.

"Who's Judith Winther? Don't be angry! *Who* is she?"

"Don't you *know*, Tessa Schneideman?"

"I don't remember."

"But you know who I am?"

"You're... Yes, you're Aron's... son. I wrote letters... You were sad, you sat in a kitchen... Snow, there was much snow. I'm so tired – don't leave me... Judith Winther... she worked at the post office in Taihape... Is that her?"

"She's very old now."

"Does she know...?"

"She doesn't know where you are, or that you are..."

"I'm so tired... so tired."

Her voice died away, and he thought at first that she feigned. But when he had listened a long time to her even breathing he got a blanket and spread it over her. He let the hours pass in the armchair by the window. Just such sleep had streamed over him once when reality had pressed him into a much too little room. It had kept him as in a chrysalis during an indefinite time in the Madhouse. Mercy in the form of fog and escape. All the more threatening shapes and thoughts that surrounded him in every direction were dissolved, like tablets in a glass of water. An obscure piece of work had got its start in the inner regions. The spring afterwards became a curious time: it was as if he had crawled up on a beach. As if he stood there still dripping darkness. But with clear sight. In clean air. And the voices were distant. Like an orchestra rehearsing on the other side of a large body of water.

Tessa sat up with a start.

"Charles! Charles, where are you? Why am I here?"

Desperately she looked round the room; she got up and staggered over to the mirror.

"What are you luring me into?"

"Tessa!"

"I must go home to Charles. Oh, no, he's in the hospital…"

"Tessa! Mrs. Winther lives on Tinakori Road."

Why should he say that now!

"I mean, she…"

"And what would I say to her? What would we talk about? Relive old memories, perhaps. Is that what you want? Is that why?"

"Mrs. Winther had to move from Taihape for your sake, Tessa. If you're sorry…"

Tessa picked up her purse, straightened her dress jacket and yelled:

"She wouldn't like me anyway. As I am now. You understand that yourself, don't you…"

She tried to shatter the reflection in the mirror with her eyes and fled out the door.

And in her flight she dragged with her a whole row of days. Sidner sat in a room empty of air, without being able to move. But he did not know Tessa had really disappeared before she stood before him again. Another person, another voice.

I COULDN'T FIND my way home. I hate you, Sidner. I walked along the streets and came to the area where I lived, and suddenly couldn't remember what number was on the building. What the name of the street was. It's true. I was standing still, right in the eye of a storm. Everything was blank around me, there was nothing to remember, nothing. It lasted only a moment, but it was enough for me to see! That's why I hate you, because you came here. When I opened the door of *that* house and stood in the hall, in a sort of dream-time, a total black-out. There wasn't *anything* I knew with certainty was mine. Not a fingerprint, not a book that smelled of me. I tried to recall conversations, remember faces. Nothing, Sidner. So many years, and not one memory! The bedroom was as clean as in a furniture catalogue. The kitchen had covers on the stove's burners. Not a bread crumb on the counter, not even a trash bag that smelled. At last I turned and left. When I came to the beach it started to blow. My hat blew off. My shoes chafed and I kicked them out into the water. I remember I suddenly felt my purse and how I opened it, staring down at lipsticks and keys, at nail scissors, at I don't know what, but they were things that didn't tell me anything. I'm sure the water was happy to get them. Two days I walked along the shore. I slept and woke in an absolutely empty room; once I ran into a Maori family that lived on the beach, they were washing clothes, a child sat on the mother's back, she was washing clothes on a washboard, the child rocked up and down, up and down, and it was as if it were the first time for a long time I had seen a person move naturally, a person who did something with her body, and I ended up sitting there until they came and talked to me, gave me bread, spread a blanket over me. Over me? I didn't know who I was, the name Blake was fastened on me on one side like a kite, the name Schneideman hooked on another, but not visible, not to begin with… but then images came from out at sea, it blew hard, it struck against my face; Sidner, I'm so cold, may I lay down on your bed, I can't go to Charles, not now, he's worried, I'm sure. That he could stand me! Sometimes I've been so afraid he wouldn't. I've heard how I sound, how badly I puncture him. He's been so brave. "Love, you can certainly never get enough of that," he says. With a completely sincere laugh. No, for that matter, they were so untruthful, those laughs. How much love have I really given him? I start with fright every time he touches me. Stiffen in every muscle, lie still until it's over. He doesn't hurt me, he does nothing to me at all, but I've never asked him to come, never have I *wanted* him, wanted his hands or embrace, give me a blanket, Sidner, my hands have burnt out on his chest, I haven't allowed him to touch me between the legs, forbidden point after point of my body, what good have I done him? My speech has died away, well, it did that before I met him, my adjectives have gone out, my exclamations, it's dwindled so. What time is it?

"It's midnight."

"And I woke you. Lie down beside me, I can't let you sit there… I'm probably obliged to you, to undress."

"You don't owe me anything."

"It's not certain I'm naked even under my clothes. Give me a chance, Sidner, for God's sake."

"Who shall I give a chance?"

"All of me. The frozen Mrs. Blake and the lost Tessa Schneideman. It's not certain it will work, perhaps I can't love, give me a chance."

"I'll lie beside you. But I can't…?"

"Because of Charles?"

"Not any more."

"If we were to make love, would it perhaps be with him I was lying, in any case? I've never known any other man, you see. He doesn't bother me, he's good. Am I hateful? Wash the hatefulness off me."

He sat on the edge of the bed, freezing.

"Wasn't your hair dark, then… at that time…"

"Yes; is it important for your fantasy image?" She pulled him down to her.

"No," he said, "it's not."

But as if the gates of wrath were opened wide on their hinges and he saw he had arrived, and now it would happen: images of revenge came over him. Now, you, Aron, now I am committing the sin of sins. I am erasing you from the world.

"I'm terribly frightened, Sidner."

"Me, too," he mumbled. "There's so much that's in the way. It should have been my father who received you. He should have hung the jewel around your neck."

"What happened? Sidner, really, I remember nothing. He was on his way?"

"Yes. He jumped overboard somewhere on the way here, that's all I know. Maybe he didn't dare approach you."

"Judith Winthers wrote about me? Did she do that? Where does she live now? Is she bitter that she never heard from me?"

"I believe so; she had to quit her job because she helped you. She was persecuted, your brother and others… when you went crazy."

"Hold me in your arms."

"You and I: abandoned by the same person."

"I became so frightened when you came and said you were from Sweden. I recognized your name, but I didn't know what it meant. I've repressed everything, everything. Been afraid all these years that it would catch up with me again."

"Do you know what you wrote about the jewel when you sent it?"

"Yes, I think so, but it's vague, it's on the other side of that nightmare which is my past. I swore then I would never think about it. I've succeeded, but at the expense of…"

"Have you never even reread Papa's letters?"

She trembled, did not answer, but now that he was used to the dark he saw her eyes gleam; she pulled his arms tighter about her.

When Aron did not come. When she went home to Robert in her new dress. Was like a roar in her head. The rain soaked her. Dripping, she stood in the room and pulled out all the letters, her books. Read aloud for Robert:

> *My heart aches, and a drowsy numbness pains*
> *My sense, as though of hemlock I had drunk*
> *Or emptied some dull opiate to the drains*
> *One minute past, and Lethe-wards had sank:*
> *'tis not through envy of thy happy lost*
> *But being too happy in thine happiness –*

If it was the same day or not she could not recall. But there was rain. Robert took her letters, the books – he was drunk – he threw them out into the yard: "Here you have your goddamn trash." The rain was in torrential streams, he stomped them down into the mud with his boots. Keats, Shelley. She saw the pressed roses between the pages, and the boots saw them and tramped, tramped in the soft lines, and then it came like a flash of light in chaos: the laughter. At first far away like a timorous finger of winter where it lifts corners of the darkness, exposing a rose-colored twilight and the laughter gets out, it is tossed out into the wind, into the rain, it staggers through the weather, gropes over her, finds her openings and goes into veins in her heart in her throat and she lies on the ground with her hands around the books, her fingers down in the mud and there the laughter takes her completely, and Robert's boots meet her face, her breast, her abdomen. She does not dodge out of the way, but rolls in the soft, warm mud, eats it, rubs it in, tries to get up but Robert kicks her back, she falls to the

ground, her head cover falls off, she remembers that, her hair
snakes out in the mire. She hears nothing, she is so far into herself
she does not understand his gasped words, they are much too big,
they stretch out over the field, up toward the mountains, huge,
harsh words that cannot reach into her but pass by her exterior, it
would take a year to understand a single syllable, she thinks while
Robert tears off her underwear and taking the letters sticks them
into her crotch she faints she regains consciousness

To

She gets up, there is no one there in the yard, the house is dark
and the sky has gone away and left darkness, she walks out toward
the sheep, a jingle here another there, stumbles in a rabbit hole,
remains lying there it is not cold

YOU

in the sheep's coats there is warmth for her fingers blood lays
her cheek against sheep after sheep creeps between them pressing
cheek and breast up and feels the blood flowing there are stains on
each and every one of them she knows that she feels that

You GODDAMN

and the red-stained flee towards the hills but when dawn comes
she sees the blood there is blood enough for everyone it comes out
of her mouth from her arm from her breast falls with her arms
around an ewe here you have my red rose she says

WHORE

remains lying

LETTER FUCKING

until morning and a church bell down in the valley where once
her parents were buried does not move her. She can see Mrs.
Winther's post office the pain between her legs turns around opens
herself all the letters crumpled up in this month's blood

pulls out the rags nothing comes

CUNT

once he was a child at her side at a funeral held each other by
the hand which was cut off at the sawmill and all the years that

waking silence furtive glances from behind when she stands at the stove longing for her books longing for the school skirts of the same age down by the road the creeping evening hours the door she always locked around her the key in her belt and the mirror where she looked increasingly

IN VAIN

out and no God to share with someone the hymns she tried behind the barn when the church bells had rung and she thinks about hands holding books behind the barn by the hawkweed poor flowers when he is angry and is going to hit her and no one to flee to and crawls further in the rain with separated legs because of the pain finds her way to a well but there is none and then awakes at Mrs. Winther's in the flowery bed the doctor but she could not stop laughing.

When I heard Robert was dead I dared recover. I remember I went to a brook behind the house where I lived then (I believe it was with friends of Mrs. Winther). I washed, combed my hair, clipped my nails. It was a strange feeling: when someone came I made myself dirty again: I was afraid of having to take any responsibility, but I had begun to see and develop a sort of strategy for annihilation. One day I went away, put up at a hotel, bought clothes, went to the hairdresser, colored my hair, bought makeup – for the first time in my life – sat at a mirror and painted *over* Tessa Schneideman. It was a tough job, there were so many possibilities to test. The shape of the eyebrows, the appearance of the lips, color of the skin. Hand gestures. I sat in a restaurant observing other women, how they teetered along on high heels, how they swayed their wrists; it was frightening to see how affected most of them were, how studied. What tricks there are to be concealed! What hysteria over cracks in the mask, how they stopped them up, plastering over them so no darkness could leak out.

The hospital needed a lot of employees then, so I became Sister Tessa. I met Charles Blake there. He lay on his back in his bed, with his leg hanging up in a sling. I felt his pulse, he sparkled with thankfulness, was completely harmless. In detail he told about Europe, about innocent behavior that filled him with guilt: how he once stole a paper knife with mother-of-pearl inlay in an abandoned house; how he killed chickens on a farm because he and his companions were hungry. He told about heaths and pine trees, about the cynicism of his coarser fellow soldiers, about the letters home to his mother. Sleep now, Mr. Blake, I said. Don't worry yourself about it, war's like that. But how could I be seized by the intoxication of stealing, Sister Tessa? Even if it was only a couple of times. Mr. Blake, your situation was certainly severe, but don't think about it any more. You're so understanding, Sister. I have such confidence in you. I must tell you something, Sister. I dreamt about you last night. Hope it was a pleasant dream, Mr. Blake. Call me Charles. Could you think of marrying me, Sister? You don't need to answer now.

He couldn't kick me where he lay. I prayed to God his leg would never become straight again. He never touched anything inside Sister Tessa's exterior.

Perhaps I'm not the world's most exciting man. But I'm honest and safe.

I thought: if he touches me I can kill him. That was my security. To have an object to kill for the rest of my life. It's true, Sidner. So I said yes. And woke up mornings with my arms tied around my body, my legs pulled up, trussed up. The weight of being forced to wake up every morning with those involuntary deprecating movements of my arms when I pushed away his kind hands. Constricted me like a lemon.

I was so angry over Robert dying before I managed to kill him. Many times in Charles's presence I discovered a gesture that had remained in me, a gesture directed at Robert, but from which Charles had to defend himself. The poor thing! My spiteful remarks when he approached! How I de-eroticised the room, the bed, the landscape when he wanted to touch me. Wash your

hands, Charles! I say. What a headache I have, I say. Then he's extinguished.

Rocked in the groundswell between both her names, rocked
in the swell between belief and indifference, between smile and
bitter lips, between the past and the present, between hot and cold,
between long silences and many words, between vigil and sleep –
she pressed against him, child and woman, she let her fingers touch
his chest, but without passion, without attendance, as if he held
his arm around her thoughts, crackling, shattering like the ice far
out on the sea's horizon one cold night in the north, a head of
shimmering crystals under his hand in a room on an island so far
away that every step out from here, in whichever direction would
convey him homeward. But one never comes home, if one has
not been away. If there in "the other place" one has not found a
smile, an experience, that changes one, and he had not yet found
anything which could resolve his perpetual waiting for the world's
presence. They lay here outside each other's gates, listening to the
rising wind which caused the windows to tremble, which made
the stars flicker outside the panes; they knocked carefully at each
other's grief, but the walls were still too strong for words to be
heard, signals to reach their mark, so they could open for each
other.

Afterward he got up and fetched the diamond boat, fastened it
round her neck.

"Now the hard part begins," she said.

❊ VII ❊

MAIN STREET was the street of the sun.

It lay in such a way that every morning the sun could be reflected over its entire length. It fit exactly between the low wooden buildings, their shop windows full of shining apples, clocks, and ladies' undergarments. The sun made the mannequins at Kahn's smile, a quick smile, just before people came out their doors to squint and welcome a new day. Main Street begins in the east at the Square and ends over in the west at Cross Way and Long Street. Streets like Long Street must exist, too; streets with deep shadows. People must live here, too; but those who do long to warm themselves in the light of Main Street, to bring words home to their shadows. The paving stones glistened in the blue haze and in these first minutes of dawn had a hue of violet and green because here, too, were trees, leafy yards, heavy crowns stretching out over the white fences.

It was also the street of the peacocks. Hundreds of them pecked at the seeds that came from the countryside on the wheels of milk carts, or were shaken off stuffed sacks of grain on open-sided wagons making their way to the Mill on Bathhouse Street; they promenaded like church wardens, quietly with twitching necks, picking over the sidewalk stones in front of the bank, in front of the Manor House and at Werner's Paint Store.

How could it otherwise be so clean? How could one otherwise understand that exquisite color of turquoise and ultramarine, of jade and lapis lazuli that lingered during the morning hours, right until Clas Löfberg opened his shop, rolling the green and white-striped awnings down over his windows, and the exhaust vents of the New Café offered their fragrances of fresh bread and almond buns?

The peacocks had been there just a moment ago, had with-drawn from visibility only exactly as much as was needed so as not to disturb those who did not want to see. They were just outside, and sometimes I could feel their tail feathers fan open and brush my leg when with my schoolbooks I traipsed up to the school on Åmberg Hill, taking the shortcut by the district police superin-tendent's yard to look at, just look at, his golden-yellow plums that secreted a satisfying sweetness.

I knew Main Street was the street of the rich – not because they owned money, but because they owned the sun. The shop own-ers had united in that, built the street for its beams, and the rite with which they honored the holy rays consisted of standing door-to-door with their hands behind their backs, nodding along the street, so the morning greeting spread all the way from the Yarn Shop on the Square to the Crafts Shop at Cross Way. And that is eternally true.

The peacocks have always been here "just a moment ago."

What difference did it make that they disguised themselves as pigeons or sparrows? It never fooled me.

And on the balconies with their delightfully ornamented rails and arches hanging like drops among Virginia creeper and climb-ing clematis, little white-haired ladies sat waving and dropping tickets, letters and sweets wrapped in handkerchiefs of finest silk. What difference did it make to me that this manna from heaven was concentrated in a single letter, one single time, when one morning I strolled along the street with Mamma? I did not know then how lonely she had become through my birth. I did not know that the letter with its invitation was the first sign she had been re-accepted by her former friends; did not know either that it was too late for her, or perhaps it had never been time. But I re-member how she looked up at the balcony and smiled a huge smile that coincided with the light on the street; remember how she raised her hand upward, long fingers in the air: "Thank you, it would have been exceedingly pleasant, but unfortunately we

haven't time." Afterward we went home to the red Parlor and
drank tea.

Mamma and I lived in a cloud of tea. We each had our armchair
of red velvet. We had crocheted cloths and always a fresh bouquet
of flowers from Halldin's Nursery down by the river. There were
chrysanthemums, roses, and freesia. I liked the mild scent of the
freesia the best; she always let me smell them when she cut their
stems and put them in water. Her fingers straightened out the
damask tablecloth over the peach-red table-top. She "offered" me
a seat. We contemplated the shining silver spoons, slowly stirred
our cups, which had blue festoons in the shape of flowers. We
breathed in the steam, smiling at each other, and that was the only
thing that happened, for we were Waiters. Uneventfulness was a
privilege because she believed it would pay: one day a golden egg
would arrive in the mailbox, even if it was disguised as a postcard
from Sidner with exotic stamps on it and with a picture of a smoking volcano or steep cliffs descending into the sea. In every case I
imagined she believed as I did. Slowly she twirled the spoon in her
cup, making a comment now and then about the Coffee "the others" drank. "It is such good fortune, my boy, that one isn't addicted to such dishwater." I loved the word "addicted," it raised
the two of us above the community's slurping, smacking, clatter-
ing herd, whom I never really encountered. Sometimes she let me
visit Beryl Pingel or even Sleipner; some isolated times I managed
to go into the hotel's Kitchen to visit the Sauce Queen and beg
for a cookie or sandwich; but I noticed she did not like it, and I
was an obedient child, completely encircled by her anxieties and
pronouncements. The word "addicted" made us different, and
she winked at me, for I would be her confidante in her way of seeing the surrounding world.

When we drank our tea we found ourselves in a particular room
outside of time, a holy place, and even if sometimes it happened
that some customer, some vaguely known person, was allowed to

sit down in the third chair the two of us transported ourselves to a still more intimate room where we dropped our secret code words. "Shall we perhaps offer a little Ceylon today, Victor? Don't you think it would be suitable in this weather?" Or: "I hope you can serve us, Victor, some of the smoked." Then when we were alone she shrugged her shoulders and laughed: "You know, it's actually casting pearls before swine to offer that. Or what do you think?" There is so much I associate with these tea times: her puff sleeves billowing like small clouds at her shoulders, a high neck, white and clean. There is stillness and expectation of the mail at the window open to the street.

It is also to vulgarize it to say we "drank" tea. We "celebrated" it. It was a mythically repeated act which followed a strict ritual dedicated to maintaining us in a state of participation with something not visibly present, with which, to all appearances, she did not bother: life itself.

With saucer in hand and lifting the cup to her lips, which still trembled with beauty, she used to raise her eyes toward the window. I say "toward" because I often doubt she saw the window, the nearby briar thicket outside, the maples on the other side of the street; she satisfied herself with the idea of the window.

"What wonderful weather today. It's as if it were made for a walk along the lake."

Eventually I learned to wait, to hold back my desire to shout out my Yes, for she always continued:

"If I didn't have so much to do now."

Then, when I had also learned not to interrupt, she felt relieved and could take hold of her dreams, following them through the willow thicket hanging out over the water. She could set her feet on the imaginary grassy slope where meadow saxifrage stood white in the spring. With her hands she could stroke trunks of the birches by the Lake House and paint a really pretty picture of the sunset, describing how we stood together and were global.

"If you continue in that direction, a long way, you'll come to New Zealand (which I would not have done at all). Precisely on the other side of the world. Just think if we were to go there and…" She smiled before she took possession of her most beautiful phrase:

"… and pay a surprise visit!"

With that, tea time's profession of faith was pronounced, the summit was attained. To pay a surprise visit meant to break out of the grayness of reality, abandon connections, to be new. How afraid was she really? I do not know and I had not seen through her then; I only remember how we gave each other a moment's palpitation of the heart and superior passion while we regarded the view that such a phrase had opened: the world spread at our feet, like a fan of promises. The sea stirred, it glittered and teemed with dolphins and flying fish, and somewhere among the tropical plants someone had stiffened at sight of us, someone who now dropped everything he had in his hands and rushed toward us to take us in his arms.

But we were not even standing outside the house.

We had not taken a single step; and the cup sank to the saucer and the saucer to the table, and the table had legs and underneath that was the floor. I, poor, sinful mortal.

"He would probably not be happy. Oh, for you, of course, but what would I do there?"

"Don't say that, Mamma!"

"Oh, yes," she said, "one must be realistic and not dream away like this."

But I, who had been lured out into the world of dreams and could not defend myself, had got my eyes caught on that imaginary sea. She had created it from tea and tranquillity. I drank from my cup and closed my eyes. The waves no longer glittered as clearly as a moment ago. A cold breeze came right through my field of vision, a serpent moved in the tropical vegetation.

I was too young, of course, to understand that was a ponderous retreat, even for her, an arduous route into fabrics, buttons, and eyes.

"Although you can afford to do it one day. You'll stand there and... Do you think the tea was good?"

"Yes, Mamma."

"Go get the Nordic Family Encyclopedia, we'll look at the pictures." We had done that many times, but as when one listens to music one could relive the mystery of looking up the section about New Zealand: the photographs never ceased to gleam, the glossy pages were like the inside of her arm.

"There you have the South Island's mighty mountains. They're over three thousand meters high, covered with perpetual snow. You must be dressed warmly, even though it's so far south, because down there on the other side of the equator south is the same as north for us."

It was difficult to draw conclusions from such a statement.

"Is that where Sidner lives?"

"No, he's on the North Island. Perhaps here."

Her fingers touched mine when she stroked the glossy, smooth paper.

"See how many sheep there are."

We had left the bah-bah stage, so I thought of saying:

"But don't you see them, too, Mamma? Don't you have to be warmly dressed, too?"

But I understood I had to manage by myself down there when I grew up, and perhaps *that* was the underlying message of these holy holiday moments.

So what others call uneventfulness is something shimmering like the brocade in her dress when she crosses her legs, when she lifts her hand to her cheek, a ring glimmering near her temple. When she then asks me to clear away the tea tray and I, therefore, understand we are leaving that room, it does not matter to me: we are still there, each on his own chair of velvet. The steam rises from the cups as the months turn into years.

"WHEN IS SIDNER coming back?" I asked one day as we walked along Main Street. I said Sidner because I did not know he was my father. The word father had no meaning to me. I was still busy disentangling myself from her blouse bodice, just recently having caught sight of the world, and it consisted in large part, of course, of the transparent freshness of her blouses, consisted of shimmering mother-of-pearl buttons and an amber necklace that flashed when I sat in her embrace, twisting it between my fingers. It consisted of the fragrances from her various perfumes, which she let me smell by lowering her earlobes to me. I was a part of her. To introduce something so strange as a "father" would have been improper. She was my morning and evening. She was the waking side of dreams and the dream side of wakefulness; now she held my hand in hers and when I looked up her throat made a turn toward the Ladies' Wear Shop's mannequins, and I saw a contemptuous wrinkle between her eyebrows when she scrutinized the mannequins' out-stretched fingers and the (to her taste) cheap clothing, a contemptuousness which I would later learn to recognize as her shield against sinking. She was *exalted* by contempt for the cheap and provincial, and she did not see her own captivity in that, had no ability to break out of it by her own strength. She turned to me:

"You little Telemachus!"

Naturally she was not aware of what she subjected me to when she laid that myth's form about me. As when a ginger snap cutter is laid in the dough and pressed, she severed me from the street, the houses, and the immediate.

"Why do you say that, Mamma?"

"Oh," she answered, the corners of her mouth playing nervously, like small waves out at sea. She gave herself time to sweep back a strand of hair that had fallen on her forehead; she greeted a passerby with a reserved nod, stopped a moment at a new shop window to look at herself: it was the Crafts Shop. Then we turned, her skirt swinging. Space grew around the silence with that oh! the wrapping on the present, the paper with the string. Or was it just that she forgot to answer, sailing away alone on her dreams? Probably so. A simple question had been transformed into two, into ten, into an endless series of questions that has no end and in whose labyrinth I still wander. A breeze in the lindens, a presentiment of a world outside her. I gripped her hand harder to keep her from forgetting herself.

"It's a long story," she said without answering. "Now let's go in here and buy us each a pastry. You get to choose just what you want."

I do not believe she answered me that day, perhaps not that week either: something else always came in the way. Details that she held in front of herself.

Time does not mean the same thing to a grownup as to a child. A strange name had carved a place in my soul. The princess cake sat there green and coated with powdered sugar, the tea cups steamed, and I carefully asked why Sidner took such a long time.

"Oh," she answered again. The whole of that childhood is filled with her deprecatory Oh! It was as if it escaped her at a sort of crossroad where she could never decide which direction she should choose. Her knowledge of Odysseus's perils and wanderings cannot have been great before I compelled her to read the book. Isolated names fluttered by, I suppose. Nausicaa, the island of the Phaeacians, Scylla and Charybdis, Cyclops. But it would surprise me if she had ever given herself time to read it, or any other book, completely and for herself. Of course, she would gladly live in foreign places, like the Greek archipelago, as earlier she had ridden through Pamir with Sven Hedin by a sort of visionary attendance, the more distant the better. To be sure, she fed

on the distant, on the uncontrollable, gathered strength to live
further through believing herself to be participating and through
graciously presenting these brilliant fragments to an admiring
world, even if it consisted of one small child. But she did not possess patience. Of course, she was also afraid to give other than
vague answers, because she had a strong intuition when it concerned touching on truths that were dangerous for her. Now she
dodged:

"He's on the way home, quite certainly."

"But *why* does it take such a long time?'

"It took ten years for Odysseus."

So she had stumbled over the threshold of her musings again
and wished it had been unspoken.

I have no history. I am forced to create it from fragments, from
images of intense memories, but I need totality. Perhaps she *had*
read the book. Or also, I am confusing that with my own later
reading memories. But one thing I know: she loved Sidner-
Odysseus as long as he struggled homeward, or was absent, so intensely that sometimes she again became medial and with closed
eyes told me what he was doing on "the seas." I do not know if
they were "real" performances when she stepped behind the curtains of her eyes, searching among suitable set pieces with the
voice of an actor fumbling in the gloom. Sometimes Sidner-
Odysseus found himself among wild mountains where solitary
sheep farms lay, sometimes she transported me to a shore bordered
by palms where she pointed out Sidner who, unaware of our presence, made a fire and roasted a wild boar or stag. He always found
himself in great danger. In a cave lived a giant with one eye, the
Cyclops. He had imprisoned Sidner to eat him up. But he −
Sidner? Odysseus? − had invented a stratagem, running a tree
trunk right through the giant's eye, thereby freeing many others
as well. Here there were plenty of witches, women who looked
good from one side, but who, for example, did not have any back,

or wore tails. All of them were out after him, sang beautiful songs and wound their arms about his neck. I sat breathless as she told these stories, and when we borrowed the book from the library my first reaction was that Odysseus had stolen Sidner's adventures; then I convinced myself that *this* was what travel was about. He who sets off must be prepared to take giants in hand, sinuous women and seductive song, and actually nothing has refuted that theory.

But even so, I eventually tired of hearing her end her tales with an inconclusive "Oh, I don't know how it went then" and see her stroke her temples, as if she had a headache. I wanted to know how it actually was behind the few words on the postcards, or in the letters she received and where the crumbs consisted of "Sidner sends greetings" or "Sidner went fishing and caught a gigantic fish." I had to know who I, Telemachus, was.

What bedtime stories! She sat on the edge of my bed in her robe reading, at first hesitantly, as if she pleaded with me that this was boring, incomprehensible, and utterly too full of difficult words, but since I never showed signs of exhaustion she continued right to the end.

> *But my heart is rent when I think upon the hero Ulysses*
> *who, far from his loved ones hath long suffered affliction*
> *on a far-off, seagirt isle, with its lofty forest*
> *the navel of the circle of the sea.*

Her own eyes filled with tears and we held hands while the radiant-eyed Athene, lightly approached, like a breeze over sea and the infinite earth.

> *Soon she stood in Ithica, and at the gate of King Ulysses,*
> *on the threshold of the courtyard, she stepped forth with spear in hand*
> *in the semblance of a stranger, Mentes, leader of the Taphians.*
> *Now she saw the scornful suitors, for they were in the courtyard*

outside the door, taking their pleasure at draughts,
all sitting on hides of oxen they themselves had slain.
Hastily, heralds and cheerful pages labored there,
some were mixing water and wine together in bowls,
some were wiping the tables with porous sponges,
then setting them forth, and some were carving meat.
The fair Telemachus saw her long before the others,
for among the band of suitors he sat with a heavy heart,
thinking continually of his renowned father, if he might
ever return and clear his house of the crowd of suitors,
take his dominion again and himself command in his abode.
Sitting there among the suitors with these thoughts, he saw Athene:
immediately he hastened to the gate, feeling vexation
that a stranger should stand at the door waiting so long;
and so coming forward, gave her his hand and took her spear,
and with winged words spoke to the goddess and said:
"Hail to you, oh guest, welcome here! You may later say
what your errand is, when first you have enjoyed a meal."

What a message she came with, that radiant-eyed goddess:
Sidner was alive. He was on his way, and she said I resembled him,
and through Telemachus, the judicious youth, I answered:

"Since you ask, my friend, I will tell you quite plainly.
Certainly my mother has said he is my father, but it is impossible
to know for myself, for no man has yet witnessed his own descent.
Oh, that fate had vouchsafed me to have as a father
one of those fortunate men who ages among his own possessions.
Now, however, I learn I have as father one who of mortal men
is most hapless, for, to be sure, it was of that you asked."

My room had wallpaper in a flame-colored pattern: when
Mamma left, leaving the door ajar so the light fell in a streak across
the floor and I could hear her sit in a chair in the Parlor – and what

she did there I have never known; those times I was up to pee and saw her, she sat completely still, without reading, without knitting – then the wall paper was transformed into a map of islands, channels and seas. Sidner struggled out there, and perhaps he was my father, and to that Mamma had nodded, but as it were without significance; and if he was, he became a gift, something to wait for when the storms had subsided. And if he was my father, then Mamma was my mother; and if Sidner was Odysseus, Fanny was Penelope, and I adjourned

"into sleep with so many thoughts in mind."

"Where are all your suitors, Mamma?"

I sat in my chair at the tea table, a crystal of curiosity in the tranquil twilight, where through the open window one could hear a neighbor raking his gravel path with long, even strokes before the church bells rang in the Sabbath. Mamma straightened the curtain, dusted the window sill, shook the dust rag outside, moved the bouquet of freesia (those mildly scented flowers that make themselves known only during silence, reminiscence, and expectation), to the piano where she remained standing to look at me.

"Oh! How can you think such a thing?"

I did not understand how she could say that. A true Penelope implied a number of suitors rummaging about in hallways and parlors; here it was always empty. She had transported me halfway into a world where everything was put in its place, became visible and well-arranged, where the outcome could be evident as soon as Sidner returned. I was Telemachus, I was a participant and would aid him in the final conflict. But there had to be a conflict first. Now she was destroying the delicate spider web of thoughts she had built around me, since she took her thoughts from the grownup world of false propriety and incomprehensibly forbidden burdens to which I did not yet have access. She hurried forward in her own corridor of sensibility and threw her arms about me:

"How can you believe such a thing of me!"

When does one see a human being for the first time? When does she detach herself from one's own conceptions and become an independent person?

I had expected something completely different: that the pattern would continue to be consistent. She, fidelity and expectation; I, passing the test of manhood. What joy would have ruled, if she had said:

"Oh, they slip in here at night. Haven't you noticed them?"

I stared at the piano. No one had played a single note since Sidner left, only Mamma's dust rag had glided now and then from dark to light, from light to dark.

"Then you're lying, Mamma."

We looked at each other from two separate lands, and sentries and presented arms detached themselves from our respective mountain passes and bridge abutments. We did not understand each other's language for the first time. Just then we had nothing in common. She said from her country:

"How can you say that?

And I from mine, almost with tears in my eyes:

"You *must* have suitors, Mamma. Like Penelope."

"Oh, that's what you mean."

But it was partially too late.

I had a very vague concept of what a suitor actually was, but now when I was on the point of acting of my own accord, outside her will and reach, I understood that to fight with Sidner and be vanquished by him a suitor must play the piano. "Uncle" Källberg who wound clocks and tuned pianos became my first victim. He was a very old man with a white mustache and eyeglasses hanging down his nose. When I met him one day after school and he, as usual, asked me to say hello to Mamma, I said that she would gladly have her piano tuned.

"You don't say, are you the one who's started playing?"

"I'm going to," I answered. "If it suits you, next Saturday? It has to be well tuned when Sidner comes back from his trip."

"Uncle" Källberg scratched his nose.

"I would think so. When is the big day of arrival?"

"It's not definite yet," I said, as if I were one of the decision makers in the question.

I sat on a chair by the door when he arrived. To Mamma I had said that "Uncle" Källberg wondered if he could drop by and tune the piano, and Mamma had looked a little puzzled but not said anything against it. With a smile on my executioner's face I pointed at the silent keys so he saw the tea cups and cake dish at the same time. We were alone in the Parlor, Fanny was busy closing the shop, and I carefully noticed his hands that rooted in the open piano; they were old and wrinkled. In the great final battle he would be an easy victim, if it concerned archery or piano playing. When then Mamma and he sat with tea I eagerly waited for him to think of something that would qualify him as a suitor, like laying his hand on her knee or whispering something in her ear – in short, something I would not like, something that excluded me; but nothing happened. Källberg talked about his wife's bad legs and Mamma was sorry. He ate our cakes, which I myself had put out, but he was not even gluttonous; the meeting was a fiasco, but I did not think of giving up.

"Can we have a party, Mamma?"

"Well, why do you want to do that?"

"We have, you know… such a nice place," I said, instead of saying that the silence no longer satisfied me.

"But I don't know anyone."

That could have been true, of course, but I appealed to the mythical past when Sidner had sat at the grand piano.

"You can make Jansson's temptation and those little meatballs. Like before. And then those who can play will come. Cantor Jancke for example."

"Yes, he has some culture."

"And the Hagegårds."

"Perhaps so. Of course, they have children, so you would have someone to play with."

I snorted. I did not play. At school I kept to myself for the most part and never understood why it was fun to run after a ball or play hopscotch; I crept with books in my desk and under my coat; I read during recesses and the world of books was much more fantastic than the real. Fanny's poison had already started to work.

"You're going to have your red dress on. And then we'll have place cards, you'll sit in the middle so everybody sees how pretty you are."

"What others do you think, then?"

"I'll think about it."

I crept along the streets, casting my "judicious" eye in through shop windows along Main Street to find suitable victims. The community immediately looked completely different, the people received new functions, different faces. They were appraised, confiscated, promoted, repudiated. I became bold and inventive when it concerned coming to grips with a candidate. Opened the door to Clas Löfberg's shop. When at last he had time for me I asked if he had seen Mamma. Kalle Österberg had a visit from me and had to grant the use of the toilet behind his store. The enormous "uncle" Kahn with his aquiline nose, bushy eyebrows, and flowing hair could not lend me a bicycle pump. And then there was the barber, Jönsson from Skåne. He was considered a "good eater" and it might come in handy. He was round as a ball, with rolls of fat on the back of his neck and under his chin; his hands were short and flabby. He rocked back and forth on the floor of his barbershop in a white coat, speaking in the Skåne dialect. Furthermore, he had the only mustache of its type in Sunne and it looked really foreign, short, sharp and perhaps dyed, because it gleamed with a strange red color. Oh, I could see him sitting at the table, tasting and enjoying our wine and our aspics, and our revenge would be dreadful. Actually, I regretted his bitter fate because it was a feast to go to him for a haircut: his blue and green bottles smelled good, he had scores of magazines, and I always hoped there would be a long wait so I would have time to read the Katzenjammer Kids and breathe in the sweet smells from bottles and tubes. We had not managed to read through the whole *Odyssey* yet, so I was uncertain if he really had to die; perhaps a

little gash and a terrible gaze would suffice. Mamma looked surprised when I presented him as a prospective guest – why him?
We're not on visiting terms, you know, and his wife is very sick.
That Jönsson had a wife had never crossed my mind, but I did not
see any direct impediment in wives. Of course, I could not reveal
the dreadful truth behind my plan, but said I thought his laugh was
so funny. As the Gods on Olympus represented various tempera-
ments and attitudes towards life, I wanted my guests to be as
different as possible. There was a teacher, too, who lived not so
far from us, about whom Mamma had said he was "dreadfully
lonely." His name was Bergman and he received an altogether
different appearance the day Mamma dropped her comment. He
was a tall and lean man, always wore well-pressed clothes, shiny
black gloves which he held behind his back. When meeting people he politely lifted his hat without smiling. He was a mathemat-
ics and physics teacher at the junior high school, and from the
drops of answers uttered earlier I understood that he, like all lonely
people, except children, was dangerous. Before Mamma said that
about his "dreadful loneliness" he had seemed to be one of the
pieces of the puzzle of adult life who certainly fit in somewhere,
but now I could not refrain from following after him and studying him closer. And see! I saw that "dreadful loneliness" in his
whole face. I read it in his serious eyes, the wrinkles on his forehead, the falling angle of the care-worn lips. I saw loneliness in his
gloves, his hat, the crease of his trouser legs. It was devastating. At
a distance I felt "dreadful loneliness" approaching like a cold wind
on a warm summer day. When he had disappeared into his apartment above the Cederblad sisters and lit the yellow light behind
drawn curtains, all the yellow lights in town became "the light of
loneliness." He ate his dinners at the hotel, and the dining room
which before had sparkled under the cut-glass chandelier, where
the symphony of colors on the Sauce Queen's smörgåsbord had
played on my most sensitive strings, now became an abode of the
lonely. With "dreadful loneliness" he was separated from the

larger dough and made into someone special, as person after person is separated when one gets to know them.

I notice how through Mamma I became class conscious: I did not so much as furtively glance at people who were outside that middle-class world to which I did not know we belonged. But the future guests were not allowed to wear work clothes or have creased faces; they were not allowed to speak the Värmland dialect because they had to be able to converse with Mamma. I did not wrinkle my nose at those "others", but meetings with them always occurred under definite conditions, in their own functions. Outside their functions they did not exist. To fetch milk from the tenant farm was a great pleasure, it smelled of hay and milk warm from the cow, chains rattled, and the cattle's lowing and the chickens' cackling was a sinfully pleasant experience; as it was to talk to Jansson, hear when he sang his sailor's songs from the seas he always longed for; yes, I liked it. But those who worked there belonged there and could not be taken from there. It was unthinkable to embarrass them with our behavior, with our smells, with our words. Of course, I did not know either how they regarded me when I came with my empty milk bottle, in my exaggeratedly clean clothes, which I was anxious about getting dirt on; do not know how they saw my fear of the animals or how my precocious words fell in the cow dung like sugar pills. The children who belonged there always fell silent when I came in, fled and undoubtedly did not even make comments about me: kept quiet about me because I was of another sort.

But within the middle class I thought I had a free choice: I imagined right up to that evening that if one could pronounce the word "exquisite" as Mamma did, then one belonged, then no borders were closed. But I was wrong. When I seemingly aimlessly tossed out different suggestions I suddenly got to hear that there were upper boundaries, too. The really rich or the seemingly rich she refused to acknowledge. "Such fine people," she said and turned away. "We don't have anything to offer them," and suddenly my world shrank to a narrow slit. The fault with Bank Manager Valentin was evidently that he had often been in Stockholm and gone to the Opera, that his wife bought food in Karlstad. Another had been on an air trip to Italy and now loved "lasagne." This shrinking world did not disappoint me, because disappointments emerge from deceptions and I had not been subjected to such. It was surprise I felt; my body crept closer to me. Detachment. Separateness.

Mamma, elevated to a true Penelope, stood by the sink and I offered to dry the glasses, which would now be an instrument in the battle, not against anything or anyone, but for Sidner.

"Haven't you given up on that idea of a party yet?"

"No, Mamma."

I wanted to see shining weapons, harder movements as counterbalance to all the feminine I was surrounded by, but I did not dare say exactly that; since in some way had I *seen* her fragility and loneliness, it would have been to reject her.

"But surely we can wait until Easter?"

"As long as it happens."

Would Sidner stand there in the doorway then?

> *But Telemachus with purpose had given Odysseus*
> *the place beside the paved threshold inside the hall,*
> *where he had placed a simple seat and one of the smaller*
> *tables. He dished up a portion of food and poured*
> *wine in a double goblet of gold, began to speak and said:*
> *"Here can you sit and partake in the revel with these men!*
> *Affronts — or violence — from all the suitors' side I myself*
> *shall prevent. For this is no public inn, but the house of*
> *King Odysseus who acquired it, and to whom I am heir!"*

It cost her a great deal to dare. Her anxiety was greater than I thought since she had such a lovely way of carrying herself, and her smile was so strangely dreamy and attractive that it ought to have drawn suitors to itself like bees to a hive. Nothing was allowed to come too close to her, something must have hurt her very badly once.

But there was a party, and there were three and four parties. None of my guests (for they were mine, she had no others to suggest herself) came too close to her. I sat in a chair by the door with a vain hope that my dreams would be sufficiently strong to entice Sidner home. It had become important to me, perhaps for only one reason. The memory of my walks with him was fading away, of course; as time passed, the war had meant that he was away for long periods, but one I remember: we were walking along the churchyard wall. It was summer and the linden trees were in bloom. It was blowing a bit, and I said: "May I walk in the lee behind you, Sidner?" A caravan of trucks comes along the road. Tanks, yellow in color. Soldiers are sitting on the platforms; they wave. "Sometimes I dress like that, too," says Sidner. "Because there's a war. And when there's a war all borders are closed. Then you can't travel abroad. During war nothing is as one had thought." And suddenly in my memory he says: "Architecture is frozen music." Sidner has a book in his lap. "There's an old fellow by the name of Goethe who said that." And then we both laugh. Then Sidner says: "Our speech is like frozen music, too. Our fantasies are frozen music. But only you and I know that." "Doesn't Mamma know that, too?" "I don't believe so. This is your and my secret." And I had further associated: "Just think if everything we say is letters that take room in our mouths. Like icicles. And you talk them out of your mouth so it won't get completely full everywhere." And Sidner says: "We have to be careful that we don't make a mess with our words." Then Sidner is gone from my memory, but I had continued to think about that. What would those thoughts be like, if they came out? Or the things one said very quietly? And the soldiers who swore. And then all of that would thaw out and become music! Therefore I believed everything one thought and said had to be pretty. I used to go out alone and *compose*. I sat leaning against the churchyard wall and said pretty things. I said *Fanny and Sidner*; I said *wild strawberries* and *Eva-Liisa*. It had to sound as fine as when Sidner played. Yes, one other thing Sidner also said: "It can take a very long time before what you say thaws out. Sometimes it doesn't become music before you're grown up." "Why's that?" "Because you're frozen inside. Although you don't know it yourself. But one day, when you're really sad or really hungry for something and completely alone, then you can notice how all of a sudden your old words become music." Perhaps I looked sad because he added: "Although for some it goes very fast. The important thing is that you're always waiting for that to happen. You must *believe* that." So I sat there, believing for all I was worth, dreaming about music which never came. And that had to do with Sidner. In the end it had to do with his not coming.

I do not remember much about the party. I remember Fanny managed to turn all attention away from herself by asking Jancke to play the piano, which was not any fun at all. I remember how Fanny forced me to show the drawings I had done. They stroked my hair and told me how clever I was.

I STARTED TO DRAW by mistake.

One day I am on my way to get milk up at the Tenant Farm. Twilight is indignant over the strife between remaining light and approaching darkness which try to get a waist-lock on each other in the crowns of the maples; oblique, gilded dark beams glide between the trees. It is muddy on the road after the rain, my shoes are thin, I have to pass the field where the bull is standing. His chain is lying in helixes in the grass; I do not know how long it is and the bull's eyes disclose nothing. Then the bull steps on it and gets closer. At once I am alone on the earth, the faces glimpsed in the cow shed window have disappeared, somewhere someone is pulling down the sheets and the sphere of heaven lies dark and tight on all sides of the field. I run, but fall and remain lying there, and the bull's enormous body rushes by. I want everything to be over soon and lie still, waiting, but soon see that the bull is standing at one edge of the field; he pulls and prizes, and I see his horn has caught in the sphere of heaven, bored in deep and cannot come loose. Heaven creaks and screams, the gods become incensed so saliva pours down on earth through huge cracks, there is enormous running about up there, soon heaven will break into pieces, fall down over the earth and crush it, I manage to think: how fast does a prayer go? But I get on my feet and rush in through the cow shed door and there they stand, Bergström and Jansson, looking out the window, observing heaven and earth and the bull, who puts his feet against the ground and finally manages to free himself. There is a large hole in heaven, and through the hole darkness pours down over the bull.

"What a damn nasty storm," says Bergström, and I am thankful to him for pretending that he has not seen what happened.

Mamma does not understand at all when I tell her, but says: "Draw it so I can see."

With crayons I make a drawing of the bull and the hole and the pouring darkness. Draw strong yellow strokes to mark the cracks in heaven. I make the darkness violet, I make the bull brown, I draw myself naked as a light bulb in the grass. Mamma sits a long time in silence holding the drawing in her hand. She finally looks up and says:

"You're an artist, Victor."

Immediately her life has received a direction: from that day she establishes another sort of activity. First she goes to the frame shop and orders glass around my drawing and places it on the wall in the Parlor, turns a lamp on it. I myself am very satisfied and do not notice until long afterward how I allowed myself to be taken prisoner by her admiration. When I come home from school, paper and crayons are always lying on the tea table; she smiles and asks what I have experienced during the day, and I innocently tell her about plums at the district police superintendent's and she asks:

"How big were they? What color? Draw them so I can see." I draw. I color. But she is the one who is skillful:

"Just think, I've forgotten what he looks like, the police superintendent. Is he a little fat man?"

But, of course, he isn't at all. I draw him tall and slender, with glasses and thick hair. He stands behind his plum tree, peeking out at me so I won't steal anything. He is standing in autumn red light holding a plum in the palm of his outstretched hand. The plum is radiant, I draw it larger and larger in each sketch because soon it will be winter, and all fruit grows in memory. I draw the pigeons on Main Street: a compact mass of blue-gray violet mounds drenched in morning sun; draw Mamma and me where we walk. Mamma's skirts stand like sails of green or blue around the child, wrap it up, as if in waves,;sometimes my face sticks out of the material so just my eyes are seen. Yes, I draw fabric in quantities since there are quantities when she asks me to sketch her face, her body where she sits at her sewing table, hemming up a dress of velvet or silk. The undulations in the fabric billow and live; it is so amusing and enjoyable to follow the complicated play of the lines. We admire each other colossally, we are one mirror image and one reality:

"You sketch so well, Victor."

"You sit so prettily, Mamma."

I illustrate Odysseus's adventures on the seas, and since I see no other sea than in books I resort to fabric for help, get a roll from the shop and lay it across the floor with books or boxes under it so the fabric will look like waves, and the fabric is red so the sea is red. High waves, little boat: Sidner's black beard, his eyeglasses. Odysseus meets Nausikaa. A hundred balls in the air, of which the sun is only one. Rocks on the beach. Real rocks which I search out along the roads until I have a large collection in my room. Cyclops when he has the tree trunk through his eye. Telemachus and Pallas Athene. Mamma takes part, arranging my still-lifes and my scenes; it fills her lonely days. She has her sights set on my future.

And she's in a hurry.

One day she presents me with a painter's smock she has sewn: a long, white smock that makes me look like a dwarf doctor.

"Prince Eugene has one of these when he paints."

I am given an easel and oil paints; I enroll in a correspondence course where one starts by sketching spruce cones and boats from the front. I like doing little flat-bottomed rowboats with rings of water around their prows. Birds that start up from their nests, birds diving. She is scrupulous about sending in letters and my efforts, which return with astonished exclamations from the teacher; she has surely written letters telling about me because she overelaborates everything.

"When you begin at the Academy we'll move to Stockholm." Or: "After your time at the Academy I believe we'll go to France, to the Riviera. Van Gogh painted there. Cézanne."

Books come into the house. Things of great value which we browse through together at tea time. It is important not to dog-ear the pages, that hands are washed. Mamma learns a great deal herself, reads about the artists and conveys thrilling stories about their poverty and suffering before they attained great renown. She buys a camera and photographs me where I sit in front of the easel in my smock. I look really ridiculous, a monster of refinement and pompous manners, but I was a child and had no idea what a prisoner in her conception of the world I was becoming. Yes, there is a terrible photo of me, my head at a bit of an angle and a paintbrush raised before my eyes, measuring a picture of sail and sea, which I had never seen with my own eyes, but must have stolen from some impressionist.

I never protested against anything that happened at home, but when she began drawing other people into the painting and I heard her boasting in front of customers in the shop, when she folded aside the heavy drapes and asked them to step into the parlor to look at me, an awakening irritation began to tickle far down in my consciousness. Of course, she possessed no real knowledge about art: it was her dreams of renown that drove her to force me all too fast, so that at last I came shuffling along behind the sleigh of her notions, like a wounded moose calf.

"Here's my little Impressionist," she burst out in raptures and asked some little old lady, who was in to buy underpants, to sit down on a chair and meet great art. But Sunne was too small and too confined to accommodate such phrases; they began to roll after me, like balls of fire, when I was in school or on my way home.

"I hear you've got one a those coats like a doctors's!"

"When ya gonna go ta France an' git famous? You 'n' yer high 'n' mighty fart of a ma!"

It caused dreadful pain to encounter such language. I ran away crying and saw "how my ma *farted*"; I had nothing to defend myself with, she never put any such weapons in my hand. So, I hurried home and buried myself in her beauty.

"*La France a quatre grands fleuves. La Garonne, La Loire, La Seine et le Rhone.* Now repeat after me, Victor! *Les murs sont blancs. La maison est grande. Le ciel est bleu.*"

"*Les murs son grands. Le ciel est bleu.*"

JUST ONE MORE CHAPTER before I close the world of childhood, if childhood is indeed that time when the colors we will later use are assembled on our palettes. It was August and the orchards burned of scents from ripe apples, phlox, and bushes heavy with currants. The streets lay clean after a nocturnal rain, and when I leaned out the window I could see the legs of a man who was busy taking down the sign from above Fanny's shop: we were going to move to Stockholm so I could be "nearer art."

To take leave is to sum up, to sum up is a sort of taking leave. I was now fifteen years old and famous within a radius of three kilometers for my light-saturated, exotic landscapes, which I had shown in an exhibition at the People's Hall; but I had braces on my teeth and an awkward body, which prevented me from smiling smugly over that fact. During the summer we had been in France and Marc Chagall's words still hurt. I stood before the easel in my ridiculous Prince Eugene smock and painted the view from the window. It was to be my "farewell painting," Fanny had said, and I obeyed with a grimace. Sails against the light, figures under foliage, horses in pastures! What light and what shadows! What mechanics and what falsehood! But I still had nothing against it. Packing crates stood round about me. My horrible paintings, which Fanny had persisted in giving gold frames and bracket lamps, lay packed among bundles of velvet fabric, covers, and cloths. The spots from the pictures were yellow, the holes from the hooks gaped like wounds. I had no one to take leave of: I had always been cut off from my schoolmates' language and games, and only with the greatest distaste had she allowed me to work a month in the cemetery so I could earn a little of my own money. Naturally, she was afraid I would be infected by the language of the world, and perhaps she was right. It was an enormous relief to go weed and rake among the graves and to get to listen to the talk during lunch hour, but I was always punished when I came home and she, as though wounded over not being allowed to give me money, forced me down into the bathtub to get rid of "the smell," I don't know of what, and then got to see me strut about the apartment in white shirt, well-pressed trousers, and a tie drawn tight as a noose round my neck. Now she was running around the community, bidding farewell and making herself a high and mighty fart, probably telling her stories about our French summer, about my future as an Artist and about the successes that waited just around the bend. I can see all that now, afterward: the world had only started to pick at me and it is not certain I would have allowed myself to be influenced, if it had not happened just then, at that point in my life, that there was a knock on the door.

I *believe* I knew who he was. He was a tall and powerful man with a black, short-trimmed beard. He wore glasses and looked tired. He stood in the doorway a moment without saying anything. Then he smiled, came forward, and laid his arms about me: "Victor, my son!" but I who had not managed to get the brush out of my hand managed to draw a long blue streak across his pale suit. And so it came about that the first thing I said to him was: "Sorry!"

There is a river in my consciousness. When I first sat contemplating its course I knew I had already seen it. It swings out of the jungle a few hundred meters from the tree where I am resting; it divides and encircles a low-lying island with dry elephant grass, which sometimes bows down to a rhinoceros's advance: then there is snuffling and mumbling in there and the elephants standing right behind me in the morning light lift their trunks and test the air, then return to eating. The river runs by beaches of Naples yellow; the current is strong against one's legs; kingfishers swirl above the water, flash and dive. Huge sky where the tops of the Himalayas hang free from the ground, as in a painting by Magritte.

Behind my back a mustard field blooms, one and another white oxen pass with their creaking carts on the way north, and over on the other shore Nature plays her bird concert: the peacocks scream, golden mallards quack, the herons, storks and cranes trumpet. Sometimes the shadow of a crocodile, sometimes the sound of leaves falling from the tree. But this is not about all that. It is that "RIGHT HERE THE RIVER WIDENS." Right here its course becomes quieter; from here it is possible to travel by boat all the way to the distant sea.

And I paint a blue streak across my father's back and say: "Sorry!" – and right here the river widens and has a quieter course, and I am no longer just fifteen years old, I am fifteen plus his thirty-four; my history widens backwards and forward, but it will take some time before I know what I have experienced. Sidner looks around the room: empty are the chairs where suitors should have sat. Penelope has aged and does not dare be sought after.

"So that's what you look like, Victor! You never even sent me a card, as I asked you to so many times. Are you angry with me because I disappeared?"

"I don't understand. I never got any letters," I say.

Perhaps Fanny had loved Sidner as night and absence. But she was not capable of having him too close to her. That afternoon when she stepped through the doorway and saw him, she fainted. It was a long time before she dared awaken. I kept out of the way on Sidner's advice: I understood that the deceit she had perpetrated against me would be hard for her to explain; it would have to be a thing between the two of them. I went out, drifted along the lakeshore, confused and wholesomely weak: suddenly I had a father and with my father a whole history.

"Have you seen Sleipner and Victoria? Torin?"

I shook my head. They were, in Fanny's eyes, not "fine" enough; they had soon given up inviting me in. I nodded when I saw them, that was all. She said I should watch out for Torin. Eva-Liisa, then? My aunt? Had I ever visited them? No. Talked on the phone? No. Did I play the piano, then?

"It's been quiet here ever since you left, Pappa."

I had been a caged bird on a velvet perch. When I came home toward evening I went right to the easel and tore down my canvas. Cut it to pieces in front of her. She and Sidner sat each on their own packing crate. It was the first time I had seen "naked life": the face that was always well made up had dropped its luster, the makeup had drained off, and she looked at me with big desperate eyes. She had lost control and cried herself into old age. It went so quickly I thought it took place before my eyes. I caressed her as I used to, but it was another person I touched, not my "exquisite" mother. She would never manage to paint that face on again.

I was shy and afraid of Sidner those first days, but there was so much to talk about. He was going to stay in Sweden for three months and would visit Eva-Liisa and Splendid, who lived in Arvika. One day he also wanted, he said, to pick lingonberries. We hung buckets on our bikes, filled bags full of sandwiches and thermoses and set off toward Stöpafors.

He was married now. He was choir master in a church in Wellington. He was not rich because his wife had suffered from a bad nervous condition, but now that she was well enough he had risked traveling. They had no children. Therefore, he said, it would be fun if I wanted to come stay with them sometime.

He rode beside me on the gravel roads. The web of the myth had scaled off; he was reduced to a human being. But that did not bother me: I myself was raised from caged bird to person. He wanted to teach me to play, he said. Give something more of what he was. We filled our buckets and roamed farther into the forest.

"I've written so many letters to you," he said. "Maybe they're in one of her boxes. I've written a diary, too. As a sort of explanation."

All those arias expelled from the straightforwardness of the in-
exorable course of events that has chosen to summarize and to
touch the invisible root system of my conceptions! I was born in
a net of pictures to which I must be true. Sunne's streets: membranes against darkness. An echo chamber that set my speech in
motion. But where does this impulse come from to make airtight
every millimeter, every second of my origin – which began, of
course, long before my own birth? Why am I so obsessed by the
Mystery of Beginnings? By charting those seemingly insignificant
moments that spin down in the past and, like felines, suddenly
throw themselves forward, scratching marks in that day: why? To
be sure, I am not afraid to die, for life arranges death, as death has
once created my life.

Our history catches up with us, and it caught up with me that
day in the forest when, to my great surprise, I discovered that I was
already born but had not taken part and done anything about it,
had not listened, had not become one of the notes. I was already
born and had not noticed it. Life had been in progress, not just the
fifteen years that were my own, then, but twenty, thirty years, all
the way back to Solveig's death in a curve in the road, in another
summer, in another room. I was born there. There my journey
had begun. The strength death created had thrown me here, in
among the trees. I had expected life would be somewhere else.
That it was a question of searching it out, following my family's
custom. Now, so long afterward, I am often gripped by vertigo
over how random those steps were that led us correctly, that led
me *forward*. But it is the same sort of vertigo that reaches me every
star-clear night when I go out into the darkness and look up, feeling how the earth moves in its immense universe, and I know I
must cling firmly to the ground yet a while longer. And let the
music that gives us hope ring out.

And between the trees a sort of explanation was revealed.
I know one walks by many signs; I feel the transgressions of

inattentiveness, the snares of indifference. But here was the unavoidable fact: as if music began to radiate from Sidner's helpless
gestures, we suddenly heard a voice speaking loudly and strongly:

And there were in the same country shepherds abiding in the fields,
keeping watch over their flock by night. And, lo, the angel of the Lord
came upon them, and the glory of the Lord shone about them: and they
were sore afraid.

The forest was filled with instruments, the trees whirled and
were transformed into violins, viola di gambas, and bassoons, and
a chorale rose up:

> *Break through, oh lovely light of morn*
> *and let the heavens dawn!*
> *You shepherd folk, be not afeared,*
> *because the angel tells you:*
> *that this weak babe*
> *shall be our comfort and joy,*
> *thereto subdue the devil*
> *and bring peace at last.*

The music wove a net around me, became walls and ceiling in
a mighty building in whose scaffolding I clambered about: an in-
complete cathedral that strove higher and higher. And between
the bars of the scaffolding I saw: pines, a forest mere. I heard the
birds farther away and beside me, completely still, Sidner stood
smiling at the two ungainly old creatures before us on the edge of
the mere: on either side of a portable gramophone, both naked,
in pink skin, sat Torin and Glorious Birgitta. A little fire smoked
under a coffee kettle. Glorious Birgitta painted watercolors. She
bent forward and dipped her brush in a water glass, drew several
strokes and leaned back with her head at an angle. Traces of her
activity were visible on the trunks of the pines, small banal pic-

tures of the mere, of the pink-hided Torin, who was reading a book whose title I could not see. Her gold tooth shone and I wanted to take those few steps over to them: here was where it was, then.

It was here he disappeared to. To a green tent hidden under a clump of trees. Clogs outside the tent, clothes on a line! Water striders danced on the still surface, a fish splashed and the music continued to grow. When I moved from the boulder behind which we were hiding, Sidner pulled my arm. He put a finger to his lips and signalled to me that we should draw back.

Yes, he pulled me into the forest's silence:

"Victor. Never tell Torin, or anyone, what you've seen! They need that love space for themselves. Be content with knowing. With you and me knowing. Be content with having seen it, just once. Know that such a thing can happen on earth."

ABOUT THE AUTHOR

A clergyman's son, Göran Tunström was born in 1937 in Karlstad, Sweden, in the Värmland province that has become the geographical and spiritual center of much of his writing. He published his first book of poems in 1958, and his first novel, *Quarantine,* in 1961. *The Christmas Oratorio,* which appeared in 1983, was awarded the Nordic Council's Literary Prize and established Mr. Tunström's reputation throughout his native country. He was awarded the coveted Selma Lagerlöf and Aniara prizes for his 1986 novel, *The Thief* (forthcoming in Verba Mundi), which affirmed his stature as a major European writer. Mr. Tunström, who lives in Stockholm, is also the author of seven other novels, as well as of several volumes of poetry and drama.

ABOUT THE TRANSLATOR

Paul Hoover, a translator and actor, was educated at Pikeville College, the University of Pittsburgh, and the University of Stockholm. His previous translations include theatrical works by August Strindberg and Göran Tunström. He lives in Brooklyn, New York.

THE CHRISTMAS ORATORIO

was set in the electronic version of Monotype Bembo. This typeface is based on the types used by Venetian scholar-publisher Aldus Manutius in the printing of *De Aetna,* written by Pietro Bembo and published in 1495. The original characters were cut in 1490 by Franseco Griffo who, at Aldus's request, later cut the first italic types. Originally adapted by the English Monotype Company, Bembo is one of the most elegant, readable, and widely used of all book faces.

Book design and composition by Elizabeth Knox, New Haven, Connecticut. Printing and binding by Haddon Craftsmen, Scranton, Pennsylvania.